Taking Chances

Taking Chances

Molly McAdams

ωℳ

WILLIAM MORROW

An Imprint of HarperCollins*Publishers*

TAKING CHANCES. Copyright © 2012 by Molly Jester. All rights reserved. Printed in the United States of America. No part of this book may be used or reproduced in any manner whatsoever without written permission except in the case of brief quotations embodied in critical articles and reviews. For information address Harper-Collins Publishers, 10 East 53rd Street, New York, NY 10022.

HarperCollins books may be purchased for educational, business, or sales promotional use. For information please write: Special Markets Department, Harper-Collins Publishers, 10 East 53rd Street, New York, NY 10022.

FIRST EDITION

Designed by Diahann Sturge

Library of Congress Cataloging-in-Publication Data has been applied for.

ISBN 978-0-06-226768-9

13 14 15 16 17 OV/RRD 10 9 8 7 6 5 4 3 2 1

1

MY FACE WAS stretched in a wide grin as I looked around my bedroom one last time. I was doing it, finally going to live my life however I saw fit to live it. I'd grown up with only my dad, and I loved him, but he didn't know how to be a parent. The only part he seemed to get was the word "no." I promise I'm not just being a whiny teenager, that really was about the extent of our conversations. He is always around me, rarely talking to me and always silently expecting me to be perfect. Not that I could blame the way he is, he has been in the Marine Corps since he graduated high school, and apparently he's really good at what he does. The guys that came through his units respected him, and he always exuded pride for them. He'd kept me home-schooled which resulted in me going to work with him every day and doing my work in his office. I learned early on that if I didn't understand something, it was just better not to ask. He'd look up at me from under his lashes with a raised eyebrow, sigh, and then go back to whatever he was working on. I was expected to finish by the time he started drills in the morning so I could go out there with him, but he still never said a word. The only interaction I really ever had was with his Marines. If anyone were to ask, I would let them know in a heartbeat I was raised by a bunch of immature jarheads that I adored, not by my father.

And now, after eighteen years of struggling to achieve a perfection that couldn't be reached in my father's eyes, I was finally going to let loose, have the college experience—whatever that was—and hopefully find out who I am in the process. I could have easily gone to a college here, but to say that my dad was strict would be the biggest understatement of my life, and I wanted to experience things I knew I wouldn't be able to if I stayed here.

"Are you sure you want to do this Harper? There are plenty of excellent schools in North Carolina."

I kept my eyes trained on his. "I'm one hundred percent certain Sir, this is what I need to do." Did I mention I'm only allowed to call him "Sir"?

"Well," he looked past me at my window, "it will be different around here." He turned and walked out of the room.

And that's as good as it was going to get, to be honest, it was one of the longest conversations we had in a few months. Four sentences. It was surprising that he could talk to his guys all day long, but we start talking and he's out of the room within minutes.

My phone chimed and I smiled again, my "brothers" weren't thrilled I was leaving for California. I'd been getting calls, texts and messages on Facebook since last night begging me not to go. Now that I was older and closer in age with most of them, the guys no longer tried to raise me; they saw me as their sister or friend and taught me everything I needed to know when it came to other guys like them. It always made me laugh that most of them preferred to spend time with me rather than heading off

base during their liberty, but I think they liked that I wasn't one
of those girls that tried too hard to get their attention. Not that
they didn't like that kind of attention, but apparently I was a
nice break from the rest of the women they dealt with.

J. Carter:
*DON'T LEAVE ME! I'm going to go insane without you
here to keep me company.*

Me:
*I'm sure you'll be fine Carter. Prokowski and Sanders
seem to be taking it a little harder than most too . . . you
can comfort each other ;) Or you can always take up
one of the base skank's offers. They're sure to keep you
better company than me.*

J. Carter:
I think I got herpes just thinking about them.

Me:
*Ha! Ew. I gotta go, Sir's done loading up my bags in the
car.*

J. Carter:
*I'll miss you something fierce Harper. Have fun, don't
forget about me.*

Me:
Never.

Jason Carter was twenty and had been in Sir's unit for about
a year, he and I had become close quickly. He was my best friend

and if I was on base when they had liberty, he was always one of the guys that opted to spend time with me rather than hunt down women with some of his other friends. I had always been sad whenever one of the guys transferred to another base, unit, or finished their time in the Marine Corps. But I'm pretty sure Carter would have been one that would kill me to see go, so I wasn't surprised that this was the sixth time he's asked me not to leave within the last hour. He couldn't have said it better, I would miss him something fierce too. I glanced around the house I'd grown up in one last time before meeting Sir in the car. That house was definitely something I wouldn't miss.

Almost twelve hours, two cars and two planes later and I was standing in my dorm room at San Diego State University. My new roommate hadn't checked in yet, but from the e-mails we'd sent back and forth over the last few weeks, she lived close and would be moving in a few days from now. I picked my side of the room and hurried to settle in before taking a shower and falling onto my bed. Glancing at my phone I noted it was almost two in the morning and groaned, if I was back home I'd already be on base with Sir. It had been a long day of traveling and unpacking and it took all the rest of my energy just to curl up in my comforter and fall asleep.

"HARPER? HAAAAARPERRRRRR! WAKE up!"

My eyelids opened just enough to see a smiling face directly in front of me. I shot upright and brought my arms up, my entire body already tense.

"Whoa, whoa! It's me, Breanna!"

"Do you have a death wish? Don't do that!" She'd better be happy I had still thought I was dreaming, growing up with my dad meant always being on the defensive when waking up.

She giggled and sat on the edge of my bed, "Sorry, I've been trying to wake you up for the last five minutes."

Weird, I was usually a really light sleeper. "I thought you weren't coming 'til Sunday?"

"Well technically I'm not, all my stuff is still at home . . ." She gestured to the still bare other half of the room, "but my brother and his buddies are throwing a huge party tonight and I figured I'd see if you wanted to go."

The closest I'd ever come to a party was the stories I heard from the guys on base. I tried not to show my excitement and shrugged indifference. "Sure, when is it?"

"It doesn't start until nine or so, so we still have a few hours. Want to grab dinner?"

"Dinner? What time is it?!" I grabbed my phone and didn't even look at the time, all I could see was the twenty missed calls from Sir. "Crap, I need to call Si—um, my dad back. But after that I'll get ready and we can head out."

Breanna didn't move from my bed so I decided to just let her stay there, I'm sure after she heard him yelling she'd leave. I caught the time just before I hit the send button and gasped. I'd slept for almost 16 hours, he was gonna kill me. As assumed, he answered on the first ring starting off in a disapproving lecture about not letting him know I'd made it to California and that I was okay, not answering my phone, and how bad of an idea it was to let me come here. I murmured apologies at all the appropriate times, and tried to ignore Breanna's laughing at the conversation. We may not ever talk, but when he was pissed, it wasn't something to take lightly.

"Oh my God, time to cut the apron strings, don't you think?"

I blew out a sigh of relief that the conversation was over, "Yeah, well, I'm all he has left."

"Where's your mom?"

"She died."

Her hand flew to her mouth, her eyes wide. "I'm so sorry! I had no idea!"

"Don't worry about it," I waved her apology off, "I never knew her."

She simply nodded.

"I know my dad though, this is just the first time I've ever been away from him, and I think he's worried. Now that he knows I'm alive, I probably won't hear from him again for a while."

Breanna still wasn't talking. This happened every time I told someone I didn't have a mom. Instead of trying to tell her not to worry about it again, I got up and got dressed for the party. Thankfully, my thick auburn hair was already naturally straight so I was ready in no time. Grabbing my purse, I turned to see Breanna's horrified expression.

"Wh-what?"

"Is that what you're going in?"

Shrugging, I looked down to my long jean shorts and black and gold infantry shirt. "Yes?"

"Oh no." She was now looking in my wardrobe, checking all my clothes. "Okay you and I are both a size two, how tall are you?"

"Five feet two." Yes, I know. I'm incredibly short.

"Just barely shorter than me . . . hmm. Okay come on, we're going to my place to get you changed."

"Is there something wrong with this?"

She raised one perfectly shaped blond eyebrow at me, her blue eyes narrowed, "Let's just say I'm going to throw out your entire wardrobe and take you shopping tomorrow, because we obviously don't have time tonight. I'm guessing we have to get some make-up while we're at it?"

I nodded. To be honest, I'd never felt like I'd needed make-up. Not saying that I think I'm really attractive or anything, just never saw the need. I'd been blessed with a smooth complexion and had wide gray eyes hidden behind long dark lashes. I always thought anything else would have been too much. Plus, I'm sure Sir would've had a fit if I'd ever bought any.

We grabbed some sandwiches from a deli and before I knew it, I already had my make-up completely done and Breanna was holding different outfits up to my body. She settled on a faded, torn denim mini skirt that looked like it would barely cover my butt, and a black spaghetti strap.

"Okay put these on, and no peeking yet!"

"Is there something else to go over this undershirt?"

"Undershirt? No, that is the shirt!" She looked at me like I was crazy before walking into the bathroom.

Thankfully, the spaghetti strap was pretty long allowing me to pull the skirt down enough so I didn't think my butt was showing, but I'm pretty sure I'd never been this exposed outside of my bathroom in my life. If she was a couple inches taller, how on earth did she even wear this thing?

"Ooo. MUCH better!"

"Are you sure? I feel like I'm naked." I was still trying to tug the skirt down.

"Hah! No, you look hot, I promise." She spun me around until I was facing a mirror.

"Oh, crap." Sir would kill me, but I had to admit I think I liked it. Just as I thought, the skirt barely covered a thing, and it was impossible not to have cleavage in this shirt. I guess I had a nice chest, but when almost every top you own is from the Post Exchanges on base, there isn't ever an opportunity to see anything. I turned to look at my backside and smiled a little bit before facing forward again. "Oh my God, look at my eyes!"

"I know, don't you love them?"

"You're a genius Breanna." I looked at my smoky lids, and even thicker eyelashes making my eyes look like dark thunderstorm clouds.

"Well it's pretty easy when the model has your face and body. Mind if I steal your lips and eyes for the night?"

I laughed but was still mesmerized by my new reflection. "I can honestly say I've never worn anything like this, and this is my first time ever having make-up on."

"Are you serious?" She looked appalled.

"My dad is a career Marine. I've never even *touched* make-up. Hell, I haven't even been to a mall." I giggled when her face dropped to one of horror.

"I guess this means you won't be opposed to me taking you shopping tomorrow then?"

"If you can make me look this good for a simple party, I'd let you pick out all my outfits."

She squealed and clapped, turning to grab her clutch. "Yay! Okay, let's go snag a couple guys."

I stopped walking, eyes wide. I don't know how to talk to a normal guy, let alone snag one. "Uh, I'm not exactly great with the opposite sex. Like, I've never had a boyfriend or anything."

"Whoa, what?!"

"What part of Marine for a father didn't you understand? I don't think I've ever even talked to a guy that wasn't a Marine."

"Okay, timeout. Are you being serious? Have you ever been kissed?" She gasped when my lips pressed into a hard line. "Oh honey, I promise to fix at least that by the end of tonight."

My cheeks flamed as I quickly followed her out to her shiny graduation present of a car.

"HEY BREE!"

"Hi Drew." Breanna hugged an already intoxicated looking guy that opened the door. "Drew this is my new roomie Harper, Harper this is Drew."

"Nice to meet you," I mumbled. Before I knew what was happening I was being lifted up in a bear hug. I gasped but refrained the urge to kick him.

"Always a pleasure to have fresh meat here," he said with a wink before putting me down.

"Easy tiger, she's off limits to you!" She mock glared and poked him in the chest.

"Aww, come on Bree, don't be a cock block."

Raising an eyebrow I almost smiled at him. He wasn't even attractive and was holding a blow up doll.

"Nu-uh, no one that lives in this house is allowed to touch her. I know how you all are. So play nice, kay?"

Drew grumbled and walked away to refill his plastic cup. Breanna leaned in to speak in my ear, "I'm not gonna lie and tell you they aren't all like that, practically every guy that lives in this house is just as bad as him, and most of the guys that will be here tonight are too. I'll tell you who's safe and who isn't."

I smiled at her, "Thanks Bree, I'll owe you." Not that I needed her to tell me to stay away from guys like him. Sir let me around the Marines not only because they were like the brothers I never had, but he knew I would never end up falling for someone who would talk like that in front of a girl.

She scrunched her brows together and teased me, "Duh. Want a drink?"

Agreeing, I walked with her to a group hovered around one of the kegs. After getting a beer and forcing half the cup down to get the bad taste over with as fast as possible, I followed her out to the back yard to meet more people. I don't remember most of their names, but I got picked up and carried around more times than I cared to count, and was gawked at by every guy I met. Bree assured me it was because I looked good, but I was already wishing I'd worn a sweatshirt and jeans and cursing my tiny frame. Breanna seemed so at ease with the way guys were touching her and raking their eyes over us, and I didn't understand how she could do it. I no longer felt beautiful, I felt exactly like what Drew called me. Meat. I was halfway through my second beer of the night when I was pulled onto the dance floor by Bree and a few others.

I'd never felt so out of place in my life. Just watching the way these people were groping each other was making my cheeks burn, I tried to follow Bree's lead but I ended up just stumbling around from people rubbing up against me. I turned my head to see the most recent encounter and found myself being glared at by the most beautiful blue eyes I'd ever seen. Taking in the rest of him I could see I'd gotten in the way of his dry humping with a busty blonde and tried to quickly move away. Pointing to the kitchen when Bree tried to stop me, I slowly made my way through the packed bodies and out of the living room.

"What's up Harper?"

I turned to see Drew standing beside me. "Uh, nothing. Just had to get out of that," I said pointing over my shoulder.

"You don't like to dance?"

You call that dancing? "Not really my thing."

Drew put an arm on each side of me trapping me against the counter and pressing his body into mine. "Is there anything else I can I interest you in?"

Not you. "Is there a bathroom I can use?"

As soon as I asked, a bunch of guys started chanting and I turned to see what the fuss was about. My eyes about bulged out of my head when I did. The same guy I'd last bumped into on the dance floor was now taking shots out of a girl's mouth, running his tongue and lips all over her neck and chest between each one. When he sprinkled more salt on her, I realized why he'd been licking her. After the third one he looked right into my eyes and winked before putting his mouth to the fourth glass. I shook my head and didn't even wait for Drew to respond, I went off to find the bathroom on my own. After opening the doors on two couples having sex, I finally started asking more people where to find one. Once I got in, I locked the door and tried to calm myself. I may have heard disgusting stories from my brothers trying to get a rise out of me when I was young, but hearing it and seeing it are two completely different things.

I stayed in the bathroom until people started pounding on the door and dashed down the long halls trying to avoid looking at the doors to the other rooms I'd already opened. When I rounded a corner I ran right into a broad muscular chest and almost fell on my butt before he caught me.

"I'm so sorry, I—" I shut my mouth when I looked up and saw those deep blue eyes again.

He smiled and I momentarily got distracted by his perfectly straight, white teeth and full lips. Cocking his head to the side, I saw the recognition flash across his face that was soon replaced by a sexy smirk. By the way my heart started pounding, I was sure he'd perfected that look years ago. "Now who are you?"

I blinked and tore my gaze from his mouth and tried to move around him but his hands were still holding me in place.

"What, you're too good to tell me?"

I thought about the two girls I'd seen him with, and for the first time since running into him, realized there was a new blonde with her arm wrapped around his waist. Wow three girls within half an hour. I raised an eyebrow at him, "Apparently."

He and the tall blonde both scoffed. After releasing my arms he crossed his in front of his chest exposing even more muscles and a good bit of half sleeve tattoos on both arms. His stance may have looked intimidating if his face didn't appear so shocked and amused. "Excuse me Princess?"

Narrowing my eyes I started to shoulder my way past him, "You're right, *excuse* me."

He let me pass and I made my way back outside, to where

most of the activities happening didn't make me want to shut my eyes and turn away. Bree said we'd be here all night, and I know it's childish, but all I want to do is hide out. I found a couple chairs in a dark corner of the backyard and plopped into one. It's obvious I'm not going to be a fan of parties. I pulled out my phone and texted Carter.

> *Me:*
> *So . . . I don't understand why you guys get so excited about parties*

> *J. Carter:*
> *You at one?*

> *Me:*
> *Yep.*

> *J. Carter:*
> *Are you drinking?*

> *Me:*
> *A little.*

> *J. Carter:*
> *. . . please be careful. I know better than anyone that you can take care of yourself. But you've never had alcohol before. Don't let anyone hand you an open drink, and don't set yours down ever.*

> *Me:*
> *Okay Mom.*

J. Carter:
I'm serious Blaze. Be careful.

I smiled at his nickname for me. I was known for blushing.

Me:
I will. Miss you already.

J. Carter:
Same here. No one left this weekend, we're all too upset knowing you're gone.

Me:
I doubt that. You're probably on a date right now, already forgetting about me.

We texted for hours and I realized the party had thinned out immensely by the time Breanna found me.

"Harper! What are you doing out here by yourself? I've been looking for you forever."

"Sorry, guess I'm not as good at this as you."

Huffing, she fell into the chair next to me. "You'll get used to it, once you know more people you'll have fun. Did you talk to anybody?"

I shook my head, "After I left you I only saw Drew and some other guy."

"There were a lot of guys here, you're saying you only saw two in the last few hours?"

"Not that, he just . . . stood out I guess." Not only because he'd given me a nickname I'd lived with and hated my entire life, but he is easily the most attractive guy I've ever seen. He had that bad boy model look going for him, and unfortunately he knew it.

"Really? And who is this mystery guy?"

"Apparently he isn't really a mystery." I laughed, "I saw him with three different women in like thirty minutes. He was kind of a jerk too." Not exactly, but I didn't like his entitled attitude.

"Sounds like my kind of man!"

I looked over at her, shocked.

"Kidding Harper! Kidding, oh my God you are too fun to mess with. Well, not to say I didn't have my hands all over a few guys myself, but at least that was over the course of four hours." She laughed and stood up, offering me a hand. "Come on, practically everyone's already gone."

"Are we going back to the dorms?"

"No way, crazy! I never drive if I've had anything to drink within the last three hours. It's a rule."

"Sooo . . . where are we going then?"

"Well first we're gonna find my brother, and then we'll crash in his room."

"What? No! I'm not sleeping in his room."

"Chill Harp, it'll just be you and me in there. I always get his room after these parties." She pulled me across the lawn toward the back door.

I groaned and tried to keep up, almost losing my flip flops on the way.

"YYYEEEAAAH, Bree and fresh meat are sleeping over tonight!" Breanna bounced over to where Drew and another guy I didn't recognize were pouring shots and grinning while staring at my chest.

"Well, well. If it isn't the princess."

My body tensed and I frowned when I saw him approaching. Narrowing my eyes, I plastered on a fake smile. "I almost didn't recognize you without a tramp attached to you."

Drew and the other guy snickered.

Leaning into my ear he harshly whispered, "Would you like to change that? I'm not up to my limit tonight yet."

Gah, why did he have to be so hot? My body was practically humming with how close he was. I leaned away and replied with the most innocent expression on my face, "Oh I'm sorry, but I don't have any STDs, I'm not your type."

Drew started choking and Breanna spit her next shot all over the counter. Sputtering and choking, she finally composed herself enough to chime in, "Chase, you better stay away from my roommate. I told the guys she's off limits."

I tore my eyes away from his to look at Bree, "You know him?"

Everyone started laughing except for the guy standing next to me. His eyebrows were raised and his perfect mouth was slightly open. I guess women don't turn him down often.

"Well I'd like to think so, he *is* my brother."

Oh. Crap. Heat instantly spread to my cheeks and I took a step away from him. Now that I'd been informed, I realized I should have known it. They had the same blond hair, blue eyes and killer smile.

"Wait, Harper is this the guy you said was a jerk?"

My eyes widened and I looked at the ground.

"You said I'm a jerk?" Chase laughed and turned to the bar, "She's the one that just practically called me a dirty man-whore."

"Don't be rude to my friends Chase!" Breanna took another shot then punched his arm, I doubt he felt it though.

Without saying anything else I went back outside to my chair in the dark corner of the yard, and stayed there until the music was turned off. As a rule, I don't let guys push me around, but I felt horrible that I'd said that to my new roommate's brother. Not to mention we were currently at his house and about to stay in his room. I planted my face in my hands, elbows on my knees and groaned at myself. I should have just kept my mouth shut.

As if he knew I was thinking about him, Chase fell into the seat next to me. I removed a hand and looked into his dark blue eyes.

"You hiding?" That stupid sexy smirk was there again.

"Is it that obvious?"

He looked around the empty backyard, then glanced back to me, "A little." He stretched out his long legs and sank farther into the chair, "Tell me, what's a princess like you doing at my party?"

I bristled and literally had to bite down on my tongue. "I'm not sure what you mean, but I was invited." It came out a little harsher than I'd meant it to, but I wasn't about to apologize for that.

His smirk was gone, and he looked pissed, "You don't have to be invited to come to the party, but if you didn't notice, you don't exactly fit in here, *Princess*." He sneered.

My mouth dropped open with an audible pop, I quickly shut it. He was right, I didn't. But seriously? Rude. At least when I was snide, you could hear the sarcasm.

"If the way we are disgusts you so much, feel free to stay at school next time." Standing quickly, he shot me one more glare before turning away.

Aces. I've been here a little over a day, and my time here in California was already starting off so well.

"Chase," my voice stopped him, "I'm really sorry, I was out of line."

He turned to look at me, head cocked to the side. When he continued to look at me with a confused expression I went on.

"I was raised not to back down to people, but what I said was too much. So, I'm sorry. I don't know you, I shouldn't judge you."

A huff of a laugh escaped his chest and I saw the corners of his mouth slightly tilt up. He shook his head, still looking confused and now a little stunned before he took off around the side of the house.

This was going to be a long night. If I had any idea where we were, I'd try to walk back to campus.

"Haarrrrrpppeeeeerrrr!" I looked over to see Breanna stumble out the back door. "Harper, come inside, everyone's gone!"

When I got close she hooked an arm through mine and led me into the living room. "So did you kiss anyone tonight?" She raised both eyebrows and it looked like she had to struggle to keep them there.

"No," I muttered.

The same guy she'd been taking shots with when I left yelled from the kitchen, "I can help with that!"

I shook my head and started to answer when Bree spoke again. "No, no, no. I told you guys, she's off limits!"

"Come on Bree, what's your deal?"

She leaned forward and fake whispered, "Cause she's *pure.* Completely. Pure."

My jaw dropped and I grabbed her wrist as she went to tap my lips with her finger. "Breanna!"

Putting her hand back to her own lips she held one finger in front of her mouth. "Shh! Harper don't tell them!"

A little late for that. I was completely mortified. I wanted to be angry at her, but she could barely stay standing, I doubt she would remember any of this tomorrow. Looking up, I saw four guys standing there staring at me with wide eyes before busting up laughing. I needed someone to kill me. Now. No, first I needed to get out of here. Then someone needed to kill me.

One of the guys I hadn't met was wiping tears from his eyes, "Oh my God! Princess, is she serious?"

Glad to see they all adopted my favorite nickname. Was there something about me that just screamed *Give me a nickname*? I couldn't even respond, my throat had closed up and I thought I would actually cry for the first time in years. Unhooking my arm from Breanna, I made a beeline for the front door, intent on trying to find my way back to campus. I stopped when I realized Chase was blocking the hall that led to the entryway, he was the only one in the room not laughing. Instead, his lips were mashed together and he was shooting daggers at his sister.

"Please. Move."

He moved, but it was to grab my shoulders and steer me back toward the living room. What was he doing? I dug my heels into the carpet trying to scramble back in the other direction.

"Don't touch me!" I hissed.

"Just trust me," he growled in my ear, walking me past everyone still laughing at Bree's slip.

When we hit a hallway I hadn't been down tonight, one of the guys from the kitchen yelled, "Looks like Chase is gonna take care of that problem for you Princess!" That brought on a new round of hysterics.

Chase paused for a second, cussed under his breath and started forward with me again. When we got to the end of the hall he stopped in front of a door, and pulled out a key to unlock it before towing me in. When the light flipped on, I blinked until I realized we were in a bedroom, I gasped and tried even harder to get out of his grasp. If I could just turn a little, I could have him on the floor in a few seconds. But his grip was firm, I couldn't budge at all.

"No! Get off me!"

"Not until you stop trying to hit me!"

I stopped but stayed tense as he waited for almost a minute before releasing my arms. Once he did I turned on him and backed away.

"Calm down Princess." He sighed sounding uninterested, "I'm not going to do anything to you."

"I really wish you would stop calling me that," I said through gritted teeth.

He rolled his eyes and went to a drawer, after throwing a pair of basketball shorts at me he walked back to the door. "Put those on, I'll be back."

"Why?"

"Did you want to sleep in that skirt?" He bit his bottom lip, his eyes glued to my legs. "I swear I won't mind it, I figured you'd be uncomfortable though."

"Breanna said I would be in a room with her tonight, and if that's not happening I'd rather just go back to the dorm."

"I can assure you she'll be sleeping in the bathroom. I'll give you a minute to change, I'll be right back."

"I am not sleeping with you in here."

"Look, you're seriously hot, that alone is going to have them chasing after you. But top that off with the few words you've even said that shows me just how snarky and sweet as hell you are, that is one hell of a tempting combination. Trust me when I say they're going to want to change what they just found out about you. So if you don't mind, I'd rather make sure that doesn't happen."

He slammed the door shut and not more than three seconds later I could hear him yelling at the guys in the kitchen and telling Breanna to fend for herself tonight. I was standing there in his basketball shorts and Bree's spaghetti strap when he walked back in and locked the door.

"That was rude, she's your sister. She should be in here too."

He looked at me incredulously, "Are you serious? You're gonna defend her after she just spilled that?"

I shrugged my shoulders and put the skirt on a chair, keeping my back to him so he couldn't see my cheeks flaming again. "She's drunk. I'm sure she didn't realize it."

"That's not an excuse." His voice was soft as he pulled down the covers, "Come on Harper, get in."

The way his voice wrapped around my name sent a warm shiver through my body and I had to fight to keep my eyes away from his now-bare chest as I crawled into his bed. Even the quick glance at his sculpted chest and abs had my heart racing. After he flipped off the lights, I felt the bed sink down from his weight and I sat up.

"What are you *doing?*"

"What do you mean?"

"You can't get in here with me!"

He chuckled, "It's my bed, I'm sure I can do what I want."

I know he couldn't see me, but I glared at him anyway. Flipping the cover off me, I grabbed a pillow and sank down to the floor.

"Get back in the bed Princess."

I scoffed at my nickname but didn't say anything. I could feel his eyes boring into my back and after what felt like an eternity, heard him sigh and the bed shift. I wanted to ask for a blanket but was too stubborn to ask. Next thing I knew I was in the air.

"Oh my word! Put me down!"

He dropped me onto the bed and crawled over me.

"Chase! No!"

"Calm down, I'll stay on my side. We can even put a pillow between us if it'll make you feel better." He snickered.

I grumbled and scooted to the edge of the bed. Obviously I've never been in a bed with a guy before, and the fact that he was inches away had my whole body shaking. "I swear if you touch me, I'll go Lorena Bobbitt on you."

It didn't take him long to figure out what I was referring to. He put a pillow over his face to muffle his booming laugh. "Oh my God! Princess! You're my new favorite!"

"That wasn't a joke."

His body was still shaking with silent laughs as he moved closer and trailed his fingers up my arm. "One of these days, you'll be begging for me to touch you."

I couldn't tell if my next shiver was out of pleasure or disgust but I still growled at him and slapped his hand away. "I'm serious Chase. I'm not like all those girls I saw you with tonight."

"That's an understatement." He rolled back to his side of the bed and sighed, "Get some sleep Princess, I'll see you in the morning."

2

MY EYES SHOT open the next morning when I felt something squeeze me. Looking down I saw tattoos trailing down to a muscled forearm that was wrapped securely around my waist and gasped when I remembered I'd slept in Chase's bed last night. I jumped out from under his arm and off his bed in a move so fast it had my head spinning. My heart took off again as I took in Chase's shirtless body. His tattoos expanded up his shoulders and for some reason I wanted to trace them with my fingers and splay my hands across his well-defined abs and chest. Dear me, this man was gorgeous.

Chase sat up cursing until he realized who I was. "Jesus Princess! You almost gave me a heart attack. I thought I had a girl in here." He flopped back onto his pillow, raking his hands over his face.

That snapped me back to reality. "Chase?"

"Hmm?"

"Sorry you didn't seem to notice, but I *am* a girl."

He dropped his hands and scowled at me but still proceeded to slowly take in my body. My cheeks were bright red by the time he looked back up. "I noticed last night, trust me." My question mark face must have prompted the rest of his response. "I meant, I thought I let a girl stay the night with me."

"Uh . . . ?"

"Someone I'd been with Princess. I thought I banged a girl and let her stay here."

"Oh."

He snorted. "Sorry, is that too much for your PG ears?"

"No, I just don't understand why that would be a bad thing."

Sighing deeply he propped himself up on an elbow and looked directly into my eyes. "Girls I screw around with aren't allowed to come in my room, let alone stay the night. This is the only place that is mine, and I'm not about to share it with them."

"So you sleep with women and then make them leave?" I didn't even want to ask *where* he slept with them.

"No, I *screw* women . . . and then make them leave."

I shook my head and walked toward the door, "You're a pig."

He laughed once without humor and watched me leave.

When I got out to the living room I saw Breanna at the kitchen table with a housemate, as soon as they saw me the conversation stopped. I hadn't known I could feel even more awkward, guess so.

Looking at me sheepishly, Bree stood from her chair and pulled me toward the living room. "Harper, I'm so sorry. Brad just told me everything." Her voice broke at the end. "I swear I would never intentionally do something to embarrass you. I know we just met but I've been looking forward to living with you and I can't believe I hurt you like that after just meeting you."

"Really, it's fine. I've heard enough stories that I figured you didn't know what you were doing."

"It's not fine! You should hate me."

I nodded and looked over at Brad who was grinning at me. "Well I don't plan on seeing any of these guys ever again, so there's no use in making you suffer with me." I smiled at her, trying to make light of the situation.

Although I was still humiliated, I'd never been one to hold a grudge, and I wasn't about to start now. I had wanted to come start a new life here, and even though I seem to have taken five steps back, I was still determined to make this the best experience ever. Embarrassing moment or not, it's not like I had a lot of options here. Either let this get to me and cower away from people, or hold my head high and push forward.

She still looked sullen and it was making me uncomfortable. "Well at least people don't think I'm a whore."

That brought on a smile which turned into a light laugh. "You're a glass half full kind of person, aren't you?"

"Definitely."

Hugging me tightly before walking back to her cup of coffee she said, "At least let me buy you one new outfit."

"Hah! I won't stop you. Are you sure you're up for that today though? I figured you wouldn't be up for much of anything after last night."

"Sweetie, I'm *always* up for shopping. Go change, I'm ready when you are."

I walked back into Chase's room to find it empty, after shedding his basketball shorts I quickly stepped into Bree's skirt. Before I could pull it up, the door swung open and Chase walked in.

"It's really a shame you don't let anyone see that sexy little body."

Blushing fifty shades of red, I pulled them up and turned to face him.

"Calm down, you don't have anything I haven't seen before." He cocked his head and raised an eyebrow making it disappear under his shaggy blond hair. "Not saying I wouldn't want to see yours."

"Bite me." I pushed past him toward the door.

"Is that an invitation?"

"Not even close."

He grabbed my waist, and pulled me against his chest, his nose skimming along my jaw, "One of these days Princess, I promise you."

I turned to scowl at him once more, "I would never be desperate enough to want you." Okay that was a lie; my breaths were already quickening just feeling his sculpted body pressed against mine.

His smile was slow and sexy, "We'll see."

BREANNA AND I were lying on our beds in the dorm room after an epic six hour shopping trip at an outdoor mall. As promised, I let her pick out all my outfits, and she paid for one of them. Now that we were done, I was regretting how much money I'd spent, but I'd just bought fifteen different shirts, four pairs of jeans, a couple pairs of ultra-short shorts and skirts, three sexy but cute dresses and five pairs of shoes. After that was done we headed to Victoria's Secret, and I blushed my way through the entire store while she picked out all my new underwear, bras and sleeping clothes. Our last stop of the day was at Sephora where we basically purchased my own make-up counter after Bree swore to teach me how to put it all on. And for all that? I think I did pretty well. The only thing Sir had let me do growing up was work at one of the Post Exchanges. Not that kids my age were generally allowed to, but everyone knew our situation so I started there when I was twelve and had saved every cent.

"I'm. So. Exhausted."

"It was so worth it though! Now you're finally ready for college."

Looking at the garbage bags full of most of my old clothes I laughed and let my head fall back onto my pillow. "I think you're right."

"Now we just need to get you comfortable being around cute guys and you'll be golden. What's your type?"

Your brother. "Um, I'm not sure I have a type."

"So no preferences? Hair color, eye color, skin color? Athlete, geek, musician?"

Rugged surfer, with dirty blond shaggy hair, impossibly blue eyes, the most breathtaking smile you've ever seen and cover him in tattoos. I'll take that, please? "Nope, none. We'll just have to start from scratch."

Just thinking about his tattoos had me biting my lip and fantasizing again about tracing them with my fingers. He was exactly the kind of guy Sir would hate, so naturally I was drawn to him.

"Hey Bree?"

"Yeah?"

"There's kind of something I've wanted to do for a whi— You know what, never mind."

She sat up on her knees bouncing, "No you don't! You have to tell me now. You've wanted to do what?"

"Well there's a lot of things. But it'd probably be a bad idea to do them all at once. I should spread them out, and think about them more."

"I'm waiting Harper."

I sighed and scooted up against the wall, "I want to get a couple piercings."

"Pfft, I thought you were about to say something juicier than that." Figures she wouldn't be excited, each of her ears had four piercings.

I frowned at her.

"Okay, okay! What piercings do you want?"

"Um, I don't know what they're called. But here, and here." I pointed a finger to my upper lip, and another to my ear.

"Oh cute! Your lip is called a Monroe, and your ear is a tragus. I actually really want my lip pierced too! Do you want to go get them done together sometime?"

I looked down before stealing a sideways glance, "Could we maybe go right now? Eighteen years of not being able to do what I want, I'm kind of impatient."

"Harper, I'm pretty sure we're going to be best friends." Without another word she shot off her bare mattress and headed for the door. Guess that means we're going.

I'm really glad she knew the area, because she drove right to a tattoo parlor, and after chatting it up with the piercer, we were sitting in his room picking out the studs before I could even think about this possibly being a bad idea. To my surprise, I wasn't even nervous 'til I was sitting on his chair and he was putting the markers on me. "Oh my God, Breanna I need your hand."

She laughed and sauntered up to me.

"Don't laugh, you're next." That shut her up.

"Okay deep breath in." The piercer said, "Annnnd blow out." After he finished putting the one in my ear, he opened up a new packet and got to work on my lip. "Another deep breath in . . . and blow out."

My eyes were watering, but thankfully it was done. I glanced in the mirror and a huge smile crossed my face, I absolutely loved them.

"Oh my God those are perfect for you! Ahh. I'm so excited for mine now!" Bree had also decided to get her tragus pierced so we both were getting two, but she and the piercer had agreed her bottom lip would be better for the way her mouth was set.

Another ten minutes and hers were done, I made her eat her words when she grabbed my hand at the last minute and squeezed until I thought I'd never get the circulation flowing again. We paid the guy and ran to her car, looking into the visor mirrors before we left.

"Are your parents going to mind?"

"What? No way. Have you seen my brother? They love his tattoos so they aren't going to care about this. Besides I'm pretty sure I couldn't get them mad at me even if I tried." She laughed, "Let me guess, daddy's gonna be pissed?"

"Ha! Yeah, I'm almost positive he's going to try to rip them out. Good thing I'm not going home for ten months!"

"Ten months?! What are you doing for winter break?"

I shrugged, "Stay here. It wouldn't be much different than being there. We don't spend much time together if we're in the same house."

"Jeez Harper, you had the most depressing childhood didn't you?"

"Not really, I mean it's all I've ever known. I thought it was normal until a few weeks ago when you and I started e-mailing." I think I need to stop talking about my past, because I always seem to depress everyone. "So . . . dinner?"

She smiled and turned to glance at me, "You read my mind roomie, let's grab some burgers then we can stay at my house tonight. We'll move my stuff into the dorm tomorrow."

3

AFTER ORIENTATION THAT next week, classes had started this last Monday and the first week had flown by. Breanna and I both loved our professors, and thankfully they didn't seem like they'd be too hard. I hadn't seen any of the guys from Chase's house, but that was my fault, I'd been avoiding them until today. Bree always ate lunch with them and though I'd made excuses the first three days, I was tired of eating alone in my room already. I'd never admit it out loud, but after Bree left for her first class this morning, I changed my outfit three times and spent extra time on my make-up. My entire body was shaking just think-ing about seeing Chase and I still had to sit through a class, thankfully I only had one today, and that was the last one for the week. Just as class let out, I received a text from my roommate making sure I'd be there today because she was already holding a seat for me. No getting out of it now.

"Hey, hey! What's up Princess!"

"Princess! Where've you been all my life?"

I bit back my groan and smiled at the guys as I sank into the seat next to Bree, I tried not to let my disappointment show when I didn't see Chase there. No sooner had I cursed myself for spending the extra time trying to look perfect today, than two hands appeared on either side of my plate and I felt a hard chest press against my back and warm breath against my ear.

"Have you been hiding from me, PG?" He chuckled when he felt me shiver.

"Why, you miss me?"

"Of course. You're my favorite, remember?" His nose brushed along my neck and I almost turned into a puddle right there.

I sighed dramatically and leaned away from his intoxicating presence, "Sad to say you're not mine."

"You sure about that?" He tapped a finger on my arm that was now covered in goose bumps.

"Chase! Stop bugging her, go sit down."

I blinked over to Breanna, remembering we were at a table with a group of other people. Chase sat a few seats away and I was grateful to be able to think clearly again. I looked around the table to see Chase's four housemates, two other girls I knew to be girlfriends of Brad and Derek, with another girl I'd never seen before who was openly glaring at me. After shooting her a dark look I continued my inventory of the rest of the table, on the other side of Chase were two guys I had seen at the party, but didn't know their names, and across from them was a pair of gray eyes smiling at me. I dropped my face to look down at my salad and counted to five before slowly lifting only my eyes to find him engaged in a conversation with Chase. Raising my head a little to get a better look, I took in his short buzzed hair, warm smile and single dimple on his right cheek as his laughter boomed across the table. His build was slightly bigger than Chase's, and the way his shirt stretched across his chest and shoulders, I'd bet he was perfectly muscled. Dear God, and I'd thought Chase was the most attractive guy I'd ever seen. This guy was . . . just wow.

"See something you like?" Bree leaned into my side, looking down my line of sight.

"What? No."

"Uh huh, that's why you're biting the crap out of your lip. He's looking at you again."

My head shot up, causing the mystery guy to smirk as his eyes met mine. I felt my cheeks start to burn and forced my head back down and toward Bree.

"How do we know he's not looking at you?"

"Ha! I knew you were staring at him." She grinned and took a massive bite of her burger.

"Wow, that's attractive."

She tried to talk around the mass in her mouth, "You're just jealous you didn't get one too."

Looking down at my salad I grimaced. My stomach was flipping so much now I don't think I could eat at all. "Do you know his name?" I whispered in her direction. Before she could answer, Drew interrupted.

"So Princess, how come we haven't seen you lately? It's been like two weeks, I feel so unloved."

I laughed and rolled my eyes at him, "Oh I'm sorry, did your girlfriend deflate already?"

The entire table burst into laughter and Derek was slapping him on the back while trying to keep his drink from spewing out of his mouth and nose. A couple of the guys started making fun of "Mindy the doll," and I was glad the attention was away from me.

Bree leaned back towards me and whispered, "His name's Brandon, he lives with the guys too but he wasn't at the party."

"So you know him well?" I wanted to look at him so bad, but didn't want to risk being caught staring again.

"Not really, he's only a Junior, and he lived in the dorms last year. I just met him this week during lunch."

"Only a Junior?" I asked confused.

"Yeah, the rest of the guys are Seniors."

"Oh." I looked up at her but gestured toward Brandon with my eyes, "Anything going on . . . ?"

She smiled and nudged me before sitting up straight, "I've already got my eye on a couple other guys."

I nodded remembering that she'd been talking about some guys in our dorm all week that she had classes with. Hearing my name, I glanced up to see Chase's fork paused halfway to his mouth, his jaw set tight, and his eyes burning holes in Brandon who was talking with one of the guys across from him. When he was done killing him a million different ways, Chase's eyes cut across to me and his entire face relaxed. He nodded slightly and resumed eating.

"Party tonight, you girls game?"

Bree snorted, "Seriously Zach? When have I ever not been there?"

"Princess?"

Bree answered for me, "Of course she'll be there." Then she whispered to me, "It won't be anything like the first one. There probably won't even be twenty people there. They save the big parties for Friday nights."

"Fine," I grumbled.

"Looking forward to sharing my bed with you again, PG."

I shot a hard look at Chase, heat flooding my cheeks. He was looking at Brandon with his head cocked to the side, one eyebrow raised. *I* could even see the challenge in his stare.

"Thanks, but I'd rather share a bed with Drew's blow-up doll."

He turned his glare toward me and I struggled to keep my eyes narrowed at him. Is it bad that all I could think about was how his lips would feel on mine? Before I could think on it too much, the girl that had been glaring at me earlier moved around the table and sat on his lap, pressing her mouth to his neck before trailing her lips along his jaw. His hands instantly gripped her hips, but he never took his eyes off of mine.

"I'd be happy to share that bed with you Chase." Her bubble gum voice made me want to gag. I'm pretty sure I hadn't even sounded like that when I was five.

After she brought his mouth to hers, I spared a glance in Brandon's direction to see him studying me. It wasn't uncomfortable, and it didn't last nearly as long as I would have liked it to, I could have sat there looking at him for hours. I wasn't used to feeling anything for a guy, and now I couldn't stop going back and forth between him and Chase. Butterflies in my stomach with one, and hot shivers with another. I almost laughed out loud when I realized how stupid it was to feel anything for Chase, his current position with the brunette proving why. Brandon on the other hand, I knew nothing about. Other than his laugh, I hadn't even heard his voice. Ugh, I'm ridiculous, one guy is a whore, the other I haven't even spoken to.

Saying good-bye to everyone, I picked up my bag and began walking away as a deep husky voice called my name. I didn't stop walking, but looked over my shoulder in time to see Brandon walking around the table toward me, and Chase holding the brunette's head away from his as he watched us, she just continued onto his neck.

Falling into step with me, he held out a hand, "We haven't met yet, I'm Brandon Taylor."

Dear Lord that voice could warm me on the coldest day of the year. "Harper Jackson, nice to meet you."

He smiled as he held the door open for me, "You too. You seem to know the rest of the guys pretty well though we're just meeting, they said you're Bree's roommate?"

"Uh, yeah. I am, but I don't really know them well. I've only talked to them for a total of about ten minutes before today."

"Really?" The corners of his mouth twitched up, "You seem to make quite an impression in a short amount of time then."

"Oh I definitely made an impression with them." I muttered.

He looked at me quizzically but I shook my head so he wouldn't push it. We stopped walking when we got to the path that would take me to the dorms and him to his next class. I turned toward him and shamelessly took in his worn jeans resting low on his narrow hips and fitted black shirt before going back to his face. I hadn't realized how tall he was when we were walking out, but he had to be at least a foot taller than me. His height and muscled body made me want to curl up in his arms, it looked like I'd fit perfectly there. I nervously bit my bottom lip while I watched his cloudy eyes slowly take in my small frame. It didn't feel like the guys at the party, looking at me like I was something to eat. His eyes made me feel beautiful, and it thrilled me that they were on me. *Thrilled me that they were on me? Get a grip Harper you just met him two seconds ago.*

"Come on PG, let's go." Chase grabbed my arm and started dragging me away.

"Chase! Stop!" I yanked my arm out and shot him a dirty look. "What is your problem?"

"I'm taking you and Bree to the house, and you need to pack for the weekend so let's go." He grabbed for me again but I dodged his hand.

"The weekend, what?"

"You're staying with me, go pack."

I narrowed my eyes and started to turn toward Brandon, "Fine, hold on."

"Harper."

"Go away Chase, I'll meet you in the room in a minute. Go find Bree."

He moved to stand closer behind me so I just sighed and gave Brandon a lame smile. "Sorry, apparently I have to go. I'll see you tonight?" I don't know why I asked, he actually lived there.

A sexy smile lit up his face as his hand reached out to quickly brush against my arm, "See you then." With a hard nod directed toward Chase, he turned and walked away.

I stalked past Chase and didn't look back at him the entire way to my room. He stood in the doorway as Bree and I packed for the weekend, which made me uncomfortable because I couldn't ask her which outfits I should wear. I threw in things she had gushed over at the mall, a few pairs of underwear, sleep shorts, make-up and all my bathroom supplies before finally saying anything to him.

"Why don't you be a dear and carry this for me." My tone was laced with anger, and he seemed to find it amusing.

I tried to squeeze by him but he caught me around my waist and pulled me close, his breath warm as he whispered in my ear, "Anything for you sweetheart."

My heart pounded and my legs started to shake. I stayed in his arms a second too long and he noticed. I pushed him off me as soon as I saw that cocky smirk take over his face. "God you piss me off."

"Whoa, whoa. Did you just say 'piss'? I'm not sure if that's PG approved." He laughed when I glowered at him and stormed away toward the parking lot.

As soon as we got to the house, Bree was talking to some guy on her cell in Chase's room which left me alone with Chase. Not wanting to deal with him, I grabbed the remote and spread out on the couch trying to find something other than him to hold my attention. I made it a point not to look in his direction again.

Sighing, I flipped through the guide a few more times without finding anything interesting and just turned on the news. Sir would have been proud.

I hated that I knew Chase was looking at me, or where he was in the room. Why does my skin have to tingle over a guy like him? It's not that I didn't want it to, because to be honest, he's all I could think about the last two weeks. But I've already heard all about his one-night-stand reputation from people at school, and from the stories his sister told me, I shouldn't even want to be with someone like him. He was with different women all the time, I knew what happened in the café was completely normal and Bree said he hadn't been in a relationship for four years because it "just isn't his thing." Apparently girls felt privileged to have been with him at all, I would hate to be anyone's one nighter. He walked over to the couch and I tried to still my heart when he lifted up my legs and sat down, putting them back on his lap. No need to let him know how being near to him had me coming undone.

"So I see my sister is already influencing you poorly."

Not like I expected a deep meaningful conversation, but I hadn't been expecting that. "Do I even want to know what you're talking about?"

"This." He leaned over to touch just above my lips. Damn the stupid shivers that course through my body when he touches me.

"What, you don't like it?"

"I never said that, it's hot as hell." He let his fingers trail across my jaw before sitting up with a smirk, "But I'm disappointed you'd let her start talking you into stuff already. Figured you weren't one to give in to people like that."

My mouth dropped and I pulled my knees up to my chest so I was no longer touching him. "Not that it's your business, but I was the one who wanted them and brought it up. I didn't know at that time that she would want to get them too, and I certainly wouldn't let someone talk me into something like that. Glad to know you think so highly of me." With that I left for his room only to find it locked. I didn't want to go back in there and face him, but I didn't want to stand here like an idiot either. I heard his phone ring and listened to his voice retreat as he went outside before deciding to go back to the couch. I had barely sat down when he was next to me, arm extended with phone in hand.

"It's for you." His mouth was set in a firm line and I noticed his jaw tick from the pressure.

"He-hello?"

"Sorry to have to go through Chase, but I wanted to talk to you."

I glanced back at the phone and saw Brandon's name, smiling I brought it back to my ear and relaxed into the cushions. "I don't mind, what's up?"

"I have a few hours before my last class, would you like to grab a coffee with me before?"

I wanted to say something along the lines of *Yes, please! I want nothing more than to sit there and look at your smile for the next couple hours!* Instead, I kept it simple. "I'd like that. Did you want me to meet you somewhere . . . ?" Does he know I don't have a car?

"I'm on my way to the house, I'll be there in five."

"See you." I smiled and handed the phone back to a stone-faced Chase. I ran back to his door and pounded on it so Bree would unlock it.

"Brandon's coming to pick me up for coffee!" I all but squealed.

"I'll call you back!" She pressed end and pointed at me, "I knew it!"

"You knew he was going to call?"

"No, I knew you liked him!"

I scoffed. "Bree, I don't even know him."

"But you want to?"

"Uh, did you not see him?" He was ridiculously attractive,

and had that rugged look that made me quiver. "And oh my goodness that smile."

"Oh sweetie, you are so falling for him already."

"Crap, Bree I'm nervous. I don't know how to talk to guys."

"You talk to Chase and the other guys just fine . . . ?"

"Yeah, but that's because they're more annoying than anything. And so far Brandon isn't, plus he's incredibly gorgeous." I smiled when she elbowed me.

"Just try to see him like the rest of them, they all love you, and I'm pretty sure he's already completely taken with you; so you have nothing to worry about!"

"If you say so. Do I look okay?"

"Yeah you do! I meant to say something at lunch, you look stunning!"

I laughed at the fact that just this morning I'd been dressing for Chase, and now here I am getting excited about going to coffee with Brandon. And by excited, I mean frantically nervous.

"What's funny?"

Oops. "Nothing."

She wasn't buying it.

"It's just no one's ever asked me to go anywhere with them," I lied, "and I'm getting all excited over coffee. I feel stupid that I'm eighteen and I still haven't been asked on a date."

"Well I have a feeling that isn't going to be true much longer." Just then we heard Brandon calling for me. "See you when you get back!"

I took a deep breath before leaving the room to meet up with him. Heat zinged across my cheeks when he smiled at me. Did everyone here have to have an absolutely perfect smile and teeth? Thankfully, I'd inherited my mom's teeth, they naturally looked like I'd had braces for years.

"You ready?"

I nodded and ducked my head in an attempt to hide my blush.

Unfortunately, I'd also inherited that from her. I followed him out and jumped into the passenger side of his black Jeep that looked perfect for off-roading. There wasn't much of an opportunity for talking, unless I wanted a mouthful of hair, so I sat quietly until we pulled into a parking lot. I grabbed the door handle but stopped when his hand touched mine.

"Wait," he said with a smirk before jumping out and jogging to my side and opening my door.

Dangerous-model-looking god *and* a gentleman? I raised an eyebrow and smiled, "Well thank you."

"Of course." He tucked my hair behind my ear and a slow smile spread across his face as he took it all in. "Maybe I should put the top back on."

My face fell and my eyes grew wide.

"Oh! No, I didn't mean it in a bad way. Far from it, I swear."

I was suddenly fascinated with the pavement.

He put his hand under my chin until I looked at him again. "Harper, I'm sorry for the way that came out. You're already the most beautiful girl I've ever seen, but I swear the way your hair looks right now . . ." he trailed and his eyes heated, "I'm gonna be fighting guys off you for sure."

He said I was beautiful. My smile grew wide and I put the rubber band I'd been digging out of my purse back in, "I doubt that, but thanks."

Brandon just shook his head and led me toward the doors with a hand behind me. I wanted him to touch my back with his big hands, to feel their warmth on me. But he never closed the distance, just guided me. We got our drinks and went back outside to sit on the patio before we said anything else. It was nice that he didn't feel the need to fill the silence, plus it gave me some time to calm my nerves.

"So tell me about yourself," he began.

"What do you want to know?"

"Everything." One corner of his mouth turned up, his dimple barely showing.

I shrugged "There's not much to tell, my life has been incredibly boring."

He laughed softly before continuing, "Okay fine, family?"

"I grew up with my dad, no siblings. Was homeschooled my whole life, I think just so he could keep an eye on me."

"Wait, you were homeschooled?"

"Yes . . . ?"

"I'm sorry, you're just not what I'd pictured a homeschooler to look like."

I laughed. I wonder if he saw how I looked when I showed up a couple weeks ago, he would still think that. "I guess I'll take that as a compliment?"

His warm eyes and smile confirmed that I should. "Where was your mom?"

"She died giving birth to me." I was expecting him to get awkward and start apologizing profusely, instead his eyes were soft and his mouth barely tipped up in a smile.

"My dad's gone too. He was on one of the planes that crashed into the twin towers."

My heart sunk. I never understood why people felt sorry for me. Yes it hurt knowing I'd never meet my mom, but I hadn't had the chance to lose her. She was already gone. But this? I would never understand Brandon's hurt, and I didn't know how to try, but I wanted to take it away. What I did know, was that he didn't need my condolences right now, so I reached my hand across the table and rested it on top of his. He made slow circles on my thumb causing my entire hand to heat up.

"Tell me about him."

He glanced up and my breath caught at his expression. If a masculine man could be described as beautiful, then his expression was just that.

"He was amazing. Hard worker, but always home for dinner with us. Brought my mom flowers every other weekend, never missed one of our games. Taught me how to play football and surf. He made sure to let us know we could have anything we wanted if we worked hard enough for it. I always wanted to be like him when I grew up. Everyone loved him, he was a great man."

"Sounds like it. I'm sure he would be very proud of you."

He smiled at me and sat back into the chair, looking at me intently.

"What?"

"I've never had someone ask me that. Normally people just tell me they're sorry and get uncomfortable. It's awkward and to be honest, gets kind of old."

"Does it bother you that I asked?"

"Not at all. It's nice to talk about him sometimes. Your dad ever talk about your mom?"

"Um, not exactly. Just said enough to let me know I reminded him too much of her. It never made sense to me, he always kept me close, like with the homeschooling, but he always made it clear he didn't want me." I snapped my mouth shut before I could say anything else. I exhaled in relief when he didn't ask me to explain that further.

"Well it's his loss."

Yeah, try telling him that. He was stupid enough to let a bunch of horny Marines raise me. "Are you from around here?"

"I'm from Arizona, just south of Phoenix. My dad's side of the family doesn't live too far away though, that's kind of what brought me here."

"Do you see them a lot while you're in school?"

He shrugged and tilted his head to the side, "Usually once a month. What about you?"

"My dad's been in the Marine Corps since before I was born, he's stationed at Camp Lejeune."

"And what brought you to SDSU?" He leaned forward, his elbows resting on the table.

"You want my honest answer?"

"Of course."

"I wanted to get as far from home as possible, and I love the beach. Plus, the fact that it wasn't too far from another base was the only way I could get Sir to agree."

"Well I'm glad you're here Harper."

My stomach warmed hearing his deep voice say my name. "Me too."

We stayed there for the next hour and a half talking about everything from favorite movies and foods to school and aspirations. Brandon was easy to talk to, and I had a feeling Breanna was right, I was already falling. Hard.

4

ONCE I GOT back, Bree and I took over Chase's room to get ready for tonight. I ended up in a pair of daisy dukes and a black off the shoulder t-shirt that I absolutely loved. I left the shadow neutral, put on some eyeliner and mascara before putting my long hair in a low ponytail. Bree came up and pulled at my hair making it look a little messy before she gave her approval of my overall look.

"You excited to spend the weekend with Brandon?"

My heart was racing and I was smiling like an idiot just hearing his name. I glanced at my left hand that was still tingling from Brandon holding it on the way to Chase's. "Yes! I just hope he doesn't think anything is going to happen because I'm staying here."

"You mean like *happen* happen. Or am I missing something?"

"No, I'm pretty sure you got it."

"It's not like you're staying with him, you'll be in here with me."

I nodded and looked to the door then back to her, "Do you think the guys will tell him?"

"Tell him what?"

"About me being a virgin?" I whispered the last part, I didn't know if he was home yet and I didn't know where his room was.

She snorted and grabbed her perfume to spray us with, "Who cares if they did. It's like you said, at least you're not a whore, and trust me when I say this Harper . . . guys love knowing a girl isn't sleazy."

We heard the voices get louder in the living room, so after another quick glance in the mirror, we made our way out to join them. Bree had been right, there were only about twenty people here, and they were all currently surrounding the bar where Zach was chugging a massive drink. I glanced around and saw Chase's face pressed into some girl's neck and Brandon walking in from one of the halls. We smiled widely at each other as he came to stand by my side.

"Hey beautiful."

My heart practically beat out of my chest. "How was your class?" I softly nudged his side.

"Long, but I'm glad I'm done for the week."

"Same here, it'll be nice to always have three days to relax."

He nodded and leaned closer, "So you guys will be here all weekend?" I caught a ghost of a smile on his lips.

"At least through Saturday." I tried not to lean into him when I caught a hint of his cologne. I couldn't place the scent, but it was perfect for him.

"Can I ask you something?" He glanced over his shoulder before meeting my gaze again.

"Of course."

"Is there something going on with you and Chase?"

I leaned away to look at his face. Was he serious? "No . . . why?"

Brandon looked to the side, "No reason. I was just curious."

My face fell. "Brandon. What happened?"

"Nothing." Brandon sat there for a moment studying my glare before conceding, "After I dropped you off, he called to tell me to stay away from you."

"*What*?"

"Yeah, said that you're taken and he reminded me *again* that you've slept in his bed and would be this weekend."

Taken? Hardly. I pointed to where Chase was sticking his tongue down the same girl's throat and laughed. "Well you tell me, does it look like there's something going on?" I turned toward the living room and he followed. "As for sleeping in his bed, he said he was 'protecting' me from the other guys, and I swear to you nothing happened."

"Will you be staying in there this weekend?" He didn't sound angry or possessive, simply curious.

"Most likely, but it will be with Bree. He won't even be in the room." I hoped.

"And you aren't dating anyone?"

I turned to look at him over my shoulder, "Not yet."

His smile turned playful as we sat down on the couch, "So I don't need to stay away from you?"

My breaths were coming faster as I stared into his warm eyes that were only inches from mine, "I really hope you won't." I caught myself leaning in closer to his face and saw his eyes look at my lips then back to mine as they turned to liquid steel. Before our faces could touch I was yanked back and thrown over Chase's shoulder as he yelled for the beer pong game to start.

"CHASE! Put me down!" I couldn't even enjoy the fact that his hands were touching my bare thighs. He'd just stopped what could have been my first kiss, and his shoulder was really un-comfortable against my stomach.

"No way! The Princess needs her throne!"

I started beating my fists on his back, which just made him laugh harder and smack my butt. Ugh, this was the worst position to be in, I couldn't even get a good pressure point to hit. "If you don't put me down I will make good on my previous threat!"

He laughed for another few seconds before remembering the night in his bed, immediately his laughter stopped and I was set down. But of course, I couldn't have the last word. Gripping my arm firmly, he pulled me toward the front door before bringing me close to his body so he could whisper roughly in my ear.

"I don't want you with him." He growled and his grip tightened. Gah, even that sent shivers of pleasure through me.

"What is your deal with him? Is there something he did that you'd like to share?"

"He's not good enough for you."

I shook my head and failed at yanking my arm free, it was starting to get painful. "How do you know what is and isn't good for me? You don't even know me!" I hissed.

Warm hands were on my shoulders then, and though he dropped my arm, Chase looked more pissed off than he had before. I knew he'd been gripping me tight, but my arm was now throbbing where his hand had just been.

"I thought I told you to back off man?" Chase's voice got louder, I swear I could practically see his feathers ruffle.

I could tell Brandon was standing in an intimidating stance, but he seemed perfectly at ease making soothing trails up and down my arms. "I don't really think that's up to you."

Chase looked at me softly, his voice still harsh, "You hurt her, I swear to God I'll break your neck." With that, he pushed past us and went back toward the kitchen.

That was a little much. "Ridiculous." I blew out a breath I hadn't realized I was holding and turned to look at Brandon. "Before you ask, I have absolutely no idea."

He laughed and wrapped his arms around me, pulling me close to his chest. "And you're sure nothing's going on between you?"

"Positive. He probably just views me as his sister, so he's a little protective."

"Hah! I'm pretty sure he doesn't see you like he sees Bree."

"What do you mean?"

I didn't think it was possible, but somehow his voice got even lower and all I wanted to do was close my eyes and listen to him talk. "You're gorgeous, funny and just all around amazing. And what makes it worse is that you don't even see it. All the guys had been talking about you before I even got here, and after today, I see why."

"No they weren't Brandon." I rolled my eyes.

He raised his eyebrow and smirked, "I wouldn't lie to you. Harper, trust me when I say he doesn't want to be your brother, but I'm not about to let him try to be anything else."

His mouth was on mine then and my entire world stopped. One hand gripped my hip, and the other snaked around behind my neck, anchoring my face to his. His full lips were soft but firm as they moved against mine. Pulling back slightly to look into my eyes, he smiled and softly brushed his lips across my own twice before kissing me again, lightly sliding his tongue against my bottom lip. I gasped and gripped his shirt, pressing my body closer to his. A groan escaped his mouth as our tongues met, sending goose bumps across my body. Our breaths were ragged when we broke apart, and I could see myself falling in love with those lips. The pad of his thumb brushed across my cheek as his liquid gray eyes searched mine.

"Harper come on it's our tu—woops! Sorry." She hardly looked sorry as she sat there smiling at us.

"What Bree?"

"Oh! Um, it's my turn at beer pong. I want you to be my partner."

Okay that was the second time I'd heard the words "beer pong." What on earth is that? "I don't know how to play."

"Well, duh. But you're not going to learn by standing back here making out."

I blushed and ducked my head again, Brandon just chuckled beside me. "Okay, let's go."

All the guys tried to explain the game to me as Konrad—Bree's fling for the weekend—and Drew set up the table. I nodded and started to worry when they did half a beer per cup. If these guys were good, I was going to be falling over in no time.

I leaned into Bree to whisper, "Are the cups supposed to be that full?"

"Not even close, they're doing it because Drew wants to get you drunk. Let's just hope they don't make many."

"I'm pretty sure he's going to get what he wants." I felt sick already and I hadn't even had a sip yet.

Apparently, it's true what they say about beginners luck, because I only missed one shot, and only had to drink two cups. Even with those, I was already feeling good and laughing a little more. I know, I know. I'm a lightweight. They set the cups up again, this time there wasn't much in each, and Brandon stepped up with Derek.

I raised my eyebrows and smiled slowly, "Ready to lose?"

"I've never lost before. Bring it sweetheart."

The boys went first, and each made it. We drank the first two before both landing our shots as well. Brandon made his, Derek didn't. Bree and I both made ours. I started gloating, but then they both made their shots. I'm really glad Konrad and Drew weren't this good. Bree made hers and I lined up. Just before I let go of the ball, Brandon stretched his arms above his head and arched his back. His shirt raised a little exposing a perfectly muscled V that met his boxers, which were barely visible above his jeans. I missed that one. He laughed and fixed his shirt.

Cheater. I whispered to Bree as Derek drank a cup and she burst into laughter. Everyone looked at us like we were crazy, so we just shrugged our shoulders. Brandon raised his hand, and as he did I bent over acting like I was looking for something on the floor, purposefully turning so my butt was facing him. He missed. When Derek went for his turn, Bree bent slightly at the waist, giving them a better view of her cleavage, her hand trailing along her chest. His ball didn't even hit anywhere on the table, which landed him a hand across the back of his head from his girlfriend. We were cracking up as we both made our next shots. Before the guys could go, two guys I didn't know came up behind us and made sure we couldn't "cheat" again, not that it made a difference. We were all laughing so hard from everyone still attempting to distract the other side, that no one made their next few shots. Although the first half of the game flew by, it took me and Bree four more turns to make our last two cups.

"I'm done. Someone else can take my spot." I laughed and backed away from an advancing Brandon.

"You think you're funny, huh?"

I nodded and continued my retreat but he caught my hips and firmly pressed his lips to mine, when our lips parted he picked me up and started walking me toward the couches. I wrapped my legs around his waist and kissed him as passionately as my tipsy self would allow. I whimpered when he caught my bottom lip between his teeth as he sat on the couch. Good God, was this what I'd always been missing? Or was my blood heating and my heart racing just because it was Brandon? Grabbing his broad shoulders, I melted against his body, his muscled arms holding me tight. Our tongues met again and he gripped my hips tighter when I arched my body into his. Before I could protest from his lips leaving mine, he started making a trail across my jaw and down my neck, my eyes shot open when a familiar voice broke through the haze Brandon's lips and tongue had put me in.

"So much for the PG rating." Chase sneered as he made his way toward the back door with the girl from earlier.

My eyes went wide when the party came back into view; I had completely forgotten we weren't alone. Looking down at the position Brandon and I were in, I quickly climbed off his lap and sunk down next to him, trying to keep my eyes off Chase.

Brandon looked at me confused, "Wait, 'PG' is a rating they gave you?"

I blushed fiercely and looked at my hands. I guess the guys hadn't informed him.

"What, she didn't tell you? Princess over here was as virgin as someone could possibly get until she met you. Now she's just simply a virgin, I guess we can raise it to PG-13 until later. I'm sure she's ready to get rid of it all together. Maybe you'll have better luck than I did."

My breath was coming quickly for a completely different reason now, and I couldn't meet Brandon's eyes again, though I knew he was still staring at me. Chase and his nightly tramp snickered as they walked outside and I took off for his room. I should have known he would lock it while people were here, but I was two seconds from breaking it in so Brandon wouldn't see the embarrassment covering my face. I turned into the bathroom and shut the door as I heard him and someone else approaching. Less than a minute later, there was a soft knock and Bree walked in, shutting the door again behind her.

"Will you ever forgive me?"

I looked up at her, "Forgive you? For what?"

"For telling them the last time."

"Bree you didn't tell them maliciously. You weren't even completely coherent when you said it! What he did is completely different."

She sat on the floor next to me, and ran her fingers through my ponytail.

"Did everyone hear him?"

"No, everyone was still in the kitchen, I just happened to be standing there with Konrad when they walked by."

I nodded and tried to be happy about that. "Can you get the key to his room please?"

"Harper, you can't just hide when someone tries to embarrass you."

"Breanna. Please. I can't face Brandon right now."

"Why not?"

"Did you not just hear everything your brother said? How could I after that? He'll probably start calling me PG like the rest of them." I looked at her like this should be obvious.

"I don't know him well, but from what I *have* seen this week and what you've said I would bet he isn't like the rest of them. He's seriously pissed at Chase for embarrassing you. I had to talk him down from going after him and coming to your rescue. I figured you'd want to talk to me first."

"Thanks Bree, you're a good friend. And I'll talk to him, but later. Can you please go get the key, I really just want to be alone right now."

She shut the door behind her, but a few seconds later I heard her voice coming back toward the bathroom. "She doesn't want to see you right now, just give her some time."

I could tell it was Brandon by how deep the voice was, but I couldn't make out what he was saying to her.

"Because she's humiliated! She'll come around though . . . No, if you want to blame someone, you can blame me. I'm the one who told everyone the first day she met them . . . Look, Chase is an ass, but you're going to embarrass her more if you confront him. He'll make sure of it, so drop it."

I didn't hear anything else for a few minutes until Bree came back with the key. She checked the hall before leading me to Chase's room.

"My first two parties ever, and I hide out for most of them."

"Well I don't exactly blame you for this time. But I wish you would talk to Brandon. He doesn't understand why you're avoiding him."

I laughed humorlessly and grabbed a pair of pajama shorts and racer back tank top from my bag. "Thanks for talking to him for me. I think I'm just going to go to bed."

"Really? It's only eleven."

"Yeah, we got up early; I'll stay up later tomorrow, kay?"

I grabbed my mouthwash, toothbrush, paste and clothes and ran back to the bathroom. Before shutting the door, I turned to Bree, "Thanks again Bree. If you see Brandon again tonight, will you please tell him I'll see him tomorrow?"

She frowned but nodded. After I was make-up free and clean, I put on my pajamas and climbed into the bed. I don't know how long I'd been in there, but it wasn't long before Chase came barging in.

"Can't you just leave me alone?" I groaned and rolled over to face him.

"Once again Princess, you're in my room."

"Fine, then *I'll* go." I tried to make my way around him but he planted his hands on my shoulders holding me in place. "Chase let me go!"

"Not until you talk to me."

I couldn't even throw my hands out in exasperation, "We have nothing to talk about!"

"I'm sorry I hurt you but I was just so damn mad!"

"Do you know how immature you sound right now? You decided to hurt me because *you* were mad?! What did I ever do to you Chase? And why do I always end up with your hands on me? Let. Me. Go."

"Because you won't stop and talk to me for five minutes!"

"Then you should understand that I don't want to talk to

you." He still didn't let me go, "Answer me! What did I do to make you mad?"

His face was suddenly directly in front of mine and he gripped even harder, making me gasp from the sudden pain; it felt like his thumbs were digging into the sockets. "Nothing! You did nothing, I'm not mad at you!" The scent of vodka was pouring out of his mouth, I'm pretty sure I could get drunk just from his breath.

"Seriously, you're hurting me! Get off me and leave me alone!" I didn't feel threatened yet, but I instinctively went through different moves I'd been taught in case I started to.

The door swung open and Brandon rushed in, followed closely by Bree and a few others. "What the hell, Chase?!" He roared and stomped toward us.

Brandon's fist connected with Chase's face seconds after his hands left me. I shrieked and jumped back as he fell to the ground.

"Keep your hands off her!" Brandon took a step toward me and pulled me close, cupping my face in his hands. "Was he hurting you?"

I just stared at him and put a hand over his reassuringly. I didn't need a guy coming to my rescue, but damn if Brandon punching him hadn't just turned me on.

"Come on, let's get you out of this room." He led me toward the door, stopping at Bree. "Bree I'm sorry—"

She held up a hand to stop him, "Don't. He deserved that one." She smiled at us before glaring at her brother, still on the floor. Brandon must've hit him hard. "Can you make sure Harper has a bed to sleep in tonight? I don't want him near her."

"Of course."

"And keep your hands to yourself," she said sternly, complete with a raised eyebrow.

"Yes ma'am." He squeezed me gently once before pulling

me through the crowd gathered in the doorway and hall. Once we were in his dark room he turned to face me and cupped my cheeks once again. "Are you okay?"

"Yeah, I'm fine. He wasn't doing anything other than trying to talk to me."

"He doesn't need to force you to speak with him, or to stay in the room with him. He should have let you go the first time you asked him."

"The first time?"

He sighed, "We heard everything Harper."

I groaned and let my head sink into his chest, silently thanking the dark for hiding my blush, "Awesome. I'm starting to think I'm just not meant to come to this house."

"Maybe just when Chase is here." He laughed when I playfully slapped his stomach. "I'll protect you."

"I noticed that. I think you knocked him out."

"Trust me, I didn't. I only hit him hard enough to make him think twice before touching you again." He released me so he could look at my face, or attempt to anyway, it was really dark in his room, "Did that bother you?"

"No, just surprised me. I wasn't expecting it."

"I'm sorry, it was hard walking in on you two for the second time tonight and hearing you tell him to let you go."

If I had punched him, I wouldn't have stopped with one. And here he was apologizing for standing up for me. I wrapped my hands around his neck pulling his face to mine, pausing just before our lips touched, "Don't be sorry." I pressed my lips softly to his twice, before resting my forehead against his.

"I shouldn't have done that in front of you."

I smiled into the darkness, I understand he didn't know that my entire body was warming over what just happened, but I wasn't about to tell him that either. "You're sure you didn't knock him out though?"

Brandon's rich laugh surrounded me and I sighed at the warmth it carried, "I do this for a living Harper, I'm positive I didn't hit him that hard."

"Uh, what? You do what?"

"I fight, didn't Bree tell you that?"

That was a big negative, I'm pretty sure I would have remembered something like that. "Um, no. What do you mean you fight for a living? Fight how?"

"MMA, it's mostly underground fights though. Every now and then I'll do local tournaments, but I prefer the Underground. Less rules, better pay."

Suddenly his size was a little more intimidating. He was tall, muscled and seriously rugged. But I had thought he looked like an underwear model, or an Abercrombie and Fitch model. "Huh," I replied lamely.

"That bothers you." He deadpanned.

I shook my head. Nope, still definitely turned on, even more so now. Was that weird? "How long have you done that?"

"Started going to a gym and training after my dad died, just to let everything out. It wasn't until I ran into Brad and Chase in a gym here my Freshman year that I started on the Underground."

"They fight too?" How had Bree failed to mention all this?

"Not really, mostly just train at the gym. They've done a few fights, but I haven't seen Brad fight since maybe middle of last year, Chase around the same time."

"Huh," I repeated. Man I was all kinds of brilliant tonight.

Brandon's face was guarded while he tried to understand my thoughts.

"That's kind of creepy, but kind of hot. Can I see you fight?"

He smiled widely. "If you want, I'm sure there's another one coming up in a few days."

"You don't know when it is?"

"Nope, I get a call an hour before it's supposed to happen. Other people start finding out about it after, that way there isn't enough buzz to attract unwanted attention."

"Unwanted . . . like cops?"

"You're quick," he whispered against my neck and I shivered from his warm breath against my skin, "Are you ready to go to sleep?"

Not really, but I nodded anyway. "Where are you going to sleep?"

"I'll sleep on the floor." He kissed my nose and swept me into his arms like I weighed nothing at all.

"Holy crap!"

He laughed and pulled the comforter back on his bed before lowering me into it.

"You do realize I could have done that myself?" I said a little breathlessly.

"Yeah, but where's the fun in that?" He kissed a trail from my collarbone to right behind my ear, "I'll be back in a few minutes."

I heard some drawers open and shut before he left, and though I tried to calm myself enough to fall asleep, I was still wide awake when the door opened about five minutes later revealing Brandon in nothing but a pair of work out shorts. And dear Lord that boy had an amazing body. My eyes were traveling up his torso and I thought I saw something on his chest, but before I could look close enough, the door shut and the room was dark again. He grabbed a pillow from the bed and dropped to the floor. After a few more minutes I realized there was no way I was going to fall asleep knowing he was down there. He had to be uncomfortable, and he didn't even have a blanket.

"Hey Brandon?"

"Hmm?"

I paused, and almost talked myself out of it. But only almost.

Leaning over the bed to look down at where he was, I smiled and let my hand fall down to his chiseled chest. I wanted nothing more than to run my hands all over his sculpted body, but I wanted him wrapped around me more, "I don't want you to sleep down there."

"Oh, okay." He grabbed his pillow and walked toward the door.

"What . . . where are you going?"

"To crash on Drew's floor."

"Why?"

"So you'll be okay to sleep, I'll see you in the morning Harper. Sweet dreams."

This guy beats the crap out of people on a regular basis, but is doing everything to make sure I'm not uncomfortable? My God he's perfect. I chuckled and sat up, "No, I want you in the room. I just don't want you on the floor."

"Are you sure?"

"Come here." I held out my hand and waited for him to reach me. He took it and slid in next to me before kissing my palm.

"I really don't mind sleeping on the floor if you're uncomfortable with this."

"I know." I smiled to myself as I curled my back into his chest and sighed happily. I was right, it's like I was made to be in his arms.

"Can I ask you something?"

I laughed at the same phrase that had practically started our night, "Of course."

"Why wouldn't you see me tonight? After what Chase said?"

Ugh, I'd already forgotten about that. "I was embarrassed and kind of afraid of what you'd think of me."

"What I'd think of you? Why?"

Apparently I'm the only person who sees it this way. I turned to face him, "Because I'm weird. Up until two weeks ago, I'd never been to a party, I'd never hung out with normal guys my own age, and like Chase said—"

"Am I the first person you've ever kissed?"

I didn't answer for a minute. "Yes."

He laughed and trailed his fingers across my back in random patterns, "I would have never known, you're an amazing kisser."

"You don't have to try to make me feel better."

His next laugh was a little louder, "I'm not, I swear. During the two games of beer pong all I could think about was kissing you again."

He had no idea. "So you didn't know what 'PG' meant?"

"Not at all. I figured since they called you 'Princess,' they had just shortened that with something else to 'PG.' "

"I'm not really a fan of either name." I grumbled.

"You won't hear either from me," he whispered against my neck and my whole body tingled, "I promise."

The way he was nipping at my neck caused me to almost forget what I wanted to ask him, "Does it bother you that I'm so inexperienced?"

I could feel his smile against my collarbone, his lips brushing against it as he shook his head, "No. If I'm being honest, I love knowing that your firsts will all be with me."

All? Oh God my heart was racing just thinking about being with him like that. It wasn't something I wanted yet, but I'd be lying if I said I didn't want to think about Brandon's hard body pressing against mine. "Have you ever been with someone?" The way his body stiffened, I knew he knew what I was asking.

"Yes."

"How many girls?"

He pushed back slightly and ran a hand through my hair, cupping the back of my neck with it, "Harper . . . is that really something you want to know?"

I was already head over heels for this guy, and if he decided he wanted to be in a relationship at some point, this was something I definitely needed to know. God, please don't let him be like Chase. I swallowed audibly, "Yeah, it is." We were talking about *all* of my firsts being with him after all, it was only fair that I knew too . . . right?

He blew out a deep breath and thought for a second, "Five. I'm not like some of the other guys here. I actually have relationships, so my last five girlfriends."

Five seemed like a hell of a lot to me, but then again I was glad that at least he could count them on one hand. Chase could barely count a week's worth on both hands. "Okay."

"Please don't ever be too embarrassed to talk to me." He leaned in to whisper in my ear, "I'll never intentionally make you uncomfortable. If I do, tell me. And I promise I'll never push you to do anything you don't want to."

"I know you won't, I'm not worried about that." I pressed my face into his chest and fought the urge to run my fingers across his abs. We sat there in silence for a few more minutes, I almost fell asleep from the way his fingers were trailing down my back, but I wasn't ready to finish my time with him just yet. "Where did you go when you left?"

"Did you miss me?" He chuckled into my hair, "I just took a shower."

"Oh, that was fast." Seriously? He'd only been gone a handful of minutes, it practically took me that long to wash my hair . . . not that he had that problem. Slowly reaching my hand up, I passed it over his short buzz a few times.

"Does my head bother you?"

"Not at all." If I was being honest, I loved the feel of it against my palms and fingers. I'd been wanting to do this since the moment I first saw him in the café. I continued to lightly run the tips of my fingers over his head, causing him to groan.

"You don't know how good that feels."

I crawled higher up on the bed to press my lips to first his head, then temple, making my way to his lips. He crushed his mouth to mine when I got closer and I sucked in a startled breath. He held my body close to his, the weight of him as he rolled slightly on top of me was exhilarating and I found myself trying to pull him even closer. Parting my legs with one of his knees, heat instantly pooled low in my belly when his knee pressed high up against the inside of my thighs. I shuddered when Brandon made a trail to the base of my neck.

"Harper," he groaned into my skin, "you can't do that."

I froze, "What did I do?"

He blew out a long breath before rolling back to his side and curling me into his arms. "You can't shiver like that when I kiss you. It drives me crazy."

Relieved I hadn't actually done anything wrong, I bit my lip and tried to keep the stupid grin off my face. Good to know I affect him as much as he does me.

"If we don't go to sleep, I'm going to have to go back to the floor."

I sighed in disappointment, but he was right. "Goodnight Brandon. I'll see you in the morning."

"Night sweetheart."

THERE WAS NO freak out when I woke the next day, I knew exactly who had their arm around me and where I was. I stayed wrapped in Brandon's arms for a few minutes just enjoying being there until his fingers started tracing patterns on my waist.

"I'm guessing you're awake then?"

"Well I really hope I'm not dreaming you here." Dear Lord how could his voice be any sexier?

I turned to face him and when his breath caught, covered my face with my hands. I silently prayed I didn't look absolutely hideous. I had washed my make-up off the night before, so there wouldn't be any streaks of mascara. But I'm sure there could be a ton of other things wrong right now.

He slowly peeled my hands away, "God you're beautiful Harper." His hand left mine to brush across my cheek and push back my hair. "It was too dark to see you last night, but now?" He paused and slightly shook his head. "Beautiful is all I can manage right now."

I smiled and studied his face for an immeasurable amount of time. Something seemed off but I couldn't place it for a while. "Your eyes are brown!"

He laughed and I desperately wanted to kiss that dimple, "Thanks for the observation . . . ?"

"No, no. I just thought they were gray, like mine."

"I've never seen anyone with eyes like yours. They're mesmerizing." I looked at him pointedly, so he continued, "Grayish, brownish, greenish. Just depends. They change all the time."

"But they were really gray yesterday, and now they're really brown. They don't just look hazel."

"Different lights, different shirt colors, different eyes."

"So what would usually make them green?" I was fascinated now, I wanted to see every different color they could possibly be.

"I don't know, hulk-like tendencies I guess."

I laughed and kissed his hard jaw, "Well too bad it was dark in Chase's room last night, I would have liked to see that color too."

His hands clenched into fists behind my back and I'm pretty sure he growled.

"Hey, calm down."

"Sorry," he exhaled and forced his hands to relax, "I just feel like one wasn't enough. He deserves a few more for yesterday."

Males and their constant need to be violent. Ridiculous. "Please don't. I'm fine, all he did was embarrass me."

"If he does anything like that again and I'm not around, please tell me."

I blew out a deep breath and kissed his lips to keep from saying anything about his protective nature, he was just standing up for me. "I will." Tucking my head back into his chest, I finally got a good look at it. "Hey you have a tattoo." I touched the numbers on his chest and tried to make sense of them.

"I have a few."

"What do the numbers and letters mean?" I traced them all. *U A F 175 9 11 01*

"United Airlines Flight 175. September 11, 2001."

"Your Dad."

"Mhmm."

"Can I ask you something? You don't have to answer it."

He tucked my hair behind my ear again and cupped my face, "I'll answer anything for you."

"Why was he on that plane?"

"Twice a year he had to go on a two week long business trip all over the country. He was headed for his last stop before he was going to come home." The pain in his voice was unmistakable and I instantly regretted asking.

"I'm sorry," I whispered into his chest, and placed a light kiss over the tattoo. I sat there quietly until he returned to playing with my hair and making circles on my back, even then I waited at least five more minutes before I said anything. "Will you show me the others?"

He smiled and flipped around so his back was facing me. I gasped when I saw everything on his back and shoulders. There were definitely more than a few. Tribal swirls covered the majority of his right shoulder leading toward his waist; I would have thought it looked stupid on anyone other than Brandon. It flowed perfectly over his sculpted back. A few lines of words in another language were peeking out from the bed near his ribs on his left side. Hidden between a swallow, a few stars and a Celtic cross were other designs I'd never seen before but thoroughly complimented the rest of the tattoos.

"Brandon, this is amazing," I breathed.

"You like them?" He started to turn around but I stopped him so I could keep looking. He laughed and grabbed my hand to kiss my palm. When I felt satisfied, I tugged on his shoulder until he faced me again.

"Thank you Harper," he said softly.

"For what?"

"For letting me talk about him, and knowing how to respond."

I pulled his face toward mine and looked directly into his eyes, "Whenever you want to talk about him, I'll be here."

He kissed me quickly before climbing out of bed. I instantly missed his arms around me and frowned. "Don't pout. It's cute as hell, but I want to take you out to breakfa—err . . . lunch."

I grumbled and tried to crawl out of his bed. Before I could get my feet on the ground he had my legs wrapped around his waist, and his lips were devouring mine. Our tongues touched, and thankfully he didn't seem to mind my next shiver. I laughed into his mouth when he slammed my back into the wall. His mouth left a trail of heat down my neck, across my collar bone and stopped on my shoulder. I wiggled against him when he didn't continue.

He sucked in air through his teeth and I felt his chest rumble. "Are you fucking kidding me?!" he yelled it loud enough that I flinched and I wouldn't doubt if he woke up everyone else in the house.

I shushed him, "Brandon! What's wrong?"

For how angry he seemed all of a sudden, I was surprised with the gentleness of his touch on my arm. He was breathing hard, but somehow I didn't think it had anything to do with me being pressed up against the wall anymore. He cursed again under his breath and his eyes finally caught mine when he set me down.

I inhaled sharply when I saw the hate in them. "Brandon?"

Mashing his lips together, he set his forehead against mine and closed his eyes. When I tried to look down at whatever he'd seen, his other hand slipped under my chin. "Don't." He growled. After a few more seconds he took a deep breath in and looked at my arm again. "Harper." He said through clenched teeth, "I want you to stay in here, and get ready. I'll be back soon." He firmly pressed his lips to my forehead and turned to leave.

"Brandon what's wro—" my eyes widened, "Oh. My. God."

"CHASE!" He roared as he left the room.

I stared in shock until his door slammed shut and he yelled for Chase again, then I grabbed the shirt he'd been wearing last night off the floor and took off after him, pulling the shirt over my head in the process. "Brandon! Brandon, don't!"

"Chase open the damn door!" he yelled as he banged his fist on his door.

There were already a group of barely awake people standing behind me in the living room when Bree opened the door.

"What is your problem?" she hissed at him.

"Where is he Bree?!"

Before she could answer, the back door slid open and Chase sauntered in rubbing his eyes. Had he slept outside? "What's with all the yelling?"

"You son of a bitch!" Brandon boomed as he charged toward the living room.

"Brandon!" I was standing close enough to the door that I stepped in front of Chase, who of course wasn't having that. He gently moved me behind him and I saw his entire frame tense up, ready for whatever was coming at him. "No. Brandon just stop!" I moved back in between them and held one hand out toward Brandon and put another on Chase's chest. I didn't care what Brandon did for a living, or that I had only known him for a day. I knew there was no way he would hurt me. His gentle touch just a minute ago when he was livid was proof.

"Harper, please move."

"No." I stood there with my hands still stretched toward both of them for another minute; when I felt confident he wouldn't charge Chase, I moved closer and rested my hands on Brandon's naked stomach. "He's not worth it," I whispered.

The way he was breathing reminded me of a bull. "You have got to be kidding me! He—"

"I know," I whispered so only he could hear, "I saw them Brandon. But please, don't do this right now."

"Will someone tell us what's going on?" I didn't look to see who asked the question, I'm guessing one of the housemates.

I wrapped a hand around Brandon's neck and forced him to look at me. "We'll handle it, but not like this, okay?" I kissed him softly and looked back into his soft eyes. "Let me talk to him, I'll meet you in your room in a minute."

His eyes flickered between me and Chase before he blew out a hard breath. "Not a chance." Without waiting for a reply, he scooped me up in his arms and walked us back to his room. I wanted to remind him I was perfectly capable of walking myself, but I kept my mouth shut, "I'm sorry but I'm not leaving you near him without me." He pressed his lips to mine fiercely and set me on the ground.

"I figured as much."

"I know I'm probably pissing you off right now, but—" He glanced under the sleeve of his shirt on my body and sighed, "Why did you stop me?"

"I told you, he's not worth it." I replied, "You guys live to-gether, and if you got in a fight, I'm almost positive it wouldn't end with just you two. I don't want to be the cause of that fight Brandon." I absolutely hated that I was worried about Chase. He was a big guy too, and I'm sure he wouldn't go down easily this time, but I didn't want him hurt and I had no doubt Brandon could do serious damage to him.

He pinched the bridge of his nose and exhaled deeply again as he sat on the bed, "You have bruises Harper. Bruises. Why didn't you tell me he was holding you that tight?"

"I hadn't realized he was." I lied.

Just then there was a knock on the door and Chase stuck his head in. Brandon stood up with a huff but I kept a hand to his chest and hoped he got the hint. Thankfully he did, because Lord knows I wouldn't be able to actually stop him.

"Well you just woke everyone in the house, care to clue me in?"

I felt Brandon's chest rumble beneath my fingers, ugh these guys needed to calm down. "Chase," I began calmly, "how drunk were you last night?"

"Not drunk enough to forget why my jaw hurts." His eyes wouldn't leave Brandon, I could practically see the ways he was thinking of getting back at him.

"Well you deserved that one, you were being rude."

He flung his arms out and finally looked at me, "I was just talking to you!"

Brandon brought my body to his and slowly raised the sleeves of the shirt over my shoulders, "*This* is just talking to her?!"

Chase's gaze dropped to my arms and his face paled as he took in the three distinct bruises. One on my left arm from the beginning of the party. You could actually see the individual fingers on it. And the other two from where his thumbs pressed into my shoulders during our confrontation in his room. He shook his head slightly and tore his eyes from my arms to search my face.

"Oh God, Harper. I di— I." He took a deep breath and ran a hand through his shaggy hair, "Harper I'm so sorry. I had no idea, I swear I didn't mean to hurt you."

I had known, even when it happened, that Chase wouldn't

physically hurt me on purpose. But there was no way to convince Brandon of that, and it looked like Chase was mentally beating himself up worse than Brandon could have with his fists. Despite Brandon's warning, he stepped up to me and placed his fingers on my left arm, lining them up with the biggest bruise.

"Harper," Chase cleared his throat twice before continuing, "can I please talk to you alone?"

Brandon bristled behind me but slowly turned me so I was facing him. He kissed my neck, whispering in my ear, "I'll go get us something to eat. If he does anything, call me and I'll come right back okay?"

I nodded and watched as he put on a shirt and searched for his wallet and keys. Before he left he kissed me so passionately, I almost forgot Chase was there. I knew he'd done that on purpose by the smirk on his face. After one last silent warning to Chase, he was gone.

Chase waited 'til we heard the front door close before saying anything. "Are you okay? God that's a stupid question, of course you're not."

"No, I am. I'm fine."

"How can you even say that?"

"Because I am!" Jeez, did these guys think I was that fragile? I mean, I know I'm small, but my dad is a Marine for crying out loud, I did daily drills and work outs with the guys in his unit. When they weren't doing anything, they were constantly teaching me how to defend myself. "They don't hurt, I didn't even know they were there until Brandon saw them."

"I just—I never meant to hurt you, I swear."

The pain in his eyes was too much, he hadn't done this on purpose. Before I could think about what I was doing, I wrapped my arms around his neck and he pressed his face into mine. "I know you didn't Chase. It really is okay, you were drunk, and I was being stubborn."

Groaning he leaned back far enough to look at me like I'd lost it, "Don't do that. Don't act like it's okay when it's not. You do this with everyone. And please don't make excuses for me. Yes I was drunk, and I don't always realize what I'm doing after I've been drinking, but that's no excuse Princess." His voice wrapped around my nickname lovingly, and though it threw me off for a second, I'd have to think about that later.

"Well maybe you shouldn't drink then." I joked to lighten the mood.

"Maybe I shouldn't." His eyebrows furrowed together, but he didn't look angry, just thoughtful. "Why him Harper?"

"What do you mean?"

"Why Brandon? You'd never been kissed, why'd you choose him to change that?"

It was weird to have him not making fun of me, I almost didn't know how to respond. "Why not Brandon?" I replied simply. He snorted a laugh but didn't say anything. "Why does that bother you so much Chase?"

"Because you deserve someone who realizes how amazing you are. You shouldn't have just let the first guy who gave you the time of day kiss you."

"You're acting like I gave him everything and all we've done is kissed!" I unwrapped my arms and sat down on the bed. "And who are you to judge who I do and do not kiss?"

"Please don't. Don't give him everything." He placed a hand on either side of my body and brought his face back to mine. "He doesn't deserve you Harper."

My breath was coming faster, and though I knew I should lean away, I couldn't make myself actually do it. "And who does Chase . . . you?" My voice was barely above a whisper.

His eyes flashed before he closed them and hung his head. "No. I don't deserve you either. You need someone who will cherish you, protect you and take care of you. Someone that realizes they'd never be able to find another you in the world, no matter how hard they looked." He looked back up into my eyes and we just stared at each other.

I was blown away, the emotion in his voice when he'd said that was unlike anything I'd ever heard. But we barely knew each other, there was no way he could think all this about me. He moved until his lips were hovering just above mine, and I thought my heart would stop.

"Chase . . ."

His voice was husky, and I could feel his breath against my lips. That alone was enough to make my eyelids flutter shut and my mouth open slightly. "That first night, I *did* realize I would never meet another girl like you. But you deserve someone who has waited for you as long as you have waited for them. And no matter how much I wish I could be that guy, I can't Harper."

I had to bite back a frustrated groan when he moved his face away from mine. My arms gave out and I flopped down to the bed, trying to control my erratic breathing. It couldn't be healthy to feel this way for someone. A whimper escaped my mouth when he pressed his full lips to my throat.

"You're amazing Harper. There will never be anyone good enough for you."

I secured my fingers in his hair, but didn't pull him closer. To be honest, I was a little terrified of what would happen when I did. If I kissed him right now, I don't know if I'd be able to stop. And what would that say about me? I finally had my first kiss just last night, and not fifteen minutes ago Brandon had me pushed up against the wall. The way my heart would pound for each guy separately was already frustrating me to no end, I didn't want to complicate things further by kissing Chase. And even though I hadn't known Brandon long, I couldn't stomach the thought of hurting him. Before I could move my arms back, Chase skimmed his nose up the inside of my forearm and kissed my wrist and palm before setting down my hands and walking out the door.

I stood up and tried to shake all feelings for Chase away before going to the bathroom to freshen up for when Brandon returned. When I walked back into his room he was sitting there with an iced coffee and blueberry muffin. I grinned and practically bounced over to kiss him. His stone face broke into a brilliant smile right before he caught me and lifted me off the carpet. That boy seriously liked picking me up.

"Did everything go okay?"

"Yep, he was really nice. Just apologized profusely, said it wouldn't happen again." I'd already decided what to tell him when I was in the bathroom.

"It better not." He grumbled into my hair and set me back down.

I laughed and turned to my coffee, "Thank you for this."

"You're welcome. It's not much, but I was kind of hoping I could take you out tonight."

I almost choked, "Out? Like a date?"

He chuckled and grabbed my hand pulling me toward the bed, "Yes a date. I know it's cliché, but how does dinner and a movie sound?"

"Sounds perfect!" I said a little too enthused. I slapped my hand over my mouth and turned beet red. "I'm sorry," I mumbled into my hand, "I've never been on a date."

He smiled and brushed the hair out of my face, "What was yesterday then?"

"What, at Starbucks? I thought we were just hanging out."

"God you're adorable." He kissed my forehead then lay back on his pillows. "Okay, well tonight is a date."

I bit my lip and tried to avoid bouncing up and down. I was way too excited for just a date. "When do you want to go?"

"It's almost two, we can leave at six if that's okay."

"Four hours? I gotta go then!" I leaned over and kissed him chastely before running out of the room to find Bree.

Bree was so excited for me that she left Konrad in bed to go with me to get our nails done. I'd have to apologize to him later, but I was glad she was such a good friend. I don't know why I was nervous, but I had butterflies in my stomach as I thought about tonight. She continued to tell me not to worry since I no longer had to worry about whether or not I should kiss him on the first date, to which she got a swift elbow in her ribs. Her only real advice was to not make out in the movie theater because it was annoying and unnecessary and I would most likely be sleeping in his bed again since she planned to do more than sleep with Konrad. I thought it was bad that I was already so comfortable kissing Brandon after just a day, but when she talked like that, all I could do was shake my head. At least I wasn't like that. I doubted I would ever be so comfortable with sex. We stopped by the dorm to get an outfit Bree thought would be perfect for the night, before heading back to the house so I could shower. I was almost done shaving when I heard the door open.

"Uh . . . Bree?"

I heard the toilet seat close and someone sit down on it. "Nope, just me."

"Chase! What the heck are you doing in here?" I tried to cover different body parts, but my chest alone needed two arms to cover everything, so it wasn't working out too well.

"Calm down Princess, I won't peek."

"I could've sworn I locked that door."

"You do realize how easy it is to unlock *my* bathroom door when I have the key right?"

"Can you please leave so I can get out of here?" I whined as I shut off the water. A towel was thrust through the side of the curtain and I gladly wrapped myself in it, but still didn't open the only thing separating us.

"Answer one thing first, and I'll leave." He waited for my reply, but went on when he didn't receive any, "Are you going out with him tonight?"

"Yes Chase, I am."

"Is that what you want to do, or are you trying to get back at me for telling you not to?"

"I thought I only had to answer one question?"

"Harper." He deadpanned.

"Ugh, no I'm not doing it to get back at you. Yes, I really want to go out with Brandon tonight. And if he asks me out again after tonight, I'm telling you right now I will say yes. I don't see why I shouldn't go out with him, and since you clearly don't want me, I don't think you're allowed to have a say in the matter.

He flung the curtain open and I jumped back, almost slipping in the tub. "I didn't say I don't want you. I said I don't deserve you."

"That's practically the same thing." I glowered at him, "We both know how you are Chase, you screw every female you come in contact with. I don't want to be just another girl to someone, and when it comes to Brandon, I won't be." I waited for a response from him, but didn't receive any. "If you can convince me right now, that I have a reason to not be with him, then start talking. Otherwise, you and your confusing words need to stop."

"As long as he is what you want, I'll stop bothering you." He reached out to brush his fingers across the main bruise and I watched as his eyes clouded over.

Like that wasn't confusing.

He leaned in to press his lips to the finger marks, then on my left shoulder and finally my right. Chase's eyes were dark by the time he looked back into my eyes. "I'm so sorry Harper," he whispered and leaned in close to kiss the corner of my mouth.

My knees started shaking but I somehow managed to stay standing.

"Get my number from Bree, I have to go into work tonight but if anything happens, call me and I'll be there."

I just nodded and watched him walk out. I didn't even know he had a job, but I was positive I wouldn't be calling him tonight. Nothing good would come of it if I did. If my heart was already twisting from what just happened, he would surely break it when I saw him with his next girl. I couldn't let myself get any closer to him. No matter how much I wished he was different, he wasn't, and he would probably never change. I needed to stop thinking about him and focus on my date with Brandon. I dried my hair and curled the ends before doing my make-up with Bree. She said we had to pick carefully because my green shirt was being used to bring out the red highlights in my hair, and we didn't want to take away from that. Whatever that meant. She settled for a neutral goldish color and thankfully let me do my eyeliner and mascara. I wasn't too keen to have someone else putting pointy objects near my eyes. My phone chimed and I reached for it, smiling when I saw who it was from.

J. Carter:
Blaze! How's California?

Me:
AHHHmazing. When are you going to come visit? ;)

J. Carter:
Soon as I get the okay.

Me:
Promise?!

J. Carter:
Of course. What's my girl up to?

Me:
I met someone and he's taking me on our first date to-night!

J. Carter:
Uh . . . really?

Me:
Yes, really. What, am I not dateable?

J. Carter:
Never said that . . . just wasn't expecting you to meet someone, or date or anything like that.

Me:
You could at least be excited for me.

J. Carter:
I am. Call me later. Miss you

Me:
Miss you too.

"Let me guess . . . Jason?"

I looked up at Bree, "Yeah, how'd you know?"

"Every time he calls or texts you, you stop paying attention to anyone else."

"Well I don't get to talk to him often." I shrugged.

"Uh huh. Does Brandon have some competition?"

"What? No way. Carter's my best friend. There's never been anything like that between us."

Bree just raised a blond brow at me and turned me toward the mirror.

I was dressed in a green shirt that was loose at the top but form fitting where it rested on my hips, faded jeans with the bottoms rolled up to my calves and flip flops. After getting Bree's approval of my appearance, I left the room to find Brandon.

"You look gorgeous Harper," he breathed when I walked into the living room.

"Not so bad yourself." I winked. That was a lie, he looked downright delicious. He had on a pair of reefs, dark tan cargo shorts and a black button up shirt, sleeves rolled up to his tan, muscled forearms.

He led me outside and I laughed when I saw the top had been put back on, "I don't feel like fighting guys off you tonight." He kissed me once and helped me into the Jeep. I wasn't complaining, I'd actually done something with my hair today, I didn't want it messed up.

Bree had been right, I shouldn't have been nervous about the date. We'd had so much fun laughing and getting to know each other during dinner, and the movie was hilarious. As promised, we didn't make out in the theater, but the few tender kisses he'd stolen throughout the night left me wanting more, and honestly I couldn't wait to get back to the house. Chase was long forgotten by the time we were on our way back. We walked into a party much like the first one I'd been to, and I stifled a groan. Hopefully this one didn't end the same as the others. Brandon squeezed my hand reassuringly as we made our way to the kitchen. I was whisked away by Bree to get the play by play of the date, and though she'd told me to keep it clean, she was frowning with my lack of juicy details.

"Uh, who's that?" She pointed over my shoulder and I turned and searched through the sea of people. It didn't take long for my eyes to land on a leggy blonde hanging off Brandon. I smiled when I saw him repeatedly take her hands off him.

I looked back to my friend, "Well what do you say we go find out?"

When we got close enough, I could hear her whiny voice, she was obviously intoxicated. "But Brandon I've missed youuu." She pouted at him and tried to run a finger down his chest, but he caught it and once again put her hand by her side. "We're so good together, remember? I'm sorry about this summer honey but I want you back."

Even with him pushing her away, I was starting to get insanely jealous over this girl who was most likely his latest ex. "Kendra, seriously you need to stop. We're done."

"Come on Brandon, I know you miss me too. Let's just pretend the last few months didn't happen." She leaned in to try to plant a kiss on his neck but he pushed her back and held her away at arm's length.

No wonder Brandon tried to beat the crap out of Chase. I wanted to punch this girl and she was falling over drunk. I decided it was my time to cut in, and yes I was going to lay it on thick. "Hey baby," I purred as I stepped in between the two and pulled his face down so I could cover his lips with mine. Letting my tongue trail across his bottom lip, I whispered loud enough so Kendra could still hear. "I have something for you in your room," I said suggestively.

He grabbed behind my knees and lifted me into his arms as he walked me toward his room. I caught a glimpse of the girl one more time, and couldn't help but laugh at her expression. *Game over bitch. I win.*

"Tease." Brandon whispered in my ear, "But you are adorable when you're jealous."

"Well I wasn't going to let her keep touching you. That's my job."

He grinned and pressed two loud kisses to my cheek before locking his door and setting me on the ground. He threw a pair of boxers at me and I held them up, confused.

"Unless you want to fight your way to Chase's room, that's all I have for you."

"Oh." When he turned toward his dresser again, I switched my jeans for them quickly. They were so big I had to roll them up a few times, but I loved the fact that I was going to sleep in his clothes. "Um, do you have a shirt too?"

He unbuttoned his shirt and sauntered over to me with a mischievous grin on his face. Slipping his fingers under my chin, he tilted my head up and nearly kissed me senseless. I felt his other hand trail down my side to the bottom of my shirt, and then his warm fingers were on my stomach, soon followed by his other hand. Other than the second it took to pull my shirt over my head, his lips never left mine and his eyes stayed closed. A chill ran across my body and my breaths started coming faster as I thought about his hands running over my bare body. He shrugged out of his button-up, draped it over my shoulders and resumed to running his fingers over my bare waist and stomach while I pulled my arms through the sleeves. Once my hands were back on his muscled chest he slowly buttoned it back up. I was gasping for air by the time he finished.

I flipped on a lamp and Brandon turned off the light as I sunk onto the bed. Turning back toward me he stopped mid step. "This was a bad idea."

"Why?" I sat up quickly.

He chuckled and crawled onto the bed pushing me back down and hovering over me. "You're in my bed, wearing my clothes, and your hair was splayed out across my pillows." He kissed my neck before gruffly whispering in my ear, "You look so damn sexy, I want to take you in my arms and never let you leave this bed."

"Then why don't you?" I countered huskily.

"God Harper, you're going to be the death of me I swear."
He turned the lamp back off, rolled onto his side and pulled me
toward him.

I hmphed and curled deeper into his embrace. "I love how I
feel in your arms." I sighed into his chest.

"You fit there perfectly." He squeezed his arms around me
and kissed the top of my head, "Get some sleep sweetheart."

I WAS WOKEN up the next morning to Brandon's lips on my neck.
I smiled softly and ran my fingers over his head, "I want to wake
up to this every morning." My voice was raspy from sleep.

He chuckled against my throat and placed a warm kiss on it
causing me to bite my own lip to stop a moan from escaping.
"Does that mean I get to keep you?"

"As long as you share me with Bree. I'm pretty sure she'd
kidnap me otherwise."

Brandon had gently moved the collar of his shirt I was wearing away and was smiling against my collarbone, "I went to
Kindergarten, I learned how to share with others."

I burst into laughter and brought his face to mine for a quick
kiss. "Well I don't want you to share me with everyone."

"I don't plan to." He propped himself up on an elbow and
brushed his thumb across my cheek. "I want you to be my girl
Harper."

A slow smile spread across my face and I was beaming inside.
It was Saturday morning, and we'd just met on Thursday, but it
didn't feel like this was coming a moment too soon. There was
something about this dangerous looking god that made me feel
safe and cherished. Being with him felt so right, it was almost
scary but incredibly thrilling to have found someone that made
me feel this way. Pulling his face to mine, I stopped less than
an inch from him. "I'd love to be your girl," I whispered against
his lips.

Brandon kissed me fiercely, but when I ran my fingers down his side and rested them on the top of his shorts he caught my hand and held it away. "I just woke up with the most beautiful girl I've ever seen beside me, and you agreed to be my girl. If you keep touching me . . . well, let's just say I can't make any promises."

I brought his mouth back to mine and wrapped a leg around his hip arching my body into his. I was suddenly extremely aware that his boxers on my body, and his basketball shorts were the only thing separating us, and apparently so was he. I didn't want to go further than this, I just wanted to be closer to him. Unfortunately, that wasn't going to happen. He pushed me back down to the bed and stood up laughing and shaking his head.

"I'll go make some coffee."

I pouted and fell back into the pillows. "Fine."

His mouth curved up on one side revealing his deep dimple as he leaned over to kiss me chastely. "I was planning on spending the day with you in here, but if you're gonna force me into a cold shower, we'll have to find something else."

I quickly climbed back under the covers. "I'll be good. Promise," I mumbled.

Deep brown eyes searched mine, "There's no rush Harper. You don't have to prove anything to me, or anyone else. Let's just take this slow, okay?"

My face turned bright red. "Did you go slow with the other girls?" I wasn't sure I wanted to know this, but I couldn't help but feel like the reason for him not wanting to go any further was because he didn't actually want to be with me in that way. I certainly didn't look anything like his last girlfriend, Kendra. That girl had looked like a freaking Barbie.

He sighed and dropped his head to my shoulder. "No. But I know what you're getting at, and you're wrong."

I didn't say anything, just waited to see if he'd explain, and after a few awkwardly silent moments, he did.

"I don't know how you could even think that I don't want you, I can barely keep my hands off you." He cupped my cheek and held my gaze, "We just met, but I already know there's something different about you, and I'm not about to ruin this by rushing into things. I plan on taking my time with you. Those girls, yeah I had relationships with them, but all they were was a distraction for me. I wanted to feel something other than being pissed that my dad was gone for good. I didn't . . ." he took a deep breath in and out, "they weren't you Harper." He said it like that explained everything, and in a way, it did.

My heart thudded irregularly against my chest and I couldn't stop smiling knowing that I wasn't the only one that was already in this deep. "Thank you," I whispered before pressing my lips softly to his.

We did end up spending the rest of the day in his bed, and I loved it. We turned on a movie, but had to keep restarting it because we ended up talking throughout the entire thing. Other than sweet kisses to the top of my head and nose, all we did was stay curled up in each other's arms. Brandon would intertwine our fingers and hold them close to his chest whenever I started trailing my fingers down his bare stomach, and eventually just ended up putting a shirt on. I had frowned at that, but knew it was my fault. We left the room to go to dinner with Bree and Konrad that night, and other than a quick trip to buy coffee and donuts for everyone on Sunday morning, we repeated our previous day in his bed. We were dozing off while attempting to watch another movie when Bree came walking in.

"I'll be ready to go in a few minutes, do you have all your things?"

Guess that means Konrad went back to the dorms already. "No, but it won't take long, give me a few minutes."

I started to climb off the bed, but Brandon wrapped his arms around me and pulled me back down. Bree snickered and walked out the door. After it was shut, Brandon pulled me closer to him.

"You're leaving?" he asked softly, his fingers trailing down my arm.

"Yeah, I have to go back to my dorm."

"You don't have to. I want you here with me."

My first thought was of Chase and what he would think about that. I scolded myself and shook my head, "I can't, we're not rushing, remember?"

He grumbled halfheartedly and squeezed me tighter, "If I knew you were going to leave at the end of today I would have clarified what we weren't going to rush."

I giggled against his jaw and continued on with a trail of kisses. "I know what you meant. But I can't stay here." Lord knows I would love to wake up to his handsome face every day. But like he said, we just met and I've only been out of Sir's house for a little over two weeks. If that's not the definition of rushing, I don't know what is.

"Weekends?"

"What about them?" I asked against his neck.

"Will you stay with me on the weekends? You'll probably be here anyway."

I sat up and looked down at his breathtaking face, "You really want me here? You're not going to get tired of me being around?"

"Seriously Harper? I told you I wanted to keep you here. You're right though, you do need to stay at the dorm with Bree. So if I have to 'share' you with her, then I plan on using this sharing to my advantage so I get you too."

I rolled my eyes and pushed against his chest playfully, "Okay fine. How about this? Unless something comes up, I will stay here with you on Thursdays, Fridays and Saturdays."

A huge smile showing off his perfect teeth and dimple spread across his face as he brought his mouth to mine, "That sounds perfect." He spoke around our kisses.

"I feel like I'm the kid of a divorced couple," I grumbled and he laughed.

We kissed a few moments longer until we heard Bree complaining from the hallway. Brandon hugged me tight to his chest at his door and planted a quick kiss on my forehead, "I'll see you at school, have a good night sweetheart."

The door swung open to reveal Bree with our bags slung over her shoulders and hands on her hips. "Sometime today, Harper." After we were in her car, her fake sullen mood disappeared, "Tell. Me. Everything!"

I laughed and turned in my seat so I was facing her. "I'm afraid I'm about to disappoint you again, nothing happened."

"What!" She looked between the road and me. "You guys never left his room! You can't tell me nothing happened."

I shrugged and smiled, "I'm serious, nothing happened. All we did was talk and sleep."

Her jaw dropped and after a minute formed into a perfect O, "He's gay?"

"Oh my God! What? No!"

"I'm sorry but you're going to tell me that a straight guy had you in his bed for three whole days and didn't try anything with you?"

"It wasn't that, we talked about it on Saturday and decided we aren't going to do anything for a while."

Her eyebrows scrunched together and she looked more confused than I'd even seen her, "But . . . why?"

"I think he's afraid of rushing me, and to be honest, I'm kind of glad. I can see how easy it would be to get too carried away to stop, and I feel like everything about us has already moved so fast. Not that I'd change anything so far, but I'm happy we're going to wait. When I think about it, I know I'm still not ready to go there. He's my first boyfriend, and it's only been a couple days."

"Huh. I guess when you put it that way."

"Is it safe to assume you and Konrad had a good time?"

She beamed a smile at me before turning back to the road, "I actually think I like him. Who knows, I may even try to date him!"

I just shook my head. She's just like her brother. How people could be like that was totally beyond me.

"Ooo, DON'T LOOK now, but someone's man is at our one o'clock." Bree nudged into my side as we walked toward our second class of the day.

Of course, I had to look then. I saw Brandon with a couple guys and a girl I didn't know standing off to the side. His deep husky laugh reached us then and I smiled at the sound of it.

"Well are you going to go over there?"

I stopped walking for a few seconds then continued on the path we'd been on, "No, I don't want to bother him."

"He's your boyfriend Harper! You're supposed to go bother him."

I smiled and dropped my head hoping my hair would hide my blush, "I'm just kind of worried he doesn't like me as much as I like him. I didn't think I could feel so strong about someone after such a short time, and I'm sure it's because I've never dated anyone. I'm afraid I'll be too much for him, and he'll get annoyed with me quickly." I'd seen that more than enough times with the guys on base. I knew how frustrated they'd get with their clingy girlfriends.

"Okay, I know you don't have much experience in this department, but let me clue you in. You didn't see that boy when Chase had you in the room. Guys don't go all hero over some girl they don't feel strongly about. And they definitely don't worry about protecting their innocence."

I shushed her and looked around to see if anyone was listening.

"I'm just saying, Brandon's in deep. Trust me, I don't think it's one sided."

"If you say so."

"I do. So stop trying to be invisible and—" She looked over my shoulder and smiled, "Looks like someone beat you to it."

Before she could finish her sentence, Brandon had me scooped into his arms and his lips planted firmly on mine. I ran my hands over his buzzed hair before clasping them around his neck.

"Hello to you too," I mumbled against his mouth.

He smiled and rested his forehead against mine, "I missed you this morning sweetheart."

His voice warmed my body and I bit my lip in an attempt at hiding my idiotic grin, "Only three more and then I'll be there."

Bree's annoyed tone broke through, "Uh, rude. It's like I'm not even here."

Brandon's eyes didn't leave mine, "Good morning Breanna." He gave me another quick peck and set me on the ground, capturing my hand in his.

She snorted, "He's in deep alright."

"Bree!" I hissed.

"Yeah," Brandon laughed huskily and squeezed my hand once, "yeah I am."

I hid my face in his chest so he couldn't see my red cheeks or elated expression. He wasn't having that though, his fingers tilted my chin up and he bent down so our faces were almost touching.

"My class is about to start, I have to get going. See you at lunch?"

Nodding, I kissed his hard jaw, "See you then."

He turned to leave and called over his shoulder, "Take care of my girl Bree."

My smile fell as I caught the glare of the girl from the group he'd been talking to earlier. Was she another ex? I leaned into Bree and whispered, "Hey, you wouldn't happen to know that girl, would you?"

"You mean Psycho Barbie over there? She was at lunch with us a couple days last week. You don't have to worry about her though, he kept turning her down, and that was before he met you."

Not another ex, but still another girl that wants Brandon. "Everywhere we go some girl ends up shooting daggers at me."

Bree grabbed my arm and turned me toward our English class, "Um, have you seen your boy lately? Don't hate me, but he's freaking hot. I swear he should be a model. Lots of girls are going to want him, especially the ones who go Underground and see him fight, just remember he's yours and there's a lot of people ready to kick his ass if he forgets it. Me included."

My eyes widened but she cut me off before I could say anything.

"He's not going to, I was just saying. He just let everyone in the immediate area know he's taken. Brandon's a goner when it comes to you, roomie."

As soon as she said that, goose bumps covered my body and I tensed at what that could mean. Chase. This whole being physically aware of him was getting beyond ridiculous.

"What's up sis?" He threw an arm around Bree's shoulders and walked with us toward class.

"Uh, nothing. I thought you didn't have classes 'til later?"

I couldn't look at him, but I saw how his feet missed a step after her question. "Had some things I had to take care of earlier, didn't feel like going home."

A paper was pressed into my hand nearest him and I curled my fingers around it. His fingertips brushed softly from my wrist to my elbow and I had to fight the urge to look at the trail of fire he'd left on my arm. Chase and Bree talked about something at their parents' house this weekend all the way up to the door of our class. I still hadn't said anything or looked at him.

"You ladies have fun, I'll see you later." He gave Bree a quick hug and nudged my shoulder before walking away.

After taking our seats, I leaned over toward my backpack and unfolded the piece of paper so Bree wouldn't see.

"You look beautiful today."

I crushed up the paper, slid it under the rows of seats and prayed that she wouldn't ask why I was beet red.

That night, Bree and I both got texts a little after ten. We looked at each other, confused, and rushed into getting ready when we read the messages. Brandon was going to fight within the hour, he was coming to pick Bree and me up, we'd meet the guys from the house at the place.

"Is it weird that I'm nervous to watch this?" I huffed as I hurriedly fixed my hair and make-up.

"You shouldn't be, Chase said he never loses, and the time I watched was awesome."

"But you aren't going to have to watch your boyfriend possibly get beat up!"

"I'm sure he'll be fine!" She rolled her eyes and grabbed my hand, "Come on, we have to go."

We ran outside and hopped into Brandon's Jeep, he had his iPhone to his ear and was smiling widely when he leaned over to kiss me.

Brandon gave someone an address and name of a building I'd never heard of and stopped for a second, "Yeah, it's on in forty, start calling people." After hanging up, he dropped his phone in my hands, "Hold that for me 'til it's over, would you?" He was still smiling, his left knee bouncing up and down fast.

"Uh, you a little excited?" I was terrified, how could he be so excited? It's not like I'd never watched UFC, but I hadn't known the guys fighting, and they were on TV, it's a little different.

He laughed lightly, "I've never fought this guy before, but from what I've heard, he hasn't lost and has a pretty good reputation for knocking out his opponents and I plan to show him what that's like. It should be a pretty high paying night, *and* my girl is gonna be there. So yeah, you could say I'm excited."

"That makes one of us," I mumbled under my breath. He must have heard because his next laugh was louder and he squeezed my knee.

We pulled up to a restaurant that was already closed and went around to a back door. Taking the stairs to the basement, I was assaulted by loud music and voices.

"This way." Brandon held my hand tight and I latched onto Bree as we continued to turn corners in the dark hallway. When we got to a set of doors, he wrapped his arms around me and kissed me hard. "I gotta go talk to Scarecrow, go with Bree and find the other guys before the fight starts. I'll see you when it's done sweetheart." He took off down a hall and I looked to Bree.

"Scarecrow?"

"He's the guy that puts all these on. He finds the places, sets up, decides who fights, refs, collects the money, it's all him."

"Huh. Nice name."

Breanna snorted and opened the doors, my jaw dropped when I saw inside. I don't know what I'd been expecting, but I hadn't been thinking at least a hundred people, plus the ones still pouring in from the other door, would all be smashed together surrounding a make-shift ring.

"There's Jared!" Bree yelled and pointed to a guy I'd never seen before, but just behind him was Drew and Derek.

We began making our way to the other side of the room, but we were just as far away five minutes later when the music got louder and a guy, I'm guessing Scarecrow, started riling everyone up and announcing Kale and Brandon. It was already loud enough with the music and people yelling, but it was near deafening when Brandon came out in only a pair of loose shorts. His smile was breathtaking and that dimple was enough to make any girl sigh, but then you looked down and saw his tanned muscled body, skipped the sigh and went straight to drooling. The girls that were there were screaming for him and I grinned to myself, knowing that he was mine. The music lowered a bit and the fight began.

Right away Kale threw a punch, Brandon leaned back letting it pass an inch from his face, his smile never faltering. He looked so comfortable and confident, it started to make me nervous. When people get cocky, they mess up, and messing up with this guy swinging and kicking at you? It wouldn't end well. Kale looked to be a little shorter than Brandon, but had to have at least an extra twenty pounds on him, and he just looked evil. Kale went after Brandon again, and they both started in on each other. A tall guy stepped in front of me and I had to struggle to even catch a glimpse. I was up on my toes and leaning to the side as Kale brought his leg around, I didn't even see if he'd gotten Brandon because I stumbled, falling into the guy in front of me. Thankfully he caught me around my waist before I could hit the ground.

"You alright there, Graceful?" He smirked, but his eyes were bright, I knew he was teasing.

I narrowed my eyes at him, but couldn't help but laugh. "Yeah, fine. Sorry about that!" I raised my voice enough so he could hear me above the crowd.

"Trust me," his eyes heated as he raked them over my body, "it's not a problem."

The basement filled with cheers and frustrated roars, Scarecrow started yelling into the mic, "Knock out! I can't effing believe it!"

I tried looking to see who had gotten knocked out, but all I saw were people cheering. Everyone was screaming, but no names were said, and for a few moments I was terrified that

Brandon was in that circle, unconscious. I surged forward, but Mr. Tall Guy grabbed and pulled me back against the wall I'd originally been standing by. I wanted to yell at him to let me go so I could check on Brandon, but when his hands locked around my wrists, all thoughts of Brandon flew out the window as I turned to face him.

"You look scared, baby. I promise not to bite. Hard."

"Baby?!" Oh, *hell* no. "I am not your baby." If his hands weren't still gripping my wrists, effectively pinning my arms to my sides I would have shoved him back far enough so I could show him what I thought of random guys calling me baby. I looked around him and noticed no one was watching us, and I couldn't see Bree anymore. I'd lost her when I'd originally fallen.

"No?" He tilted his head and raised an eyebrow, after a couple seconds a twisted smile crossed his face. He leaned in and pressed his body into mine, his breath reeked of beer, "Well, we're about to change that."

I understand that I'm petite and look like I can be forced, but I was not raised by hundreds of jarheads just to let some preppy douche try to tell me what I was *about* to do. Friendly strangers and guys I like, sure I get nervous around them, but belittle me or try to dominate me, and I get pissed.

"Get. The hell. Away. From me," I growled.

He responded by pressing himself harder into me so I could feel how excited he was getting. "I know you're scared, but I'll be gentle."

Sad thing was, this guy was attractive, and his outfit suggested he came from a country club home, I'm almost positive he could have any girl he wanted, and yet he was getting hard because he thought he was going to have his way with me by scaring me? I tried not to gag. He lightly licked my neck and put a hand under my shirt. My knee jerked up but he pushed back too fast for me to connect. He was glaring, but still had that stupid grin on his face. He laughed once and tried to pull me closer, but I kept my feet planted where I was.

"You're feisty, I like that. I think we're going to have fun." He winked and tried pulling me toward him again, "Let's go."

"Yeah, that's not gonna happen."

That husky voice made me sigh in relief, Brandon was okay.

"Can I help you bro?" Mr. Tall Guy asked calmly and released my wrists.

Brandon refused to look at, or answer him. The muscles in his jaw were ticking from the pressure of trying to keep his mouth shut. He held a hand up toward me, and when I went to put my hand in his, my new best friend grabbed my wrist again.

"Sorry man, but you're gonna have to find another chick to bag tonight, this one's mine."

Brandon's eyes shot toward him, his right hand clenched into a fist and his body turned to face him. This Brandon was terrifying, he hadn't even looked at Chase like that the morning he saw the bruises. I knew what was about to happen, and there's no way I was letting Brandon take this from me, so I acted before he could. I kneed the prick hard in his groin, when he bent at the waist my hands flew to the back of his head and I slammed his face into my still-bent knee. Blood instantly poured out of his nose and onto my bare leg, I let go of his head and let him fall to the ground. One hand was gripping his crotch, the other trying to hold back as much blood as possible.

"Asshole," I murmured.

Looking up slowly, I made sure to avoid my boyfriend's eyes. I think he liked being protective of me, and honestly I loved that he was, but I'm not going to cower down and play the damsel when a boy that's sick in the head treats me like that. I knew Carter and the other guys would have been proud that I used some of the moves they were always teaching me, but I didn't know what Brandon would think about it.

The few people that *had* seen the little exchange were razzing Mr. Tall Guy for letting a "little girl" bring him to his knees. I smirked at him still curled up on the ground, but my face fell when I finally looked at Brandon's wide eyes and dropped jaw. My cheeks blazed and I bit my lip, worried about what he was about to say.

He blinked and shook his head in disbelief, "Damn, sweetheart. That was hot."

I laughed and jumped over my victim and into Brandon's arms, kissing him fiercely. He still had his shirt off and was covered in sweat, but I didn't care. He was okay, he'd won the fight, and he liked the way I was able to take care of myself. He hissed and sucked in a sharp breath before setting me down.

"Are you okay?"

He was grimacing, but pulled me close, "Yeah, I'm good. Let's get out back and find Scarecrow."

When we got out of the main room and found Scarecrow and Brandon's shirt, I pulled out my phone to call Bree, but she'd sent a text saying she caught a ride with the guys. Brandon introduced me to Scarecrow who let out an appreciative whistle and clapped Brandon on the back.

"Nice catch man, keep bringing your good luck charm around, I like the money she's making me." He smiled at us and handed over a massive wad of cash.

Brandon didn't even count it, just shook his hand and wrapped an arm around my shoulders, leading me outside. I noticed the rigid way he was holding himself, and how it took him a little extra time climbing into his Jeep, but didn't ask. Instead I wrapped my hands around one of his and silently inspected him. He didn't look like he had any cuts, or bruises, but I couldn't see much of him now. I wished I'd looked earlier, while his shirt was still off.

He smiled and moved his hand from mine to place it on my thigh, "Do I pass inspection?"

I blushed and looked out at the street, "Sorry."

"Don't be, I was joking. Did you have fun?"

"Well I wasn't really able to see anything because of that guy, and then I was focused on getting him away from me."

Brandon laughed and cut off abruptly, sucking in another quick breath, "Seriously Harper, that was by far the best thing I've ever seen. I couldn't believe my girl put someone down faster than I did." He smiled, his eyes bright.

I smiled back at him and shrugged, "I really don't understand why you all think I'm so breakable. Remember, I spent almost every day of my life with a bunch of horny Marines that treated me like I was their little sister. They made sure from early on that I could handle myself against guys like them."

"Well, I'm glad for that, and I do know that you can take care of yourself. I'm sorry if I go a little caveman when it comes to you sometimes, but I've never met anyone like you. You're precious to me, and everything in me screams to take care of you."

My heart started hammering in my chest. How was it possible that he was mine? "Did you just say you go caveman?"

His smile got even wider, and I leaned over to kiss his dimple, "You can't act like you haven't noticed. I was worried it was going to start pissing you off. That's why I tried to stay calm tonight."

"I'm pretty sure you were justified every time you've done something like that. And don't worry, you're protective, you aren't possessive. *That* would piss me off."

"I don't want to own you, Harper, I just want to be with you."

"I know," I said softly, thinking about actually *being* with him, even though that wasn't what he'd been talking about. "Can I stay with you tonight?"

He kissed my hand, "I'd hoped you would."

When we got back to the house Brandon took me to the bathroom and after helping me onto the counter, proceeded to clean the blood off my leg. I left him in there so he could shower, and went into his room to put on some of his clothes. I inhaled his scent surrounding me and smiled while climbing into his bed. I'd left off bottoms, opting for one of his shirts that came down to my thighs. I hoped it would get my message across, since I didn't exactly know how to tell him what I wanted. He turned off the light when he came in and got in the bed, each movement was stiff and he winced twice.

"Are you sure you're okay?" I really had planned on waiting for him to tell me, but he looked like he was in a lot of pain.

"I'm fine sweetheart, come here."

Brandon pulled me close to him and kissed me softly at first, when I brushed my tongue across his lips he groaned and deepened the kiss. Before I could let my nerves take over, I pulled myself up and swung a leg over his body, keeping myself from pressing my body to his. I wanted him to be the one to pull me closer. His hands were on my legs, slowly sliding up my thighs and under the shirt, when he realized I wasn't wearing shorts he growled against my lips. "Jesus Harper." Keeping one hand on my hip, and bringing the other one to the top of my back, he slowly lowered me to him, freezing and cursing when I pressed harder against him.

"Okay, you're lying." I quickly hopped off and tried not to touch him at all until I knew where he was hurting.

He grumbled and placed a hand back on my thigh, "I bruised or cracked a rib," he tried to sit up and fell back onto the pillows, "or two."

"Brandon! When?"

"Kale got a pretty good kick in, but I'm positive they aren't broken."

"Well do you need to see a Doctor or something?" I started to get off the bed but he held me there.

"I promise I'm fine," he chuckled lightly, "this wouldn't be the first cracked rib I've had sweetheart. I just need to take it easy for a few days."

"Is there something I can do?"

"You can stay here with me," he kissed me softly, "and when I'm better, we can pick up that conversation where we left off."

"I'm looking forward to it." I pressed my lips to his neck and curled up against his pain-free side, falling asleep quickly.

"OH. DEAR. LORD! Bree, I can't wear this." I stared in horror at my reflection in the mirror.

"Why? You look hot!"

"I'm almost completely naked!"

"Uh, that's kind of the point of a bikini. As little fabric as possible." She was fixing her own suit and checking herself out in her mirror.

I failed at moving the top around to cover more of my chest. "Do you not have anything bigger than this? It's barely holding in my boobs."

"No that's the one with the most coverage." She threw a shirt at me before putting her own on over her suit. "Honestly Harper, you have a rocking body. I would kill for your chest, you need to embrace it."

"I'm not sure that's possible when I'm going to wear this around a bunch of guys." It was now Thursday, and we were already packed for a weekend at Chase's house. But what Bree failed to mention until the last possible minute was that the guys were barbecuing tonight and we were going to be hanging out in their pool all afternoon.

"Once again, that's the point. It's the best way to show off the goods. Brandon's gonna die when he sees you."

"I think I'm gonna die before he can see me," I mumbled.

She rolled her eyes at me and grabbed her bag and keys, "I'm sure you'll live. Let's go."

I complained the entire way there, and kept it up even after I was in nothing but the bikini and a pair of shorts walking out to the backyard.

"Harper, stop trying to cover yourself. You're not succeeding and you look stupid."

I glared at my friend, but stopped trying to cover myself. At least none of the guys were home yet. I pulled off the shorts and lay down on my towel next to Bree. She had turned on her iPod docking station on the patio and we rocked out to the songs while we tanned. We had flipped onto our backs again a few minutes earlier when a huge splash followed by freezing cold drops of water interrupted us. We both screamed and jumped up, apparently that's what they'd been going for since we were tackled into the pool as soon as we'd gotten vertical. I came up sputtering and smacked Derek across the head as soon as he surfaced.

"Are you serious?!"

"I'm going to kill you Drew!" Bree shoved Drew back under the water and held him there.

I looked over to see Zach laughing from the side of the pool, I guess he'd been the one that did the cannonball. I swam to the side and hopped out, running to my towel I picked it up to find it soaked from the numerous splashes.

"Awesome."

I ran my fingers through my hair trying to get the tangles out, and stood there long enough so I was no longer dripping. Bree was still in the pool with the three guys so I decided to go get a few more towels for everyone. I was halfway to the hall closet when Chase walked out of his room. He froze and his eyes got wide as he took in my body.

"Damn Princess. You look . . ." He cleared his throat and finally met my eyes, "wow."

I blushed fiercely and crossed my arms over my chest. "I was uh, just coming to get more towels."

He reached into the closet and pulled out a few. Dropping all but one on the floor next to me, he shook out the one still in his hand and wrapped it around my shoulders. "How are you?" He brushed his fingers across my cheek and down my neck causing me to stifle a moan.

"Huh?"

Chase chuckled against my neck and lightly pressed his lips to my throat. "That good, huh?"

I blinked a few times and pushed away from him, ignoring that smirk I loved so much, "Why do you keep doing this to me?"

"What do you mean?" He went to wrap his arms around me, but I stepped out of his reach.

"This!" I pointed to an outstretched arm, "You can't keep doing this. I'm with Brandon now, you have to stop."

His face fell into an unreadable mask and he dropped his arms to his sides.

"No more notes, no more touches, no more putting your lips on me. This isn't fair to me. Do you have any idea how crazy you're making me?"

Okay, maybe I shouldn't have asked that, his eyes lit up and that stupid smirk was back. "Really now?"

"Chase I'm serious, this has to stop."

"Give me one good reason why I should."

I huffed and wrapped the towel tighter around me, "I told you, I'm with Brandon now."

"I said a good reason Princess." He deadpanned.

"That's a perfectly good reason! And it's the only one you're going to get." I bent down and picked up the towels, when I stood back up he was right in front of me.

"Harper."

"No Chase," I shut my eyes so I wouldn't get distracted again, "Please just—just don't. I really like Brandon. Besides, you have plenty of girls who are fine with being treated like shit by you, I'm not one of them. Go find another brainless bimbo to screw and get out of your system."

I heard his sharp intake of breath, but kept my eyes closed until I was on my way back outside. Setting out the dry towels, I flopped onto my stomach and tried to forget about Chase. Brad fired up the grill a little over an hour later, and Bree was lying out next to me as the guys talked about going surfing tomorrow. It was easy enough to keep my eyes off Chase's bare chest, but the stupid goose bumps wouldn't go away and Brandon was taking forever to get here. I was so focused on where Chase was, not even five feet away, and trying to hold a conversation with Bree that I didn't even notice Brandon until he wrapped his arms around me and lifted me off the ground. I shrieked and kicked for a second before I realized it wasn't one of the other guys about to throw me back in the pool, which had happened two more times since my hallway encounter with Chase.

Brandon just laughed and pressed his lips to mine, "Mind if I steal you away for a few minutes?"

I didn't miss the fact that Chase abruptly stopped talking, "Not at all, I'm yours for the next three days."

We were in the house before he spoke again, "We need to cover you up sweetheart."

"Why? Do you know how long it took Bree to talk me into wearing this thing?"

He set me down on his bed and slowly raked his eyes over my body. Heat spread across my cheeks and I had to force myself not to cover myself. "Remind me to thank her for that later, but I don't have enough patience tonight to continue watching the rest of the guys look at you like they want to eat you."

I frowned and ran my fingers down his cheek, "Bad day babe?"

"Something like that," he snorted and dropped his head to mine.

"You wanna tell me about it?"

"It's not a big deal, just people trying to piss me off."

"Like . . . ?"

He kissed me hard and crawled onto the bed to hover over me, "Don't worry about it sweetheart, it's nothing I can't handle."

I just stared at him for a few minutes, hoping he'd elaborate, he didn't. "Fine, I'll go change so we can get back out there."

Brandon's eyes warmed and the corner of his mouth tilted up. "I just got my girl alone again, I'm not ready to share her just yet." He bit at the hollow at the base of my neck and let his teeth lightly graze across my collar bone. The shivers I never seemed to be able to control surged up my spine, causing him to grin. "I love knowing I do that to you." His husky baritone voice was enough to make it almost happen again.

Bringing his mouth to mine, I tried to take advantage of our current situation by pulling at his bottom lip with my teeth, he groaned and slid in between my legs, pressing his body firmly against mine. I pulled his shirt over his head and trailed my fingers down his back, a shiver of his own made me giggle and repeat the trail. His lips followed the bikini top's string down my chest, when he reached the swell of my breast a hand found the ties on my hip for the bottoms and started to pull the string but suddenly froze and pulled away.

"Maybe you should go change, we need to get out of the bedroom." He looked down my body again and stepped away, "Like now."

After I changed into actual clothes, we joined everyone outside as the burgers were coming off the grill and I tried not to look for Chase, who was now gone. First thing Brandon did was thank Bree for her hand in my earlier outfit, she winked at both of us before running back to the side of some new guy named Ryan. We grabbed our dinner and Brandon pulled me onto his lap, always keeping one of his hands on me. The guys started in on a small game of football once we were done, while Bree and I cleaned up all the leftover food. Brandon came bounding into the kitchen and pulled me in for a sweaty kiss.

"We're getting in the pool, you want to join?"

I looked to Bree for her answer and turned to press my lips to his again, "Sure, let me change back into my suit. I'll be out there in a second."

He shrugged out of his shirt as he walked out the back door. Bree hit me with a dish towel to get me to stop watching him.

"What? I'm allowed to look, he's mine."

She laughed and put the rest of the food in the fridge, "Well why don't you get back in that suit so he can look too?"

I smiled and rushed back to Brandon's room. I had just grabbed my suit when Brandon's phone chimed, I glanced at his desk where it sat and continued to take my shirt off. After the top was securely in place it went off again twice. Looking at the door to see if he was coming through, I stepped toward the desk and sucked in a shocked gasp. I barely managed to fall into his chair as I stared at the offensive little screen before it went black. Going through his phone was probably too much an invasion of privacy, but he's *my* boyfriend, and what I had caught a glimpse of was definitely *my* business. Bringing the screen back to life I saw he had five texts from someone named Amanda. Sliding to unlock his phone, it instantly brought up the texts and my jaw dropped. It was the girl that had been in the group with Brandon on Monday outside of class. The one Breanna had said kept flirting with him the week before. I immediately saw the picture of her face and bare breasts, as well as the one I'd originally seen of her . . . um . . . nether regions. My heart clenched as I read the three other texts,

> *Amanda:*
> *I miss you already, can barely wait 'til tomorrow*

> *Amanda:*
> *I can't wait to feel your lips all over me again*

> *Amanda:*
> *I'm ready for you*

I dropped the phone and choked on a sob. This couldn't be happening. I felt like someone punched me in the stomach and ripped out my heart. I took deep breaths to calm my stomach so I wouldn't throw up and shakily walked over to where I'd discarded my shirt. Throwing everything else back into my bag, I ran through the house and out the front door, tears streaming down my face for the first time in years. This is exactly why I wouldn't ever give Chase and me a chance. This is how his life is, but at least he doesn't hide it like Brandon seems to be doing. A sob racked through my chest as I thought about him and I had to lean up against someone's car before I continued my way down the driveway. I hadn't expected something like this from him. I was a few blocks from the house when I heard a car slow down.

"Harper?"

Groaning, I kept my head down and continued my trek.

A door shut and footsteps quickly approached me, "Harper what are you—are you crying? What's wrong?"

I angrily wiped the tears away and stepped around him, "Please leave me alone."

"What happened?" He wrapped his hands gently around my arms and bent down to try to look in my eyes.

"Nothing happened Chase, just let me go."

"Like hell, you're crying and walking through a dark neighborhood. Talk to me."

"Why are you even out here?"

"I'm going in to work, now tell me what he did."

I breathed a miserable sounding laugh, "Don't act like you don't know. You tried to warn me, you knew he would do this." My phone rang and after a quick glance to confirm it was Brandon, I ignored the call and shoved it back in my pocket.

"Princess, I promise you I have no idea what you're talking about, but I'll kill him for hurting you. Please tell me what happened." He wrapped one arm around me, and tilted my chin up with his other hand, anger and worry etched in his face.

Another cry escaped my mouth and I crumpled into his arms. He held me and whispered soothing words into my ears until my phone rang again, I ignored it. "Can you take me to the dorms, please?"

"You sure you want to go there?"

I nodded into his chest and wiped at my cheeks again.

"Kay, get in the truck Princess." He helped me in before running to the driver's side. "Is that him calling again?"

"Yep."

"Are you going to answer it this time?"

"Nope." I hit ignore for the third time.

He let go of the seat belt and scooted toward me. Cupping my face, he wiped away the remaining tears with the pads of his thumbs. "Tell me what happened."

I opened my mouth to speak but my phone rang again, "What Brandon?!"

"What the hell Harper, what's wrong?"

"Seriously? You're really going to play that game with me?" I puffed and dropped my head into my other hand.

"Sweetheart, what are you talking about? Where did you go? And where's all your stuff?"

"I left."

"I got that, but where are you going?"

Tears started streaming down my face again, "Please stop calling me, Brandon."

"Wha—Harper, why?"

"Why don't you ask Amanda?" I sneered, "I'm sure she'd be more than happy to *show* you why I left."

He cursed away from the phone, "Harper, I swear—"

I hung up and turned my phone off.

After a few silent minutes, Chase grabbed my hand in his and spoke softly, "Who's Amanda?"

"Apparently she's some girl he's sleeping with. Bree and I saw her on Monday with him and a group of guys." I wanted to smack myself. I thought he was incredible for trying to keep my innocence intact, but instead he'd just been holding off because he was sleeping with other women.

He glanced at my face, eyebrows furrowed, "Why do you think he's cheating on you?"

I told Chase about the texts and pictures I found on his phone, which brought on another round of tears. "I feel so stupid."

"You shouldn't." He paused for a second and gripped the

steering wheel tighter, "I can't believe I'm about to say this, but I think you're wrong Harper."

"Excuse me? I know what I saw Chase!"

"I'm not saying that, but he wouldn't do that to you. That's not the kind of guy he is, but even if he were, he would have told one of us. We tend to brag about girls we're with." He reasoned, "And as much as I hate him for it, all he does is talk about you."

I shook my head and leaned against the door, "Do you realize how all over the place you are? A week ago you were telling me not to go on a date with him, and now you're defending him?"

"I'm not doing it for his benefit, trust me. I don't want you with him, that hasn't changed; I just hate seeing you hurt like this."

We sat there for another minute before I reluctantly took my hand from his and opened the door, "Thanks for the ride Chase."

"Are you going to be okay? Do you want me to stay with you?"

"I'll be fine, I'm tougher than you think." I flashed an unconvincing smile, "Go to work, I'll see you around."

He frowned, but didn't say anything else. After I got upstairs, I took a shower and put on clean pajamas before falling into bed. My eyes burned from crying so much and I desperately wished I had some eye drops. A knock sounded on my door but I didn't move. I had a feeling it would be Brandon and though I was surprised it took him so long to come here, I wasn't ready to face him. My heart hurt too much. After another soft knock, a key turned the lock and the door slowly pushed open.

"Sweetheart?"

I didn't answer, I just stared at his darkened figure through blurred eyes. He flipped on a lamp and I watched his shoulders slump when he finally saw me.

"Harper." His deep voice was thick with emotion.

"Did Bree give you her key?"

His brow furrowed as he slowly nodded.

"Traitor." Wasn't she supposed to be on my side?

"You have got to let me explain, I swear it's not how it looked."

"I doubt that and it was all pretty self-explanatory, so don't bother."

Brandon took a step toward me, but dropped his outstretched arm when I flinched away, "There is nothing happening with Amanda. She's just trying to get us to break up."

"Well, it looks like she's getting what she wanted."

A horrified expression passed over his face, "No. Don't— don't say that. Please Harper."

"Just go Brandon, I'm not going to do this with you." I turned to face the wall so he couldn't see how much this was killing me. First boyfriend, first kiss, I fell too hard too fast, and now I'm getting hurt. Him being here was just dragging it out. "Go home Brandon. We're done. Good-bye."

"God, please don't say that," he said softly to himself. Leaning over onto the bed, he ran his fingers down my arm, and continued to my back when I flinched away, "I can't leave until you hear me out. She's mad that I kept turning her down, she's seen me with you this week and she told me this morning that she would make sure I ended up with her. Right after lunch I started getting these pictures, she's just been sending the same messages over and over all day."

"And you didn't see any reason to tell me this?" I asked the wall since I still wouldn't look at him.

"I thought she was going to stop, I saw her after my last class and told her to drop it because I wasn't going to leave you."

"Is that why you were in a bad mood?"

"Yes. She knew you were staying with me this weekend, I was afraid she was going to do something else."

"Meaning?"

He blew out a deep breath and moved his hand back up to my arm, "She said she'd stop the texts, and told us to have a good weekend together. The way she said it and stressed the word 'to-gether,' I just knew something was going to happen."

I sighed and rolled back to face him, his face fell when he saw my heartbroken expression.

"Harper I'm so sorry, I should have just told you earlier." He cupped my face, and though I flinched once again, he kept his hands there.

"Are you cheating on me with anyone? Not just Amanda."

"No. I only want you."

I searched his face carefully for any sign that he was lying, but didn't find any. He had been painfully honest with me from the beginning and I knew he was telling the truth now. Because of that I couldn't stay mad at him, no matter how much I'd wanted to. It had worried me how hurt I was when I'd first gotten those messages. I'd already fallen for this guy, and while it surprised me how fast I'd come to care for him, it was completely blowing my mind how much he seemed to care for me as well. Before I could tell him I believed him, his phone started repeatedly chiming and we sat silently watching each other until it stopped. I held out my hand and was surprised when he handed it over without even checking it. Opening up his messages I saw the exact same five messages Amanda had sent earlier. I typed back a response and hit send before handing it back to him.

> Brandon:
> This is Brandon's girlfriend, I don't know what you're trying to accomplish, but I'd really appreciate it if you stopped sending him pictures of yourself. He doesn't want you, and desperation isn't cute. So back off bitch.

Brandon read it quickly and managed a laugh before dropping his phone to the ground and sweeping me up in a big hug. "I'm sorry I hurt you."

"You didn't, I should have just asked you before running off."

"I really wish you would have, but I don't blame you sweet-heart." He kissed both cheeks and my lips, then leaned away to look in my eyes again, "Can you tell me one thing though? Why'd you run off to Chase?"

"I didn't, how did you know I'd been with him?"

"He called to tell me where you were."

Chase defending Brandon was weird enough, but I for sure hadn't expected him to do that. "I didn't run off to him, I left and he saw me walking back here. He gave me a ride."

He still look worried, and I thought about the already count-less times he'd asked if there was something going on between Chase and I.

Taking a deep breath in, I put a hand against his cheek and smiled softly at him. "If I can believe you about a girl that keeps sending naked pictures of herself to your phone, then you should believe me when it comes to a guy that does nothing but piss me off."

He kissed my palm and placed his hand over mine, "You're right, I just wish I would have been there for you, not him. I'm sorry it took me so long to get here."

"Don't be sorry, you're here now, that's all that matters."

He smiled and lightly pressed his lips to mine, cradling me against his chest. After a few minutes he finally spoke again, "Do you need more time alone, or can I take you back to the house?"

"You can take me back, if you promise me something first."

"Anything," he said without missing a beat.

I raised an eyebrow and smirked at him.

He nudged me playfully, "Anything *reasonable.*"

I huffed but winked so he knew I was kidding, "If something like this happens again, you need to tell me right away. My heart broke when I saw that, I don't want to go through that again."

"Done. I didn't mean to break your heart." He kissed me thoroughly before murmuring against my lips, "Anything else?"

"Yeah, I want it to just be you and me tonight."

"It will be."

"Like lock the door, stay wrapped up in each other's arms and forget about everyone else kind of night. Do you think you can handle that?"

A sexy grin spread across his face, "I'm sure I can manage."

5

"BREE, ARE YOU ready?"

"Freaking Konrad hid my bag."

"Okay?" I drew out the word.

"He didn't want me to be able to get dressed."

I laughed, "Nice. Check in the washer or dryer." I wasn't surprised that she'd replaced Ryan with Konrad at some point last night.

Bree ran through the kitchen in only a thong. Good thing all the guys had gone surfing this morning. She came back holding her bag, her eyes narrowed, "You knew he put this there?"

"Was it really there?" I laughed louder and shook my head, "No I had no idea, but a few times the guys on base would do that if someone was in the shower. Take not only the clothes they had to put on, but all the other ones in their locker and hide them in the laundry room. I saw way too many butts that way." I thought of Carter and pulled out my phone.

Me:
Miss you :(

J. Carter:
;-)

I waited to see if he'd say anything else, but he didn't. I went back to putting the blankets and food in the car while Bree changed for the beach. Brandon had made good on his promise last night. When we got back from the dorm he'd taken me into his room, not saying anything to anyone. He turned both our phones off, locked the door and curled around me on the bed. I wanted to spend time talking to and kissing him, but I'd been so exhausted from crying, I'd fallen asleep soon after. We were woken up early this morning by Brad banging on the door so they could go surfing, and although Brandon started to tell him we were having time to ourselves, I'd kicked him out of the bed and told him to have fun. Bree and I decided to go down to the beach later to surprise them, figuring we could eat lunch and relax for a few hours. I'd made dozens of sandwiches, grabbed numerous large bags of chips and drinks and loaded them all into the coolers while Bree had been looking for her clothes.

We got to the beach and were glad to see the guys still out in the water. After setting up the blankets and towels, we sat down to watch them.

"So . . . Ryan?"

"Pfft, that guy was way too into himself. I need my guy to be more into me."

"And did Konrad know he was your replacement last night?"

She shrugged, "Obviously he didn't mind."

"Obviously. Have you decided if you're going to date him?"

"I think I am." Bree smiled, Konrad had asked her to be his girlfriend, and she told him she'd think about it . . . while they were in the middle of having sex. I swear I didn't get her. "I really think I like him Harper. I'm used to guys getting bored after we hook up, but he's not like that. It's like we just can't stop going back to each other."

"Then why are you making him wait?"

She rolled onto her stomach, facing away from the water, and I followed, "I don't know. I mean I've had boyfriends before, but I just started college. I don't know if I want to be tied down right away. I'd like to explore my options."

I only sort of understood that, I hadn't come to San Diego even looking for a guy, let alone a boyfriend. But there was no denying whatever was going on between Brandon and me. With him around, I couldn't see myself not being with him. My phone chimed and I had to dig through the huge bags we'd brought things in to find it.

J. Carter:
Where are you?

Me:
At the beach

J. Carter:
Ditching classes then?

Me:
I don't have classes on Fridays. What are you up to?

J. Carter:
What beach?

I don't know why that mattered to him, there were tons of beaches in the area. He wouldn't know the difference.

> Me:
> It's just a beach that's literally all the way down the street from the school.

"Why are you frowning?"

I looked up at Bree and put my phone away, "Carter's been weird the last few days."

"Weird how?"

"Well we usually talk every day. But we didn't talk at all yesterday, and the three days before that he wouldn't answer my calls, he would just text me back right after. And now he's asking weird things. I don't know, it's just not like him."

"And nothing's going on there?"

"No . . . I told you that. I just don't understand what's going on with him."

"Well maybe he has a girlfriend now." Bree reasoned, "I'm sure it would bug her if he was always talking to you. Does Brandon know about him?"

"He knows of him, but I don't think he knows how close we are. Or were." I trailed off, I didn't know moving here would mean losing his friendship.

"Does he know about Brandon?"

"Yeah, well he knew we went on a date. I haven't talked to him much since then."

"Well there you go!"

I looked at Bree confused, "There I go, what?"

She propped herself up on her elbows, "I bet he likes you, and now that you're obviously interested in other guys, he's pulling away from you."

"Nice try." I laughed and sat up to take my shirt off, leaving me in only my tiny shorts and bikini top. "I've told you, it wasn't like that between me and Carter. He dated a lot of girls while I knew him. It just hurts that he's being distant. I mean we went from seeing and talking to each other every day, to this. I feel like I lost my best friend."

Bree looked at me like I wasn't getting it.

"Would you ever date Brad?"

"God no!" She said a little disgusted, "He's like a brother to me."

"Exactly. Carter and I were exactly how you are with Brad."

She flipped onto her back, "Oh . . . well then I don't know what to tell you. Just ask him next time you talk."

"Hey babe!"

I turned to look at Brandon and smiled, "Hi! We thought we'd hang out for the day."

He grabbed one of the towels and bent down to kiss me, "Should I thank Bree for this one too?" He trailed a finger along the fabric of the top. I nodded and he kissed me again, pressing his wet body to mine. If it hadn't been for the rest of the guys coming back and talking loud, I would have forgotten we weren't alone in his bed.

"Brandon," Konrad walked over to us, "come help me get the coolers out of Bree's car."

"Coolers?" Brandon looked at me, his head tilted to the side.

"I brought lots of food for you guys, figured you'd be hungry after surfing."

He kissed me soundly before jumping to his feet, "You're pretty perfect Harper."

My heart beat wildly as I watched him walk toward the car. My phone rang when they were headed back.

"Carter!"

"How's my girl?" I could hear the smile in his voice.

"Well speak of the damn devil," Bree muttered next to me.

"I'm good. I feel like we haven't talked in a long time. Is everything okay?"

"It's better than okay now," he said mischievously.

"Really?" I smiled at Brandon as he sat down next to me. "And why is that?"

"I'm at the beach with some of the guys."

I really had to focus on what he was saying, I was currently getting lost in Brandon's brown eyes, "The beach huh? Glad you guys got out early for the weekend. Tell them I said hi."

"I don't think you know these guys, but I'll be sure to pass along the message. So how's *your* beach?"

I bit my lip as I looked at Brandon, "Amazing. Yours?"

"It's got the best view. You know, I bet if I yelled loud enough, you could hear me from here."

I laughed, "You're so dumb."

"No really . . . put down the phone and I'll yell. You can tell me if you hear me or not." He waited a few seconds, "Come on Harper, I said put the phone down."

Rolling my eyes I conceded, "Fine, fine. Phone's going down." I put it down on the blanket and started to lean over to kiss Brandon when I heard someone yell.

"BLAZE!"

I sat back quickly. That definitely hadn't come from the speaker of the phone. Grabbing it, I brought it to my ear, "What the hell?"

"Shall we try that again?" A few seconds later I heard a distant voice yell *Blaze* again.

Glancing at my phone I realized he'd ended the call and I turned to look behind Bree.

"You okay Harper?" Brandon asked.

"Did you hear someone yell 'Blaze'?"

"Yeah," he nodded to something behind me, "the guy back there did."

I turned around and gasped. "Oh my God, Carter!" I sprang to my feet, already in a run. I crashed into Carter, hugging him tightly, "What are you doing here?!"

"Damn Blaze. Where's my Harper and what have you done with her?"

I blushed and crossed my arms over my chest, "Uh, yeah. I guess I look a little different."

He ran a finger near the piercing on my lip, "A little." He smiled and hugged me to him again. "I missed you Blaze."

"I missed you too." I said into his chest, "I can't believe you didn't tell me you were coming. I would have been at the airport to get you."

"Well that wouldn't have been half as fun as your reaction just now."

I leaned back to smile at him. He was tall too, not like Chase or Brandon, but close to six feet. His black hair was in the traditional fade the Marine's had and his brown eyes were bright. "How long do you get to be here for?"

He smiled wide and opened his mouth to talk, but was cut off. "Harper?"

Turning, I saw Brandon staring at Carter, he didn't look happy. And I could only imagine how after what happened last night with Amanda, me taking off and almost tackling a random guy while in a bikini would be a little alarming. Especially since Carter still had his arms wrapped around my waist. Stepping back toward Brandon, I grabbed his hand and squeezed, "Brandon this is my best friend from Camp Lejeune, Jason Carter. Carter, this is my boyfriend Brandon Taylor."

They firmly shook hands but didn't say anything. Awkward.

"Um, why don't we head back over there? I can introduce you to everyone else." I pulled Brandon back toward our friends while I was introduced to the three guys Carter had been with. He was right, I didn't know them, but Carter had never been to California so I didn't know how he knew them either.

I introduced Carter and the three guys to everyone, and while all the housemates and Konrad were polite, Chase wouldn't speak to, or shake Carter's hand. Just crossed his arms over his bare chest and openly glared at him. What threw me off even more, was Brandon standing right next to him, in the exact same stance. It didn't surprise me that Carter took a step back, those guys could look scary if they wanted to. Rugged looks, tall tattooed and muscled bodies. Yep. Definitely scary to someone who didn't know them. Bree looked back and forth between Carter and me with an amused expression. I knew she would grill me about this later.

When we were all seated on the blankets, I asked Carter again, "So how long is your leave for?"

"I didn't get leave." He shrugged his shoulders.

"Carter!" I gasped, "I swear to God if you went UA . . ." I knew what the punishment was for leaving base without authorization, and if Carter did . . . well let's just say it wouldn't be good.

He laughed, "No, no. I didn't. Everyone knows I'm here. I requested for a transfer to Camp Pendleton when you decided to move to San Diego, it got accepted right after you left. I got here on Monday."

"Wait, you moved here because I was moving here?"

"Of course."

"Did Sir make you do that?"

"Not at all. I just couldn't let you go."

"Oh shit," Bree muttered.

Brandon sat up straighter, I didn't have to look up to know he was glaring and sizing up Carter. This could get bad, I was about to say something when Carter spoke up again.

"I mean I can't let my little sister go across the country alone, right?"

I smiled at Carter and felt Brandon relax from behind me. Sean, one of the guys that came with Carter, looked at the other two guys then back to Carter with a confused look and started to speak, but when he looked back to me and Brandon, he shut his mouth.

"So . . . I'm sorry what was your name again? Brady?"

I glared at Carter but remained quiet. I knew he could tell me everyone's name that he'd just met. I'd always envied that he could remember anything as long as he read or heard it once.

Brandon's arm tensed around my waist, "Brandon."

"Right, my bad. So how did you meet my girl?"

"Through school. I live with Chase, Bree's his sister and Harper's roommate."

Carter's head tilted back a bit, his eyes lit up like he was just told valuable information, "Chase huh? Good for you two, I don't judge."

Brandon snorted and trailed his other hand down my arm to intertwine our fingers, "Hear that Chase? Apparently we're together."

"Ah. It all finally makes sense. Why you're always at my house and such. Guess I should take you on a date or something." Chase smirked but kept his glare on Carter.

I kicked Carter's leg and gave him a *be nice* look.

He smiled warmly at me and glanced above my head to Brandon again. "What are you going to school for?"

"I'm double majoring in financial services and accounting, and minoring in marketing."

Carter seemed genuinely surprised by this. I had been too

when Brandon told me he'd taken every core class he would need at a community college while he was still in high school, so all he had to focus on during his time at SDSU were his majors and minor. He was incredibly smart, and it only added to his appeal.

"That's admirable I guess," Carter said looking at me, "you can probably go into something to make a good living."

"I make a good living now." He pulled me closer into his body and I watched as the muscles in his forearm strained against the skin.

I rolled my eyes and was about to stop the testosterone filled interrogation when Carter spoke again.

"And how's that? You a manager at McDonalds?"

My mouth dropped and I glared at my friend, why was he being such a jerk? Brandon stiffened and I shut my eyes. Here we go.

"I fight. And I'm damn good at what I do."

I quickly glanced at everyone around us, it was like a bad movie. Everyone stopped talking and was staring at Carter to see what he would say.

"What kind of fighting? With open handed slaps and hair pulling?" Carter goaded.

"MMA," Brandon said through what sounded like clenched teeth.

"Oh perfect." Carter glanced down at me, "You managed to find an abusive hot-headed boyfriend, exactly what we tried to get you to stay away from."

"Carter!" I hissed.

"Consider this your warning tool," Carter's eye got dark, "the minute you touch *my* girl, I will end you."

Brandon started to stand up but I beat him to it, grabbing Carter's arm and pulling him with me. As soon as we were far enough away that I didn't think anyone else would hear us, I whirled around, "What the hell is your problem?!"

Carter looked a little sheepish, "I'm just looking out for you Blaze."

"You're being an asshole!"

"Well!" His arms shot out to the side, "I don't think he's good for you."

I was getting freaking tired of people telling me who is and isn't good for me. I crossed my arms over my chest, wishing I would have put my shirt back on. "And why is that Jason?"

His eyes flashed with hurt, he knew I only used his first name when I was mad at him, "Because of what he does. You heard him, he fights for a *living* Blaze. And he was having a hell of a time trying not to hit me and I just met him."

"Because you were being incredibly rude! And you're right, you two had *just* met. If you would have given him five seconds you would have seen how amazing he is. Instead, you continued to push every button you could find, and why did you have to keep calling me *your* girl. I'm not your anything and you know that."

"You're my best friend Blaze," he said softly.

"And I thought you were mine, but my best friend wouldn't have treated anyone the way you just did, especially my boyfriend." I turned to walk away but he grabbed my arm.

"Blaze I'm sorry. Please don't walk away from me, I'll make this up to you I swear."

Yanking my arm from his loose hold, I stepped closer to his body, even though I was much shorter than him, he still backed up, "Do you have any idea how much you've embarrassed me?" I put my hands on his chest and shoved him back, "When I told them about you, all I did was gush over how awesome you were and how much I missed you. Then you show up and treat them this way?" I looked down trying to get ahold of my emotions that were all over the place. I was embarrassed, angry and sad for the loss of the Carter I knew. Huffing sadly, I glanced back up at him, "Go back to base Carter and please don't call me anymore. You shouldn't have come to California."

He grabbed my hand when I turned away and pulled me back to his chest, wrapping his arms around me. "I'm so sorry Harper. I was being stupid, I just—I don't know. I guess I felt threatened by them, you're *my* best friend, and they were all looking at me like they wanted to protect you from me. It pissed me off, and I shouldn't have let it. I'm really sorry."

I sighed and put my arms around his waist, "Because they would protect me in a second. It's just the same as it was on base, Carter. These guys are really protective of me and Bree. That's why I'm so comfortable with them, it's like I went from one family of a bunch of brothers, to another."

"But you barely know them."

"Carter," I laughed lightly, "how long had I known you before you knocked out a guy from a different unit that said something about my chest?" He shifted his weight not wanting to answer, so I continued, "About two hours. It's the same."

"It's not Blaze. I want to be the one to protect you. I don't want anyone else to do my job."

"Oh my God. What is it with you guys? I don't need anyone protecting me and I'm not your responsibility."

"I know you don't," he pulled back a bit and looked at my face, "there's just something about you that makes guys go crazy wanting to take care of you."

I rolled my eyes and cursed my tiny frame, "I know. Oh!" I smiled widely at him, "Did I tell you I busted some guy's nose that was coming on too strong?"

His eyes darkened but he still smiled, "No, but I would've liked to see that."

"He just wasn't understanding that I didn't want him, and then he challenged Brandon and I knew Brandon was going to do something, so I did it first. Smashed his face right into my knee." I brought my knee up now, "See, I still have a bruise from it!"

Carter shook his head and hugged me to his chest again, "I'm proud of you Blaze." He kissed the top of my head and I tensed, not knowing what to make of that, "Do you forgive me?"

Pulling away from him, I punched him lightly on the arm, "Yeah, but you need to be nice to my friends. And you need to apologize to Brandon."

"You really like him?" His face twisted.

"Yes, I do. So be sweet!" I grabbed his arm and started walking back to everyone else, "It's Friday so there will be a party at Chase's house tonight. If you can get back on everyone's good side, you all can come over and crash after."

He stopped walking, "Yeah, what's up with that guy anyway? To be honest, I would have thought he was your boyfriend, the way he looked was like he wanted to kill me."

I laughed, "Honestly, I have no idea. You and Brandon are both wondering that. But he means well, I promise."

Carter mumbled something under his breath, but I was already rushing over to my boyfriend so I didn't hear him. Brandon stood when he saw me coming over and caught me in his arms, smiling against my mouth when I kissed him soundly.

"Everything okay?" he whispered in my ear before setting my feet on the ground.

"Yes, I'm really sorry, he isn't usually like that."

Brandon looked behind me and shook someone's hand.

"Sorry man." Carter said, "She just means a lot to me."

"I understand that," Brandon said as he stared in my eyes, warming my heart. "Come on, Harper made lunch for everyone, you and your guys are more than welcome to it."

I smiled against Brandon's chest. Even after Carter had been an ass, he was still being incredibly polite to him. We all sat down to eat, and stayed at the beach for another few hours. Everyone but Chase seemed to forgive Carter for the way he'd been when he first showed up. Even Brandon was laughing and joking with him as he invited them all back to the house for the party that night.

"CARTER!" I YELLED and ran over to hug him after slamming back another shot. This was the third Friday in a row he'd come to Chase's house with some of the guys from his new unit.

He hugged me tightly and shook Brandon's hand, "Sorry we're late, it took forever to get off base."

"Just glad you're here now."

Carter's answering smile was warm and slow, and kind of confusing. "Me too." His words were lost in the loud music, but it was obvious what he was saying. His arm was still around me, and I slid out of it, wrapping my arms around Brandon's waist.

"Let's get you a drink," Brandon said as he led the way to the kitchen.

After we all had a beer in hand, Brandon gave me a weird look when we tried for the third time to start a conversation with Carter, and he just stared straight ahead. Chase walked through the kitchen, on his way to work I'm sure, and when he saw Carter his face fell as he pushed through him to leave. Carter glanced at him and drained his beer. It wasn't weird for Chase to be rude, as far as I knew he still had yet to say anything to Carter. But usually Carter would make a snide remark to him, not just stand there and take it.

"Are you okay?" I asked, placing a hand on Carter's arm.

He glanced to Brandon, then back to me, "I'm perfect, why?"

"You're being really quiet."

"I don't have to keep you company every time I'm here, do I? As far as I'm concerned, that's your boyfriend's job."

"Hey," Brandon pulled me closer to his chest, "she's just worried about you man. You don't have to be an ass."

Carter laughed humorlessly, "*She* doesn't have a reason to be worried."

"Look," I leaned into Carter so I could speak in his ear, "obviously you've had a bad day, or week, and I'm sorry. But you need to have another drink, relax, and go find a girl or something."

"I'll be sure to do just that." He grabbed another beer out of the fridge and left the kitchen.

Brandon kissed my neck, "Just let him go, he needs to chill for a bit."

I nodded and tilted my head to give him better access, "I don't know what his deal is, he's been so different since he came to California."

"Maybe he's having a hard time getting used to his new unit."

"You're probably right." Turning, I wrapped my arms around his neck and slid my tongue across his bottom lip, I laughed huskily when he moaned, "Want to dance?"

He grabbed my hand and led me into the living room, smiling when Bree winked at me from where she was grinding on Konrad, they were finally exclusive. Pressing my back against Brandon's chest I slowly started moving against him, loving the way his hard body felt against mine. I brought a hand up to cup the back of his neck when I felt his lips on my shoulder, and placed my other hand over one of his gripping the bottom of my shorts. My body felt like it was melting into him as heat burned through me, and I was once again left with my heart racing and wanting to take him somewhere where we could be alone. When the song changed into a faster one, Bree grabbed my hand and pulled me toward her, Brandon stayed right behind me. The four of us were dancing so close to each other, I kept brushing against Konrad's legs and I knew Bree was having a hard time avoiding Brandon's. While one of his hands stayed on my thigh, Brandon's other raised up and went under my shirt, leaving it at the top of the denim I was wearing. My breath caught when he gripped me tighter, his pinky barely sliding under my shorts, the rest of his hand splayed across my bare stomach. I pressed my back against him even harder, resting my head on his shoulder and closing my eyes so all I could do was feel his body and hear the music. When my movement caused his ring finger to go below the waist of my shorts as well, my body trembled and I felt him harden against the small of my back. I don't know if it was the shots, or the music, but I brought my hand behind my back and let it pass over the bulge in his jeans every time he'd move against me. Brandon trailed his fingers lower, skimming them across my satin underwear and I let out an involuntary moan, my body aching for his hand to continue lower. Suddenly, his hands and body were no longer touching me. I turned to ask what was wrong, but I lost my voice when I saw the passion and heat in his gray eyes.

"If I don't back off for a minute, I'm going to take you right here in front of everyone."

I grinned wickedly at him and watched him mentally talk himself into walking away without me. Good thing one of us could remember that we weren't alone, I would have let him do anything to me just then, people surrounding us or not. I kept my eyes on Brandon while he walked to the kitchen, but had started dancing with Bree and Konrad again when a hand on my arm caused me to turn my head and look at an angry Carter. He tilted his head to the side and back, indicating the backyard so I followed, slowly making our way through the tightly packed bodies.

"Wha—"

Carter turned and roughly pressed his mouth to mine. My eyes went wide and I pushed against his chest, trying to scramble back.

"What the hell?!"

He was still holding my upper arms, his eyes smoldering, "Blaze, I want you. I've wanted you since I met you last year."

My jaw dropped and I shook my head, "What?"

"I love you Harper."

"No you don't, we're not like that, you know that!"

"No . . . I don't know that. I moved here for you, I followed you across the country so I could be with you."

I glanced at the people looking at us and tried to quiet my voice, "Carter, you're my best friend. Don't do this. Don't try to change things between us, let's just go back to how we were."

"Did you never understand anything I did for you? Did you not hear everything I've ever said to you?" He looked at me incredulously, "I have never thought of you as just my best friend, I even asked your dad if I could date you and he made it clear as long as I was in his unit, I couldn't. But I knew you would be leaving soon, I knew that was our chance to be together."

"Carter," I said softly, "I love you, but not like that. You even said it yourself, I'm like your little sister."

"You know I was lying. I had to because you didn't even wait five fucking seconds before hooking up with the first guy that you came across."

My jaw dropped, "Jason!" I hissed.

"Just give us a chance Blaze, I can love you and take care of you better than he can. Better than anyone can."

"I'm in love with Brandon, but even if I wasn't, I would never think of you that way. I'm so—"

His lips were on mine again, and I leaned as far back as I could. "Stop!" I yelled as I shoved him off me.

As soon as he was a few feet away, someone grabbed me from behind and pulled me back further at the same time that Brandon plowed into Carter with his shoulder, knocking both of them to the ground. Sean and another Marine, Anthony, were on top of Brandon trying to pull him off, followed closely by Drew and Zach. I shot forward but Derek held me to his chest telling me not to get in the middle of it. As they started pulling each other off, Brad came out yelling for everyone to back off. It took a few more party goers for the fight to end, Anthony and Sean held Carter back as he continued to lunge for Brandon, I was surprised to see he wasn't bleeding anywhere. Brandon just stood there with his hands down at his sides.

"What . . . nothing?!" Carter hissed, "You claim to be some fighter, let's see it!"

Brandon continued to not move or say anything.

"DO SOMETHING!" Carter yelled.

"Enough!" Brad's voice boomed across the backyard. "Get out. The three of you need to leave. Now." Looking around him he threw up his hands, "Never mind, everyone get out. Party's over. If you do not live or stay here, get out!"

Everyone started shuffling in, keeping a distance from the two Marines dragging Carter away. He was still taunting Brandon, who was now standing beside me, replacing Derek's arms with his own. He wasn't stopping me like Derek had though, Brandon's arms were full of warmth as his fingers made small circles on my side and back.

"You okay?" he asked softly, still watching Carter leave.

"I'm fine, did you hurt him?"

"All I did was keep him on the ground."

I nodded and buried my face in his chest, "I swear I had no idea about any of that."

He chuckled, "I know *you* didn't know, doesn't mean the rest of us didn't."

"What do you mean?"

"Like he said sweetheart, everything he says to you or about you is laced with how much he wants you. You just didn't realize it because you thought you were only friends."

I felt incredibly stupid. "How much of that did you see?"

"The whole thing, it just took me a while to get through everyone to you." He tilted my head up and I was surprised to see a wide grin on his face as he leaned in closer to me, "And I love you too Harper, so much."

A smile stretched across my entire face as I hurried to press my mouth to his, murmuring how much I loved him against his lips.

After everyone left, we cleaned up from the party quickly, but when the guys and Bree sat down to watch a movie, Brandon grabbed my hand in his and led me to his bedroom. Flipping off the light, he locked the door and changed with his back to me as I slipped into a tank top and shorts. When we were under his comforter, he wrapped his arms around me, pressing my chest to his.

"I'm sorry if you wanted to stay up with them, it's just been a long day, and all I want to do is be with you."

I pressed my face into his neck, placing a light kiss into the base of it, "This is perfect." After a few silent minutes I laughed softly, "I really was starting to enjoy the parties here too. I guess I'll have to go back to avoiding them, too much drama."

"One of these days, everyone will get the hint that we're not going to leave each other. They'll back off."

"I hope so."

"I love you sweetheart."

My heart soared, "I love you too."

I SLIPPED OUT of bed the next morning to use the restroom and freshen up a bit, smiling the entire time. I was still on cloud nine from Brandon telling me he loved me. I'd known I was in love with him for a couple weeks now, but I had been too afraid to tell him. I guess that was one thing I could thank Carter for, he made us skip the awkward moment of telling each other for the first time. Carter. I rolled my eyes. He'd left me ten voicemails and dozens of texts last night apologizing, and I hadn't said one thing back to him. I hated what I'd lost from our friendship in

North Carolina, but he was just too different now, I didn't know how we could even continue on being friends, especially after what happened last night. I mentally shook myself as I pulled my hair back into a loose low bun, I didn't want to think about him right now. I just wanted to go back to my boyfriend, and spend the weekend wrapped up in his arms.

After I shut and locked his bedroom door, I froze where I was, taking in the remarkable sight of Brandon. God he was sexy. His tanned upper body was bare, trailing my eyes down, I bit my bottom lip as I looked at his muscled V, leading down to his loose shorts, all but the waistband hidden by the comforter. My body started warming just looking at him, and all I could think about was running my hands and lips all over him. Looking down at myself, I made a decision to start this weekend off right. I slipped off my shorts and tank top, grabbing the gray and white button down shirt he'd been wearing last night, I pulled it on leaving all but one of the middle buttons undone. Glancing in the mirror, I decided to keep my hot pink satin underwear on, and pulled my hair out of the bun, giving it some fluff. Before I could talk myself out of it, I crawled onto the bed, one knee on either side of Brandon's body, and placed my lips to his muscled stomach. His body twitched and I pressed my lips a little higher up the next time, smiling when he moaned in his sleep. I kissed my way up his body, he opened his eyes wide when I sat firmly on his lap and nipped at his throat.

"Harper," He breathed as he stared into my eyes.

"Good morning," I whispered and covered his mouth with mine.

He gripped my hips and moved slightly, trying to get more comfortable, he moaned and I gasped when his arousal pressed against me. I rocked my hips against him and my eyelids fluttered shut from the incredible feel of it. I had no idea what I was doing, but I didn't want to stop. There was a slow burning that started low in my stomach and with each rock of my hips it grew greater. Brandon's hands slid up my bare stomach, undoing the one button when he reached it, and continuing to my chest. He sat up, pressing his lips to the swell of my breast, exploring it before making his way to the other. My breaths were embarrassingly loud, but I couldn't seem to care enough to try and stop it as he caught my nipple between his teeth. I arched my back and let my head fall back as I experienced each sensation for the first time. One of his hands trailed back to my hip to assist in my rocking, but I grabbed his hand in mine, grasping the side of my underwear and tugging on it. Realizing what I was doing, he slid me off his body and onto my back, he barely hovered above my side as he propped himself up on an elbow.

Brandon's lips were on mine, his free hand trailing from my jaw to my underwear. When his fingers stopped at the top, I took his hand and moved them just inside of the satin, to let him know exactly what I wanted. I couldn't even continue to kiss him as the burning in my stomach instantly increased when his fingers moved against me. A pressure I can't explain started building between my legs and I moaned loudly when he slid a finger inside me, moving it in rhythm with my hips.

Minutes past and the sensation got to be too much, I didn't know what was happening and part of me wanted him to stop, but the other part wasn't ready yet, "God. Baby . . . I."

His lips hovered over mine as he spoke softly, "It's okay sweetheart, let go for me."

I didn't understand what he was talking about, but when I arched against his hand one more time, my entire body racked with an intense, exhilarating explosion. Brandon's mouth on mine muted most of my pleasured cry as I gave over to the mind-blowing spasms continuing throughout my body.

That's what he meant by let go. Oh. My. Word.

Brandon wrapped his arms around me and pulled me so I was

half-lying on his chest. He kissed my temple and rubbed soft circles into my back. "I love you Harper."

I nodded against his chest, still trying to get my breathing back to normal, "I . . . love you . . . so . . . oh wow."

His silent laugh shook my body and he squeezed me tighter while bringing the comforter up around us. He peppered my cheek and jaw with kisses as he held me until my already completely relaxed body succumbed to sleep. Just before I gave in, I swear I heard him vow to love me forever.

6

"WHY ARE YOU being like this?" I hissed.

He just continued to look at me like I was the biggest inconvenience possible, and I had no idea why.

"Did I do something to offend you? You haven't said a word to me since Sunday." And it was freaking Thursday, "You have been so bipolar lately, I don't even know what to expect from you."

Keeping his mouth shut, he raised one brow causing it to disappear under his shaggy hair. Chase and I had been having the most bizarre relationship lately and it was making my head spin. Bree had been taking me to her parents' house for family day every Sunday for a month, and though it had been awkward at first when Claire, their mom, had hugged me as soon as I stepped in the door; I soon fell in love with her and her husband Robert. They were extremely loving, funny, and honestly I liked spending time with their family more than the parties at Chase's house. Especially if they were like last week's with Carter's declaration of love.

What was frustrating, was Chase's drastic mood swings. Over the last three weeks, he'd started talking to me less and less during the week, but if we were at his parents' house, he wouldn't leave my side and you wouldn't believe he was the same guy I'd met my second night in California. He was hilarious, sweet and an incredible artist. Listening to him banter back and forth with his dad usually left the rest of us in tears and he treated his mom, Bree and I with such respect, it was mind blowing. If anyone's drinks started getting low, he was already refilling it, he always made sure we were comfortable and had everything we needed, and his kisses on his mom's cheeks had to be the most loving thing I'd ever seen come from him.

The biggest shock was when I'd gone to Chase's room in his house to tell Bree I was ready to leave, and stumbled upon a sketch book. I confronted him about it later at his parents', and he ran upstairs for a minute and brought down an armful of them. He was extremely talented and I shouldn't have been surprised when he told me he was a tattoo artist at the shop Bree had taken me for our piercings. The way his eyes lit up as I gushed over each drawing tugged at my heart, and I tried desperately to push those feelings away. I'd spent a couple hours last Sunday watching him work on a few new pieces he wanted on his forearms while the whole family watched a couple movies in the living room. At some point I must have fallen asleep on the couch I'd been sharing with Chase because an explosion on the TV jerked me awake.

"It's just the movie," he whispered in my direction and ran his fingers over my cheek, "don't move yet Princess."

"Don't move? Why?"

"I'm almost done, give me another minute or two."

I heard his hand moving back and forth across the paper

slowly and waited until he kneeled down in front of the couch so his face was directly in front of mine. My breath caught and his electric blue eyes glanced down to my barely parted lips. His tongue absently wetted his lips and his teeth lightly bit down on his bottom one as his gaze roamed my face.

"Why couldn't I move?" I managed to ask when he started closing the distance between us.

He abruptly stopped and blinked a few times, "Oh, um. Well . . . here. Just don't freak out, okay? I wasn't trying to be creepy."

"You're not supposed to tell someone not to freak out, those words alone cause them to freak out."

Chase smirked, "Okay, well then don't hit me or use your pressure point training on me again."

Before I could roll my eyes at him, he brought his sketch pad up in front of me and my jaw dropped. I felt my cheeks burn and he took that the wrong way. Snatching the pad of paper back up, he cursed softly.

"I knew it was creepy."

"Chase," I breathed and shook my head in an attempt to clear my thoughts, "that wasn't creepy. Can I see it again?" When he didn't make an attempt to move I reached my arm toward the book, "Please."

He handed it over with a sigh and looked at me with a sad smile, "I'm sorry, but you looked too perfect. I couldn't let that opportunity pass."

My stupid blush came back with force when he said that and I focused at his drawing. It was amazing, somewhat embarrassing, but remarkable none the less. With the shading and the detail he'd captured of my upper body and face, it almost looked like a black and white photo. It was perfect. From my chest, throat and slightly open mouth to the way my hair fell around my face and my eyelashes rested against my cheeks, it was one hundred percent me. He even had my hand clutching the pillow under my head that was resting on his leg, as well as the blanket that had been pulled up to the swell of my breasts. Goose bumps covered my body as I realized he'd spent however long staring at, and replicating, every part of me while I'd been completely unaware. He was wrong, it wasn't creepy, it was beautiful and strangely intimate.

"Chase, it—" I cleared my throat and tried again, "It's incredible." Incredible didn't cover it.

"Yeah?"

I looked up into his eyes and smiled, "Yeah."

We stayed there staring at each other, my mind and heart completely torn in two. One half desperately wanted to act on the feelings his drawing had stirred up in me, and the other was screaming at me to sit up and scoot away from him. Before I could try to make a decision, another series of explosions came from the TV and we both jolted away from each other.

MY FACE HEATED again as the memory of last Sunday played through my mind, and Chase's annoyed look turned bemused. I pushed aside my awe and longing for that rare side of Chase and let my anger take forefront again. I don't know why he was so different on Sundays, but at least during the week he would usually say hi to me. Not that I expected him to spend more time with me since I was always with Bree or Brandon during the week, but after that moment on Sunday I was dumbfounded as to why he'd avoided me like a leper since.

"Whatever. I'm done trying to figure you out. If you want to be an asshole, go right ahead. But don't keep acting like there's nothing wrong between us on Sundays."

"We're back to this now?" he jeered.

"It's a freaking miracle. He speaks."

"You think I'm confusing? God Harper, that's rich." He laughed once and narrowed his eyes at me, "This coming from the girl who repeatedly told me to stay away but fell into my arms at the first sign of trouble with her boyfriend? Do you want me to back off, or don't you?" Chase took a step forward, I took one back and he matched it, whispering in my ear, "Why keep fighting the inevitable, baby? You want me. Even now your body is shaking because you're trying to keep yourself from touching me." Brushing the tips of his fingers across my hand he smiled, "One touch from me and you're covered in goose bumps. Tell me now that you want me to go away."

"You're such an ass." I growled and took another step back, "I just don't understand why we can't be friends all the time. I don't want to be your friend on Sunday and the girl you don't acknowledge every other day of the week. I want the same thing every day. So you decide what that is and let me know." I moved to walk around him, but he put his arm up against the wall of the hallway, blocking me in.

"I'll tell you, if you tell me."

"Tell you what?"

"I feel like I'm just one in a group of Harper's many guys, but I'm not getting the benefits. So tell me, if I act like your friend, will I get to fuck you too?"

My fist was aiming straight for that perfectly shaped nose but Chase was slammed into the wall before I could connect. Brandon's forearm was pressed against Chase's throat and his tan face was turning red with anger.

"What the hell did you just say to her?" He growled and pressed Chase harder into the wall.

Chase's only response was to spit in Brandon's face.

Brandon's other hand grabbed Chase's shirt to bring him forward while the arm that had been against his throat delivered a hard blow to Chase's stomach. Chase swung and hit the wall when Brandon moved, but he'd moved right into Chase's left hook. I started yelling at them to stop and somehow they ended up on the floor with Chase on top. Just as the other housemates came out of their rooms, Brandon knocked Chase's head to the side and Chase spit again on Brandon's face, this time it was full of blood.

"Shit, again?" Brad huffed as he ran past me and grabbed Chase's arms to pin them back. Derek kept Brandon on the floor while Zach helped Brad haul Chase toward a hall on the opposite side of the living room.

"Holy Crap Princess," Drew slung his arm around my shoulders and I shook it off, "you really drive guys crazy don't you? This has been the most entertaining two months we've ever had in this house, and it all seems to come back to you."

"Drew."

"Yeah Princess?"

"If you want to have kids at some point in life, I suggest you leave."

He tsked at me, but wisely moved away, "So touchy. Hey B, you uh, got a little something on your face."

"I'm about to let him up." Derek warned and Drew took off for the backyard.

As soon as Derek let go, Brandon was up and stalking toward his bathroom, not saying a word to me. Derek handed me Brandon's back pack and nodded toward his bedroom.

"Wait for him in there, I'm gonna go talk to him though I'm positive I already know what he's gonna say. Just give him a few minutes, and Harper?"

"Hmm?"

"Stay away from Chase. It'll make all of this a lot easier."

I blushed fiercely and nodded before shutting myself in Brandon's room. Ten minutes of sitting there alone felt like three hours. I listened to numerous doors open and slam shut, raised voices on different sides of the house and what must have been Chase taunting Brandon. Next thing I know all the guys were yelling at each other and Brandon started threatening Chase. The door opened, and I watched Derek and Drew struggle to push Brandon in.

"Chill man!" Derek puffed as he kept shouldering Brandon's chest so he couldn't leave, "He's doing it to piss you off more, just calm down."

"She's mine!" Brandon growled and pushed forward again.

"Yeah, she's yours and right now you're scaring the hell out of her. Calm down!"

Brandon turned and stopped trying to force his way out when he saw me. As soon as the other two were out of the way, he slammed the door shut and locked it, but didn't turn back to me. He rested his head against the door, one of his hands pressed against the wall.

I started to move off the bed, but his voice stopped me.

"Don't. Give me a minute."

Four tense minutes later and I stood up anyway, "I'm going to go—"

"I'll take you to your dorm." He finally looked at me and shook his head, "Never mind I'll get Derek to take you."

My stomach dropped. I had been planning on going outside to give him more time; I wasn't expecting him to want me to actually leave. Usually he was trying to stretch our "weekends only" rule, this was the first night since Saturday that we were supposed to be together, and he wanted me to go back to the dorm. He didn't even want to be the one to take me. Was he that mad at me for the fight with Chase? My throat closed up, so I simply nodded and grabbed my duffel bag.

"Uh, will you please take me to a hotel?" I asked Derek after we were in his car.

"Hotel? Don't you want to go to your dorm?"

"No, Bree's having Konrad stay there tonight. Just take me to a hotel."

He pursed his lips but didn't say anything until we were at the entrance of the closest place. "Don't be too hard on Brandon, kay? Try to forgive him, he feels really bad for doing this to you."

What? Doing what to me? Oh my God, is he going to break up with me? I didn't ask him to get in a fight with Chase, I had been about to take care of it myself. My eyes watered and I couldn't even thank Derek for the ride, afraid that if I opened my mouth I'd start sobbing.

Derek got out of his car and walked with me up to the front desk. I still couldn't speak so he told the woman in the business suit behind the counter that I needed a room for the night. When she asked for a card to go on file he pulled out his wallet. Grabbing his arm, I shook my head quickly and the tears started falling.

"I already can't believe I'm about to leave you here Princess. Give me some peace of mind knowing that I didn't make you pay for a room because of what just happened." He handed his card to the woman who was shooting daggers at Derek. Once I had the keycard in my hand, he hugged me awkwardly and stepped back, "Let someone know if you need anything."

I heard the woman mutter "Asshole," under her breath when he walked out the doors. It wasn't until I was in the elevator I realized how that must have looked to her. With my tears and what he said, that definitely made him look awful. Poor Derek.

As soon as I was in the room, I curled up onto the large bed and let my heart break once again for the man I had a feeling I would always love. He called an hour later, but I was already devastated with what I knew he was going to say, so I ignored the call and turned my phone off. Maybe he would take that as my acknowledgment of what he no longer wanted. Me.

Loud pounding woke me some time later and I had a momentary freak-out when I didn't realize where I was at first. The pounding started again and I looked at the door, I had no idea what time it was, but Brandon had called right before ten, so I knew it was really late now. Was there some drunk trying to get into what they thought was their room?

"Harper, baby open the door."

My eyes widened and I scrambled off the bed. God, I should have just answered the phone. Break up over the phone would have been much easier than face to face. Taking a few deep breaths, I unlocked the door and cracked it open.

Brandon stepped in and pulled me into his arms, roughly bringing his mouth to mine. "What the hell are you doing here sweetheart?"

Me? What was he doing, and why was he kissing me?

"I've been going out of my mind, why'd you turn your phone off?"

"I—I didn't want to talk to you."

His face and arms fell.

"I couldn't, I couldn't handle you breaking up with me."

"Whoa, wait . . . what? Break up with you? Why the hell would I break up with you?"

I floundered for a minute trying to remember everything that he and Derek had said, "Because you . . . isn't that . . . wasn't that why you wanted me to leave?"

"No!" He hunched down and cupped my face, "I thought I scared you with that fight, I thought you wanted to get away from me."

A sob escaped my chest and hot tears streamed down my cheeks again as I shook my head.

"Baby," he crooned and wrapped his arms around me again, "are you insane? How could you think I wouldn't want to be with you? Seeing your face in the bedroom, you looked terrified and I hated that you saw that. I shouldn't have lost it like that in front of you."

"So we're not breaking up?"

"God no."

A huge wave of relief washed through me, "I *was* scared in your room, but it was because I thought you were mad at me. I thought you were mad that you got into another fight because of me. And I hated that everyone had to get in on it."

"Harper, I would fight anyone, anytime for you." He kissed me softly and moved back to the door, "I'll be right back, alright?"

Before I could say anything, he was out the door and jogging down the hall. When he came back a handful of minutes later, he picked me up and without breaking our kiss laid me down on the bed.

"Where'd you go?" I asked breathlessly when his lips moved across my jaw.

"I rented the room until Sunday morning." He grinned impishly and I hurried to pull his shirt off his body.

"Princess, stop walking and just talk to me."

"Why? So you can let me know again how much of a slut you think I am?"

"I don't," he let out a half-growl, half-sigh, "I don't think you're a slut. You just caught me on a bad day."

"Let me guess Chase, you hurt me because you were just so damn mad . . . am I right?" I threw his line from a month ago back in his face and he paled.

His hand came up and brushed my hair back, holding it away from my face as he stared into my eyes, "This is why I

told you I would never be good enough for you, all I do is hurt
you Princess."

"This isn't about you being, or not being good enough for me.
I just want to be your friend, and you're making that impossible."

Friend, he mouthed and scratched his head before grabbing a
fistful of hair, "Okay, fine, we're friends. But I need you to stop
approaching me around my house and at school."

"What? Then that puts us exactly where we've been the last
three weeks, that doesn't change anything."

"It needs to be that way." He released both his hair and mine
at the same time and turned away for a second before facing
me again, "Sundays are the only day I get you. Those are the
only days when you're here with me." I opened my mouth but
he stopped me, "No, I know you're not here *for* me . . . but you're
here. And he's not." He bent his knees so we were eye to eye, "I
need these days with you Harper. But every other day, you're his
and it's not a good idea for us to be around each other then. So
stay away. Please."

"Chase . . ."

"If you think acting like you don't exist isn't the hardest thing
I've ever done, you're wrong. I hate not talking to you, I hate not
bickering like we're an old married couple and I hate not spending every day right next to you. But this is how it has to be, Brandon hates me, and Princess trust me when I say he has every
reason to. So if after everything I've done to you, you'll still even
consider being my friend, then it has to be Sundays only."

"Brandon won't care if we're friends." Okay I wasn't entirely
sure that was true.

He smiled and shook his head, "I know you're not that naïve.
Now go have lunch with Mom and Bree, then get your ass back
here so I can have my few stolen hours with you."

I walked toward the entryway but stopped after a few feet,
"Chase?"

"Yeah Princess?"

Looking over my shoulder, I held his gaze, "Will you please stop hurting me . . . in every way?"

Chase closed the distance and pulled me into a tight hug, "Go eat sweetheart."

That wasn't a yes, or no. But I wasn't going to press the issue further.

7

THE LAST THREE months had flown by in an amazing blur. I had three A's and one B last semester and was actually excited for my next classes to start. Bree was the best roommate I could have ever asked for; she showed me everything in the San Diego area, helped me ease into college life and welcomed me into her family. She was like the sister I'd never had, and I loved her dearly. We still spent every Sunday with her parents and Chase, and although it was my day away from Brandon, being part of a family was amazing, and Sundays soon became my favorite day. It hurt knowing I'd missed out on this growing up, but I was extremely appreciative of how quickly Robert and Claire took me in and grateful for my time with them.

As I had suspected, I only heard from Sir about once a month, and even then it was by e-mail. I tried to call him once a week, but he never answered and never returned the calls. It didn't bother me too much, even when I'd lived at home, I only talked to him if I absolutely needed to. Carter and I almost never talked now, I still missed the way we had been, but ending our friendship was most likely for the best. He still texts me every now and then when he's wasted, usually telling me about whatever strip club he's at, or what girl he slept with recently. And last I heard before his unit left for Afghanistan, he'd eloped with a girl he met the day before they married. I had worried that I'd pushed him into his new lifestyle, but Bree and Claire quickly pushed that worry out of my mind.

Chase and I still had our different kind of friendship. We continued to not speak during the week, and when Sunday hit, he never let me out of his sight unless I was having a girls' day with Bree and Claire. I found out quickly that he hated those days. No matter how much I wished for it, my feelings for him never seemed to go away. Actually, the sexual tension between us seemed to grow each time we saw each other, rather than dwindle to nothing like I wanted. The week of Thanksgiving break, we had run into each other in the hall of his parents' house and he stopped me so he could run his hands across my cheek and jaw, then down my throat. He gently pressed me against the wall and leaned in. Through the hammering in my chest and quick breaths, I'd somehow managed to ask him not to kiss me, and that was the last time our bodies ever came closer than a few feet of each other. I didn't understand my unwanted feelings toward him, but I was glad we seemed to find a happy medium with our friendship, and as far as I knew there had been no more fights between him and Brandon.

Brandon is . . . amazing. He treats me like I'm the only person in the world that matters and we're practically inseparable. Our "weekend only" sleeping arrangement hadn't lasted past mid-October and most nights were now spent in his bed, but we only ever slept. There have been quite a few more times where things had gotten hot and gone a little too far, but he always stopped us before we went *there*, and I loved him for it. He had told me to let him know when I was ready, and even when caught in the heat of the moment, I still hadn't said anything and he never pushed me. Bree and I went to almost all of his fights, and he had yet to lose. Every time it was over, Scarecrow would hand him a wad of cash, and every time he would shove it in his pocket without counting it. I was itching to know how much he was making, but figured if he wanted me to know, he would tell me. There were no more cracked ribs, but sometimes he would come home with a busted lip or a cut brow. I preferred the cut brow, the busted lips got in the way too often.

He had taken me to Arizona with him for Christmas, and I was completely taken with his mom and brother, Jeremy. His mom was thrilled that he was actually bringing a girl home, and to not have to be surrounded by boys for another holiday. I helped her cook, we went to get our nails done together and had a night of romance comedies after we'd sent the boys away. I could easily see myself in his family, and though that thought after only four months into our relationship scared me, it kind of exhilarated me too. I wasn't sure if I was ready to talk about marriage, but eventually, I think I'd like to head down that road with him.

Brandon planned on staying in Arizona for the entire winter break, but I'd promised Bree I would bring in the New Year with her, so I'd flown back to San Diego the day of and was currently walking out of the airport. I grabbed my phone to call my boyfriend and my heart ached at the thought of not seeing him for the rest of break. Since Brandon and I had met, we had spent at the very least a few hours with each other every day. These two weeks were going to suck.

"Hey baby, you make it there okay?"

"Yep! Just got my bag and I'm waiting for Bree to get me."

"Will she be there soon?"

"She sent me a text when I was in baggage claim saying she was a few minutes out. Actually here she comes."

"Okay, well I'll call you later then. Have fun tonight and happy New Year. I love you."

I bit my lip and smiled, hearing him say that in his deep husky voice always did funny things to my heart. "I love you too Brandon." I slid the phone back in my pocket just in time to be nearly tackled by my best friend.

"Oh my God Harper I missed you! Two weeks without you is too long!"

"Hah! I missed you too Bree. Next time I'll just have to sneak you in my luggage." After we got my things in the trunk, we jumped into her car and fought the airport's holiday traffic. "Where are we going tonight?"

"Your pick, the guys are having a party, or my parents are throwing a party. Which I promise is not as boring as it sounds. There's always a ton of people there, everyone plays poker and drinks."

"Well where will Konrad be?"

She smirked and raised an eyebrow like that answer should be obvious, "Wherever I am."

"Can we just go to Mom and Dad's? I missed them too." During Thanksgiving, Claire and Robert had told me they wouldn't respond to me anymore if I didn't act like they were my parents. It started as a joke, but it stuck.

While Bree was on the phone with Konrad, my cell went off and I started when I saw it was from Chase.

Chase:
You gonna be at the house tonight?

Me:
Nope, going to hang with the family.

"Is that lover boy?" Bree questioned as she turned the music back on.

"Uh . . . yeah." I have no idea why I lied, but it felt awkward correcting myself now.

"Did you guys have *fun* in Arizona?"

I laughed at her wagging eyebrows, "We had fun, but not that much fun. Hate to burst your bubble."

"You're going to kill that poor guy Harper! It's been like what . . . four months? Five?"

"I know, I know. I don't know what keeps stopping me. It's not like we never have the opportunity. I just . . . I don't know."

She shut the music off quickly, that was never a good sign. "Are you guys okay?"

"Yes Bree, we're more than fine, trust me! It's nothing like that, I just haven't felt like it's the right time yet."

"If you say so. But I'm serious. He's going to explode if it's not soon."

"So you keep telling me." I was dying to ask how Chase was, even if we didn't talk, we saw each other every day too. And having him text me for the first time ever just a few minutes ago had my heart racing knowing I'd be seeing him again within the next few days. "How's the family?"

"They're good. Mom actually cried because you weren't at Christmas."

"What? Are you serious?"

"As a heart attack. Your presents were still under the tree that night and she started crying, I had to take them up to my room to get her to calm down."

I didn't know what to say, I just shook my head in disbelief.

"I'm serious Harper, she was devastated!"

"No, no. I believe you. I guess I still have to wrap my head around how much they care for me. And did you say I had presents? Why?" The only presents I've ever gotten from Sir was a laptop for graduation and my iPhone. And to be honest with you, I know the only reason I got those was because I had been planning on buying them anyway and he didn't want me to waste my money. There were never presents, cards or any sentiments on Christmas, or birthdays. It's just how it was.

"Because we all love you!"

"But I—I didn't get you guys anything."

Bree's voice got really soft and she reached over to grab my hand, "We didn't expect you to. They all know what growing up with Sir entailed. We wanted to show you what a real Christmas is like." She looked at me until the light turned green again. "Did you talk to him?"

"No. I called him twice though and left messages." Jeez, I really did have a crappy home life. Even Bree's family called me on Christmas. And Brandon . . . "Oh my God Bree, I'm so stupid!" I groaned.

"What, no you're not!"

I pulled out my necklace to show her, "It's from Brandon."

"He got you a Tiffany's necklace for Christmas? Good choice!"

"That's just it Bree. He didn't give it to me on Christmas, he gave it to me before I left. I thought it was so weird because he's never given me anything, and we weren't apart after Christmas so I would've known if he'd gotten it after. But he knows what holidays were like with Sir, and that I was upset he wouldn't answer the phone. I think he thought it would upset me more if he proved how much of a jerk Sir is."

"He's a good guy Harper. I'm glad you have him."

I clutched the necklace in my hand and sighed into the seat, "Me too." We sat in silence for a minute, just listening to the radio. "So besides Mom breaking down, how were they the rest of the time?"

"Pretty good, we just relaxed a lot. Mom's trying to learn how to knit, so be sure to make grandma jokes, it pisses her off. Dad and some of his buddies went to that golf tournament."

"Oh yeah, how'd they do?"

"Uh . . . don't ask him about it."

"Figures." Dad couldn't play golf to save his life, but he apparently loved it. "And Chase?"

"I don't even know. He's so moody lately."

"Bree, when isn't he moody?"

She snorted, "No, I mean he's been way worse than usual. Literally since the day school let out for break he won't talk to anyone without snapping at them. And at Christmas, he'd barely stay long enough to even eat with us, just kept leaving. I swear that guy needs to get laid."

Brandon and I left for Arizona the day school let out. Could that—I wanted to smack myself for even thinking me leaving would have anything to do with Chase being upset. I think way too highly of myself. "Yeah probably . . . holy crap is this all for their party?" Cars were lined up blocks from the house and people were walking toward it. Thankfully we could still get in the garage.

"I'm telling you, this is their big thing every year!"

We grabbed my bag and somehow squeezed through the mass of people and made it upstairs to her room so I could freshen up and change. Bree must have let them know we were on our way because Mom and Dad were already waiting in her room to engulf me in hugs.

"Oh sweetie we missed you!"

"How you doing baby girl?"

I laughed and hugged them back, "I missed you guys too. Why are you up here? You're missing your party."

"Oh hush! We had to say hi, and plus we have some things for you." Mom bounced over and sat on the bed where there were boxes of presents.

"Oh. My. Word. You guys . . . you really didn't have to get me anything." Now I really felt awful for not getting them anything.

Bree grabbed my arm and pulled me over to the bed, "I already told you, we wanted to."

I took a deep breath in and willed myself not to cry. God, I had never been an emotional person until I moved here. Mom and Dad showing me how parents should be had made the water works come frequently, and I still wasn't used to it. Bree got me a new outfit she picked out specifically for tonight, and a Coach purse that I absolutely adored. Mom and Dad got me two pairs of UGGS, an extremely expensive jacket I'd been drooling over since Thanksgiving and a prepaid spa day for us girls. I just sat there with everything scattered across my lap and legs and stared at them through blurry eyes. I tried to speak through the lump in my throat but my *thank yous* were barely audible. Mom and Dad both kissed my cheek and walked out with Bree, who was going to save Konrad from all the older people downstairs he didn't know. I slowly put the things I wouldn't be using tonight back in boxes for when I took them back to the dorms or Brandon's room and was almost done when there was a soft knock and the door pushed open.

"Hey Princess." Good God I missed hearing his voice.

"Chase," I had to clear my throat to continue, "I didn't think you were going to be here."

"I asked if you were coming to the house," he replied hesitantly.

"Right, I just figured you meant your house."

The room was thick with the tension that always followed us around. My heart started racing from his nearness and I silently cursed myself. I really didn't want any kind of feelings for this guy, and here I was wishing he would try to kiss me again. We sat there watching each other for who knows how long before he walked over and sank down on the floor next to me, handing me a small wrapped box. "Merry Christmas Harper."

I picked it up and just stared at it, all I could say was "Why?"

"Because you're my favorite, remember?" He huffed and his lips tilted up a little, "When I saw it, there was no way I couldn't get it for you. Please open it."

So slowly I probably drove him crazy, I took off the wrapping and opened the little leather box. I gasped when I saw the ring inside there. It was a silver band that wrapped into the trinity symbol on top. I'd always wanted that symbol as a tattoo. I looked up at Chase and shook my head in wonder.

"How did you know?"

"You doodle it on everything put in front of you."

He was right of course, if I had a pen and paper or napkin, it always ended up on there at some point. I just hadn't realized anyone other than Brandon noticed that, especially him.

"Chase . . ." I couldn't hold them back any longer, tears started falling down my cheeks and I quickly dropped my head hoping he wouldn't notice. He did.

"Don't cry Harper. If you don't like it, or you don't like that it's from me I'll take it back."

My laugh sounded more like a sob than anything else. "I love it, please don't take it."

"Then what's wrong?" He tilted my head up and brushed away a few tears with his thumbs. I had to force myself to not lean into his hands, it was the first time we'd had any type of physical contact in over a month. He was a whole new kind of Chase on Sundays, but I'd never seen him like this. So gentle and kind. It made my entire being crave him.

"I've never had this before. Not just the presents . . . the love that your family has for me. I've never had it until now, and it's so overwhelming. I don't know what I did to deserve it and I don't know if I show them that too."

"You do. Trust me." He searched my face for a long time and wiped the remaining tears from my cheeks. "You're special

Harper, it's not hard to love you." Dropping his hands from my face, he stood up and left the room.

After I rinsed off my body, fixed my hair and make-up and got dressed in my new outfit, I grabbed the ring and tested it on my fingers before leaving it on the ring finger of my right hand. Looking in Bree's full-length mirror, I smiled to myself. She really knew how to shop. I was wearing a short sleeved see-through green top that was fitted on my chest and flowed down to cover my bottom, with a black camisole underneath, faded skinny jeans and my black UGGs. I wasn't the best at saying thank you, but I hoped the family knew how much I loved everything.

"Woo! You look hot!"

I spun in a circle to show Bree her creation, "I love it! It's perfect for me."

"I knew it would be." She winked as Konrad came up behind her with drinks and they sat at one of the poker tables.

I stood behind her chair and tried not to look like I was searching for Chase. All of a sudden the hairs on the back of my neck stood up and I looked to my right to find him staring at me and unconsciously biting his lip. My face flamed and I tried to pay attention to Bree losing Konrad's money instead of those lips. As Chase walked by, he grabbed my right hand and rubbed his thumb over the ring he gave me before dropping it and sitting at the other end of the table. I watched two games and reveled in Chase's booming laugh as everyone at the table ragged each other for losing money. Konrad stood up after the second game and gave me strict orders to sit in for him and to not lose his money while he went to the restroom. Guess he forgot that I was so horrible people wanted me to play with them because it was a guarantee they would get my money.

"You better just hand over all his chips now Princess, they

won't be here by the time he gets back anyway." Chase teased and flashed his signature smirk.

"It's about time," Bree whispered leaning into me.

"For what?"

"He must've finally got some. This is the happiest he's been in two weeks."

Not that I had any right to be, but I was instantly jealous of whoever he had been with. My heart clenched just thinking about Chase in that way. I felt like I was cheating on Brandon with my thoughts alone, and I hated it. Thankfully Konrad came back before I could do any damage, because not only did I not have any idea what kind of hand I had, but I could feel Chase's eyes on me every few seconds and it was seriously distracting. The tension between us was palpable, even in this room full of people and I needed to get away from him. I walked around until I found Mom and Dad sitting at another table and wrapped my arms around her neck.

"How are you guys doing over here?"

"I'm winning! Can you believe it Harper?" Mom's smile was contagious.

"No, have you been cheating?" Bree's family taught me to play, and if anyone was as bad as me, it was definitely Claire.

"Course not! But I'm pretty sure Robert is," she mock whispered.

I laughed and grabbed her empty beer bottle, "Need another?"

"Oh yes please, sweetie!"

"Anyone else?"

Three other people I didn't know said yes so I headed for the kitchen and grabbed five.

"Nu uh. If I'm not drinking, you're not drinking."

I shot a sideways glance at Chase, "Well then why don't you have one?"

"Because I don't drink anymore." He shrugged and looked around the kitchen for a moment.

"Since when?" I hadn't seen him drink in months, but I didn't know he'd actually stopped.

Chase stopped looking around and pierced me with his blue eyes, "Since I was a jackass and hurt my Princess."

He said my Princess. *My.* I had goose bumps covering my body. "Huh . . . I didn't realize."

"You're the one that told me I should stop." He said it matter-of-factly.

"But I didn't mean you had to Chase. You're grown, you can do whatever you want."

"I know. Nothing good ever came from drinking though."

Who was this guy, and what did he do with Chase? "Do you want to split one? Nothing will happen from half a beer, right?"

He slapped his stomach and raised his voice an octave, "I guess my little body can handle half a beer."

"You're so dumb. Help me with these, I'm hanging out at your mom's table." I never could call them Mom and Dad in front of Chase. Thinking about them as my parents when I had these feelings for him was beyond awkward.

We watched Claire win two hundred dollars, without cheating, and even though I kept my beer in between us, Chase never touched it. With five minutes left of the year, everyone bunched around the massive TVs all over the house waiting for the countdown to begin. I found Bree and Konrad and joined them, though I doubt they knew I was there. They weren't waiting for midnight, they already had their tongues down each other's throats.

The countdown started and when we hit "six," I was yanked back to the darkened hall and found the deepest blue eyes staring into my own. His hands cupped my face and the pad of his thumbs brushed back and forth over my cheekbones. I vaguely heard the party chant the final numbers before erupting into cheers and Chase's lips softly pressed into mine. I stood stunned for a few seconds before wrapping my arms around his neck and moving my mouth against his. When he traced my bottom lip with his tongue, I opened my mouth in invitation and he didn't disappoint. My stomach heated and I ached to press my body to his. He stumbled back to the wall opposite where we'd been and grabbed my hips, bringing me to rest between his legs. One hand went back to my hair while the other found its way to the small of my back, bringing me even closer to him and I moaned into his mouth. We poured four and a half months of longing and ignoring our chemistry into that one kiss . . . when it was over, I knew I'd never be the same. He rested his forehead against mine, and I had to press a hand to my chest, I swear my heart was about to explode.

"Harper." His voice was rough and passionate, "I will think about that kiss for the rest of my life." He held me back, stepped away and watched me for a moment, then turned to leave the house.

I stood there watching where he'd just been and tried to convince myself that had just happened. Next thing I knew I was back in Bree's room with my back pressed against the door, I didn't even remember walking up the stairs. I was still trying to calm my heart when my phone beeped and I ran for my purse, disappointment coursed through me when I saw it wasn't from Chase.

Brandon:
Happy New Year baby. I love you.

Worst girlfriend of the year award should definitely go to me.

* * *

FIVE DAYS WENT by without seeing or hearing from Chase. I hated that that bothered me. I hated that I dreamed about him. I hated that I cared at all. I'm madly in love with Brandon, so why do I have to love Chase too? I was relaxing on Bree's couch, still trying to excuse our kiss when my phone chimed. My heart kicked up a notch when I looked at it.

> *Chase:*
> *So . . . you ever going to come get that tattoo?*

The day we'd decided on our friendship, I'd come home from lunch with Mom and Bree to find him sketching on the couch. When he saw me he'd flipped the book closed and said he was working on a tattoo for me. Only problem? I wasn't allowed to see it unless I actually got it as a tattoo, and it was finished. Of course I wanted a tattoo, but at that point I'd had a hard enough time just being around him. Having his hands on me for hours would have been torture I wouldn't survive.

> *Me:*
> *When are you free?*

> *Chase:*
> *Seriously?*

> *Me:*
> *:) Make me an appointment. I'll be there*

> *Chase:*
> *We open at four today come in then*

> *Me:*
> *Do I get to know what it is first?*

Chase:
You can see it when it's done. I'm warning you now, it's going to take hours.

Me:
Chase I swear if you put something I hate on my body . . . I'll kill you

Chase:
I promise you'll love it

Me:
Don't make me regret this

Chase:
See you in a couple hours Princess

    This is exactly what I was avoiding. I didn't think I could handle him touching my body before, but now after that kiss? Aw hell, I am going to regret this. I ran upstairs to take a shower and dressed in loose enough clothing that I would be comfortable during and after. I called Brandon to let him know and he was excited for me, so I decided not to mention who would be the one doing it. He would have thrown a fit. I hated even omitting things from him, I knew what I was doing was wrong, and yet I couldn't talk myself out of it. Thankfully Bree was gone with her man until tomorrow, I knew she would be mad when she found out I went without her, but I needed to do this alone. Okay not really, but I wanted to be alone with Chase. I arrived just after four and followed Chase to his section.
    "I can't believe you actually came."
    "I know, I'm kind of freaking out."

His smile fell and he leaned in close, "Then I'm not going to do it Princess. I'll do it whenever you're ready."

"No, no. I want it today, but I'm afraid it's going to hurt and it's really hard not knowing what it is. Can you please just let me see it?"

"I'm not going to lie to you and say it won't hurt, but it's different for everyone. Some people hate outlines, some hate shading. Some people don't feel a thing, and some hate the entire process. I told you, you'll love what it is. But it's a surprise, I can't tell you."

"I'm trusting you with this Chase."

He cupped a hand around my neck and pulled me close, "I know Harper, thank you." Kissing me softly on my forehead, he dropped his hand and leaned against the counter. I already missed his touch. "Where do you want it?"

"Um . . . you said it was big, right?"

He nodded.

"Can I know how big? Because the location depends on the size."

"Turn around."

"What? Why?"

He smiled and turned my body away. "Because I already have the outline ready to go and I'm about to grab it to get the farthest points, I don't want you to see it." I heard papers shuffling for a minute before he turned me back around. "This big."

My eyes widened for a second and I took a deep breath. "Okay, I want it here." I grabbed the wax paper and put it down on my hip. "I want it to start on the far left side of my stomach and wrap around my left hip."

His eyes flashed with heat as he took the paper from my hands and rolled up my shirt just past my waist, "Lay down on your side." I sucked in a breath when he tugged the left side of my pants down a bit, "I'll keep everything covered, I promise. I just need this side further down."

"Chase?"

"Hmm?"

"You said it's going to take hours?"

"Yeah, probably three. As you can see it's big and the shading is really detailed. That part will take the longest." He set everything up before turning back to face me, "This is where you need to trust me. I'm about to put the outline on, please don't look." I shut my eyes and he laughed, "If you ever need me to stop, just tell me, okay?"

"Kay." I took two deep breaths in and out, "I'm ready, let's do this."

After the outline was on and he got the tattoo gun ready, he gave my hand a squeeze before putting his hand on my hip. "You picked the perfect spot, this is gonna look awesome."

"It better," I warned.

I froze when the needle first touched my skin, but relaxed after the first minute. It wasn't painful like I thought it would be, it was just uncomfortable. I really think the worst part is the sound of the gun.

"You okay?"

"Yep, just pay attention to what you're doing."

He laughed and continued his work. The outline was done and he was on to the shading in no time, and that's where everything went downhill for me. I'd been so focused on trying to figure out what it was from lines he was making, that I didn't even have time to think about his big hands touching me. And now it was all I could think about. I was trying to do breathing exercises so I wouldn't hyperventilate, but Chase said I was moving too much. His hands gripped and pulled my waist, hip, stomach and butt as he shaded and it took everything in me to stop the shivers that wanted to make their way through me. I ached for his hands to go lower, to feel his long fingers caress me. God this was wrong. *Think about Brandon, think about Brandon . . .* I was going through songs in my head when the gun stopped and Chase tilted his head toward me.

"Are you humming?"

"Maybe." Crap, I hadn't realized I was doing that out loud.

He laughed and ripped off his gloves while rummaging through a drawer. Walking back to me, he handed me his iPhone and a pair of headphones. "You're doing great, I'll be done soon." He pressed his lips to my neck and went back to work.

The music ended up being a great distraction from the steamy scenarios that were flashing through my mind, but more than once he had to put a hand on my upper thigh to get me to stop keeping time with the bass, and that would start the scenarios all over again. My hip was so numb I didn't realize Chase was done until he placed a quick kiss to my lips. My eyes shot open and I ripped out the ear buds.

"Am I still moving too much?"

"No Princess, I'm all done." His smile and the way his eyes were shining made my heart squeeze. "Are you ready to see it?"

"You have no idea!"

He chuckled and shook his head slightly, "Close your eyes again, I'll let you open them when we're next to the mirror."

He placed his hand on my right hip, grabbed my left hand and walked me a few feet away. Turning my body slightly he whispered into my ear, "Open your eyes Harper."

The first thing I saw was his anxious expression in the mirror. He was worrying his lip waiting for my reaction. I inhaled quickly and his body locked up when I looked down to my left side. It was beautiful. There were four large orange lilies wrapped around my hip, and I couldn't believe how amazing they looked. I stepped closer and took in the perfect shading and detail to each flower. From the sketches I'd looked at and his drawing of me, I had known Chase was amazing, but I'd never thought he could make something like this look so real. His forced swallow was audible, and I realized I still hadn't said anything. But there were absolutely no words. First my ring, and now this? Did anything get past him? I turned to face him and ran a hand through his messy hair.

"Please tell me what you're thinking."

Unfortunately, I wasn't. I crushed my mouth to his and he quickly deepened the kiss. Right away the other tattoo artists started hooting and yelling for us to get a room. I pulled back and knew there was nothing I could do about the deep blush on my face. Chase led me back to his table and put ointment and a wrap over my tattoo before fixing my shirt, he was all smiles.

"What made you choose those?"

He beamed his white smile at me, "I heard you talking to Bree and Mom about them being your favorite. And ever since that day all I've wanted to do was get you orange lilies, but I knew I'd probably get punched again. This was my way around it."

"It looks amazing Chase, thank you."

He shrugged, but he still couldn't contain that smile.

"I'm serious." I grabbed his face with both hands and brought him close, "I love it, thank you."

Chase kissed me once and skimmed his nose across my cheek. "God, you're beautiful Harper."

My phone rang then, Brandon's name flashed on the screen. "Hey babe."

"Hey, how's the tattoo look?"

"Um, it's not done yet, can I call you after?"

"I'm going out with some buddies from high school, I'll just talk to you tomorrow, kay? But send me a picture when it's done. I love you."

My stomach clenched, "I love you too. Have fun tonight." I

pressed the end button and looked up at Chase's closed off expression. "Chase—"

"So you'll need to go buy some anti-bacterial soap to clean it."

"Please talk to me."

"I'm trying. Look, here are some aftercare instructions. Don't take the wrap off for at least an hour. If anything looks wrong give me a call." He dropped the paper on my stomach and stepped back.

"Chase!"

"I have another appointment, and he's waiting. I'll see you later."

I looked into his guarded eyes and exhaled deeply, "What do I owe you?"

"Nothing. It was a gift. But I'm busy, please go." He turned away from me and walked to the back.

Aces.

EVERYONE LOVED MY tattoo, even though Bree wouldn't talk to me for about an hour because I hadn't told her beforehand or let her come with me. Chase really had done an amazing job and I wished I could fix things with him, but he'd been avoiding me since the tattoo parlor. It didn't seem to matter how we ended things lately, he always avoided me after. It was probably for the best though, Brandon would be back two nights from tonight, and I already had enough guilt eating at me, I didn't need to add more. I hated myself when I thought of the kisses with Chase, how Brandon trusted me completely and I'd gone and kissed the one guy he had always worried about.

Mom and Dad went to Lake Tahoe with a few of their friends yesterday, and Bree begged me to go to L.A. with everyone for the weekend, but I faked being sick. A bunch of them were going clubbing tonight and tomorrow and planned on splitting hotel rooms both nights. I would have wanted to go, but everyone was going with a boyfriend or girlfriend except Drew, and I didn't want to be left to deal with him. All I really wanted to do was sit at Bree's house and mope. When I moved here, I wasn't planning on falling in love with the first two guys that came along. Hell, I wasn't planning on falling in love during college at all. I wanted to have dysfunctional relationships and flings, but did that happen? Nope. I felt like Elena from Vampire Diaries. She has two insanely hot men who are in love with her and would do anything for her. One of which, she would give almost everything to be with, and the other she continues to push away, even though she can't ever actually stay away, so she won't have to admit she was in love with him too. At least my guys weren't brothers. Thank God for that.

Chase walked into the house an hour after Breanna left and stopped dead in his tracks when he saw me. "I thought you were going to L.A.?" His voice was gruff, and his face was still guarded.

"No, I told Bree I was sick."

"Are you?" He started to move toward me but stopped himself.

"I'm fine, I just wanted to be alone."

"Well I'll be gone in a few minutes. I just need to grab a few things. How's the uh—how's the tattoo?"

"Beautiful." I breathed, "Can we talk about that night?"

"There's nothing to talk about," he called over his shoulder, heading for the stairs.

I jumped off the couch and raced behind him. "Yes there is, you completely shut down and you've been avoiding me ever since!"

"I'm not avoiding you, I just have nothing to say."

"Why are you treating me like this? What did I do?"

"Nothing!"

"So this is what *you* do then? You make girls feel like they're special for a few days, then treat them like they're nothing?"

He turned on me right before he got to his room, "You're really gonna put this on me? One minute you're kissing me, the next you're talking to your boyfriend and telling him you love him!"

"What did you want me to do, not answer it?"

"It doesn't even matter Harper," he laughed humorlessly, "drop it."

"It does to me! I'm so tired of this roller coaster with you. I never know which Chase I'm going to meet up with that day. Is it going to be the cold or the funny and caring Chase? Will it be the one that's with four girls in one night, or the one that tells me how beautiful I am, does amazingly sweet things for me and notices stuff about me that no one else does?" Okay so Brandon noticed, but that wouldn't help my argument right now.

He just continued to glare at me.

"You're all over the place, I don't know how to act around you, I don't know what you want!"

"I want you! All I've ever wanted is you."

"Then why are you trying to hurt me again?"

"Because it's easier that way." His voice was soft now, and I could see the pain in his eyes, "You're with Brandon. Do you know what it's like watching you with him? Wanting you so bad, but knowing he's who you should be with?"

"But what if I want you?"

"Harper, don't."

"I'm so in love with Brandon, but I can't help what I feel for you, and I know you know what I'm talking about. Whatever this is between us . . . it's been there since we met. It's like I can't get enough of you, but all you do is push me away. It's all you've ever done!"

"Because I'm not what you need Harper!"

I stepped closer toward him, "Then why did you kiss me Chase? You knew it would change everything, and it did. So tell me, why did you do it?"

He ran a hand through his hair and blew out a frustrated breath, "I needed to." He closed the distance between us, "You're all I can think about and it drives me crazy! I would have given anything for that kiss, and I knew I wouldn't get that chance again, so I had to. I had to know if you felt something too."

I threw out my hands in exasperation, "Was that not obvious? Is it not obvious that I'm in love with you?"

His mouth was on mine then and my surprised gasp turned into a moan. He wrapped my legs around his waist and pushed me into the wall, his lips moving fiercely against mine. "Say it again." His breaths were coming hard and fast as he kissed me again.

"Chase," I grasped his face so he would look at me, "I love you."

A huge smile spread across his face before I pressed my lips to his, "God Harper I love you too, so much." He growled against my mouth.

Chase walked us into his room and fell with me to the bed. I pulled the bottom of his shirt up, and realizing what I was doing he let go of me long enough to rip it off and throw it aside. Our mouths slammed back together and he shivered when I ran my fingertips over his chiseled chest and stomach. My shirt ended up on the ground next to his, and my entire body felt like it was on fire when he kissed a trail from my lips to the tattoo he gave me. Slow enough to make me think I'd lose my mind, he took off my pants and added them to the growing pile of clothes. He pressed his body into mine, but it still wasn't enough. I didn't know if I could ever get close enough to him.

"I want you."

He groaned into my neck and nipped my collarbone, "I don't have any condoms here Princess."

"I don't care."

"Don't say stuff like that." He huffed a laugh, "I'm only so strong."

I reached for the button on his pants and struggled to get it undone, "Please Chase, I don't want to wait any longer." I whimpered when he stopped my hands. "I want you to be my first."

He sat back and searched my face, "I can't."

"You don't want me?" My eyes widened and my heart sunk. I hadn't been expecting this.

"Of course I do!"

"I don't—I don't understand."

His face was completely unreadable as he just stared at me.

"It's because I'm a virgin." It was a statement, of course he didn't want to be with me, he'd always made fun of me for it.

"Not in the way you're thinking. Trust me, I want to make you mine."

I cupped his face in my hands, "Then please," I whispered.

"Princess," his voice sounded pained, "you can't want it to be me. With what I've done . . . I don't deserve to be given something like that."

"It's yours. I'm tired of ignoring what I feel for you and denying myself of what I want."

I watched as his chest rose and fell again and again, when I looked back up into his eyes minutes later, he finally spoke, "You're sure Harper?"

"I want you. All of you."

The sense of urgency was now gone, and we took our time getting to know each other intimately. Each kiss and touch was filled with so much passion, I didn't know how anything could ever be better than this moment in bed with him. When our bodies finally joined, I cried out in pleasured pain as Chase continued to slowly, and lovingly, make me his. I now understood why I'd never been ready with Brandon, I was always meant to do this with Chase. After we were done, we fell asleep wrapped up in each other's arms.

I woke up with my head tucked into his neck and was already smiling widely, Chase loves me. Brandon's face flashed through my mind and I quickly pushed it back, I knew I would have to deal with this mess I've made, but I didn't want to think about it right now. I planted a light kiss to his throat and wiggled back some so I could look at his body and trace the tattoos I've wanted to inspect since the first night I met him. I was surprised that on his chest and the one arm I could see, he didn't have a ton of them. He had a half sleeve on the arm I was admiring, his other was now a full, but each tattoo was large enough that I could only count six separate ones. I bit back a laugh as I thought about the one that was just above where the top of his jeans sat. It said "I'm Ron Burgundy?" Apparently he'd lost a bet while watching the movie, and that was the result. I was tracing more tattoos on his shoulder when his husky voice caught me.

"Feels good." His voice was still thick with sleep.

I grinned at him and resumed my tracing, "I've wanted to do this since that first night in your bed."

"Why didn't you?"

"Well you were a little intimidating, and plus you not so subtly let me know I wasn't the kind of girl you would ever be with."

He jerked back to look at my face, "What did I say?"

"I don't remember exactly, you were just freaking out because you thought you'd let a girl stay over, and proceeded to tell me you didn't let girls you would screw stay with you." I bit my lip and met his stare, "Speaking of . . . is it okay that I'm here?"

His face melted into a warm smile and those ocean blue eyes sparkled, "I've never been happier than when I just woke up with you in my arms." He slowly kissed my forehead, nose, both cheeks and finally my lips. "You're the only girl I've ever fallen asleep with, and I want to keep it that way. You're not just some girl. I'm in love with you Harper, I wouldn't want you anywhere else."

I reached up to kiss him back, and tried to show him just how much I loved him too. I moved my mouth against his aggressively and pushed his shoulder back to the bed so I could climb on top of him, the delicious achiness in my body was fueling my desire to have him again. He gripped my hips and pressed his naked body against mine while alternating between bites and kisses down my neck. I arched my body into him and the mother of all stomach growls ripped through the quiet bedroom, I burst into laughter and sagged onto his chest.

"Is there any way you didn't hear that?"

His body was still shaking from laughter, "Not a chance." He kissed me soundly once and moved me off him. "I'll go make breakfast, I'll be right back."

"Okay, I'll come help." I started to sit up but he pushed me back into the pillows.

"Let me do this for you Princess." He rained light kisses on my jaw and sat back. "Stay here." He added severely, "I want to see you just like this when I get back."

I mock saluted him and curled into the comforter, my breath caught when he climbed out of bed.

"What's wrong?"

"Chase . . . you're beautiful."

His smile was breathtaking as he climbed back over me, "Beautiful, huh? Trying to take away my masculinity baby?" I knew he was teasing, but I played along trying to get a couple of words in between kisses.

"So sorry. I meant. Rugged. And handsome. And so. So sexy."

He laughed into my cheek and left the bed to throw on nothing but his jeans. God that didn't help much either, they rode low on his hips accentuating his muscled V and that ridiculous Anchorman quote. I took a mental picture of him and knew I would never forget Chase as he looked right now. A few minutes later, Chase walked in and I caught a whiff of bacon causing my stomach to grumble some more.

"You might want to answer that when he calls again." He dropped my phone next to me and with a sad smile walked back out the door.

I looked down to my phone and saw the twelve missed calls from this morning alone, six from last night and eighteen texts from Brandon and Bree. After reading through them and listening to the voicemails, I took a deep breath and collapsed into the pillows. I hadn't told Brandon I wasn't going to L.A., and after Bree dramatized my being sick and alone, and not answering the phone all night or morning, they had really started to freak out. I sent the same text to both of them letting them know I was fine, I'd fallen asleep early last night and left my phone in the other room. I loved them and would talk to them later after a shower and another nap. I know I was being a coward, but I didn't know what I would say to Brandon yet. My stomach fell when I got a response.

> Brandon:
> You scared me Harper, Bree thought something bad had happened. I caught an earlier flight, I just boarded. I love you so much, I'll be back to take care of you soon.

I wasn't ready for my time with Chase to be over and I had no idea what I was going to do about the two men that had my heart. Pulling the covers over my head, I resisted the urge to cry. There was no right way to go about this, and no matter what I did, I would hurt someone and lose a part of myself. Chase didn't say anything for a while after he came back with an omelet and bacon, we just sat there eating. Well, he ate. I'd had the same piece of bacon in my hand since he got back in bed.

"Baby, please say something." He pleaded as he rubbed soothing circles into my back.

"Brandon will be back in a couple hours." I finally spoke.

He hissed a curse through his teeth and sagged into the headboard with a thud. "I thought he wouldn't be back 'til tomorrow night."

"He got scared when I didn't answer the phone. Bree told him I was sick and alone, and since no one could get ahold of me . . ."

"Bree called me a few times, begging me to come check on you. Looks like they're all heading home today too."

"Chase, what should I do?" I began to search his face for answers, but he looked so pained I had to stare at my hands instead.

"I can't answer that for you Princess. No one can." After a few minutes of intense silence he continued hesitantly, "Who do you want?"

"I don't know!" I blurted out quickly, "I want you Chase, but I can't hurt him. I won't hurt him anymore than I have. I love him too much."

He flinched away like I'd slapped him.

"No matter who I choose, people will get hurt. And then what happens if I leave him? He lives in your house Chase. He'll have to see us together, it will kill him, I can't do that to him! He loves me, he hopped the first flight he could because he was scared for me and wants to come back to take care of me. How am I supposed to tell him I'm in love with someone else after that?" I took three deep breaths in and out in an attempt to calm my shaking, "If I left him for you, it would be bad for us. He'd come after you, the guys in the house would take sides. We would be miserable. My body craves you Chase, but I feel like I'm being torn in two. I just—I need a few weeks to think about this. Can you please give me that?"

His jaw was clenched so tightly I thought it might break, "Are you going to ask him to give you time too?"

"No, I can't."

Chase's eyes turned to ice and his mouth popped open, "So you're just going to go back to him? Pretend like last night never happened? You're so worried about hurting everyone else, do you even realize you'll be hurting me?" He shot up off the bed and started pacing back and forth, "Damn it Harper, don't you see that? I'm the one that will have to watch you with your boyfriend while waiting for you to figure out what you want!"

I flinched when the bedroom door slammed shut behind him. He was right, and I didn't want to hurt him either, but I didn't know what else to do at the moment. I was more in love with Chase than I'd realized, but I couldn't live without Brandon. If I thought I'd hated myself for kissing Chase, I now felt like I was dying thinking about how I'd just betrayed the man I love more than my own life. Even if I thought it was too soon, I'd over-heard him talking to his mom telling her he thought I was "the one," and I couldn't help but smile at thoughts of our future to-gether. I briefly considered a future with Chase, it didn't go far. There's no way Chase felt the same way I did for him. I'm not saying he doesn't love me, but it can't mean the same as it does for me. If I were to choose him, would he go back to being hot and cold once I did, and would he want to be with me for any length of time? As much as I wanted to believe everything he said to me last night, deep down I was terrified he'd up and leave me like he has every other girl. Brandon wouldn't do that, and he's never once treated me badly. His nearly shaved head, chis-eled face and tall beefy body may make him appear dangerous, but that boy adored me and would do anything for me. My mind was made up, Brandon is who I would choose when this day ended, in my heart I knew he was who I couldn't live without. But after what happened last night, I'm afraid I'll never be able to give him my entire heart like he deserves.

The hot steam of the shower couldn't even soothe me. I knew I could live without him, but my heart was still breaking just thinking about a life without Chase. I choked on a sob and soon my tears blended in with the water pouring on me. I pressed my hands to the wall of the shower to keep myself standing and cried harder than I ever have. Chase's hands turned me around and clutched me to him as my body shook with sobs. When I opened my eyes I realized he still had his jeans on and was completely soaked. I looked up to his face and memorized his hard jaw, full lips, perfect nose, bright blue eyes and shaggy wet hair. Even in pain, he was incredibly handsome.

"Why are you in here?"

"Because you need me," his voice was hoarse, "and if this is my last hour with you, I'm not going to waste another second of it."

He touched his lips to mine, and I met his kiss greedily. It was difficult, but we somehow managed to get his jeans off before he pressed me into the wall and positioned himself with my legs wrapped around him. I knew I was breaking my heart more, and adding more hurt to my relationship with Brandon, but I needed this last time with Chase. He slowly made love to me as the hot water continued to pour over us, and though I was no longer sobbing, a steady stream of tears ran down my face the entire time. He knew this was our last time to be together too, and the mixture of love, passion, pain and sadness made for the most beautiful experience of my life. Neither of us spoke after as we helped each other wash our hair and bodies, or when we dried off and dressed, but our eyes never once left each other's. They said everything for us in that last hour. He drove me to his house so I could pick up Brandon's Jeep, and we sat there for another twenty minutes just holding hands, his thumb making circles against my palm. I glanced down at the clock and pulled the keys out my purse with a sigh. I grabbed the door handle but his voice stopped me.

"Harper," he spoke around the lump in his throat, "I will love you for the rest of my life."

I couldn't turn to look at him, I just kept my eyes on the handle, "You will always be in my heart Chase Grayson." I walked away then, and didn't look back.

8

I GLANCED IN the rearview mirror and groaned when I saw my reflection. I looked terrible, but at least I actually looked like I had been sick. After a few breaths in and out, I put the ache to the back of my mind and focused on Brandon. He is who I want and who I need. I don't deserve him, but as long as he wants me, I'll be his. I walked to the baggage claim area and after a few minutes of waiting, saw him walking in a crowd of people. My heart tightened and I took off running toward him. I'd been unfaithful, and I was a horrible person, but I was madly in love with this man.

"Babe, I missed you!" I giggled when he immediately swept me up into his arms.

He smiled down at me and kissed my forehead, "God, I missed you too."

"I'm so glad you're back."

"How are you feeling sweetheart?"

"Better now that you're here." I wrapped one hand around his neck and trailed my other fingers across his cheekbone, jaw and lips.

"I'm sorry I wasn't last night."

"Don't be, it wouldn't have been a fun night for you." Really. It wouldn't have been.

"Is there anything we need to get you on the way back?"

A time machine so I can go back two weeks. "No, honestly I feel so much better. Must have been one of those twenty four hour things, just take me home."

I almost sighed in relief when I saw the driveway empty of Chase's truck, I couldn't face him when I walked into Brandon's room. While Brandon took a shower, I dressed in one of his button-up shirts and a pair of boy-cut underwear and climbed onto his bed. I knew it would drive him crazy, and as horrible as I will be for it, I needed to have a steamy session with him to push Chase even farther from my thoughts. Bree was right, this poor guy was going to explode if I didn't take it to the next level soon. But I hadn't been ready before, and damn if I thought I could be ready now. How was I supposed to let him love me and love him back in that way when he thought he was the first person I'd ever been with?

"Aw hell baby." He groaned as his eyes raked over me.

I faked confusion and hurt as I got off the bed, "Oh, well if you want me to change, I will."

He picked me up and slammed us onto the bed, pinning my body under his. He kissed me thoroughly and I forced myself not to compare his kisses to Chase's. I emptied my mind and focused on nothing but his lips covering mine, and his hand under the shirt on my waist. His other hand cupped under my left knee and hitched it up around his hip, when his fingers moved back to my borrowed shirt, he stopped and pushed off me. Lifting the shirt up to my waist he ran a hand over my tattoo and smiled as he brought his lips back to mine.

"You like?"

"You have no idea how sexy you are," he growled against my mouth.

I ran my hands over his head and pressed my chest to his. Bringing my other leg up to his hip as well, he pressed me deeper into the mattress when Bree came into the house shouting my name.

"You have got to be kidding me." I groaned and slapped a hand over my face.

Brandon chuckled in frustration and jumped off me to cover me with the comforter then went to find a shirt. "I needed to stop anyway." He smiled and bent down to kiss me, his now gray eyes were still burning.

"HARPER!"

"She's in here Bree." Adding softly, "You're in trouble." He left my side with a parting wink.

"Do you have any idea how scared I was? I thought you died!"

I burst into laughter, and laughed even harder when she narrowed her eyes at me. "Really Bree? You thought I died?"

"Well okay, I thought you were in the hospital but you always answer your phone, and no one could get ahold of you. What was I supposed to think?"

"Uh . . . I didn't feel good, you didn't ever consider that maybe I just fell asleep and had my phone on vibrate?"

"I thought you said it was in the other room." She deadpanned.

"It was, and it was on vibrate."

"Oh, well then . . . No."

I rolled my eyes at my friend, "I'm sorry I worried you both, and I'm really sorry that you all had to come back a day early."

I shot my eyes over to Brandon, "Well maybe not you," I teased.

"You should be, and I'm going to kill Chase." I tensed at his name, "This could have all been avoided if he wasn't off screwing some chick last night."

Dear Lord my cheeks better not be bright red right now. "Bree, it's not his job to babysit me. You can't be mad at him."

"Just don't scare me like that again, I love you."

"Love you too friend." I reached out to hug her, "And as much as I love you, I really need time with my man."

She snorted and smacked my arm, "Be good. We brought Chinese home if you guys are hungry."

Brandon sank to the bed and I crawled onto his lap. "So what would you say to grabbing some food, bringing it back here and just be alone the rest of the night?"

"I'd say it's exactly what we need." He hooked an arm under my knees and carried me out to the kitchen.

"Brandon!" I hissed, "I'm not wearing pants put me down!"

He dropped my legs quickly and tugged on the shirt I was wearing so it was longer than most of the skirts I wear. When your boyfriend is over a foot taller than you, his shirts practically become a dress. We looked through the takeout boxes and picked two of them when Chase walked through the living room. He slowed and looked at us, his eyes went wide and pain flashed through them before he could compose his face and gave us a hard nod. My jaw had dropped when I saw him and I forced it shut right before Brandon looked at me. I turned to grab silverware and chastised myself for standing here laughing with my boyfriend wearing nothing but his shirt. It was normal and needed for me and Brandon, but the exact opposite of what I wanted to do to Chase. Taking a calming breath, I walked back over and gave Brandon a playful nudge so he would follow me back to his room.

"How was the rest of your vacation?" I asked Brandon who was sitting with his back against the headboard, while I leaned against the side wall with my legs crossed onto his lap.

"Good, I really wish you would have stayed, but it was good to catch up with friends."

"I'm glad you got to. Thanks for taking me, I loved meeting your mom." I smiled to myself, remembering her bubbly personality, "She's great."

He nodded and swallowed some food, "She loves you already." He took the bite of chicken off my fork and pointed at my hand. "Where'd you get that?"

I looked at the ring and itched to hide it, not that it would do much good now. I shrugged as nonchalantly as possible and answered around a bite of food. "Chase."

His face fell and it took a few seconds before he continued chewing. "Chase gave you a ring?"

"It's not a big deal."

"A ring." He raised an eyebrow at me.

"Everyone in the family gave me a few things Brandon."

"A few? What else did he give you?"

Crap. I took my time chewing and swallowing that next bite, but forced my eyes to stay glued to his. "My tattoo."

"Chase did your tattoo? You didn't think that was something I'd want to know?"

No, I just knew you'd be mad. "I didn't know it mattered that much to you. Would you have rather me gone to someone you didn't know?"

"At least that guy wouldn't have a history of trying to take you from me."

"Babe, that never happened, and even if it had, he didn't succeed. You need to get over it."

"Not li—"

"Can we not do this please? I just got you back and I want to enjoy my night with you."

"Fine. But next time, I would really appreciate if you didn't let him touch you for four hours."

My cheeks flushed thinking about Chase's touch. Think about something else, think about something else, think about something else. "Brandon you're not—are you jealous?"

"Extremely."

"Well take it down a notch Hulk." I giggled and rubbed his arm, "Whose bed am I in?"

He continued to glower at the ring, "Mine."

I crawled off the bed and gathered up the empty Chinese boxes, hating the fact that I had just turned that around to his jealousy issues with Chase. Leaning over to press my forehead to his, I held his gaze and spoke slowly before heading to the kitchen, "Then you have nothing to worry about." I lightly brushed my lips against his, "I love you Brandon." I vowed right then to spend forever making up for the biggest mistake of my life. But how do you make up for something, when the other person doesn't know about the mistake in the first place?

LIFE WENT BACK to normal as school started again and Brandon and I continued our relationship. It had been almost two weeks since he had come home from Arizona, and we were doing better than we ever had. Chase had begun avoiding me at all costs, and though it made me sad, I was extremely happy I didn't have to see him all the time. I don't know how I would have dealt with seeing his miserable face when Brandon and I were together, which was most of the time.

It had been one of those days where Brandon and I couldn't keep our hands off each other, and it had been absolute torture waiting for his last two classes of the day to finish. As soon as they were done, he picked me up from the dorm and drove me to Chase's house. Our lips hadn't left each other as we made our way from his Jeep to his room, and his shirt, followed closely by mine, was on the floor before his door was shut and locked. Desire for him shot through my body as he lowered me to the bed and pulled my pants off before climbing on top of me. I reached down for the button on his pants as he pushed a bra strap off my shoulder and kissed where it had just been. I slid the zipper down and he put a hand behind my back, lifting my body off the bed. Planting his knees on either side of me, his other hand went to unhook my bra. He laid me back down on the bed and slowly started pulling it away when his phone rang.

"Every freaking time." He growled and snatched up his phone, "What?" After a few seconds he sat up quickly and smiled, "No way! Where? Yeah I'll be there." He jumped off the bed, pulling me with him, "Come on baby get ready, there's a fight."

"Are you kidding me?!" I hooked the bra back together and planted my hands on my hips, "You're going to stop in the middle of that to go to a fight? Tell Scarecrow to find somebody else!"

"Don't be like that Harper, this fight could easily win me three grand."

My hands paused with my shirt halfway over my head. Holy hell. "Three grand?!" I still had never heard an amount until now. The wads of cash were usually pretty big, but they could have been ones for all I knew.

"Yeah, I haven't had that high of a night in almost a month."

"In a month? How much do you normally make?"

"I don't know it changes every time." He shrugged as he pulled me out of the house, "Average is usually sixteen or seventeen hundred."

I was so shocked I stopped walking. Brandon fought anywhere from one to three times a week, and his average was *that*? "What do you do with all that money?"

He sighed and picked me up as he continued outside since I wasn't moving, "Other than some bills and buying my Jeep, I've saved all of it."

Crap. I seriously would have never known. Brandon wasn't one to talk about his money, and he didn't come across as some-one that had a lot of it either. He didn't appear poor, just seemed like your normal college student, so this was blowing my mind. "Well regardless," I said with a huff and crossed my arms after we were on our way, "I can't believe you stopped that just for a fight."

When we came up to a red light he looked to me and ran his fingers over my jaw, "I'm sorry sweetheart, I didn't mean to offend you like that. I promise after this fight we can go back and not leave the room until Monday." He started driving again and reached for my hand to kiss my palm, "Besides the call came at a good time, I had been trying to force myself to stop. I would've had to soon."

I frowned and looked out the window, I was glad he kept the top up during the winter so it wasn't too cold, but I kind of wished it was down so we couldn't talk right now. "I hadn't been planning to let you stop this time."

Brandon's hand tightened around mine and he cursed, "Harper I didn't know, I'm sorry. I swear if I had I wouldn't have taken that call." He cursed again, "I shouldn't have taken that call even if we were about to stop. That was our time together."

"I get you to myself all the time, it's fine."

"No it's not. I really am sorry, please don't be mad at me."

I smiled but it felt wrong, "I'm not. Let's just finish this and go back to the room like you said." Honestly, I wasn't trying to be rude, but I had finally decided tonight was the night. I know he hadn't been aware of that yet, but the fact that I was ready to go there with Brandon and it got interrupted set me on edge. Like maybe I still shouldn't have sex with him. I wish I'd kept my mouth shut and not told him that I had been wanting to. How did we go back to stopping ourselves after I just said that? Even though I knew I was, I wasn't trying to make him feel bad, I was just mad at myself.

He was quiet the rest of the drive, instead of his happy energetic self before a match. He held my hand and silently walked with me through the labyrinth of halls in this place. When we got to the doors that would put me in the room he kissed me softly and walked away to meet with Crow. I felt awful, he'd been so excited about this fight, and I'd put him in this sullen mood. Walking into the basement with the loud music and crazed atmosphere felt wrong after the last forty minutes, but I stood next to the box Scarecrow would be on, like I did every other fight so Brandon would know where I was.

Scarecrow gave me a big hug and started the fight, he noticed Brandon wasn't his usual carefree self but soon forgot when a seriously pissed off Brandon went to town on whoever this other guy was. I hadn't been paying close enough attention before they started. It looked like this was an oddly matched fight since the other guy wasn't doing much, and I didn't understand how it could bring in so much money. All of a sudden the guy grabbed Brandon's left hand and twisted it behind him, fully outstretched and planted a hard kick in the middle of Brandon's back. I screamed when his hand was dropped and his arm was left hanging out of its socket. He slammed Brandon to the ground, his head bouncing off the extremely thin mat covering the concrete and Scarecrow had to hold me back from running to him. The last thing Brandon needed was me running out there, but it was instinctive to go to him.

Brandon's leg came up around the other guy's chest and he slammed him down to the ground as well. Using both legs now, Brandon was choking the guy and I knew he would pass out soon. After a few tense moments the other guy tapped out and Brandon released his hold on him, slowly bringing himself to his feet. Without acknowledging the crowd screaming and cheering, he shuffled to me and Crow, grabbed my hand and pulled me to the room he'd waited in before the fight. When we got in there, he fell into a chair and gasped in pain as he unsuccessfully tried to put his shoulder back in place, I sat there covering my mouth in shock as I watched him.

"I need you." He gritted his teeth and huffed, "To take me." He huffed again twice.

"Stop talking baby, I know, I'll take you to the hospital." I grabbed his shirt and sat on the floor against his legs, "Do you want to put this on at least one arm, or leave it completely off?"

"Try to get it on."

I pulled the shirt over his head and got his right arm through the hole, I pulled it around his left arm so at least it wouldn't swing everywhere and kissed his forehead, "Is your head okay?"

"I'll be fine, I can't believe that even happened, I was just too distracted."

"Oh my God Brandon, I'm so sorry! I shouldn't have talked to you about that before a fight. I wasn't upset with you, I promise. I was just mad at the whole situation."

"It's fine sweetheart, this isn't your fault."

"Brandon," I gently kissed his cheek, "I love you, I'm sorry."

"I love you too, come here." He kissed my lips hard and I helped him out of the chair.

We started walking out when Scarecrow came running in, "Hey man, are you okay? That looked rough, you need to get checked out."

"She's taking me, I'll let you know how it goes." Brandon handed me the wad of cash he'd just received and shook Scarecrow's hand.

Five and a half hours later, we were finally getting back to Chase's house. Brandon had a slight concussion and had torn some ligaments when his shoulder dislocated, he was supposed to be wearing a sling, but he'd taken it and the wrap off as soon as we'd gotten back in his Jeep. I'd had a mental freak-out when they showed us the X-rays of his shoulder and explained he'd eventually need to have surgery on it, but kept my mouth shut. Which probably was just as bad as vocalizing my rant, because Brandon took one look at my wide eyes and clenched jaw and knew I was flipping out.

"Sweetheart, tell me what you're thinking," Brandon pleaded while I nuzzled his neck.

I sighed and rolled onto my back, "I'm just worried about you."

"I told you, I'm fine. I don't want you to worry about this, it's nothing."

"Brandon, please don't take this the wrong way, but I don't think I can watch you fight anymore. I just—" I fumbled for a few seconds trying to put my thoughts into words, "seeing that happen to you, I freaked and Scarecrow had to stop me from running out there. I can't watch something like that happen to you again. Would you hate me if I didn't go to them anymore? I'll wait for you in your bed for when you get back, but I can't watch them."

He pulled me close to his right side and kissed my forehead, "I could never hate you, especially over something like that. I'm sorry you were worried. I'm sorry you had to see that."

"Don't apologize, I'm just glad you're okay. Well, as okay as you can be right now." I sighed into his chest and he squeezed me tight.

"I love you Harper."

"I love you too. So much." I kissed him softly and settled in to finally sleep.

I SMILED AGAINST Chase's kisses while he led me back to his room, which we had barely left an hour ago. Gasping when I realized where we were, I pushed him a little bit away from me and looked around confused.

"Chase, we can't do this here! What if one of the guys walks in? Oh my God, what if Brandon comes home early?!" I could have sworn we were at his parents' house, when did we get to his?

"Don't worry Princess, no one will catch us."

A part of me was screaming that it was extremely likely someone would catch us, but when his lips touched my naked body, I couldn't seem to care enough to stop him again. I ran my fingers through his hair and pulled his head away from my stomach and back to my face.

"I guess we'll just have to try to be quiet this time," I whispered huskily.

Chase groaned and brought himself between my legs, just as I was feeling the pressure I was craving, he called my name but his lips never moved. I blinked and looked closer at his mouth when I heard my name again. That was definitely not Chase's voice. Oh God, Brandon was here!

"Chase!" I hissed, "Chase we have to stop, he's going to come in here!"

He smiled crookedly and pressed further into me, "Let him."

The door opened then, and my boyfriend's head peered in, "Brandon! No!"

Brandon simply smiled and looked at me, "Wake up sweetheart."

Huh?

"Come on sweetheart, we need to go to class."

I looked over to Chase who was now shaking my shoulder, then back to my boyfriend. What on earth was happening?

"Harper. Get. Up." I had no idea who said that last one.

My eyes flew open and I sat upright, my face smashing into a naked chest. "Brandon!" I nearly screamed.

"Jesus Harper! Calm down." Brandon's arms wrapped around me and he kissed the top of my head. "Are you okay?"

I pushed back on his chest to look at his face, then around the room. Brandon's room. "I think . . . I was dreaming."

Dreaming was an understatement. Up until the end, everything had seemed so real. Everything *felt* so real. I was still completely turned on for crying out loud! I felt sick to my stomach that I'd had a dream of cheating on Brandon. I was still fully dealing with the guilt of *actually* cheating on him, I didn't want this too.

"Was it bad?"

"Um, no. No it was fine." Not fine, not okay. Why can't I stop thinking about him?

"Are you sure? Your heart is racing and you're drenched in sweat babe."

"I'm good, it just freaked me out a little."

Brandon shrugged, "Okay, well go get ready, we have to leave for school soon."

I grumbled, but he lifted me out of the bed and set me down in the bathroom. Brandon had been doing a few physical therapy workouts with his trainer for his shoulder and was doing much better. There was only pain after working out but he was taking it easy and had told Scarecrow he had to miss the last two fights. I didn't know when he was going to go back, and didn't ask. Honestly I didn't want him to, but there's no way I would ask him to stop doing something he loved. After I was mostly ready for the day, I walked into the kitchen and froze. Chase was standing with his back to me, talking to Bree. He must have heard me enter the room because his back tensed and he straightened from crouching down to speak with his sister.

"Uh, good morning." It almost sounded like a question.

Bree glanced around Chase, her smile widening, "Morning doll! How'd you sleep?"

Chase barely cast a glance over his shoulder, saying nothing. That hurt.

"Pretty well, you?"

"Excellent." She bit her lip and her face flushed.

"Ugh, seriously Bree? Save it until I'm gone at least." Chase made a gagging noise and walked out.

My dream hadn't done his voice justice, at all. That was the first time I'd actually heard him say anything in weeks, and unfortunately it wasn't directed toward me. I watched him retreat down the hall then turned to start the coffee pot.

"So Harper, anything you want to share?" Bree asked suggestively.

I froze. Crap. He'd told her, how could he do that to me? And why did she sound so freaking happy? My voice shook, "What do you mean?"

"Hmm . . . let me see. You and Brandon were pretty cozy and he carried you away at seven last night, your lips completely locked the whole time. What do you mean 'what do I mean?' "

Oh thank God. I exhaled and the tension left my shoulders, "We were tired."

"Oh come on! Don't even try to tell me you guys didn't finally do the bunny dance in bed last night."

"The what?" I turned to face my friend and burst out laughing, "Breanna. Where the heck do you get these things?"

"That's beside the point! Fess up!"

"Sorry Bree, we really didn't do anything." I smiled and grabbed the now full pot.

"Still?!" Her head fell heavily into her hands, "Harper, how can you still be torturing that poor boy?"

"I'm just not ready yet, and he respects that. Unlike *some* people I know." I looked pointedly at her, she just rolled her eyes.

"I have a feeling you just don't want to tell me about it. Keeping all the juicy details to yourself." She hmphed and crossed her arms over her chest.

She had no idea how right, and yet how wrong she was.

"Well, *I* have a feeling you're going to continue to be disappointed for a while longer. I'm not ready to be with him like that, end of story. You'll be the first person to know when I finally decide to have sex with Brandon. I'll even give you the heads up before I tell him."

"Promise?"

I had chosen my words carefully so I wouldn't be lying to her, "Promise."

She sat there studying me as I poured creamer into the mug, "Maybe it's just because you don't know what to do!"

"So tell me, how's *your* sex life Bree?"

"Ohmygodamazing!"

I smiled and leaned against the counter. Yep, I was now a pro at getting the attention off myself. I listened to her not-so-private life until Brandon came into the kitchen to grab his cup of coffee as well.

"She talking about Konrad again? I swear she brings it up more than he does, and that's saying something." He kissed the tip of my nose and moved so he was against the counter, my back against his chest. I wiggled into him more, trying to mold myself to his warm body that could have only been made for mine.

"To be fair, I brought it up, but I think she's trying to make up for our lack of a sex life." I laughed lightly and turned to look at him.

"We'll get there when we're ready." He shrugged, but I saw the hunger and longing in his face. We still had close calls, but hadn't brought it up again since that night in his Jeep. Torture was definitely a good word for what I was always doing to him.

Bree finally got onto a different subject a few minutes later when I was on my second cup of coffee, but I could barely focus on what she was saying anymore. I shook my head as if to clear it and leaned forward a little, hoping it would somehow help. It didn't. I swear it felt like I was in a Charlie Brown episode, but in slow motion. It now sounded like she was talking under water and I was confused when she started to get up from the table and walk toward me, her face alarmed. Why did she look so scared? I heard a muffled crash and something hit my leg, it stung but I couldn't look down at it, though I was definitely leaning forward enough to try. Brandon caught me just before my face hit the tile and I lost consciousness.

I heard people saying my name and figured I must be asleep again, I thought I'd opened my eyes to see who was in this dream, but I still could only see darkness. Suddenly, someone was yelling my name in my ear and my eyes shot open.

"Oh my God! Are you okay? What happened?!" Bree was right in my face and if I could have moved back, I would have.

Why was Brandon suddenly so uncomfortable? I mean, his body is hard as a rock, but it was a comfortable rock that I curled into practically every night. Not whatever this was behind me. I turned my head and my cheek met the cold tile. "Am I on the kitchen floor?"

Brandon came running into the kitchen with Chase and Brad, all three looked concerned.

"She's awake?" Brandon looked to Bree as he knelt down next to her.

"Yeah, just happened," she replied.

I tried to sit up but my head was so heavy I barely got it two inches off the ground before I gave up, my head smacked against the tile, "Ow."

"You need to stay down there sweetheart. How are you feeling?"

I looked at Brandon's hand reaching to cup my cheek, then back to Bree. "Did I fall asleep in here?"

Bree actually laughed and grabbed my hand. "Not quite. You passed out."

"I did?"

"Yeah Harper, scared the crap out of us too." She scolded me, but looked relieved.

Brad walked back into my line of sight, "Couch is ready, get her over there."

I knew from experience any of these guys could lift me by themselves and carry me around, but for some reason all three decided to move me to the couch.

"I'm fine, you're all being ridiculous."

"Sweetheart, you were out for—"

"I get that, but I'm fine now." And I was. I felt like I could get off the couch and go make breakfast. Speaking of . . . my stomach growled as I thought of food. I pointed at my stomach and smiled at the four of them, "See, I'm fine."

Brad was pressing on my leg, making me wince, Bree was watching his hand and Chase and Brandon were staring at me. Both clearly still worried.

"Uh, Brad? Could you ease up? You're hurting me."

He smiled sheepishly and removed the bloody towel away from me.

"What the—"

"You dropped your mug and a big chunk sliced your leg pretty good." Brandon filled me in as he pressed his lips lightly to my neck. "How are you really feeling? And don't lie to me," he whispered into my ear.

I looked up in time to see Chase hang his head and step away, slowly shaking it back and forth. One half of me yearned to go comfort him, and I tried not to let it show.

"I'm great, really. I feel like nothing happened."

He seemed to consider that a moment before finally helping me sit up.

"See? Just fine." My head swam and I felt nauseous for a second.

Brandon smiled and kissed me softly, "I'll go make you something to eat then, that's probably what it was. You didn't have dinner last night."

"Or lunch," Bree interjected and I blushed as Brandon scowled at me.

"Bree?" he said.

"Yeah?"

"Can you go with her while she takes a shower? Just in case it happens again."

"Sure, come on Harp, you look disgusting."

I smiled at her, "I love you too Bree."

I took a shower, without incident, and practically inhaled the eggs and toast Brandon made, even though it was enough for Bree and I put together. By the time we were finished, I'd already missed my only class of the day, so naturally Bree and I decided to go shopping. Brandon wasn't ecstatic, he was trying to keep me in bed, but once I had eaten, I felt better than I normally did so he reluctantly let me go. We'd barely gotten into the second shop when Bree put a hand on my arm and turned me toward her.

"Are you okay Harper?"

"Yeah. Why? What's up?" I breathed heavily.

"Um, well we just walked like one hundred feet and you're practically doubled over trying to catch your breath."

I raised an eyebrow and started to speak.

"Okay fine, that was a little exaggerated. But you're bright red, sweating and you *are* breathing hard."

"Well, it's really hot today, but other than that I feel fine."

"Harper, you're wearing a short sleeved shirt and it's fifty degrees outside."

I paused, "Really?" My heart had finally slowed down so I took a deep breath, relishing in the feel of my lungs filling to their capacity.

She grabbed my hand and towed me toward the car. I couldn't even complain, I felt fine but man all I wanted to do was take a nap. When we got back, Brandon jumped up to greet us, worry etched all over his face as he took in my heavy breathing and red face.

"Did she pass out again?" he asked Bree.

"No, but she wasn't doing well."

"What do you mean? Did something else happen to her again?"

"*She* is right here, and nothing happened. I just need to take a nap. If you guys are done treating me like a child, I'd like to get to that." I pushed past him and headed for his bed.

It wasn't either of their faults, and they really didn't deserve to have me snap at them. But I was frustrated with how rapid my awesome feeling had turned into barely being able to keep my eyes open and practically drooling at the thought of taking a nap. I climbed into Brandon's bed, fully clothed and was out before I could consider taking my shoes off.

The rest of the weekend consisted of me feeling fine, and Brandon and Bree fluttering around me like I was going to collapse at any given moment. I breathed a huge sigh of relief when Sunday came and went. Bree, Claire and I had a girls' day since Chase bailed on family day again, and Monday I was back in class. Things were already calming down with Bree and Brandon since there were no more weird episodes, and I was certain they'd get over it completely if I made it through the day. And get through it, I did. I'd had so much energy that day, I practically skipped to each class and Bree had to hold me tight enough to keep me walking. Thankfully, Brandon seemed to be completely over the fainting spell too, because when I got back to his room that night, he immediately tossed me on the bed and attacked my mouth and clothes. I hadn't had one of these steamy sessions with the love of my life since Wednesday, and it was long overdue.

9

"So Chase isn't here again."

"I know, Mom and Dad have to be getting annoyed with him. He's missed the last few family days."

He has missed five, not like I was counting or anything. I haven't seen him once since over a week ago when I passed out, and other than that I'd only caught a glimpse of him three times since our good-bye one month and two days ago. I know, I'm pathetic. "Maybe I shouldn't come to family day Bree. I might be the reason he doesn't come around anymore."

That made her finally look up from her laptop, "Why would you say that?"

"I don't know, maybe he doesn't like that I'm intruding on family time." My heart ached for him, and I wish it didn't. I wanted to marry Brandon, it finally hit me two weeks ago and I'd never been more sure of anything in my life; so the fact that Chase still had a hold on me at all frustrated me to no end. Since the night Brandon had come back from Arizona, I'd never once regretted my choice in choosing him. I don't know how to explain it, but when I thought about my future, he's the only man I ever saw. But I needed to say good-bye to Chase for good, I just didn't know how to do that yet.

"You're not intruding." She huffed a laugh and went back to some video she was watching, "I swear you fit in this family better than he does. I wish I had another brother, I'd make you marry him so you could be my sister."

I choked on the chip I'd just put in my mouth and walked out of the pantry to gulp down some water. When I got it dislodged from my throat, I hopped onto a barstool and dug into the bag again.

"You're eating again Harper?"

I paused for a second, then shoved the handful of chips in my mouth. "Yeah?"

"You just ate two burgers not even thirty minutes ago." Bree was looking at the bag with disgust. "I've never even seen you finish one."

"I know," I sighed and rolled up the chip bag, "I'm just so freaking hungry these last two days, I think I'm going to start soon."

"No you're not," she said sure of herself. "We still have a little over a week." Bree and I were together so much, we had synchronized. And trust me it wasn't a fun week for anyone.

"You sure?" I swear I felt like it had been forever since I had one.

"Mhmm." She burst into laughter and started clicking on the video again, "Oh my God Harper, come watch this."

I stood next to her but didn't register what we were watching, I was too busy trying to remember when my last one had been. Bree had to be wrong, because I don't remember having our monthly chocolate and romance comedy fest lately. I hated them and she never let me get out of that, but when was the last time we'd had one? I had to go find my phone, I had a calendar on there where I tracked my periods. I unconsciously started eating the chips again thinking about times when I avoided anything other than chaste kisses with Brandon. It didn't hurt his feelings, he knew what was going on when I got in those moods.

"Well look who decided to join the party. Mom and Dad are already asleep."

I slowly turned to look down at Bree, was she talking to me? She had paused the video and was leaning back in the chair, arms folded across her chest, shooting daggers toward the living room. Following her line of sight, I dropped the bag when I saw him standing there.

"I was busy, Harper can I talk to you?"

"Uh," I glanced back at Bree's annoyed but confused expression, "yeah. Yeah I guess." I took two steps before gripping the counter, "Whoa." Crap not again.

"Are you okay?" They both rushed to me and I held a hand up to stop them.

"I'm fine, I just got dizzy for a second." I took a calming breath, "Thought I was going to faint again."

Bree tilted her head to the side and looked at me curiously, Chase was in a fight with himself on whether to help me stay standing or not touch me at all.

"How do you feel now?" Bree questioned.

"Fine, I guess. That was really weird."

"Chase, maybe now isn't a good time."

"No I'm good Bree, I'll be right back." I followed Chase out to the driveway, and though I wanted to close the distance between us, I stayed a few feet away. "Hi." I said pathetically. How would I ever tell him good-bye if I was already struggling with myself to not kiss him?

He blew out through his nose, "Hey Princess."

"Where have you been?"

"Working a lot, classes, surfing. That's about it."

I nodded my head and looked at my feet, "Your family misses you."

"Do you?"

"Of course I do Chase." How could he think I didn't?

"Harper I've given you more than enough time. I can't stand to stay away from you anymore, I need to know who you choose."

"You're really going to do this now? Bree could be listening from the front door!"

"Yes, now. I need to know."

"Chase how can you even ask me to choose between you two?" I hissed through my teeth and met his glare, "You left me, like you always do. You expected me to think you still wanted me after you've completely avoided me for a month?"

He threw his arms out, "I was giving you time! You asked me to give you time!"

"I didn't want you to avoid me like the plague, I wanted you to fight for me. To show me that you loved me like you said you did."

"I do love you Harper, and that's why I gave you that time to think about things without me interfering."

I took a step back and he matched it, after a few silent moments I finally answered him, "I'm sorry Chase, but I can't."

"No. No, no n—"

"I can't be with you. I love Brandon, I'm sorry," I whispered.

"Baby don't say that. I will fight for you, I will. Please just give us a shot."

"A part of me will probably always love you too, but I can't take chances with you Chase. You'll leave me one day, and it will kill me when you do."

"Wha— No! I wouldn't, I swear I wouldn't." He reached for me then and I let him hold me.

"You can't stay with any one girl, that's just how you are. And that's fine Chase, it's fine. You're with different girls every night, but when I think about love I think about forever. You can't give me that, so I'm not going to hurt myself by only having you for a short time."

He lifted my face and stared into my eyes, his were filled with unshed tears and the sight of it almost knocked me off my feet, "I haven't been with anyone but you since you started dating Brandon. I knew then there would never be anyone else like you, and I wasn't going to waste time being with someone else."

I wanted to believe it, and truthfully I did. He was never with girls anymore, but that didn't change anything. Chase had left me again. No matter what he said, he would always leave me. I gently kissed the corner of his mouth and stepped out of his arms, "I love you Chase."

"Baby please, don't do this!"

"I have to, I'm sorry."

He held onto my hand, "Why? Why can't you be with me?"

I didn't answer. I'd already told him everything there was to know about why I couldn't let myself be hurt by him.

"Are you sleeping with him too, Harper?"

"Why does that matter?"

"Please," he closed his eyes and took a deep breath, "just tell me if you are sleeping with him."

I wanted to tell him it wasn't his business, but of course that didn't come out, "I've only been with you." He let go of my hand then and I made it halfway up the drive before it hit me. Oh. My. Word. My eyes went wide and I sucked in a startled gasp. Oh God, oh no.

"What? What's wrong?"

"I have to go." I almost shouted as I ran for the house.

This couldn't be happening. I took the stairs two at a time and rushed into Bree's room searching frantically for my phone.

I ignored the text from Brandon and pulled up the calendar. She hadn't been lying, I was supposed to start in a week and a half. I flipped back to last month and saw I never put in when I'd started, because I hadn't. There on the calendar were the ovulation days, and smack dab in the middle were the two days I'd been with Chase. I shut off my phone and cursed when Bree came into the room.

"Are you okay? What did he say to you? I swear he's such an ass!"

"N-nothing. It's not him, I just feel kind of dizzy again."

"Well what did he want, he left after you came flying in here like a bat outta hell."

Think Harper, think. "Um, he was just . . . asking about a tattoo Brandon wants."

She stood there staring at me for a minute, she didn't believe me and I didn't blame her. "Is there anything I can get you?"

"I just need to go to sleep." And freak out for a while without your knowing eyes on me.

We decided not to go back to the dorm tonight, and got ready for bed there. I buried my face in the pillow and chanted over and over again that I was wrong, this wasn't happening, it was just a dream.

Waking up the next morning, I jumped out of bed and hummed to myself while I was in the shower. I had just been stressing last night, and forgetting about my period from the previous month. I would have freaked out when I originally missed it, and I hadn't so I was just making it seem like I could be—nope not even gonna say the word. Bree said she was going to start breakfast, and after I got dressed I skipped down to meet her.

"You look like you feel better." She grinned while she poured the egg yolks into the skillet.

"I do! I don't know what was wrong with me last night. Probably just too much junk food."

She grunted, "That's an understatement. I've never seen you eat that much."

I laughed but stopped abruptly. What in the world? "What is that smell?"

Bree stepped away from the stove and took a few hesitant sniffs. "I don't smell anything but the eggs."

"Ugh, are they bad?" I opened the fridge and looked at the date on the carton. They still had a week and Bree and I had picked them up just yesterday for Mom. I shut the door and walked to the cabinet to get a glass. When I stepped behind Bree I was assaulted again by the smell of the eggs. I barely made it to the kitchen sink before throwing up everything from the night before. Aw hell.

Bree held my hair back and got me a glass of water when I finished. When I finally looked up at her I was surprised to see her pissed off. Her mouth was mashed into a straight line, arms folded over her chest, an eyebrow raised. She wasn't stupid, she'd put it together.

"Are you kidding me?" She screeched, "You didn't even tell me you'd had sex with him!"

I started shaking and fat tears were falling down my face, "This can't be happening." I sobbed and slid to the ground, "I'm just sick, right? This isn't happening!"

She sat on the ground in front of me and pulled me into a hug. "Shh, it will be okay." She rubbed her hands over my back in comfort, "Have you taken a test Harper?"

"No, no I can't," I sobbed, "I can't be."

Heaving a sigh, she stood up and pulled me with her. "Well then maybe you're not." Her sad smile told me she didn't believe that for a second, "But we're going to find out. Come on," she grabbed two large water bottles out of the fridge and handed them to me. "Start drinking these, I'll drive."

We didn't say anything the entire drive to the drug store.

When she pulled into a parking spot I just shook my head and handed her my card. Five minutes later she came out with a bag full of boxes and handed them to me. I stared at the bag, and after a minute started reading directions.

"You knew Bree, didn't you."

She sighed and grabbed my hand, "I figured."

"How?"

"A lot of things. You've been eating a ton, last night wasn't your first dizzy spell. You get out of breath when we walk to class, and you refused to leave Brandon's side when *I* was having our week of hell last month. I kept thinking it, but every time I brought up sex, you told me you still weren't ready. And then today . . . well it was just the final piece of the puzzle."

I didn't say anything else, just continued to down the water and try to stop my entire body from shaking. When we got back to Mom and Dad's she waited in the bedroom while I used a stick out of each of the four boxes. If I was going to find out, I wanted to be sure. Bree held me while I bawled my eyes out later from the results. There had been a smiley face, a "Yes," a plus sign and a "Pregnant."

"What am I going to do?" I pulled the comforter over my head and curled myself into a tight ball.

Pulling back the comforter, my amazing friend held my chin until I looked at her, tears streaming down her own face. "We're going to tell Mom," I started to refuse that but she continued, "I promise she won't be mad at you, she'll just be sad for you. You know she got pregnant with Chase when she was seventeen?"

I shook my head, they looked young, but I hadn't known that.

"Well she did, she'll understand Harper. She can make an appointment for you and after that, you'll have to figure out a way to tell Brandon." She sighed and ran her fingers through my hair, "He's a good guy, he'll take care of you."

A new round of sobs shook my body, "I can't. Tell Brandon. He's not. He's not. Bree I didn't. Didn't lie to you."

She waited until I had quieted down and my breathing had returned to normal, "What do you mean?"

"I didn't lie to you Bree, I never had sex with Brandon."

"You cheated on Brandon?" She gasped, "With who?"

"I can't. You'll kill me Bree."

She scrambled off the bed and stared at me in horror, "You slept with my BOYFRIEND?!"

Oh crap, "No! No I swear I didn't! I would never do that to you Bree, I don't like Konrad like that at all. Oh my God, how could you even think that?"

Huffing, she grabbed her chest and forced herself to sit back down, "Well there's no other reason I would hate you enough to kill you. I'm sorry I thought that."

"Don't, don't be sorry for anything. I did this, I created the mess. Bree I never meant to hurt Brandon, I swear. I love him, I really do."

"But?" She prompted.

"I love someone else too. He's begged me to leave Brandon, but I couldn't." I choked on the last words.

"How could you not tell me about this? How could I not know . . . you're always with Brandon, I don't get it." She started, "Wait. You're *always* with Brandon, when did this even happen?"

"The night you all went to L.A.," I replied softly.

"You weren't sick?" She was mad I'd lied to her again.

"No, I just wanted to mope over him alone, and then he was there."

"Where?"

"Here."

"At the house? You invited him here?"

"No Bree, I didn't invite him over." I watched her confused face, and after a few minutes I could practically see the light bulb click on.

"Oh shit." She breathed, "You and Chase?"

I didn't respond, I just waited for her to start screaming, but it never happened.

"Why didn't you tell me Harper?" Her face was filled with hurt.

"I don't know," I answered honestly, "I hated myself for doing that to Brandon. I could barely deal with it by myself, I didn't know how to tell anyone else. I wanted to tell you, I did. But since he's your brother, I thought you'd never be okay with it."

"Does he know that you love him?"

Nodding I tried to speak around the lump in my throat, "He loves me too."

After a few silent moments she spoke again, "It makes sense. We've all been so worried about him over the last few months, he's been distant and grumpy. Now that I'm thinking about it I can't believe no one realized he's only ever happy when you're both here." She paused for a second, "What did he say last night?"

"He wanted me to make a choice between him and Brandon. I'd told him last month before you guys got back I needed a few weeks."

"Did you choose Brandon?"

"Yeah." It was barely a whisper, "If Brandon hadn't ever been in the picture, I still couldn't be with your brother. I love Chase, but I know he'd leave me. Whenever he gets mad or upset he'll avoid me for long periods of time. But Brandon *is* in the picture, and I just couldn't imagine myself leaving him." I laughed but it sounded off, "All I wanted was to avoid hurting him, and now this? I'm going to crush him Bree. I'm such a horrible person."

"A little." She tried to laugh, "You're going to have to tell both of them."

"I know, there's no way around this. I've never slept with Brandon, and Chase knows I've only ever been with him. Once Chase knows what's happening, he'll always be around me. You know he won't leave my side, and Brandon will find out he's the dad." My body felt like ice, "Oh my God Bree I'm going to have a baby. I'm going to be a mom. I don't know how to do that, I can't be a mom I don't want the baby to grow up like I did!" I was on the verge of hyperventilating. "I can't do this. I can't do this. I'd be a horrible mom, Bree. I don't want to do this!"

"No you won't! You're going to be a great mom Harper, no one has a bigger heart than you do. Yeah you grew up with a crappy father, but you won't be like him." She gripped my wrists and waited 'til I calmed down once again, "And it might be hard to believe, but Chase is great with little kids, all our cousins love him and he's always taking the babies so he can hold them. Between the two of you? This baby is going to be extremely loved, and of course Mom, Dad and I will be there to spoil him or her to no end."

I actually laughed, really laughed. "I hope you're right. This is going to be a really rough next few months, but I'm glad you'll be here with me Bree. You're like my sister, and I'm sorry I didn't tell you earlier."

She waved my apology off, "I just can't believe that dumbass didn't use a condom!"

"Err, that's my fault. He wanted to stop because he didn't have any and I kind of begged him to anyway. And the second time—"

"There was a second time?"

"The next day. Anyway that time I don't think either of us thought about it. I had just found out you all were coming home, and even though I told him I needed time to choose, we both knew I wouldn't choose him. And it just happened."

"Okay, okay I don't want details. He is still my brother."

Mom peaked her head in through the door, "I just got back from the store, I figured you two would be in class by now!"

Oh thank God she didn't hear what we were talking about. Until Brandon knew, I didn't want anyone else to know who the father was. "Uh . . . hey Mom?"

Her face worried, "Oh Harper honey, what's wrong? Have you both been crying?"

Bree squeezed my hand and we sat up on the bed, after a reassuring nod from her I looked back to her mom and took a deep breath, before any sound could come out I started crying again. Somehow between the sobs and hiccups I managed to mutter, "I'm pregnant."

Claire wasn't mad, just like Bree predicted she was only sad for me. We all cried while she held me and only looked mildly shocked when I said it wasn't Brandon's. Actually, she looked relieved when I told her. Bree and I shared a confused look but didn't say anything. Thankfully she didn't pry when I asked if I could tell her who the dad was after Brandon and I were already broken up. She swore other than Robert, she wouldn't tell a soul and then was off to call her OBGYN to set up an appointment. Her only request was that Bree and I strongly consider moving out of the dorm and into their house.

"It will be safer for you and the baby, and this way we'll be able to make sure you eat nutritiously," she'd reasoned.

Bree and I didn't care, if we weren't at Chase's house, we were almost always here anyway. The dorm was mainly only used if we were pissed off at Konrad and Brandon. And after I spoke to Brandon, I had a feeling I wouldn't be welcome in the house anymore.

"Oh and you should call your father."

That . . . was going to be a difficult conversation. I called him right away, twice, and he didn't answer. Not like I expected him to, I haven't actually spoken with him since the end of August, but I would have rather told him over the phone than via e-mail. Unfortunately, that was my only other option. I grabbed my laptop and typed out a quick e-mail explaining what I'd just found out and that I was sorry if I disappointed him. I asked him to call me so we could talk and told him I loved him. I knew he would respond soon, so I sat there and waited for it. I should have expected his response, but even Bree let out a string of choice words and ran down the hall screaming for her mom to tell her what he'd said.

> *You made your choices, you'll have to live with them. If you keep it, you are no longer allowed in my house. This semester is already paid for, but if you want to continue your education you can find your own way. I'm busy now Harper, I don't have time to deal with you.*

I felt like I'd been punched in the stomach, but I knew being upset over the dad that never wanted me was pointless. I forced a smile when Bree and her mom came back in. "Well, that's two down . . . three more to tell."

Claire's eyes filled with tears but she nodded her head, "Your appointment is a week from Wednesday sweetie."

"Thanks for helping Mom," I mumbled.

We spent the rest of the day moving out of the dorm, even though they didn't let me do much. I kept assuring them that I felt fine, but despite my attempts, I ended up supervising every-thing. Mom gave me the guest bedroom and said if the father ended up being a prick, I could live with them and set up the nursery in there too. I looked to Bree who was all smiles; at least she was sure Chase wouldn't bail. I didn't think his parents would let him not be there for the baby, but whenever I got the nerve to tell him, I would make sure he knew he didn't have to be anything if he didn't want to.

I didn't see, or hear from Chase until that next Wednesday. I had already been so flustered all day about the appointment, I didn't even notice he was there until I ran into him. Literally. Bree, Mom and I were texting back and forth, they were trying to calm me down, and I had been so focused on my phone I plowed right into him and a group of other guys.

"What the he— Princess?"

Retrieving my phone from the ground, I stood back up and turned to leave as fast as possible. I couldn't see him, not today.

"Harper, wait up!" He caught my arm and spun me around so I was facing him. "You're not even going to say hi now?"

"Hi." My voice cracked and I kept my eyes to the ground.

Chase gently placed his hand under my chin and lifted until I was staring at him through unshed tears. "Baby what's wrong?"

God I didn't want to hear him call me that. Memories of our times together flashed through my mind and my cheeks instantly filled with heat. "Nothing," I cleared my throat and blinked back the tears, "it's just allergies or something."

His look told me he wasn't buying that, but didn't push that subject further. Stepping back he hung his head and sighed roughly, shifting his weight a few times, "I haven't seen you around my house much. I know you don't want to be with me, but don't feel like you can't be there, I won't bother you and Brandon."

"That's not why I haven't been there. I um, I broke up with him."

Chase's head snapped up, "You did? When, why didn't you tell me?" He was failing miserably at trying to hide his elated smile.

"A little over a week ago. But it hurt me more than I could ever explain to do it, and I need time to get over that. I can't just rush back to you because Brandon and I aren't together any-more."

He cupped my cheeks and hunched down so he was almost

eye level, "I love you, I'll give you all the time you need. Unless. Unless you don't want me anymore?"

I pressed my face harder into his left hand and closed my eyes, inhaling his clean masculine scent. "I've told you, I will always love you Chase, but I'm still not sure you won't eventually leave me. Because of that fear, I don't know if I can be with you. And some things have changed since we talked last, you might change your mind about me altogether."

"That's not possible."

I pulled his hands off my face and wrapped his tattooed arms around my shoulders. After placing a kiss on his throat I buried my head in his chest, "I wish that were true." My life had drastically changed in such a short amount of time. For obvious reasons, I'd had to break up with Brandon and now Chase and I were going to have a baby. Because of the turn of events, I found myself wanting a life with Chase more and more, I wanted him to be there for me and his baby. Here, wrapped up in his strong arms, I could almost let myself believe it might happen. But Chase was about to graduate college, he was a tattoo artist and spent most of his mornings surfing. I couldn't see him settling down with me and our baby.

"It is Harper," his voice cracked when he said my name, and tears started falling down his face, "I love you so damn much, why can't you see that?"

Oh God no, please don't cry again. My eyes instantly watered again looking at him. I couldn't mean this much for him to start crying in public at the thought of us not being together, could I? "I have to go, I'm sorry."

"Harper please. Please don't just walk away, talk to me baby."

I kept my head down and walked around the corner to meet Bree near the parking lot. Her eyes widened when she saw the two of us together and took in the trails of tears on both our faces. I glanced around and people were looking in confusion as

Chase begged me to stop. I probably would have stared too, if I saw a six foot three inch gorgeous man covered in muscles and tattoos crying. He didn't seem to notice or care. I shook my head once at Bree and she reigned in her expression.

"Harper, please talk to me!"

I reached Bree's side and turned to him, "I will. We *will* talk, but right now I have to go."

A choked sigh escaped his throat when I lifted my hands to wipe away his tears. "Promise?" I nodded and he whispered, "I love you." He kissed the inside of my wrist and watched me step back. Bree lightly brushed her hand against his arm and he jumped back, he looked nervously between the two of us but slightly relaxed when she smiled at him. He hadn't even known she was there though her arm was wrapped around my waist. Now that he'd seen her he took in the few people staring at us and ducked his head as he walked away.

When we were in her car, Bree grabbed my hand and looked at me, "I've never once in my life seen Chase cry. There is no doubt in my mind he is completely in love with you Harper, you have to tell him you're pregnant and he's the dad."

Never seen him cry? That made me feel even worse since I'd made him cry three times in the last month and a half. "I will, just not today. First, I need to tell your mom that he is."

She bit her lip and looked at me, unsure. She didn't think I ever would. I'd told her mom, Sir and Brandon all in the first day of finding out, but it had been over a week and I still hadn't talked to Chase.

"Let's go, we need to get to lunch so I can tell Mom."

She smiled, cranked her car and drove us to the restaurant. I thought about that night with Brandon on the way over. Besides Bree, he was the only one who knew about Chase, and I was still surprised he hadn't said anything.

*　*　*

"SWEETHEART, WHAT'S WRONG?" Brandon grabbed my hands and led me to his room.

Looking at the worry in his eyes just made this harder. I hated myself for doing this to him, and I hated what I was about to do.

"Come here," he wrapped me in his arms, "tell me what happened."

I placed my hands on his chest and pushed until he let me go. "Maybe you should sit down."

"I'll stand," he said warily.

"Brandon, I—" Just do it Harper. Just like with Mom and Sir, don't skip around it. I stopped and took a deep breath, "I ch—. . . I'm pregnant."

He bent slightly at the waist, looking like I'd literally just punched him in the gut. "That's not possible," his said confused as he sagged onto the bed. "We haven't even—" His face fell and his breath came out in a huff, "Oh my God. Did you cheat on me?"

It was pointless to keep trying to wipe my tears away, they were coming too fast. "Brandon, I'm so so—"

"You cheated on me?!"

I bit my lip and nodded my head.

"And you're pregnant?" He sounded completely defeated. I would have rather he been mad, it would make this so much easier.

"Yes."

He ran his hand over his buzzed hair and down his face, "Who? Never mind. I already know."

"How? Did he tell you?"

"I'm not stupid Harper. I see the way you look at him when you think I'm not watching, and you bite your lip and space out whenever you look at that damn ring."

He did know. "Brandon, I'm sorry! It was just one weekend, and I hate myself for it!"

"Does he already know?" He glanced up to meet my eyes.

"No." It barely came out above a whisper.

We stared at each other for an undetermined amount of time, both silently crying, before he asked me one last question, "Why Harper?"

I wanted to make up an excuse, say we were wasted and I regretted it, but he needed to know the truth. "I love him too Brandon."

He flinched and shut his eyes.

"I know I don't deserve this, but would you please not tell him? And if you're going to be angry at someone, please be angry at me. I did this to you."

"You did this to *us* Harper." Slowly standing, he made his way toward the door and opened it, "I won't say anything. I've always known how he felt about you, and if you chose him, then there's nothing for me to be mad at him for. But I need you to leave. Now, please."

He wouldn't look at me as I left, just held the door with a tight, shaking grip and tried to calm his breathing.

"I'm so sorry," I whispered before leaving.

I GLANCED UP, surprised to see we were already at the restaurant. "Well . . . here goes nothing."

"How do you think she's going to take it?" Bree ran a hand through her short blond hair.

"Ha. I was hoping you'd tell me."

"Uh, no. This is the one situation I haven't known what to expect."

I looked at her in horror, "What if she hates me? What if they kick me out Bree?"

"They wouldn't do that to you, and my parents could never hate you. I just don't know how she's going to take it."

We stopped talking when we walked in and were greeted by the hostess and hugs from Mom.

"Oh, I'm just so excited for the appointment! We'll be able to get a due date, and if you're far enough we can hear the heartbeat!" She was clapping and bouncing.

Aw hell, this was about to all be real. "Is it okay if I'm not exactly thrilled right now?"

"Sure it is honey, but you've already gotten over the hard parts. This is when it gets exciting."

The waitress took our drink orders and we ordered our food without even looking at the menu. This is where we always came on our girl's day. We chatted about school, Konrad and Bree, if I planned to go back to school after this year ended, which I didn't, and started to talk about if I wanted a boy or a girl.

"Uh, Mom? I saw the baby's dad today."

Her mouth formed an O, "Did you tell him?"

"No not yet, I thought I should probably tell you who he is first."

"Well I don't see why you had to tell me first unless . . . do I know him?" Her eyes were large and she looked like she was holding her breath.

"Yeah. You could say that."

Bree tried to cover her laugh with a cough and grabbed her iced tea to take a sip.

Like a band aid Harper, just rip it off. I took a deep breath and blurted out, "It's Chase."

"Oh thank God!" Claire exclaimed and put a hand over her chest.

Bree spewed out her tea and my jaw dropped, as well as my spoon. "What?!" we screeched in unison.

She shushed us and looked around for a second before leaning over the table, "You have no idea how much of a relief this is." She held up a hand to stop my question, "My son is in love with you Harper, he has been for a while now. That's why he doesn't come to the house on Sundays anymore. He came to us a month or so ago and said as long as you were with Brandon, he couldn't handle being around you anymore, said it was too hard."

I swear my jaw dropped even more.

"When you said you were pregnant, I knew he was going to be devastated, but when you told me Brandon wasn't the daddy, I hoped it was Chase's. Don't get me wrong, I wish this wasn't happening to you two while you're so young and not married, but what's done is done. He'd even talked about maybe moving away after graduation. I knew he would do it if he found out you were having a baby, especially with some random guy."

"Mom! Why didn't you tell me? I didn't know I was the reason he wasn't coming around, you must have hated me! Why did you let me move in?"

"Because we love you Harper. Just because he wasn't dealing with it well, doesn't mean Robert and I were going to stop loving you. Even if he did move away, that wouldn't have been your fault. Just his choice."

"Holy crap." I huffed and sunk into my seat.

"Ditto," Bree chimed in.

"Harper sweetie," Mom began, "you have got to tell him. If he finds out you're pregnant from someone and doesn't know it's his, he'll be gone."

I love him, I don't want him to leave. But his possible leaving has been stopping me all along. Claire was wrong, Chase would know it was his, but he'd still be gone. "He isn't going to want a baby, I can't take him walking away from me. I love him, this baby just proves that, but I'm terrified he will leave me one day. He's always doing that Mom, one day he's in love with me, the next few weeks he refuses to speak to me."

"He stays away because it kills him to watch you with Brandon. When you would go to his house, he always came to ours so he wouldn't have to see you guys together. I never knew you two had even spoken to each other about this. All he does is talk about you in a way that suggested you didn't know he loved you. He won't leave you, I don't think you realize he's never even spoken about a girl with us, until you showed up last fall." My face must have shown I didn't believe that, "Regardless if he's ready for a child or not, he's the father, he has to help you."

"No!" I said a little too loudly and quieted my voice, "No. I want him to want to be with me, I will not force him to endure this with me. My entire life Sir has resented me, I'm not going to go through the rest of it with Chase doing the same."

"He wouldn't," Bree cut in.

"He might." I looked at each of them and said sternly, "I'll tell him soon, but you have to let him make this choice."

They both agreed and had huge smiles on their faces. I wish I could feel the same. We finished lunch, paid the bill and headed to my first appointment. The first part we sat in the office and spoke with the Doctor, an extremely nice younger lady named Dr. Lowdry.

"When was the first day of your last menstrual period Harper?"

"December twenty ninth," I said confidently.

"And do you have an idea of when the baby may have been conceived?"

"I do, it was either January twelfth or thirteenth."

The Doctor grabbed a plastic wheel and moved it around for a minute, "Okay well then your due date should be October fourth, so what do you say we have your first ultrasound? You're practically eight weeks, we'll be able to hear the heartbeat."

Mom smiled and clapped her hands and Bree looked like she was doing math in her head. We followed her to another room and after changing and positioning myself on the table, the lights were turned off and the ultrasound started. At first all I saw was a gray screen with a dark circle in the middle, then she zoomed in and I saw what looked like a gummy bear on the screen. Mom's breath caught and my eyes widened.

"That's your baby!" Dr. Lowdry said smiling and pressing different buttons. "Let's get some measurements here . . . yep! I'd say you are seven weeks and six days."

Oh my word this is real. It's real isn't it? Yep it's real. There's a freaking gummy bear growing in me! I think the Doctor was pointing out the head and arms, but I couldn't listen too much, I was beyond mesmerized by the screen.

"Harper!"

"Huh?"

The three of them laughed, I wonder how long they'd been trying to get my attention.

"Are you ready to hear the heartbeat?"

I looked over at Dr. Lowdry's warm smile and nodded my head. She clicked a button and my entire world changed. We all held our breath as a whooshing noise filled the room. It wasn't what I was expecting, it was really fast and didn't sound like what I thought a heartbeat should sound like, but there was no mistaking that's what it was. Bree grabbed my hand and Claire reached for some tissue to wipe her eyes. I couldn't see the screen anymore and I realized I was crying, so I closed my eyes and listened to the most amazing sound in the world.

"I'm going to be a grandma!" Mom cried happily.

"Oh my God, I'm going to be a mom."

Dr. Lowdry flipped on the lights and handed me the pictures of the ultrasound, "Now will Dad be joining us for these? It's usually best if the fathers are here for everything."

I didn't know what to say without sounding awkward, thankfully Claire spoke up, "Oh, my son will definitely be here next time."

Man I hope she's right.

Once the rest of the appointment was done and we picked up my prenatal vitamins, the three of us headed for a pedicure before going home and waiting for Robert to come back from work. Mom couldn't wait until tonight, she had called him on the way to the appointment to let him know Chase was the dad, and apparently he was just as relieved. Crazy. When we sat down for dinner that night, he got misty eyed when we showed him the photos and joked with me about making him a grandpa so young. Everyone was smiling, including me, I just wish Chase could have been there too.

DON'T ASK HOW I did it, but I managed to only see Chase six times over the next four weeks, and I still had avoided having the talk with him. Mom and Dad were worried that he was going to find out and bolt since my clothes were getting tighter now and Bree was just flat out pissed.

"Harper, he hasn't been with another girl since August, and you're still worried he's going to leave you? You guys aren't even dating and he's committed to you!"

"I know, I know. But it's not so easy to just be with him Bree. I can't do that to Brandon yet."

"Brandon already knows!" she reasoned.

"Yeah, but think of it this way. What if you got pregnant with someone other than Konrad. Even if you told him, would you be able to just start dating the other guy? Walking around the school on his arm, in front of Konrad?"

She didn't answer.

"No, you wouldn't. Because it would be cruel to Konrad and though you broke his heart you would still love him too."

"You're still in love with Brandon? Well then tell Chase it's Brandon's baby and get back with Brandon."

"What? No! That's sick. I could never do something like that to Brandon. That would be even worse than the conversation where I told him I was pregnant! It's like HEY! Let me twist the knife I stabbed in your heart."

"Okay true. But you have to give Chase a chance here, just tell him, but say you guys need to lie low in public."

"I know I'm already hurting Chase by blowing him off, but are you hearing yourself? That's bad too Bree. It would be like he was my dirty secret and I didn't want anyone else to know. It already takes everything in me not to run into his arms when I see him to tell him everything, and you expect me to tell him I'm pregnant with his baby and that we need to still stay away from each other? It's fine if I'm miserable, but I can't do that to him too."

"I didn't think about it like that, but you have to figure out something."

I sighed and fell onto the bed, "I know Bree. Trust me there's nothing you can say that I haven't already thought of. After that ultrasound, all I can think about is telling Chase. It's like my whole perspective changed and I'm finally ready to take that chance with him. But I know I have to wait a little bit longer. I owe it to Brandon to give him some time to get over his hurt, and I owe it to Chase to be able to fully be in a relationship with him once he knows."

She laid down next to me and grabbed my hand, "But when will it be enough time for that? When you have a beach ball under your shirt?"

"No. I couldn't let Chase find out that way, that wouldn't be fair to him either. And I know what you're about to say, I'm starting to show a little, so it has to be soon." I wasn't showing much yet, it just looked like I ate a massive meal, but it was looking more like an awkward bump with each passing day, and soon people would start talking.

"It hurts me to see you guys apart, but I understand what you're saying sweetie."

We both sat up to see Mom standing in the doorway, I guess she'd heard most, if not all of the conversation.

"Since he's my son, I obviously think about his happiness before Brandon's, so naturally I only think about how this is hurting him. And while what you're saying is extremely mature for your age, I'll be happy when all this is behind you two and you can live your lives together."

I hated that I was still hurting so many people. It was apparent Claire was hurting for Chase, he still wasn't coming around much, I'd messed up more than I thought. "I'm sorry Mom. I promise I'm not trying to hurt him or any of you. I'm just trying to figure out the best way to fix all of this, so when we do start a relationship, it's perfect."

Bree squeezed my hand and Mom came to lay down on my other side. "I don't think you're trying to hurt people sweetie, we just only see one side of this," Mom said with a sigh.

"I'm sorry for getting on you Harper, I just see how miserable you are without him, and I didn't understand why you were putting both of you through this when it's clear you guys want each other so badly. That wasn't fair of me."

"It's fine Bree, you guys are still right, I need to tell him soon. This is just a lot harder than I thought it would be."

We sat there in silence for a while until Mom glanced at her watch and stood up, "So I guess it's safe to assume he won't be at the appointment today!" She laughed and the tension slowly left the room. "Well that's fine with me, I'm selfish and want to be there to see it."

I sat up, "You aren't going to come to the appointments when Chase does? I need you two there." I looked between her and Bree.

"No sweetie, you may not understand it yet, but the first time he's there, trust me when I say you'll want it to just be the two of you."

"Okay? Well I'm ready whenever you guys are."

Bree jumped up and pulled me with her, "I'm ready! Let's go see my niece or nephew!"

I laughed and looked at my stomach, "You hear that? We're coming to see you Gummy Bear!"

Claire and Bree both laughed as we walked to the car. I was thrilled to see my baby again, but my heart hurt knowing Chase wouldn't be there, that he didn't even know about it. Next time, I promised myself, he'll for sure be there next time.

We were silent throughout the appointment as we watched my gummy bear, who now actually looked like a baby, sleep in my stomach. The heartbeat was strong and once again I closed my eyes so the only thing I was aware of was that beautiful sound.

"Well, let's make another appointment for four more weeks, you'll be sixteen weeks then and if baby is cooperative we might be able to find out the sex of the baby," Dr. Lowdry said as we walked out of the room.

"Really? I'm sorry I just didn't realize we could find out that soon!" I definitely needed to tell Chase. If there was one appointment in particular I wanted him there for, it was to find out if we were having a boy or girl. I told Claire and Bree as much when we got in the car and they both sighed happily knowing within a month Chase and I would be together. I wanted to bring up the fact that we still didn't know if he would want the baby or me after he found out, but they were so dang happy I couldn't bring myself to sour the mood again. "I'd like to give him some time before the appointment, just in case he needs to think about things, but I never see him anymore unless we're at school and I don't want to do it there either. Do you think if he hasn't come around on his own by my birthday, we could invite him to whatever we're doing? I'll tell him then."

"I can call and tell him he has to come to family day this Sunday sweetie."

"No Mom, I don't want him to be forced to come over. I would prefer if he comes to see me on his own, but if he hasn't by then, then we can invite him to dinner or something. I doubt he'd miss my birthday."

"April fifth . . . two weeks? These are going to be the longest two weeks of our lives." Bree groaned.

"Hey I just set a deadline for myself, I thought you would be a little happier than this," I joked with her.

"I am, but whenever I see him now I'm going to be freaking out, knowing that he's finding out soon."

"Well we don't see him much, so hopefully you won't have many freak-outs."

Okay so there weren't *many* freak-outs, but there were three more than I was expecting there to be. Which meant there were a total of three. All at school. The first wasn't a big deal, Bree and I were running to a class and we saw him walk out of the building. He reached out to brush my hand as we ran past, his face lit up with a gorgeous smile as Bree and I barely managed *hellos* before pushing open the door to the lecture we were late to. The next two were borderline dangerous, considering my current state.

"Damn Princess," Drew laughed. "You trying to pack on a few pounds there?"

I froze when Chase smacked him across the back of the head on the way to his seat. I hadn't been *trying* to eat for two, since I knew there really wasn't a reason to yet, but I was so hungry all the freaking time. This was just the first time Chase had been around, and the first time anyone had said something besides Bree and her parents. My hand immediately went down to my stomach, thinking he'd somehow see the bump even though I was hidden behind the table. Thankfully Bree snatched my hand and put it to my side before I could look awkward covering myself. Which, by the way, I was definitely doing more of, all my tight shirts were starting to show my now obvious bump, so everything I wore was loose or flowy around my hips. I wasn't in maternity clothes yet, by any means, I was just being careful until Chase knew. Brandon's eyes darted quickly to mine and with a hard sigh he got up from the table and left. I wanted to die.

That had been the first time I'd seen Brandon since we'd broken up, and it had been emotional to say the least. I'd stopped dead in my tracks when I saw him sitting at the table, but Bree had told me I needed to do this at some point. I knew she was right, but seeing him again made me want to take him away somewhere and beg him to take me back, even though I'd just told Bree I could never do that to him. I did love Chase, and I knew that if I were to be with anyone, it needed to be him. But I was still completely in love with Brandon. I wouldn't tell Bree this, but I still thought of him when I thought of my future, if he were to ask me today, I would marry him. But obviously that day would never come now. That thought ripped my heart to a million pieces, even though I'd done this to myself. Throughout the tense five minutes we'd been at the table, I'd watched him for four and a half and I continued to watch him until he was out of the café.

"Bree," I whispered leaning into her side, "we might need to leave soon before *I* freak out instead of you."

As if on cue, Derek's girlfriend, Maci, and one of her other friends sat down at the table. "Wow Harper, you look amazing today." Maci said with wide eyes, "I mean, not that you aren't pretty all the time, but I swear you're glowing."

Bree's intake of breath was audible. Crap. I couldn't stop myself, I glanced over at Chase and breathed a sigh of relief when I saw he was simply smiling at me. I smiled nervously, but Bree shot out of her chair, causing it to fall backwards.

"We have to go!" she explained while everyone looked at her like she was crazy.

I walked away with her, and once out of earshot finally spoke, "Subtle Breanna. Very subtle."

"I'm sorry, but I swear I thought someone was going to say something! Can you even believe that just happened?"

"No," I breathed, "you're right, it was weird to have them bring up those things within a few minutes of each other. I got nervous for a second there too. Did you notice anyone else at the table? I only looked at Chase. He definitely didn't get it, but that doesn't mean no one else did."

"Just Maci. I'm glad no one brought up the fact that you're always wearing loose shirts."

"Honestly Bree, I think we're the only ones that know that, and it's because we both decided it was for the best. I think we're just freaking out because we know I'm . . . well . . . you know."

"Probably. Ugh, only three more days, and then he'll know."

I almost started hyperventilating.

"Chill Harper! Breathe."

"Oh God, I haven't even thought of how to tell him!" I looked around quickly to make sure no one was staring after my outburst.

"Calm down friend," Bree stepped closer, "it will be easy, you told everyone else with no problems."

"That was different, they were easier because I was already upset with myself. But he's the dad, and though I'm still upset with myself, I'm happy about the baby. Different. So different."

"What's different?" Konrad pulled a squealing Bree in for a big kiss.

"God babe! You scared the crap out of me." She slapped his chest but brought him in for another kiss.

He smiled and looked at me again, "Sup Kid, what's different?"

"Uh, I just. I just saw Brandon, it was weird."

He nodded and wrapped his arms around Bree's waist. "Ready gorgeous?"

Bree looked at me, eyebrow raised, "You good?"

"Yeah! Yeah, I'm fine. See you guys after class." I flicked my eyes to Konrad who, thankfully, didn't think anything was wrong. Jeez I needed these three days to fly by, not telling Chase was becoming ridiculously hard, especially with thinking everyone was going to somehow find out.

I saw Chase for the third time the day before my birthday, and it was when I'd been rushing out of a class to hurl in the next available bathroom. Of course I hadn't been sick for three days, and then it decides to reappear and he's right there. I was throwing up violently into the toilet when his hand started making large circles on my back. When the morning sickness had taken full effect and turned into the every-few-hours-sickness, I'd worn my hair in a messy bun every day so I wouldn't have to worry about it. Though it had definitely tapered off, I was grateful I'd been running late so I hadn't had time to do anything else with my hair. I was already humiliated that he'd just watched that, but having to clean vomit out of my hair in front of him would have made it ten times worse.

"Go away." I groaned and spit into the toilet.

He walked away but came right back with a cold wet paper towel. "Here you go Princess," he said softly.

I took it and wiped my face before wiping my mouth and stood up to face him. "Thanks."

"Are you okay? Do you want me to take you somewhere?"

"No, I'm great." Weird, I know. But every time I finished throwing up, I felt like nothing had ever happened. Actually I was kind of hungry again.

"Great? You just threw up Harper."

I looked into his blue eyes and immediately regretted it. Tearing my eyes away I walked to the sink to rinse my mouth out, "I know, and now I feel fine."

"If you don't want me to take you, at least let me call Bree so she can take you home. Speaking of, when were you going to tell me you moved into my parents' house?"

I spit out the water, turned the faucet off and popped a piece of gum in my mouth. I was now always prepared with at least two packs of gum. "Does that bother you?"

"Not at all, but I just found out this morning that you've been living there over a month. I would have come around more if I knew you were there and not hiding from me in your dorm."

"I haven't been hiding from you Chase."

He hung his head, "You sure about that?"

Looking at Chase with his head down, I fought the urge to tell him everything. But now wasn't the time for all of it, I couldn't tell him in a dirty bathroom that we were having a baby. "I've just been busy, and you haven't been around much either. You haven't come to a family day in months."

He laughed humorlessly, "As before Harper, I'm giving you the time you asked for."

God I had to stop asking him to give me time, he flat out disappears when I do. Guys need to understand that sometimes, we mean exactly the opposite of what we say. I may need time, but I damn sure want you to show me that you want me. "Oh."

I grabbed my backpack and waited for him to follow me out of the bathroom. Thankfully no one was around, I'm sure it would look awkward for us both to come out of the girl's room. We walked out of the building and spotted Bree waiting with Konrad not far away. Her eyes grew wide and she turned to talk to Konrad. I'm sure to prevent another freak-out.

"Harper, can you tell me one thing?"

"I'll tell you anything Chase." Except for the fact that I'm carrying your baby.

"Have I—have I missed my chance?"

"What do you mean?"

"I mean with you, *us*. Did I miss my chance?" His face was scrunched together, he looked terrified that I would say yes.

I stepped up and wrapped my arms around his waist, "I'm sorry that you would even have to ask that. I wish you knew how much I love you Chase, it's just been a hard time for me." He pulled me closer to him and I tried to push my hips back without him noticing. "I didn't know you were still giving me time, I figured I'd already lost you." My voice caught at the end. Oh my word, I hadn't realized until those words came out that I actually thought that. Was that the real reason why I hadn't been able to tell him yet?

"Aw hell baby. That's not possible." He kissed the top of my head and squeezed me tight. "What's been going on? Is it still because of Brandon? Or did something else happen?"

Just then Bree walked up. "We need to go Harper," she said softly.

I looked at her, hoping she understood that she couldn't have had better timing. There's no way I would tell Chase here, but I couldn't stand to keep talking to him without saying something about the pregnancy. Once again, Chase quickly dropped his arms and stepped back when he saw her. I wanted to roll my eyes but resisted. She heard him say "I love you" last time, and he still thought he had to hide it from her? *One more day. One. More. Day.*

"See you." I touched Chase's arm before turning to Bree.

"Bye Princess."

10

"WAKE UP, WAKE up, wake up!" Bree shouted the next morning.

"Ugh! Bree, we don't have class for four hours. Go away!"

"No way! It's your birthday you have to get out of bed!"

Oh right. Birthday. "No one cares, go back to sleep." I grumbled and pulled the comforter over my head.

"We do, now get your ass up!" She ripped the comforter off the bed completely and threw it to the floor.

"Sometimes, I just want to punch you."

She beamed a smile at me, "I know. You love me!"

"That too."

I followed her down the stairs and almost peed myself when Mom and Dad yelled, "HAPPY BIRTHDAY HARPER!" They were putting pancakes, eggs, bacon and presents on the kitchen table when we walked in.

Jeez, could these people be any more wonderful? First Christmas, now this? We ate together and when the dishes were done I opened my presents. Bree got me three shirts that I could wear now, and when I was "ginormously huge," Mom and Dad got me

another pregnancy book as well as a baby names book, a Juicy
bracelet and a green Coach baby bag from all three of them.

How would I ever thank them for so much more than just the
presents? "Thank you. You guys are so amazing, I love you all."

I was bombarded by hugs and I couldn't help but wish for
Chase's arms too. I smiled when I remembered today was the
day. Since Bree and I didn't have school tomorrow, we were all
going out to dinner tonight, then coming back to watch movies.
I read through the fourteenth week of *What to Expect When You're
Expecting*, bookmarked my spot with the most recent ultrasound
picture, thumbed through the baby name book then hopped in
the shower to get ready for my day. This was the first time I'd
been excited about having a birthday, and I wanted to look cute
for it. So I took my time with my hair and make-up, making sure
I looked perfect for my day, and for when I told Chase. I dressed
in my favorite pair of dark Lucky jeans, flip flops and one of
the new shirts Bree got me. It was dark gray v-neck, long and
form fitting, but seriously stretchy. Yep, I'd for sure be able to
wear this throughout the whole pregnancy. I almost took it back
off when I saw my defined bump showing through the stretchy
material, but figured it was time to stop hiding it. People may
not notice that my boobs were getting even bigger, but if anyone
looked down, they'd definitely know what was going on. When I
walked into the kitchen Mom and Bree were thrilled at my outfit
because they knew this could only mean one thing and Mom
came up to pat my baby bump.

"See you tonight girls! Love you!" She had the widest smile
I'd seen since we told her Chase was the father, and it was unde-
niably contagious.

We were almost to our first class and I did a double take to a
chair sitting outside the door. I slowly walked up and grabbed
the bouquet of orange lilies, tucked into the side was a note with
my name on the envelope. I looked at Bree who was looking

around confused, and I joined in with her. There were people
I vaguely knew all over, but other than Bree and Mom, only
two guys knew about these. And neither of them were around. I
opened the note and a huge smile spread across my face when I
read the masculine handwriting.

"Happy Birthday Princess"

I bit my lip and looked harder for a tall, tan, built, tatted up
guy with shaggy blond hair, bright blue eyes and a killer smile.

"Who are they from?" Bree grabbed the note out of my hands.

"Chase, do you see him?"

"No. That boy I swear, who knew he could be sweet?"

After another quick look, I reluctantly followed her into the
classroom. No sooner had we sat down, than my phone chimed.

> *Chase:*
> *You look beautiful today.*

> *Me:*
> *Were you watching me?*

> *Chase:*
> *Maybe. I finally got to give you your lilies.*

> *Me:*
> *You already gave me my lilies a few months ago, remem-
> ber?*

> *Chase:*
> *I couldn't forget that day even if I tried.*

> *Me:*
> *Well you could have given these to me yourself you know.*
> *I would have liked to see you.*

Chase:
It was worth it to see that smile on your face.

Me:
:) Thank you for my flowers. I love them.

Chase:
What are you doing for your birthday?

Me:
Dinner with your fam tonight, movies at the house after.
You're invited.

Chase:
I'll see what I can do.

Once again, it wasn't exactly a no, but it wasn't a yes either and I tried to not let that disappoint me. Cryptic words were kind of his specialty.

"Gah, look at you Harper," Bree whispered.

"What?"

"You already totally have that preggo glow, and now your face is lit up like the freaking sun after texting my brother."

I looked at her confused, "How did you know I was talking to him?"

She narrowed her eyes at me, then raised her eyebrows. "Like I said, your face is lit up like the sun." Nudging my knee, she turned to listen to the Professor.

I smiled at my flowers one more time, and tried to follow her lead. Class flew by and we went to lunch to meet up with everyone, Chase wasn't there, but a very shocked looking Brandon was. All the guys had given me big bear hugs, and after an uneasy hug from Brandon he froze and backed up slowly, his eyes trained to my stomach. It had finally been real for me at the first ultrasound, but I don't think it'd been real for Brandon until he saw the bump pushing out from my hips. My stomach churned and my heart ached thinking of the love I'd lost, but I knew I had to get over it. I was the one who had messed up, I needed to get over it so I could get on with my life too. None of the girls got to the table until we were already seated, and even with Brandon's wide eyes staring at where my stomach was hidden from the table, no one else saw the evidence. Since the restaurant was just down the street from campus, after lunch Bree and I went to a boba shop close to the school and did most of our homework before we had to leave for dinner.

We met Claire and Robert at the restaurant at six, and tried to have a great time sans Chase. Claire shared funny stories about her two pregnancies and hilarious things Breanna and Chase had done when they were little. We were all cracking up and wiping tears from our eyes by the time the waiter came with the bill. I checked my phone again and my shoulders dropped when there still wasn't anything from Chase. Claire talked to him today to invite him to dinner, and he'd flat out refused to come. I didn't understand. I thought after our few words yesterday that things were going to turn around, and then after the flowers today, I'd been positive they were. My heart sunk but I tried to keep a happy face for the people that loved me. Apparently I wasn't doing a good job, Claire reached over the table and grabbed my hand, her face sad.

"Sweetie don't worry about it, please. This will all work out, I'm sure of it." But for once, no one looked like they believed it.

I nodded and flashed a smile, "Movie time?"

We looked at each other awkwardly, but left and headed for home. Bree had an arm slung over my shoulders talking about how much of an ass Chase is when we opened the front doors and all sucked in gasps. There were orange and white lilies covering every table and counter. Chase. A smile broke across my face as I looked around the entryway, dining room and living room for him, Robert let out a low whistle of appreciation and shut the door. My smile died as soon as I heard him in the other room.

"Are you fucking kidding me?! How could you guys keep this from me?" Chase's voice boomed from the kitchen as he rounded the bar and stalked toward us through the living room. "Where the hell is he? I swear to God I'm going to kill him!" With his tall muscular build, tattooed arms and outraged face, he definitely looked like he could kill someone. I grabbed Bree's arm and shrank back into Mom, pulling her with me. Until now, I'd never been scared of Chase, even that night he'd given me bruises.

"Chase!" Robert barked and stepped in front of us, "Calm down, what is going on?"

"I saw the books, I saw the effing ultrasound pictures!"

I flinched. Aw hell, it wasn't supposed to happen this way. Since he hadn't come back to the house in months, we'd left everything on the kitchen table ever since that first appointment.

Robert crossed his arms over his chest, "And?"

"And!? DAD! Bree's knocked up and all you can say is 'and'?!"

Bree snorted and took a step away from me, crossing her arms over her chest, "Please. I'm not as stupid as you, I'm not pregnant."

"Breanna!" Claire hissed through her teeth. She gave me an apologetic look for her daughter but it was true and I know Bree hadn't meant it as an insult toward me.

Chase shoved one of the ultrasound pictures in Bree's face, "Then what the hell is this?"

I stepped up next to her, took the photo out of his hand and spoke softly, trying to hide my shaking. "It's mine Chase."

You could have heard a pin drop. Chase's face had softened

as soon as he'd seen me, but turned into one of shock when he registered what I'd said. After a few minutes, a grin that reached his eyes spread across his face as he searched mine.

His eyes slowly trailed down to my stomach and grew wide, "You're pregnant Princess?"

"Yes," I whispered.

He lifted his head to smile at me and dropped it again, gaze fixed on my bump. This time no one stopped me when I let my hand fall to cover it lovingly. "Is it—is it mine?"

"Of course it is."

"We're going to have a baby?"

"Yes."

"This is our baby?" He reached for the photo in my hand.

I smiled, "Yes."

His expression was so beautiful, tears instantly poured down my cheeks. "We're having a baby."

I laughed through my tears and nodded my head.

Chase ran a hand through his hair and huffed out a laugh. He looked from the picture to my stomach once more, "I love you so much," he breathed and closed the distance between us, crushing his lips to mine.

I didn't care that his family was watching, I threw my arms around his neck and let him lift me off the ground. After I was good and kissed, he set me back down and dropped to his knees. Running his hand over my gummy bear bump, he lifted my shirt and kissed my bare stomach twice. A sob broke out of my chest and I looked at Claire who was freely crying and leaning into Robert. Even Bree was wiping a few tears away.

Chase stood back up and cupped my face in his hands, "Why didn't you tell me?"

"I was scared," I shrugged, "I still am."

"You don't have to be scared," he whispered and kissed my nose, "I'll take care of us."

I looked up at the family, "Can you guys excuse us for a minute?"

Grabbing Chase's hand, I led him up the stairs and to his room. I hadn't been in here since that heated night and I was hit with flashes of it when we stepped in. I sat on the edge of the bed, but he pulled me down so I was curled up into his side. He brought my hand up and played with it over his chest, alternating between intertwining our fingers and bringing them down so he could kiss my palm.

"I can't believe we're going to have a baby."

I blew out a hard breath, this is what I'd been waiting for and secretly hoped I could have skipped altogether. "About that . . . Chase—"

He groaned, "No, don't do this again, please."

"Just hear me out, okay? You're twenty two, you're about to graduate college, I don't want to take your life from you. If you want to live your life, I won't stop you. Just because this baby is yours, don't think that means you're forced to be with me . . . with us." I pulled myself up so I could look at him, "I want you to be with us, don't get me wrong. But I will let you go if that's what you need."

"Are you done?" He was smiling.

"Yes."

"Harper, I love you more than I could ever explain. Meeting you changed my world. Even when I thought you would never be mine, I couldn't continue to live a life I knew you hated. The night you told me you loved me was the best night of my life, up until tonight. I never want to let you go again, I want to be with you for the rest of my life. I want to marry you someday Harper." He paused and searched my eyes, "I would do anything for you. I don't know what to do to make you believe me, but I'll spend forever trying to show you."

"You want to marry me?"

"You have no idea how much." He brought me back so I was half laying on his chest.

"Not just because I'm pregnant?"

He kissed me softly, "Not at all. I gotta admit, it's a little bit of a shock, but I've always thought about being with you and starting a family. And even though it's sooner than I thought it would be, I'm so freaking excited that it's happening. When should we be expecting him?"

"Him?"

"Yep, it's gonna be a boy."

I laughed and ran a hand through his hair, "I'm due October fourth."

He mentally counted the months and smiled widely when he was done. "So six months, huh? Do you want to take next year off from classes?"

"I can't go back to school."

"Of course you can, I'll help you."

"No, not that. I know you would." I bit my lip and laid flat on the bed, "I told Sir that I'm pregnant."

He squeezed my hand once, "And?"

"He uh—isn't going to pay for school anymore and he said I'm not welcome back home."

Chase cursed under his breath, "Are you serious? We'll figure it out, if you want to finish school we'll make it happen."

I could make it happen if I wanted to, but Gummy Bear had changed all my wants in life. "Really, I don't even want to go back after this semester, that's not why I'm sad. I just hate how he is. I hate how he resents me for being born."

He pulled me back into his side and stroked his hand up and down my side, "It's not your fault. He's a douche and it's his loss for missing out on an amazing daughter."

"I was afraid you'd resent me too, for getting pregnant. You wanted to stop and I pushed you."

"It's not like you had to push hard, I wanted you so bad."

I nodded and ran my fingers over his chest.

"I don't resent you Harper, I never will."

We sat there for a while longer, just holding each other and sharing sweet kisses. Bree popped her head in to let us know the movie would be starting soon and left right after to give us a few more minutes.

"Harper, I want you to be mine, and not just because we're having a baby, though I'll warn you, I'm about to tell everyone that we are." He smiled and kissed my nose, "But I want to be able to hold you in public, I want to show everyone that you're taken and you belong to me. That you'll always belong to me. Are we done torturing each other by staying apart?"

"Are you done leaving me?"

He hovered just above my lips, "I'll never leave you again sweetie."

"Then I'm yours." I closed the distance and kissed him hard.

11

Now that Chase knew about the pregnancy, and was completely on board, everything was so much different around the house. Everyone was happy, Chase was there daily and was even able to drag me to his house a few times so I could hang out with the guys, but it had been more than uncomfortable. Brandon had been there twice, and he knew that Chase was now in the know as well. The look on his face when he saw us together the first time almost killed me. Chase had flipped out when I started hyperventilating, but I wouldn't tell him what was going on. The second time, he'd gotten the hint and only took me around when he knew Brandon wouldn't be there. If that upset him, he never once mentioned it, and he definitely didn't show it. I think he was so happy we were finally together, nothing could put him in a bad mood. And I was happy too, I honestly was, I loved Chase and I loved the expecting daddy role he'd already taken on. Every day I fell more in love with him, but it didn't lessen the love I still had for Brandon. Instead, it was like my heart grew to hold both. Well, all three, if you count my Gummy Bear. Chase never asked me how I'd told Brandon what happened, to be frank, I think he didn't want to know. Deep down, he had to know I still loved him, and that was probably the reason for him to pull me in the opposite direction every time we saw Brandon after that second encounter at the house. I wanted to talk to Brandon, alone, to see how he was doing with all of this. But I wasn't sure I'd be able to handle the conversation, so I continued to talk myself out of it.

We were just getting into the ultrasound room and Chase couldn't stop smiling and was practically bouncing up and down. Dr. Lowdry had seemed excited to meet him and updated him on everything that had happened in the first two appointments, as well as what to expect this appointment and the ones following over the next few months. When the lights turned off and the ultrasound started, I finally understood why Mom had told me I'd only want to be here with Chase. This was . . . an out of body experience. It was magical. You could practically see the love and joy flowing through the two of us. Instead of closing my eyes to listen to the heartbeat, Chase and I stared at each other for a couple minutes just smiling and listening to our baby.

"I can't even believe how perfect of a position your baby is in right now! That is unreal." Dr. Lowdry laughed as she clicked some keys to snap a few pictures. "Now, did you *want* to find out the sex of the baby, or do you want it to be a surprise?"

"I already know." I smiled at the screen, there was no mistaking it.

Chase laughed and squeezed my hand tighter, "I told you baby. I told you it would be a boy."

We both looked at Dr. Lowdry, "It is a boy, isn't it?" I asked. I mean, it *looked* like it was a boy, but I wasn't the professional.

"Oh he is definitely a boy." She laughed again and took a few more pictures as he rolled slightly.

Chase leaned over and kissed me sweetly, whispering against my lips, "I love you," he glanced down to my stomach and back to me, "and our son so much Harper." He brushed his thumbs over my cheeks and kissed me again while Dr. Lowdry turned on the lights.

She handed us our new pictures and we walked out of the building. As soon as we reached the parking lot Chase grabbed my hand and pulled me back to him, slamming his mouth against mine. I giggled and wrapped my arms around him as he leaned me against his truck.

"That was . . . that was absolutely amazing!" He laughed and kissed me again.

"Having you there made it so special, all I could think about the last two times was how I wished you were there to experience it with me. I'm sorry it took me so long to tell you."

He shook his head and opened the door for me, "No *sorrys* today, I love you and we're having a son. Today is only allowed to be an *I love you* day."

I smiled and got in his truck, completely blissed out. We stopped to grab some lunch and started heading home, so I was confused when we pulled into a Ford dealership. "Uh . . . ?"

"So I've been thinking," he started and grinned mischievously at me, "you're going to need your own car soon, and I happen to know that you want a blacked out Expedition."

"Chase . . ."

"I *may* have had one brought to this dealership."

"No you didn't." My jaw dropped and I looked out the windows.

He shrugged, "I said I may have. Never said I did."

I smacked his arm and hopped out of his truck, he met me on

the passenger side and pulled me into his arms. "Are you being serious?"

"I am." He pressed a feather light kiss to my neck, "But we can look around and see if there's something else you want."

"Babe!" I gasped, but reigned in my excitement, "I can't buy a car." Okay that was entirely untrue. I'd worked at least forty hours a week almost every week for six years and saved everything I'd made until I moved here, and even then Brandon had always been trying to pay for things I'd been about to buy. I still had well over ninety-eight percent of my savings. Even though Sir was cutting me off, I could have easily finished my school with what I still had, but I was having a baby, and I didn't work anymore. I needed to save as much as I could for him and getting a house. Not that Chase knew how much I had, like Brandon I wasn't usually one to talk about my money.

"Maybe not, but *we* can."

"You want to split it?" I asked confused.

He laughed and his eyes lit up, "Not exactly. Okay you can tell me if this is moving too fast, but since I plan on marrying you soon," he raised an eyebrow to make sure I understood what that meant and I inhaled audibly, "I wanted to put you on my bank account so you have access to my money."

"Chase, I don't need you to do that and I don't need you to buy me a car."

"I know Princess, but I want you to have access to it. I make decent money at the shop, but Bree and I were also given a lot when Dad's parents died. So I have more than enough in savings to take care of the three of us, and to buy you a car. It's not a big deal."

I bit my lip and shifted my weight, "I know you want to, and to be honest it kind of excites me that you want to share all that with me. But I'm saying . . . I *really* don't need you to. If we're going to share your bank account, then we should share mine too."

"Harper that isn't necessary." He smiled and wrapped his arms around me, but blanched when I whispered how much I had in savings. "Are you serious? Just from working on the base?" I nodded and he let out a low whistle, sounding like his dad, "Well damn babe. That's great, and if you want to add it to our accounts that's fine. But I'd rather not touch that money, we can save it for emergencies, just let me take care of you."

"Okay." I pressed my lips to his and sighed into his arms.

"You ready to look for a car?"

I grinned and jumped back, "Nope! No need to look, I already know I want the Expedition!"

Chase laughed and pulled me into the showroom, after talking to a couple people they brought my car around and I tried not to squeal. It was black with black rims, black leather seats and completely decked out. I was in love with this car. Chase let me do the test driving and I was bouncing up and down as we did paperwork for over an hour. My jaw about hit the floor when Chase paid for the entire thing right then and there. I mean, I knew he'd had more money than me, but to just pay for something like that seemed crazy to me. Even the guy giving us all the documents to sign raised an eyebrow when Chase said it would all be taken care of then. When we were finally finished, we drove to the bank in our separate cars so Chase could add me to his accounts and I could add my savings to our now-joint savings account. Thankfully I'd already been using the same bank as him, so it didn't take too long, but I thought I was going to have a stroke when I saw how much money we had combined. There was no reason a twenty-two, and nineteen year old couple about to have a baby and still in college should have that kind of money. Hell, most fifty year old married couples didn't have that kind of money. I now understood why Bree bought me Coach purses like it was no big deal. Because apparently, it *really* wasn't.

We drove back to Mom and Dad's house, and after showing off my new car to everyone, sat down for dinner and told them our exciting news from the baby appointment this morning. They were all ecstatic and we pulled out the names book right then and started going through them, highlighting names we liked, and bursting into laughter at some of the more ridiculous "Hipster Baby Names." About an hour after dinner, Chase leaned over the back of the couch to wrap his arms around me.

"Can you do me a favor?" he whispered low in my ear, my body instantly covered in goose bumps from his tone.

"Anything," I breathed and tilted my head away so he could press his lips to my neck.

"Go pack a bag for a few nights, and meet me down here in ten minutes." His lips left my neck to move to my ear, his voice dropped even lower and went all smooth and sexy, "You won't need many clothes."

My eyes widened and cheeks flamed. "Are we going to your house?" I was a little disturbed, we hadn't touched each other in *that* way since the weekend I got pregnant, and I didn't prefer to do anything in a house where my ex-boyfriend was.

"Nope, but it's a surprise, I can't tell you."

"You and your surprises." I laughed and rolled my eyes, "Okay ten minutes and I'll be ready."

I rushed upstairs and grabbed a bag stuffing it full of toiletries, and very few clothes. When I say few, I mean I only brought one extra outfit. And a pair of sleep clothes, though I knew I wouldn't be using them. I was back downstairs and in Chase's truck within seven minutes. We drove for quite a while, but the time passed quickly while we talked about things we had planned for our son's future. My mouth formed a large O when he pulled into a beautiful bed and breakfast in Dana Point.

"Oh my God," I whispered as I slowly got out of his truck, "Chase, I don't know how you're ever going to be able to top today. Finding out we're having a boy, buying me a car, joining our bank accounts, and this?"

"I promise I'll always try to top this, but I did want today to be perfect." He grabbed our bags and I followed him in. When we were in our room, he pulled me into his arms and locked his dark blue eyes with mine, "I know what I said earlier, but don't think we have to do anything this weekend. All I wanted was to have three nights of just you and me, I don't expect anything."

"I know you don't, but I want this too, Chase." I grabbed the bottom of his shirt and lifted it up, letting him finish taking it off. When it was on the floor I let my fingers glide down his chest and stomach, resting at the top of his jeans. I began unbuttoning them, but his hands stopped me.

"You're sure Harper?"

I laughed and pointed to my stomach, "Um?"

His face went blank, "Just because we're having a baby doesn't mean we have to do anything."

"Chase. I didn't mean it like that. But yes, I am sure. Now stop trying to stop me and let me love you."

He chuckled and brought his face to mine for a brief moment, then stepped back to let me finish undressing him. When I was done, he started his slow, torturous undressing of me. I was shuddering in heated anticipation long before he'd even gotten my shorts off. We stood there taking each other in, completely naked, not touching each other until he bent down to kiss my gummy bear bump, then my tattoo and finally standing up to mold his mouth to mine. He picked me up and set me on the bed, climbing on top of me so we could resume exploring each other with our lips and hands until we were both breathing so hard from the intense touches, I was begging him to take me. It was slow and passionate, and just as I'd remembered our first two times.

The rest of the weekend had been amazing, it wasn't just one big love fest, though we did get completely carried away a couple times each day when sweet kisses quickly turned heated, which of course turned into more. But the majority of our days and nights were spent holding each other and talking about everything. From our time apart, before and after the weekend in January, to our time together now, and what we wanted later. By the time Sunday morning came around and we only had a few more hours left, I was pouting, not ready to give up this precious time.

"We can do this every weekend, if you want." He kissed the top of my head and ran his fingers through my hair.

"Tempting, but then it would lose its appeal. It wouldn't be a perfect romantic weekend getaway; it would just become our weekends."

"True. I'm not ready to give this up yet though."

I exhaled softly and crawled up the bed so I could look in his captivating eyes, "Me neither, but we need to go back to real life now."

"Well not *now,* we still have a few hours." He grinned and flipped me onto my back, "I'm sure we can find something to do in that time."

I sucked in a breath when his lips started making a sensual line from my throat, across my chest and down my stomach. He bent one of my legs, letting his hands slowly trail down the inside of my thigh before doing the same to the other. He kissed his way back up to my lips and pressed himself into me, biting back a groan. His hand wrapped around my back and pulled me closer to him as we moved together, enjoying the last time we'd have privacy for this for some time to come. When we were finished, we lay there holding each other, whispering our love for one another before reluctantly leaving the bed and packing up to leave.

* * *

"HEY PRINCESS, CAN you come by the shop?"

I glanced at the clock and pursed my lips, "I'm going to dinner with Bree in a little over an hour, but I can swing by really quick. Did you need me to bring you anything?"

"Just yourself. Brian's mad because you haven't been around. And we have a new artist, she wants to meet you after hearing all our stories about you."

"I was just there last week!" We both laughed into the phone, Brian was another tattoo artist I hadn't met until after Chase and I became a couple, and he'd decided right then that I was having his baby and that Chase was seriously confused. He was one of Chase's closest friends there, and after meeting his bomb-shell of a wife Marissa, we'd all hung out several times. Even Marissa asked how Chase's child was doing. "I'm leaving right now, see you in a minute."

"I love you."

"Love you too Chase."

I stiffened when I saw an older woman sitting on Chase's counter, laughing flirtatiously with him, her hand on his arm, her leg brushing his every time she'd swing it. Chase saw me and his face lit up like he was looking at the most amazing person in the world, and I was confused that he hadn't looked like he'd been caught with his hand in the cookie jar.

"Come here babe!" When I got closer he wrapped his arms around me and kissed me soundly before turning me to the woman, "Harper this is Trish, Trish this is my beautiful Harper."

"It's nice to meet you Trish." I held out my hand and my face fell, eyes narrowing when she refused to say anything back or take my hand. She was blatantly giving me a once over with a nasty smirk on her painted face. "Or not," I mumbled and dropped my hand. It reminded me of the day Chase had met

Carter, except Chase hadn't even noticed what was happening, he was looking behind me talking to Jeff. I looked at Trish quickly again before turning away to join the guys' conversation.

If I had to guess, she was still in her twenties and was painfully beautiful. She looked like a tatted up pin-up girl, and even if she hadn't been touching Chase, she would make me uneasy. I was pulling back from hugging Jeff when I heard a loud voice bellow from the back room.

"Do I see my baby mama?!"

Chase and I laughed as I accepted a big hug and kiss on the cheek from Brian.

"Where have you been? You're keeping my son away from me now?"

I patted my stomach and grinned, "Never, why else would we be here?"

"Sup little BJ." Brian rubbed my stomach and mock-punched Chase in the arm.

"Uh . . . BJ?" I questioned, eyebrow raised.

"Yeah, Brian Jr., that's what we're naming him."

Chase, Jeff and I burst into laughter, "Did you already ask Marissa? I'm pretty sure she doesn't need another Brian to take care of," Chase joked and pulled my back against his chest so he could wrap his arms around me and kiss my neck.

Take that Pin-up Barbie.

The four of us talked for a few minutes until Brian and Chase got customers, I turned to see Trish still hadn't moved from her spot on Chase's counter.

I had to leave anyway so I walked up and tried to make nice. "Well it was nice meeting you, I'm sure I'll see you around." I offered my hand and once again, she didn't take it.

"I'll make sure to *take care* of your boyfriend for you when you're *not* around." She straightened and her smile became genuine, "Hey buddy, great girl you've got here!"

"Yeah, isn't she? You gonna stay and watch babe?"

I clenched my teeth and turned to look at Chase. "No. I need to go meet Bree, I'll see you at home."

"Alright, let me walk you out." His customer was still looking at a book, so he wrapped an arm around me and led me outside. "Thanks for coming, they've all missed you."

I nodded and grabbed for my keys.

"You okay?"

"Not really. No." I took a deep breath in and out, "I don't like Trish."

I've never once told Chase or Brandon I didn't like a girl they were friends with. Sure I'd gotten jealous when girls would hang off Brandon, but I'd usually just cut in and stop it. The pictures from Amanda had been a whole other story, but with both guys, I wasn't one of those girlfriends who told them I didn't want them hanging out with certain girls, because I knew I wouldn't listen to them if they told me not to hang out with certain guys. Carter being a prime example. It was pointless to be like that, and it made you look insecure. But I could not stand the woman in there.

"What? Trish is awesome, why don't you like her?"

"It might have been the fact that she refused to return my greeting, *or* that she let me know she was going to 'take care' of you while I'm not around."

Chase laughed and pulled me in close, "Aw, Princess, she's just joking with you. You don't have anything to worry about, she's gay."

"I promise you, she isn't."

"Yeah she is, she told me yesterday."

"Okay Chase." I shook my head and hugged him back. He was really going to fall for that? I knew flirting when I saw it, and I knew exactly what she meant with her little comment. If he wanted to believe she was gay, then by all means. "I really do have to go, I love you. See you when you get home."

He kissed me softly, pulling away far enough to look at my eyes, "Cheer up baby, I love you too."

I grumbled to myself the entire way to meet up with Bree, and after giving her a play by play of what had just gone down, she called the pin-up girl a bitch and said we'd have to go check her out on another night to see if she'd do that again. I smiled widely at my best friend. She always had my back. I was trying to stop choking on my tea and laughing from Bree's ridiculous scenarios of beating up Trish when Derek, Zach and Brandon walked in to the café.

They ordered their food and caught sight of us while they were waiting and came over to say hello. Zach and Derek hugged both of us, but Brandon just stood there never saying a word. He wasn't coming across as rude, all you had to do was take one look at his face and you understood why he wasn't adding to the conversation. His hazel eyes were full of so much pain and longing, I couldn't stop looking at them. It was like a train wreck you didn't want to see, but couldn't take your eyes off of. He opened his mouth, but quickly shut it and walked over to the to-go counter to grab the food and leave. Derek gave me a sad smile and kissed the top of my head before towing Zach outside.

"You still love him," Bree stated when they were gone.

I looked at her, afraid she was going to get mad at me, but she reached across the small table and grabbed my hand.

"It's okay Harper, no one expected you to fall out of love with him. It's a difficult situation."

"I hate what I've done Bree."

She nodded and squeezed my hand, "Do you still love him as much as you did before you broke up?"

I could have easily lied to her, but she would know, and she didn't deserve to be lied to anymore by me, "More. So much more."

"You love Chase too, right?" When I nodded she leaned forward to add, "And are you happy with him?"

"I am Bree. I don't know how to explain how conflicted my emotions are."

"You don't have to friend. I think I'm starting to understand it, and I'm sorry you're going through this. This is one big cluster-fuck you've created, but you're dealing with it the best you can." I opened my mouth but she stopped me, "I know you love Chase and I know you're not using him. I didn't have to ask that to be sure, I was just trying to see your reaction to each one. I know you'll be happy with my brother, and you'll love him better than anyone ever could. But I understand that you'll never get over Brandon, we all do . . . Chase included. People fall in and out of love all the time, and sometimes people have numerous loves throughout their lives. But you have two epic loves and no matter who you were with, I don't think you'd ever get over or forget the other."

"Do you think I'm a horrible person?" Because I sure as hell feel like one.

"Not at all. And you shouldn't either." She raised a perfectly shaped brow at me. She knew me so well.

THE NEXT NIGHT we were sitting around the kitchen table, picking at fruit and listening to Bree recap on a story of some crazy person she'd run into downtown while she was with Konrad. Chase laughed out loud and asked Bree if she'd given the dancing homeless person money when I felt something weird. My entire body froze and I glanced down to my stomach.

"Are you kidding? Of course we did! That lady was hilarious, there was no way we weren't giving her money." Bree got out of her chair and tried to recreate the dance for us.

Chase laughed and again that weird feeling happened. I froze again, and glanced down before taking quick glances at everyone else. I don't know why I'd think they would be aware of whatever was going on inside me, but no one was looking my way. I was staring at my rounding stomach and only partially paying attention to what Robert was saying. As soon as Chase started talking, there were two somethings and I gasped, reaching out for Chase.

"You okay?" they all said at once.

"Say something Chase," I whispered, eyes still glued to my shirt.

He leaned close, trying to look at my face, "Sweetie, what's wrong?"

I sucked in a deep breath and started laughing, "He's kicking! He's kicking whenever you talk!"

Chase fell out of his chair and to his knees, his hands covering my stomach. He leaned close to my belly and started talking slowly to him. I felt another kick just as Chase's head shot back, his eyes wide, "Oh my God!" His face instantly went back to my stomach and he continued to talk and laugh whenever he felt the nudge.

Everyone took their turns with their hands on my stomach, and by the time Chase went back to having his hands on me, there was only one more kick. "I think he rolled over." I don't know why I was whispering, but Chase had been the only one talking, and his voice had been so low it felt weird to break that silence. "That was incredible!" I laughed as Chase stood up to kiss me long and slow.

"My thoughts exactly," he whispered and went back to kissing me.

When we told Dr. Lowdry about that the next morning, she raised her eyebrow. "Wait, you're saying everyone else felt it too?"

"Yes," we said together, still smiling.

"I'm sorry, I guess I just hadn't realized that at first. Harper, normally moms feel the baby move around fifteen weeks, but for first time mothers it's normal not to feel anything until you're twenty weeks. Which is how far along you are, correct?" I nodded and she continued, "So you're right on track with that, but normally no one else can feel it for another two and a half weeks, at the earliest."

"Huh." I glanced to Chase, then back to her, "Is that a bad thing?"

"No, no. Definitely not bad, it's just a little early is all. Let's have an ultrasound and get the measurements." When we were in the room she took the measurements, then took them again, "Your baby is about nineteen centimeters, well closer to twenty."

"Okay?" I had no idea if that was normal or not.

"Usually he would only be around eighteen right now, so it looks like he's developing pretty quickly. Almost two weeks ahead of where he should be." Dr. Lowdry went to her computer and checked some things, "He was right where he should have been at your last visit," she said mostly to herself.

"I'm not trying to be rude," Chase was gripping my hand, "but you're kind of scaring me. Is it a bad thing that he's developing quicker than most babies?"

"No, I don't want you to think that. He's perfectly healthy, all this means is there's a possibility that Harper won't make it to her due date. I'm not worried about her delivering *too* early, but we'll just continue to monitor his growth. At *most*, I'll have to put her on bedrest in a couple months or she'll go into labor a few weeks early, which also wouldn't be bad, as long as he's fully developed. At *least*, she'll make it to her due date and have a big baby. Either way, there's nothing to be worried about."

We both breathed sighs of relief, thanked her and took our new pictures back to Mom and Dad's. We looked at the baby names book for a little bit, but decided to close it. We still had ten names that we liked, but Chase said he wanted to wait until he was born to decide on the names. I watched a movie in his arms until Chase had to go into the shop, so I left to go pick up dinner for everyone. Chase wasn't expected home until two or so in the morning, so after dinner I hung out with Bree, Mom and Dad for a while and fell asleep well before Chase even got off work.

12

GRADUATION WAS THIS Sunday, so as a good-bye to everyone, the guys were throwing one last huge party at Chase's house Friday night. Chase told me he'd stay at his parents' house with me since I wasn't planning on going, but I practically kicked him out, telling him it was the last time to really be with all the guys before everyone moved back home. Bree had been a little easier to get out, since she was planning on spending the entire weekend with Konrad before he moved back to Oregon, but still whined when I refused to go with them. Thankfully, Mom completely understood why I wanted to stay away, and supported my decision to make them go. I mean, it's a little trashy for a five and a half month pregnant teenager to go to a party where everyone was wasted and playing drinking games. I knew if I had gone, Chase and Bree would constantly be at my side to make sure I was fine, and I wanted them to enjoy this. Once they were all gone, Mom, Dad and I ordered Mexican food and piled onto the couch to watch movies and feel my gummy bear dance around and kick the crap out of me. Normally we couldn't make him move unless Chase was talking to my swollen belly, and even then he mostly just rolled now. But Mexican food was the sure way to make my boy dance. Over the last two weeks, the kicks had become stronger, and there were only a few times when other people couldn't feel him too. The second movie had just ended when Bree texted me.

> Breanna:
> Umm . . . that girl that Chase works with . . . what's her name Trick, Trixie, Tramp?

> Me:
> LOL! Trish . . . what about her?

> Breanna:
> She just showed up.

> Me:
> Ugh. Seriously? I can't stand her. Why is she at a college party anyway? Wait, who invited her?

> Breanna:
> My thoughts exactly. I'm guessing Chase did.

> Me:
> Aces. Well keep an eye on her, let me know. Skank.

> Breanna:
> Will do friend! You can always still come over . . . ?

> Me:
> Nah, I'm about to go to bed. Besides, I don't want Chase

*to think I don't trust him, because I do. I just don't trust
her.*

Breanna:
*Kay, I'll let you know if something goes down. Night love
you.*

Me:
Love you too, thanks.

It bothered me more than I wanted it to, but I wasn't about
to ask Chase why she was there. It's not like the parties were
exclusive to SDSU, but I'm pretty sure he said she was twenty
eight, and he knows I don't like her. Like I said, I wasn't one of
those girlfriends who didn't allow him to have female friends,
because he definitely had plenty, but they all knew we were together, and none of them ever flirted with him after our pregnancy announcement. Trish obviously didn't care that he was
taken or about to have a baby with me. She'd text him in the
middle of the night for no reason, the few times I'd been to the
shop since first meeting her, she was always still in his section
laughing and touching his arm, even if she had clients waiting.
And let's not forget how she asked him almost daily to come to
her place after the shop closed for a late dinner—Chase said no
every time—or all her new tattoos that she'd *only* let Chase do.
Chase said she was just like one of the guys, but I'm female, I
was now positive she wasn't gay and knew what she was doing,
and it pissed me off.

I barely slept that night. Despite telling me he would, Chase
didn't come home, which meant I couldn't get comfortable without his arms around me, I hadn't heard from him and *Chase.
Didn't. Come. Home.* Not like he never stays at his house anymore,

it is his house after all, but almost every night we fall asleep in
the same bed whether it's here or there. Thankfully most nights
was here since I still don't feel comfortable flaunting my relationship with Chase in front of Brandon. But we still ended up
there and the few times we did were carefully coordinated so we
wouldn't run into him.

I continued to tell myself that Chase probably decided to actually drink last night since it was his last party with those guys,
and to be happy that he didn't drive drunk. And it's not like I
need him to give me a full report when we're apart, but this time
I knew Trish was at that party, and that is what really bothered
me. At least Bree didn't text me again, which meant nothing
happened, but that just didn't seem to matter to me right now.
I had already taken a shower, gotten ready for the day, made
breakfast and was currently going through the baby names book
with a different colored highlighter to narrow down the names
even more, and it was only seven. I breathed a sigh of relief and
scolded myself for acting paranoid when Chase texted me.

> Chase:
> Hey beautiful, come by the house, I have a surprise for
> you.

> Me:
> Surprise? Really now.

> Chase:
> ;-) Yep, see you soon.

I frowned at the screen. Chase never did smiley faces. I shook
my head . . . paranoid, absolutely paranoid. I needed to cool it,
or I was going to drive myself crazy. Grabbing my keys and hop-
ping into my Expedition, I drove to his house trying to figure

out what the surprise was, and why he was up so dang early. I tried to remain quiet so I could sneak into his room without waking up anyone, but Brandon's husky voice caught me.

"Hey Harper, where were you last night?"

I turned to see him sitting on the kitchen counter, coffee mug in hand. My heart dropped when I looked into his gray eyes. I wanted to curl up in his arms and take back the last five months. "Uh, thought it'd be a little awkward considering." I waved a hand over my stomach.

"Oh, yeah." His eyes stayed glued to my small round belly, "Yeah, I guess. How is that going?"

"It's good," I said softly, watching his face carefully while I said the next words, "It's going to be a boy."

One of the days when we were in Arizona for Christmas, I had been in the kitchen with his mom cooking barefoot. Brandon started teasing that all I needed now was to be pregnant, and it would be a perfect picture. I had thrown an oven mitt at him, which he dodged and brought back over to me, wrapping his arms around me and kissing my neck. He promised he'd been joking but said whenever we did have kids, he wanted a boy to name him after his dad. I hadn't been ready to talk about marriage with him at that point, but in the joyful mood of that day I had laughed and promised to pop out a boy for him ASAP. Even through the laughing, he got a wide smile and his eyes sparkled. My heart squeezed at that memory.

He blew out heavily and closed his eyes, probably remembering that day too. "That's uh, that's great Harper. I'm happy for you."

My little gummy bear turned over and delivered a sharp and painful kick. I gasped and my hand flew to my stomach, I hadn't had one that hurt until then.

Brandon jumped off the counter and rushed to me, "Are you okay? What happened?"

I laughed and waved him off, "I'm fine. He just kicked me, it hurt a little and caught me by surprise."

"I didn't think they could kick that hard yet."

I tilted my head and smiled at him, I wasn't sure how he knew that it *was* still early. "Yeah, well the Doctor said it isn't incredibly common for the baby to move this much yet, but she figured since he's still so healthy and a little on the big side already that it was fine, and he would most likely come early. How did you know that though?"

He smiled sheepishly and ducked his head, it was such a strange thing to see on a man that looked like him, "I've been looking it up."

My heart warmed, "How did you even know how far along I was though?"

"I overheard Chase talking to Brad about your due date." His face fell at the same time my little gummy bear started in on a string of softer kicks.

"Oh there he goes again!" I grabbed Brandon's hand and put it on my stomach.

I don't know why I did it, that wasn't fair to do to him. I was silently cursing myself for unintentionally hurting Brandon even more, but his face lit up as he whispered he could feel them. We stood like that for a couple minutes until I remembered Chase was waiting for me, and might walk in on this. He didn't care when the guys he lived with or worked with would rub my belly, but I'm sure he would throw a fit if he saw Brandon do it. I stepped away, but kept smiling at him so I wouldn't come across as rude.

"So um, why are you up so early?"

He blinked and looked up from my stomach before going back to retrieve his mug, "Couldn't sleep last night, so I went surfing this morning."

"Good waves?"

"They were decent." He shrugged, "Why are you here this early? I thought Chase left for his parents' last night."

"No, he stayed. He texted me not too long ago asking me to come over. Speaking of, I should probably go let him know I'm here." Brandon and I hadn't shared more than a handful of words since our breakup, and I honestly would have loved to sit on the couch and talk to him for hours, there was so much I wanted to say to him.

Brandon nodded slowly and flashed a quick smile, "It was good to see you Harper."

"You too." I walked to the hallway entrance and turned back to find him watching me with a sad expression, the same one he'd worn every time I'd seen him in the last few months. "I never meant to hurt you Brandon, I hope you know that."

I hurried down the hall and turned the knob to Chase's room. It was locked so I knocked and stood there for a few seconds, pressing my ear to the door to hear if there was movement. There wasn't, he probably fell back asleep since it took me so long to get here. With a sigh I turned back and walked into the kitchen where Brandon was rinsing out his mug. He turned to leave and started when he saw me.

"I thought you were going . . . ?"

"His door is locked, he probably fell asleep again."

"Oh." He looked toward the hall on the opposite side of the living room that would lead to his room, then back to me, "I could make you breakfast? I don't have anything going on today."

"Don't worry about it, I already ate. I'm probably going to—"

A door opened down the hall and my jaw dropped to the floor when I saw Trish walk out in nothing but underwear and Chase's favorite concert shirt. She rubbed her eyes and stretched, causing the shirt to rise up farther.

"Was someone knocking?" she asked groggily.

Oh. My. Word. No effing way she just walked out of Chase's room. I spared a quick glance to Brandon whose face was getting red with anger and staring at the hall, then pushed past Trish to walk into Chase's room that now had the door wide open. Chase was asleep in bed in only his boxers, his arm stretched out where I guess Trish's body had just been. All the air left my lungs and I had to grab the door frame with one hand and the knob with the other to keep myself standing.

"Harper?" Brandon breathed behind me.

I turned and tears started streaming down my face when I saw him. I'd hurt him so badly, cheated on him and crushed him though he'd never once done anything but love me. Now here I am looking at my boyfriend and the father of my unborn child after a night with another woman. I would expect Brandon to smirk, say that karma's a bitch, and I deserved this. Instead his face was worried when he looked at me, and downright murderous when he glanced at Chase. I stumbled away from both of them and down the hall, stopping short when I saw Bree. She was standing across the living room from me with Konrad, both looking like they just woke up and didn't understand why Trish was in the kitchen. Bree did a double take when she saw me, Brandon now behind me again, and her eyes went wide as her head slowly turned back to the kitchen.

"YOU BITCH!" She screeched and lunged toward Trish, Konrad barely caught her arms and slammed her back to his chest. "You whore! He's about to have a baby!"

A painful sob broke out of my chest when Trish simply smirked at me, then Breanna. "I ha—I have to—I have to go." I grabbed for my keys in my purse and dropped them. Before I could bend down to get them, Brandon grabbed them and ushered me toward the front door.

He walked me to my car and opened the passenger door, "Get in, I'm not going to let you drive."

"Harper!" Bree yelled as she ran down the driveway, "Harper, are you okay?"

"Why would I be okay?! I thought you were watching them!"

"We were, I swear we both thought he went back to Mom's so we went to sleep."

I covered my face and leaned into the seat, "God, I knew this would happen."

"Let me take you to Mom's Harper."

"I can't Bree, I can't go there yet. I can't tell her about this."

She unbuckled my seat belt and pulled me into a hug, her tiny frame shaking with sobs. "I can't believe this is happening Harper, I'm so sorry. I swear we were watching them, I swear!"

"I believe you, it's not your fault." I let my head drop to her shoulder, "I always knew he would leave me."

"I'll castrate him for this, Harper."

I took in a deep breath and sank back into my seat, "Bree stop. This was his decision. I was stupid to think he would want to be with me and raise this baby." Bree started to talk but I cut her off, "Can you tell Mom and Dad please? I can't face them yet, and I don't think I can tell them."

"Where are you going to go?" She spoke through the lump in her throat.

"I don't know. I'll come home, just not yet. I can't handle possibly running into him right now."

She eyed Brandon warily from where he was in the driver seat, then looked back to me, "Call me. Just because he messed up, please don't leave us, we all love you too Harper."

"I won't, promise. I just need a few hours to think, I'll see you tonight. Love you Bree."

"I love you too friend." She squeezed my hand before shutting my door and stepping back to Konrad, tears still pouring down her face.

"Drive Brandon, please. Just go anywhere."

He cranked the car and turned to leave the neighborhood, my phone chimed before we'd gone more than a block, it was a message from Chase. Against my better judgment, I opened the text and slapped my hand over my mouth to cover my disturbed cry.

"Harper?!"

"Just drive!"

I powered down my phone and threw it to the back of the car, it hit the back seat with a loud smack. Closing my eyes didn't help, all I could see was those freaking pictures, so I forced them open and tried to concentrate on each individual house, tree, lamppost and car we passed. It wasn't working. All I saw was Chase and Trish, his hand cupping one of her naked breasts, eyes closed tight, lips locked. The next picture, his lips pressed to her neck, her head tilted back and mouth parted in ecstasy. Chase's forearm and below were cut off by the bottom of the picture, but from the way his arm was going down the middle of her body, I had no doubt where his hand had been. A small part of me noticed the irony that *Brandon* was now driving me away from the house after seeing pictures from *Chase's* phone, but this was different. Brandon hadn't actually cheated, Amanda had just sent pictures of herself to break us up. Chase was definitely in, and participating in the pictures I'd just gotten, and our relationship was much farther along than just a week with Brandon.

After a few more minutes of driving, Brandon spoke, "What was it?"

I stared at the road ahead of us, and then out the side window. I let another minute go by before I responded, "Photos of them. Together." I knew Trish was the one who took the pictures, since her arm was stretched out, and I was positive she was the one that sent them from his phone, but that didn't change anything. It still happened.

Brandon's right hand clenched the steering wheel 'til his fingers were white, his left ran over his buzzed hair, down his face and stopped at his mouth. "I'm so sorry Harper."

I snorted and turned my head to stare at him, "Why? I deserve this, it's what I did to you."

"No you don't." He said sternly, "You don't deserve this at all." He put the car in park and turned it off.

"Where are we?" I looked at the cliff overlooking the ocean, it was a beautiful view and there were benches near the edge.

"I came here a lot after I found out about you and Chase. I'm sorry, I can take you somewhere else, I just didn't know where to go."

"This is fine."

"Uh, if you want to sit out there, I'll wait in here. Or if you want to sit in here I can go outside."

"I'll go out there, you don't have to stay Brandon."

He gently grabbed my hand, "I'll be here, and I'll let Bree know where you are." When I looked down to our hands he dropped mine and forced both of his onto the steering wheel.

Nodding, I took off the seat belt and made my way to one of the benches. I sat there silently screaming. I screamed at Trish for continuously putting herself out there for my boyfriend and ruining everything. I screamed at Chase for doing this to our son, for breaking my heart, and leaving me for another woman when he promised he wouldn't. And mostly I screamed at myself, for hurting Brandon and being stupid enough to think that Chase and I could be together for any amount of time. After the anger subsided, the hurt came back full force and I cried and held my stomach, promising our son that I would make sure he had the perfect life. I'd been prepared for a life with my baby, one where Chase didn't want to be involved, but the last two months he'd been so convincing in playing the part of expecting daddy that it hurt to think about doing this alone. Regardless of

what Claire and Bree said, Chase was their family, and he came
first. I didn't know if I'd still be welcome to stay there, and for a
few moments I panicked while I thought about where I would
go, but I knew when the time came, I could take my money back
out of the account and go wherever I needed. I would figure it
out and we would be just fine. My gummy bear and me. I cried
until no more tears would produce, then sat there some more
trying to come to terms with what happened and how different
things would be from here on out.

Brandon sat down next to me and spoke softly, "I need to take
you to eat something."

Was he serious? The last thing I was thinking about was food.
"I'm not hungry."

"That's fine if you're not," he sighed and turned my head so
I was facing him, "but you're pregnant Harper, you *need* to eat
something."

"I told you at the house, I just had breakfast."

"It's almost five." His tone was soft, careful.

I quickly looked at the sky and the placement of the sun. He
was right, we'd been here for over eight hours. Now that I knew
how much time had elapsed, I started noticing my back was stiff,
my bottom was completely numb and my stomach was growl-
ing. I tried to stand up but was struggling after being in one position for so long. Brandon wrapped an arm around my waist,
pulled me up and helped me to the car. We drove to Panera and
Brandon led me to a booth in the back and sat in silence until
most of my sandwich was gone.

"Do you want to talk about it?"

Claire had told me dozens of times since they "adopted" me
into their family that I really needed to start sharing my feelings. Said it would kill me one day to keep them all bottled up.
I'd laughed at her then, but started opening up more and was
surprised to find how much better I felt when I did. "Um, sure,

I guess." I watched Brandon's patient expression for a few minutes to make sure I wasn't going to break down in the restaurant. That must have been why he brought us to the back. "I'm angry. Not just for myself, but for the baby. It's one thing to leave me, it's another to leave him. Even if he were to say he still wanted to be in his life once he was born, I'd always worry that he'd just hurt him in the end too. I want him to have two parents that love each other and love him. You understand that more than anyone."

Brandon simply nodded.

"I'm upset that he did this, but I don't know why I am. From the beginning, I knew Chase wasn't the kind of guy to be in a relationship, and then after that stupid weekend with him, I kept pushing him back because I knew one day he would leave me. From the first day I met him, we'd push each other away and he would ignore me for long periods of time. His family told me it was because I was with you, and he couldn't stand to see us together. But I didn't know that until you and I had broken up, and even then wasn't sure I believed it." I knew I shouldn't say this next part, but it was like I couldn't stop talking now that I'd started, I had wanted to talk to Brandon about everything, and apparently I was going to do it now, "I regretted that weekend with him instantly, I couldn't believe I'd done that to you. I was so in love with you," I choked up a bit and had to clear my throat and take a calming breath to continue, "and for some stupid reason I was in love with him too. I always had been, and hated it. I wanted him out of my mind, out of my heart and out of my life.

"All I wanted was you. But I messed up, I gave in and took that chance with him even though I knew it would eventually hurt both you and me. When you came back from Arizona, I promised I would never do anything against you again, that I would love you and try to be worthy of your love too. Unfortunately, as you noticed, I couldn't stop thinking about him. It would drive me crazy, thinking about you and our future, thinking about how much I couldn't stand Chase, and then of course how much I loved him despite my hate for him. I would go around and around, but I knew what I wanted, and it was a life with you. I had just started to realize I wouldn't get over him until I had my closure with him, but a part of me was afraid of what would happen when I saw him again."

Brandon was still silent, but his eyes were shining with tears he was working to hold back.

"Then I found out I was pregnant, and I knew it was my punishment for what I'd done to you. Like the universe didn't want me to get away with what I'd done, and my conflicting feelings, without paying for them. I had to tell you immediately, I already hated keeping that weekend from you, I wasn't going to be able to keep this from you too. You deserved to know before he did, you deserved to hear it from me in the beginning, rather than see the evidence and put two and two together. And you deserved to have a little time to try and move on with your life before I told Chase and you had to see us together."

"The time didn't make a difference Harper." He paused for a moment before continuing, "I have been wondering something though, and after hearing you just now, I'm more confused than ever. You don't have to answer if you don't want to."

"I owe you every explanation."

He ran his hands over his face and curled one over the other's fist, resting his forehead against them. "I understand that you love Chase, and when we were together you loved both of us, but you wouldn't take that next step. I was fine waiting as long as you needed, I thought you weren't ready, and then all of a sudden you're pregnant with Chase's baby? Why was it okay with him and not me? And then after, you still wouldn't be with me, but you're saying you wanted a life with me, not him. I just don't understand."

This was going to hurt him, "I hadn't been ready, and then that night with Chase happened and it clicked. I remember thinking *this* was exactly why I had never been able to take that next step with you." Brandon flinched and mashed his lips together, "I'm sorry Brandon! I'm so sorry, I'll stop. I was just trying to be completely honest with you."

"No, keep going. I need to know this." He watched me study his face, trying to figure out if I should continue, "Harper, please, don't hold anything back."

Taking a deep breath I thought back to where I'd ended, "Well, um, after you came back, I couldn't bring myself to go there with you. I already knew that you were who I wanted to be with, but I kept telling myself I couldn't do that to Chase, and was afraid that if I were to be with you, it would just be to clear my conscious. None of that was true, a huge part of the reason I couldn't bring myself to have sex with you after I'd been with Chase, was because you were still under the impression that I was a virgin, and you'd been so patient with me. Then that one night, I was ready, and Scarecrow called and you got hurt. That's why I was so frustrated on the ride over, I'd finally decided I was ready and I still couldn't be with you. I took it as a sign that I should wait. I figured then that unless you knew the truth, I couldn't tell you I was ready. And obviously, I didn't have a clue how to tell you, or if I could tell you. Then all of a sudden it didn't matter anymore, I had to tell you what happened, and I knew it would crush you."

"It did."

"I wish you knew how sorry I am."

"Why are you telling me this now Harper? Is it because of what Chase did?"

My stomach twisted thinking of him and Trish, "No, I've wanted to talk to you about all this for so long. But I didn't know how, or if I could and didn't think you'd ever give me a chance even if I tried. And honestly, I think Chase has been making sure we don't see each other."

"Why? You'd already left me for him, you guys are having a baby together."

I shrugged. Brandon knew why, I just didn't want to have to say it out loud. "Have you been seeing anyone?"

"No." He snorted, shook his head and looked toward the other tables before back to me, "I don't know how you never seemed to realize this, but I was madly in love with you Harper."

"I did know that," I said softly.

"I've never loved anyone that way, I know it was early in our relationship, but I knew I was going to marry you someday. I've dated plenty of girls, and held long relationships with a few, but none that ever could be compared to you. That's not something you just move on from, no matter how badly I want to." He took a deep breath as his face fell and stayed silent for a while, "I still can't see my life with anyone but you. I still love you Harper, baby included."

Why did he have to say these things to me? This would be a bad conversation to have at any time, but now, after what just happened with Chase, it's dangerous. If I didn't put an end to this conversation now, I'd be running into Brandon's arms in just a couple minutes. I can't give in to the white knight syndrome, not that a relationship with him would ever be that. I love Brandon. But I hurt him to be with Chase, and now Chase hurt me. I can't just go back to Brandon because Chase dismissed me. I'd be like a ping pong ball, bouncing back and forth to whoever is most convenient at that time.

"I love you too. I hope to someday marry someone as amazing as you. You are going to make someone extremely happy Bran-

don, and I'm sure I'll hate her because she got you." I smiled at
him softly, "My reason for moving to San Diego was to get away
from my life and to find out who I am, and I haven't even given
myself the chance to do that. I met you just weeks after moving
here and fell in love with you instantly, I was afraid my feelings for you were so strong only because you were my first kiss,
first boyfriend, and first love . . . but we both know that's not it.
What we had, was something rare. I screwed that up and almost
immediately went into a relationship with Chase. I need to find
out who I am outside of a relationship, before I can ever attempt
another one. And you need to find someone who will treat you
better than I did. You need to move on Brandon."

I got out of the booth and pulled my purse straps onto my
shoulder. Brandon stood too and hesitantly brought me in for
a long embrace. I tried to memorize the feel of his warm arms
around me, his muscled chest moving against my head with
every breath he took.

"In order to start this, I need to stop running from everything
and everyone. Can you please take me home? I need to talk with
Mom and Dad, and confront Chase. If he's even there."

Brandon's smile was sad when he let me go and led me out
of the restaurant. Other than a quick call to Konrad to see if he
could catch a ride with him after he dropped me off, the ride to
Mom's was silent. It wasn't completely uncomfortable, we were
both just too lost in our own thoughts to even try to have a conversation. After pulling into the drive and getting out of the car,
Brandon scrounged around the back until he found my phone
and handed it back to me. We were still silent for the few moments we stood there glaring at Chase's truck before heading
toward the front door.

"Will you promise me something Harper?"

"That really depends on what it is," I answered honestly.

His sexy smirk was back for a second before his face grew

serious, "If you guys move past this, please don't go back to him just because he's the father."

I looked deep into his green eyes and hoped he saw the truth in my response, "I promise."

"I'll wait out here for Konrad, I don't think it would be a good idea for me to see Chase right now."

"Thank you for everything Brandon, I'll see you later." I hugged him and let him cup my face for a few moments before walking in the door.

"Harper?!" Bree's concerned voice reached me before I saw her round the corner and crush herself to me, being careful not to touch my stomach, "I've been so worried about you."

"Wasn't Brandon talking to you?"

"Yes, but that's not the same." She pulled away and I noticed her tear streaked face.

"I'm sorry Bree, I really just needed time to myself for a while."

"I understand."

Konrad came up behind her and kissed her on the cheek, then pulled me into a soft hug and kissed the top of my head. "Is he outside?" I nodded, "I'll take him back then, I'm sorry this is happening Kid."

I lightly laughed, "You know, since I'm having a baby, I'm not sure you can keep calling me Kid. Besides you're only two months older than me."

Bree and Konrad both rolled their eyes at my failed attempt to lighten the mood. They kissed quickly and she grabbed my hands as he walked out the door. "You ready, or do you need more time? He won't bother you if you do."

"No, I need to do this."

We walked into the living room, and I almost chickened out when I saw Chase sitting on the couch. He lifted his head when he heard us come in and started to stand but Robert held him down. His eyes were puffy and red, and his cheeks were still wet. Robert tried to smile warmly at me, but it came out more of a grimace, and Claire looked like a wreck. She wrapped her arms around me and began crying. It took me a minute, but after recounting Bree's worry that I wouldn't come back, I realized why everyone else was upset too. Mom and Dad thought I would leave and take their grandchild with me.

I squeezed her waist and whispered so only she could hear me, "I won't take your grandson away from you Mom, promise."

"Oh honey, I'm glad for that, but that's not what I'm worried about. I'm hurting for you Harper, I love you as if you were my own daughter." She kissed my cheek, then the three of them left, leaving Chase and I alone in the room.

"Baby—"

"Don't. Call. Me. That," I hissed through gritted teeth.

"Harper please, I messed up." A choked sob escaped and his tears started falling harder. "I don't remember anything, you have to believe that I wouldn't do that to you."

"Why her Chase? The one person I hate! How could you do this to me? How could you do this to our baby?!" I fell into a chair near me and kept my eyes on him.

"I didn't. I mean I don't know, I don't remember anything! I was at the party and the next thing I know I'm waking up to Breanna and Konrad screaming at me and Trish is in my bed with me. But I swear I wouldn't touch her, I wouldn't touch anyone. I love you!"

So the tramp got back in his bed after we all left, completely distraught? Classy. "You really expect me to believe this? You *know* how I feel about her Chase, and then you invite her to a party I just happen to not be at? Everyone thinks you came back to me last night, and yet she walks out of your room this morning wearing your shirt and you were practically naked in the bed?"

"I didn't invite her, she invited me over again and I told her no with the excuse of the party. I didn't know she was going to show up."

"Why did you have to have the party as an excuse? Why can't I be excuse enough? You should have told her a long time ago that she needed to stop, that you were in a relationship and going to be a father and her flirting with you wasn't okay! Instead, you let her continue to flirt with you and invite you over to her place in the middle of the night. When I was around she would be hanging off your arm, and you think I'm going to believe that you didn't sleep with her when I *wasn't* around?"

"I thought she was gay! But I wouldn't sleep with her baby you have to believe me!"

"You're still sticking with that? That is exactly why I don't believe you, you can't even tell me the truth when you know I've seen the pictures."

His face fell, and eyes grew wide, "What pictures?" He whispered horrified, when I didn't answer he shot off the couch, his deep voice so loud I almost covered my ears, "WHAT PICTURES HARPER!?"

"Come on Chase, they were taken with *and* sent to me from your phone."

He yanked his phone out of his pocket and checked it for a minute, "I don't see anything," he mumbled.

I powered up my phone and waited for it to stop chiming from the dozens of texts and voicemails I'd received from Chase, Bree and Mom. When they were done I opened the texts from Chase and scrolled through the ones he had sent me after waking up this morning, until I got to the pictures. I held my phone out and waited for him to come get it. He took it with a shaking hand and after a moment that felt like a lifetime sucked in a sharp gasp.

"Oh God. No. No, no I wouldn't." His legs gave out and he hit the ground hard.

"Well, you obviously did." My voice was shaky, but I kept myself calm.

"I don't remember this, I wouldn't do this to you! You know I love you!"

"Maybe you were just that drunk."

"I didn't drink last night, I swear! Ask Bree!"

"Chase," my voice was low, almost soft, "just stop lying to me."

"I'm not lying!" He scooted closer to me and placed his hands on my thighs, "Please believe me!"

I removed his hands and took a deep breath, "Chase, if you still want to be in the baby's life, I would love that. But I can't continue to be in this relationship, besides, we both know it has been doomed from the beginning."

"No it hasn't!"

"I can't trust you Chase. Especially after this."

"Harper. We. Are not. Breaking up." He gripped my hands in his, his whole body shaking. "I was going to propose to you after graduation tomorrow!"

I recoiled at the thought of him asking me to marry him while he'd been cheating on me. "We need to." I continued, "You obviously still want to live your old life, and I need to not have to worry about what you're doing when I'm not with you."

"I don't want my old life! I don't want anything without you! You are my everything Harper. You and our baby are my everything." His head fell into my lap while his body was overtaken by sobs.

I sat there silently and ran my fingers through his shaggy blond hair until he calmed down and looked back up into my face, "Maybe sometime later, after you've had a chance to think about what you really want, we can give us a shot again."

"Princess please, *please* don't do this. I can't lose you."

"You don't have to," I whispered, "we can remain friends, you can be at all the appointments and I will continue to live

here if that's what you want. But Chase, you have just shattered my heart, over what will probably only be one night with
Trish. Because of that, I can't be yours right now. I can't be the
naïve girlfriend at home with a baby, while you're off with other
women."

"I won't be, I only want you."

I sat there a moment, concentrating on deep breaths in and
out, "It's going to take a lot for me to believe you again Chase,
but I'm willing to give you the opportunity to earn my trust
again. We're going to have to start over as friends though."

"I don't want to be your friend Harper!"

"It's that or nothing Chase." I tried to keep my tone composed
for the both of us.

"Baby I'm so sorry. I promise I wouldn't have done that to
you, I don't remember anything from last night."

"I told you, I'll give you a chance if you want it. But I need a
few days before we can try to be friends. I really—I'm hurting
Chase, I feel like you just confirmed every fear I've ever had of
being in a relationship with you. And I'm still not sure how to
begin to deal with this."

He kissed me firmly, and cupped my face, "I will get to the
bottom of whatever happened. I love you Harper, more than
you could ever imagine." He brought his mouth to mine again,
and I let our lips move against each other for a few moments.
I couldn't help it, I didn't know if or when we would have this
again.

Chase's phone rang, snapping us out of the moment. He
started to press ignore, but did a double take and answered,
"WHAT THE HELL DID YOU DO TO ME?! DO YOU
HAVE ANY IDEA WHAT YOU'VE DONE?!" He stormed
off into the kitchen, face bright red from anger, "No! You just
ruined my life, do you understand that?! Don't fucking apologize to me! Harper is the only person you should be apologizing

to, but understand that if you *ever* contact her, or me for that matter, again, I will make the rest of your life a living hell!" He ended the call and threw his iPhone against the wall, shattering the case and sending pieces toward me. "Oh God, Harper. I'm sorry!"

I shrunk into the chair when he came near me, he still looked like he was about to kill someone. When he saw my movements, his face fell, his anger quickly fading.

"I have to go, before I mess this up more." He brushed his knuckles along my jaw, "I'm sorry for everything. I can't say that enough Harper, I'm so, so sorry. Please don't end us though, I will earn your trust again somehow, just don't do this."

"Don't make this harder for either of us, you know how I feel. Let's give it a few days, and we'll see if we can start again as friends. No matter what happens to us Chase, I want you in his life."

"I love you Princess." With tears falling freely from his eyes, he kissed me quickly and walked out the door.

13

I DIDN'T REALIZE it was over and people were gathered around us until Bree pulled me up so I was now standing. We looked at each other, not knowing what to say, not knowing what to do. Mom was gripping both of our hands like a lifeline while Dad was standing behind her, holding her upper arms tight enough to support her. Some of their extended family came up and we all broke apart to accept hugs from them. I didn't know who most of them were, though they all knew me. There wasn't a dry eye in the church anyway, but when they looked down, or placed a hand on my stomach, new rounds of hysterics would burst out of them. It seemed too much to bear to everyone that I was holding the only piece left of him in this world. Chase.

It had been four days since the accident.

Four days since he told me he loved me, and I didn't say it back.

Four days since he died.

TWENTY MINUTES AFTER Chase left, Mom, Dad, Bree and I were sitting around the kitchen table talking through everything that had happened that day. Everyone was more shocked than I had been, but then again, they hadn't been there for every maddening moment of our relationship throughout this last school year. Bree's phone rang, and I knew it was Konrad by the way she answered it. I glanced at the clock, he should be back with my car soon from dropping Brandon off at Chase's house.

"No," she whispered, face drained of color, eyes wide, "no you're lying. That's not funny babe."

I tilted my head toward the phone and almost jumped out of my chair when she screamed bloody murder.

"NO!"

"Breanna!" Claire hissed. "Calm down!"

Bree was now staring at the phone, horrified, "We have to go!" She screeched and ran out of the kitchen, "WE NEED TO GO!"

The three of us stayed at the table until we heard the front door slam shut and her car start up. Bree was screaming from the car for us to hurry, fat tears falling from her eyes. Robert opened the driver door and pulled her out, depositing her in the back seat which I slid into after.

"Oh my God, oh my God, oh my God! DAD GO!" She screamed, cradling her head and rocking back and forth slightly.

I rubbed my hand across her back, and after I shared a confused look with her parents, he finally backed out of the driveway.

"Breanna honey, where is it I'm going?" He was talking soft and melodic, like she was a patient and he was the therapist.

She rattled off an intersection through her sobs.

Mom turned around from the passenger seat and pulled Bree's hands from her face, "Breanna, you're being dramatic, calm down and tell us what's wrong."

Bree's phone rang again and she pushed the talk button, but didn't say anything. I grabbed the phone and managed to get it out of her death grip, checking the screen first, I brought the phone to my ear and spoke, "Uh, Konrad? Wha—"

"He's not waking up! I can't get him out, there's blood everywhere and he's not waking up!"

"Who Konrad?"

"The ambulance is pulling up, you need to hurry!"

I heard him screaming for whom I'm guessing were the EMT's, and then the call ended. I realized then that we could hear sirens from the car as well and looked up to see we were only a few blocks away now. Bree was still harshly whispering unknown words.

"I think he might have wrecked my Expedition?" I guessed, still confused. Then it hit me. Brandon. He was supposed to be taking Brandon home. Oh God no. Please no. Don't take him from me.

We rounded the corner and saw the ambulance, fire truck and three SDPD cars blocking off part of the street. Dad drove down the street enough so he could park, and not block the rest of traffic, and that's when I saw everything. Konrad being pulled away by two police officers, struggling to get back to Chase's truck that looked like it was fused to the front of an eighteen wheeler. A scream that rivaled Bree's ripped from my throat and I bolted out of the car before it had stopped. I ran past the officers holding Konrad and made it by another few before a fireman caught me and swung me away from the wreck.

"CHASE!" I screamed and wailed on the man to put me down, "CHASE!" Everything was so silent, yet so loud at the same time. I couldn't hear the sirens, I couldn't hear the shrieks and sobs from his family, I couldn't even hear my own voice anymore. I can't describe what filled my ears, only that it was deafening.

I continued to struggle to get to Chase, and somehow realized I was no longer being carried away. I must have fallen to the ground and now two people were holding me so I couldn't get back up. I saw Konrad crushing Bree to his chest a few feet

away from me, both sobbing and falling to the street as well. I
didn't know where Claire and Robert were, but I couldn't make
myself look around for them. My eyes snapped back to the truck
as a few men pulled Chase through the passenger side door. He
was limp, his blond hair and body covered in blood. A surge of
adrenaline shot through my body and the next thing I knew I
had pulled away from the people holding me and was running
toward where they had put him on a stretcher in the street.

"Chase! Wake up! Please wake up!" I grabbed his lifeless
hand before a female EMT could begin to remove me from the
area again. I screamed at her and reached back toward him,
"Don't leave me like this! Wake up Chase, *please!*"

I was taken to the back of a police car where an officer was
trying to calm me down, and find out my relationship to the
victim. I couldn't concentrate on him anymore, the high pitched
silence was back. I looked over to Chase's family where they
were standing next to a couple officers. Robert was the only
one speaking, Claire and Breanna were clutching each other as
Konrad was being taken to a second ambulance so the medics
could tend to his arms. He had torn them up pretty severely
when he tried to get Chase out of the truck. Another medic
walked up to the family and spoke to the officers, I didn't need
to be near them to know what he said. Bree's jaw dropped in a
soundless scream and Mom fell to the ground while Robert bent
at the waist, gripping his chest with one hand, his hair with the
other. My arms cradled my belly as my little gummy bear gave a
soft kick. "Daddy's gone baby," I whispered.

KONRAD WAS DRIVING back after talking with, and dropping
Brandon off at Chase's house, he had seen the whole thing.
Chase blew through a red light, never once slowing down, the
driver of the semi had been going almost sixty miles per hour.

"If there is anything we can do for your family, please let us know." A couple I vaguely remembered from the New Year's Eve party hugged the four of us and turned to leave.

My eyes glanced over to the coffin and I felt the air leave my body. I'd been careful to keep my gaze on everything *but* the coffin, and now that I was looking at it, I couldn't seem to stop. I gripped Bree's arm and struggled to catch my breath.

"Breathe Harper." A deep voice commanded as someone wrapped their fingers around my wrists.

My breaths came but they were coming too fast, and my ears were ringing. Chase was in there. Chase was in that box, dead. It was my fault, why did I let him leave that night? Big hands cupped my cheeks and turned my face, effectively tearing my eyes from the front of the church. As soon as the coffin was no longer in my sight I squeezed my eyes shut and focused on my breathing.

"Good girl Harper, keep breathing." Thumbs brushed tears away from my cheeks, "Just keep breathing."

I opened my eyes to see worried hazel eyes staring back at me. "Better?"

I nodded and wrapped my arms around him, pressing my face to his blue shirt, "Thank you for coming Brandon."

He rubbed soothing circles on my back until I unwrapped myself from him and latched back onto Bree. Ever since I'd been dragged out of Chase's bed this morning to attend the funeral, I felt like I constantly had to be touching someone, to make sure that this was all real. I desperately wanted to go back home, curl up in Chase's bed, breathe his scent in and numb my heart and mind again. This was all so much easier to deal with when I didn't feel anything.

Bree's next intake of breath was audible and her entire body tensed. "You have a lot of nerve showing up here."

Trish was standing next to Mom, who after looking at her body covered in tattoos and pin up girl looks, put two and two together and stepped away. "I need to talk to you Harper." She choked back a sob.

Brandon and Konrad moved so they were in between us. "I'm not sure that's the best idea, and this definitely isn't the place," Konrad warned calmly.

She peered around Brandon, her eyes pleading, "I have to talk to you, you don't understand." Trish burst into tears and took a step toward me, "You have to know."

Pushing through the guys, I stepped up to her and waited for her to say whatever it was she felt was so important she would confront us here.

After a few moments of Trish trying to contain her tears, she finally began, "He didn't cheat on you, he loved you all he ever did was talk about you. I admit, I was jealous and I thought you had gotten pregnant on purpose, so he would have to be with you." She looked nervously between Chase's family and myself, "That night at the party, I uh—I drugged him." My face fell. What was she saying? "Those pictures weren't real. He was completely passed out." She cried into her hand, her body now trembling, "I'm so sorry, you will never know how sorry I am."

My palm connected with her face so hard, the sound bounced back to us from the walls of the church. "None of this would have happened if it weren't for you!" I screeched and brought my hand back again, but Brandon caught it and held both arms down at my sides, "He's dead because of you!" I began sobbing and crumbled in Brandon's chest.

"I think you should leave now," Konrad growled at her from my side.

I shouldn't have slapped her, I shouldn't have yelled at her, but I couldn't stop myself. Because of this woman, the Graysons lost a son and brother and my baby would never meet his father. Because of her actions, Chase's last conversation with me consisted of me telling him I didn't trust him, breaking up with him, and keeping myself from telling him I loved him. Because of Trish, my heart shattered, and Chase's stopped. I would never forgive this woman for taking him from us.

People came by the house for a couple hours after the funeral, continuing with their condolences, bringing meals and telling stories of Chase. Once everyone left, Dad, Mom, Konrad, Bree and I held each other, said *I love yous* over and over, and cried. Everyone split to take naps sometime later, Konrad with Bree, Dad with Mom, and me with my gummy bear. I was aware of the time passing, the room changing from light to dark, Mom bringing food and sitting there until I finished it all, and Bree coming in every few hours to lay next to me and cry. Other than necessities in the restroom, I didn't leave the bed for quite some time. I couldn't find a reason to, I just wanted to be surrounded by his things.

Brandon sat down on the bed, I don't know when it was, I just registered there was light coming through the windows.

"Hey sweetheart," he whispered and let his fingertips trail along my back.

I tried to ask why he was there, but I hadn't used my voice in who knows how long, and it was so hoarse and low I was surprised anything came out at all.

"You need to get out of bed Harper. You're going to take a shower, we're going to get you out in the sun, and you're going to try to resume your life."

Shaking my head, I roughly whispered, "I can't."

"You need to. Chase wouldn't want this, and you need to take care of your baby." I opened my mouth and I swear it's like he read my mind, "Eating and taking your vitamins isn't enough. The funeral was five days ago Harper, you need to get out of this house."

"Why are you here? And why aren't you in Arizona?"

"Bree called me. They're all worried about you Harper. This family is hurting, but they're trying to cope and move on. You need to too."

"I don't know how," I sobbed, "this is all my fault."

"No it's not, this isn't anyone's fault." Brandon pulled me onto his lap and cradled me to his chest.

"I should have told him I loved him. I shouldn't have let him leave. I should have trusted him. He died thinking I hated him!" I soaked his shirt in my tears as I continued to tell him everything I wish I could have changed from that day.

Brandon sat there silently rocking me back and forth until my sobs quieted and my tears ran dry. A few minutes later he climbed off the bed, with me still in his arms and walked me to the bathroom. He set me on the counter and turned the shower on, testing the water after a few minutes. Bree must have been waiting for this because she walked in moments after the water had started running. Brandon pulled me off the counter and kept his hands around my shoulders until I was steady. When he was convinced, he kissed my temple and walked out, saying he'd be waiting downstairs.

Bree helped me undress and shower, I couldn't even find it in me to be embarrassed by her having to care for me like I was a toddler. Actually, I think a toddler would have been easier. I just stood there not moving or helping at all. I had to admit though, I felt more alive after pouring out my thoughts to Brandon and the shower, than I had since I saw Chase get pulled from his truck. We dried my hair, Breanna put make-up on my face and picked out an outfit for me to wear. I would have been perfectly happy with wet hair, sweats and a bare face, but according to her, unless I began taking care of myself I wouldn't start healing. What those two things have to do with each other? I have no idea. But she just lost her brother, and she seemed to be doing much better than I was, so I didn't complain or ask questions.

I heard sighs of relief when I walked down the stairs and immediately went into Mom's arms, then Chase's grandmother's. Claire's mom had decided to stay with us for a while, I just hadn't realized she was still here. I apologized for hiding from them and promised to start living and taking care of myself. Once again, I'd failed to think of everyone else, I had only been concerned with my own hurt. We all sat around the kitchen table talking while Mom kept shoving pieces of fruit my way. I really wasn't hungry, but I knew she was worried so I kept eating everything that was set in front of me. Konrad walked in an hour later and after a lingering kiss to Bree, he hugged the rest of us and patted my stomach. I'd forgotten he was living here now too. After the accident, he'd decided not to go back to Oregon. From his wet hair, I'm guessing he'd just gotten back from working out and showering.

"You guys ready to go?" he asked, pulling Bree up from the chair.

"We're going somewhere?" I tried not to frown, they were all right, I needed to get out.

"Just having a day out, you girls need it."

Bree and I looked at each other and started walking for the door. Mom and Nana had their own day out planned and gave us strict instructions not to come back until the earliest, ten. Thirteen hours away from the house, and away from Chase's things. I had to take a few deep breaths before continuing out the door. Brandon sat in the back with me, but stayed against the door on his side and I was glad for it. I appreciated how he'd been there for me since last Saturday morning, but I was afraid with how much I'd fallen into his arms during my emotional break downs, he would think I wanted him physically closer to me all the time.

Other than the music that was turned down low, the car ride to the beach was completely silent. We trudged toward the shore,

Bree and I continued walking until we were a few feet from the tide while Konrad and Brandon set down the blanket and stood waiting for when we came back.

"I'm sorry I checked out Bree, I haven't even asked how you're doing since the funeral."

"I'm dealing," she sniffed and wiped at her cheeks, "you?"

I thought about that for a few minutes, "I'm really not sure. I thought I preferred being numb, but I can't live that way forever. Even after this short time since you and Brandon rescued me, I can see how bad it would be for me to continue on like that."

"Chase wouldn't want us to be like this." She grabbed my hand and echoed Brandon's words from earlier, "It's going to hurt for a long time, probably forever, but you know he'd kick our asses if all we did was sulk."

I cried out a small laugh and squeezed her hand tighter.

"We need to try to move on Harper, for him."

"Then that's what we'll do." I sighed.

Konrad took Bree for a walk when we joined back up, and I settled onto the blanket with Brandon.

"Brandon?"

"Hmm?"

"Don't take this the wrong way, but why are you here?"

His face fell slightly, "Do you want me to leave?"

"No. No, of course not. But you should be in Arizona, you should be dating again. Not here comforting the girl that broke your heart."

"I told you last weekend—"

"I know what you said, but I can't be anything more than your friend Brandon. You should be out finding someone that will make you happy."

"Harper." He sighed and lay back on the blanket, one arm behind his head, the other draped across his stomach where his shirt had ridden up.

"You have no idea how much I appreciate you being here, but I can't do this to you."

"If you don't want me around, then I'll leave Harper. But not because you think you're holding me back from something."

"What about Arizona? What about your mom and Jeremy? You need to go home."

He glanced over at me, then back to the sky, "I was going to tell you that morning in the kitchen, before the day went to hell. They moved out here to be closer to my Dad's side of the family."

"So they're here in San Diego?"

"Carlsbad. Mom bought a house and shipped everything here over the last month, once Jeremy's school year ended, they moved."

"Oh."

"Look Harper, if all you want from me is a friend, then that's what I'll be. But you need me, I'm not going anywhere."

I leaned back on my elbows and closed my eyes, letting the rays soak into my skin, "I need you to live your own life," I whispered.

"I am." He rolled over and got on his knees, leaning over me. "This is where I want to be, *I* need *you* too."

He softly kissed his way from my forehead, to my temple, to my cheek and finally my neck before his whole body went rigid and he sucked in an audible breath. Getting up, he shrugged out of his shirt and started toward the ocean. I tried not to look at him, but my eyes betrayed me. While he walked toward the water I admired the muscles that stretched across his strong shoulders and arms. He was far enough away now that I couldn't be sure, but I thought I saw some more tattoos, and frowned when I saw a large bruise on his waist spreading to his back. Not that I had a right to know anything about his life anymore, but I hadn't known he started again. I'd never asked him to stop fighting when we were together, but I think my freak out after the fight that had landed him in the hospital had pushed him to quit. After walking out a ways into the water, he dove under some waves and tread for a few minutes before coming back to shore and the blanket.

"I'm sorry, I shouldn't have done that."

I knew what he was apologizing for, though I didn't want him to. I couldn't handle him pressing his lips to me again either, but I hadn't responded to the kisses, and he knew we could only be friends. "For cooling off? You should be, it's hot out today and I don't have a suit." I turned to look at him, his face was guarded, but his eyes were thankful.

"We can go stand in it, if you want?"

Bree and Konrad were still nowhere in sight, and it *was* actually really warm today. "Okay." I stood up and headed out, thankful Bree had picked out shorts for me today, that way I could go in a little further without soaking my clothes. "Oh my God, it's freezing!" I screeched and backed away. "I change my mind, it's not that hot out."

Brandon grabbed my hand before I could make it far and slowly pulled me back into the water. I squealed again when it hit my ankle but bit the inside of my cheek and kept going.

"Still bad?" He grinned and I almost lost myself in that smile. I hadn't seen him smile wide enough for his dimple to show in a very long time, I was glad for it now.

My teeth chattered and I nodded my head vigorously, I started to wrap my arms around my waist when I felt something, "Ha! I don't think he likes it much either."

"What's he doing?"

"Come here." I put one of Brandon's hands on my stomach and watched his face over my shoulder. His strong chest and abs were pressed against my side and I allowed myself to relax into him. My gummy bear continued on his kick boxing lesson for a few minutes, and I smiled at feeling him move inside me. I'd been so out of it, I hadn't even been paying attention to if he moved.

Brandon continued to stare at my growing belly, his hand slowly moving so the kick hit perfectly into his hand each time. "I think you're wrong," he said softly.

"What do you mean?"

"I'll bet he's happy you're in the water. He's gonna be a little surfer when he gets older." He smiled sweetly at me.

"Oh is he now?" I touched the other side of my stomach and spoke, "Hate to burst your bubble little guy, but Mommy doesn't know how to surf. Sorry."

"I'll teach him."

My heart kicked up in pace, this conversation with the way we were positioned was now too intimate. Brandon must have realized it as well because he dropped his hand and stepped back a few feet.

"So," he said breaking the silence, "you said you think he'll be early?"

"Yeah. Did I tell you the Doctor said he was measuring big and developing quickly?"

Brandon nodded.

"Well there's that, and I mean, I know everyone's bodies respond differently to pregnancy, but I'm a lot bigger than I'm supposed to be. I'm afraid I'm gaining too much weight."

"You still look perfect, nothing about you has changed except for your stomach growing out."

"But I looked at pictures of other expecting mothers, and I'm as big as the women that are twenty eight weeks. And that was when I looked over a week ago when I was only twenty two weeks. I didn't even really look today," I frowned when I realized how long it'd been since I paid attention to what was going on with my gummy bear. I didn't even know where my *What to*

Expect book was anymore, "but this shirt is tighter than it was . . . I think I wore it the day before the funeral."

"Harper, I promise you look beautiful. I honestly think you've looked more beautiful over the last couple months than I've ever seen you. And that's saying something. You're probably just going to have a big baby, I mean Chase was over six feet, it makes sense. Just be glad your son won't be short like you."

I laughed, and it felt so good to laugh I wish it would have gone on longer. "Jerk." I socked his arm pathetically. "I'm average height . . . kinda." Brandon loved how small I was, since my body fit perfectly into his when we curled up with each other. But that didn't stop him or any of the other guys from constantly making fun of me and Bree for being short. It wasn't my fault Brandon was over a foot taller than me.

He held his hands up in mock surrender, "Just saying. Can you imagine having a boy that small? Girl, sure, but not a boy."

"I guess you're right." I smiled and reached out to interlace my fingers with his, immediately dropping my hand to my side when his look made me realize what I was doing, "I'm kind of tired, I'm going to take a nap."

Brandon stared at me with an expression I couldn't name before he sighed and turned toward the beach, "I'll come with you."

I stood there, heart aching, "This is why we can't do this. I can't be around you without slipping back into how we were."

"I want—" He breathed heavily through his nose and dropped his head, fists on his narrow hips. "Harper," he began again, turning to face me and stepping close, too close, "that should tell you something." His big hands curled against my cheeks and I had to force my head not to respond.

When he was standing this close, I couldn't think clearly. Covering his hands with my own, I pulled them down and stepped away, "I can't Brandon," tears started falling down my cheeks, "I can't handle this. Not right now." He just died. The father of my baby *just* died. It didn't matter if I loved Brandon too, that would be a slap in the face to Chase's memory and his family. I started back up the beach and when I spotted Bree and Konrad watching us, took off running toward them.

Bree hugged me fiercely, when I pulled away she gave me a knowing look. I didn't ask what she thought she knew, just helped them fold up the blanket so the four of us could go out to eat. Brandon didn't touch me again, other than to hug me good-bye late that night. It hadn't been awkward during lunch, the movie or dinner, we still spoke and laughed with Konrad and Bree, we were just aware of that invisible line we had to make sure we didn't cross.

14

THE FRONT DOOR shut and my heart started racing. I forced myself to remain calm and slowly finish getting ready for the day, but my body was aching to go downstairs. Brandon had come over every day since operation Get Bree and Harper Out of the House two weeks ago, and I'm reluctant to admit I craved the hours he was here. He tried to give me space by spending a good chunk of time with Konrad, Bree and Mom, but whenever I would glance up, his eyes would be on me and I always seemed to gravitate toward him. Having him near made my days better and chest lighter, as soon as he left for the night I'd struggle with anxiety until I could curl up in Chase's old bed and grip one of his shirts that smelled like him. I felt pathetic, but I was getting a little better each day. We all were.

"Harper, you decent?"

My breath whooshed out of my body and I gripped the vanity counter. That voice. God, that voice was like home to me. "Yeah, I'm in the bathroom."

He rounded the corner and handed me a mango protein smoothie, "If you already ate, you don't have to drink that."

I did, but I was already hungry again and greedily sucked down some of the delicious icy mix. "Thank you," I said with a moan.

Brandon laughed and rubbed my stomach, "What's up buddy?"

"He's feisty this morning." I took another sip and started braiding my hair over the top of my head and down to the side, putting the long length back in a messy bun before grabbing my cup again. "How are you?" My eyes met his in the mirror and he didn't answer at first.

"I'm good." His husky voice was soft. He offered his hand and helped me stand up, wrapping an arm around me, "How are you Harper?"

"I—I'm fine." I glanced at his chest rapidly rising and falling, then his mouth and finally back to his eyes, "Thanks for coming today."

"I'll always be here." His fingers brushed along my bare neck and he leaned down slowly.

"Brandon, don't," I pleaded.

He stopped abruptly and removed his arms as he took a few steps away, "I'll uh, be downstairs."

"Brandon."

"Yeah?" His back was still turned to me.

"I can't be with you." *I want to so bad, you'll never have any idea how bad,* "We can't keep doing this to each other."

"I know, I just . . . I know." He sighed and walked out of my room.

"I love you so much," I whispered once the door was shut.

After a few minutes, I walked downstairs and cursed myself for putting my hair up when my cheeks heated at the sight of him. He smiled softly and gestured for me to join him at the table where he was playing cards with Konrad and Bree.

"Morning friend."

"Morning Kid."

"Hey guys, good morning." I rubbed my stomach and sat next to Brandon, when the other two went back to their conversation, I grabbed his hand and leaned into his side, "Please don't be mad at me. I just can't do it."

He rubbed his thumb over the top of my hand, squeezed it and let it go, "I'm not mad at you, I'm frustrated that I can't stop making you uncomfortable."

If only you knew how much I wanted you to kiss me, "Don't be hard on yourself. Let's just go back to how we've been, okay?"

"Alright." He attempted a smile and peaked at my cards, "Thank God we're not playing with money."

"That bad?" I grimaced but was glad for his change of subject and mood.

"Bad? Harper, you don't even have a pair. So yeah, it's bad." He smiled wider and that dimple flashed at me.

My breath caught. If I was smart or selfless, I would ask him to leave right now and not come back. But I was the opposite of both, I needed him more than I was willing to admit to myself, and I wanted him here even if I had to ignore my feelings.

THE HARDEST PARTS over the next month had been clearing out Chase's station at the shop, and packing up his room at each house. I found the ring he had been planning on proposing with, but couldn't bring myself to open the white box. I'd handed it off to Bree so fast, and she'd left the room before looking in it. Mom and Bree put it in a safe; we'd all agreed to keep it, even though I still refused to look at it. Other than those times, our hearts all continued to heal and grow stronger, right along with my little gummy bear. He and my stomach were both measuring bigger than the thirty weeks I was, as of today, and Dr. Lowdry was now positive I wouldn't make it the full forty weeks. Bree put a basketball in her shirt, and I was still bigger than that. I had frowned when I saw the picture, but everyone laughed and said I was the cutest pregnant woman they'd seen. My legs and arms hadn't changed a bit, my hips were not even a fraction of an inch wider, the only difference was my chest and stomach. To prove their point, they took a picture of my back, I looked like normal Harper again . . . until I turned to the side or faced front. We were all making bets for when the baby would be born, Mom said August twenty-third, Dad and I said September third— which was Labor Day—mostly as a joke, Brandon's vote was September fifteenth and Bree and Konrad thought I should have to go the full forty weeks plus some with October eighth. The majority of our time together was spent with at least one person's hands on me, since Gummy Bear was constantly dancing, rolling around and practicing karate in my belly.

Mom and Dad were taking a lot of weekend trips lately, and Breanna and Konrad were almost never seen without the other. Though we were all healing and fully back into our normal lives, everyone was still very aware of how fragile life was, and were always trying to spend it with their significant other. With that in mind, each one of us, including Konrad and Brandon, had tried contacting Sir in some way to see if he would take back his words and let me into his life. Not one of us had gotten through or heard back from him. Two weeks ago, I had finally told everyone to just stop. Sir was stubborn and he wasn't going to change just because six people hounded him for a few weeks.

Mom and Bree were having way too much fun picking out clothes and nursery items for Gummy Bear, and buying maternity clothes for me. I was like their own personal life-size doll. I didn't complain though, it was fun and it made them so happy, so I continued to go along with everything. The only time the extended family could get together was Fourth of July, so we'd had an early baby shower when they were all in town for Mom and

Dad's annual party. The only girls I'd been friends with other than Bree had all graduated at the beginning of June, so there weren't a ton of women at the shower, but we'd all had so much fun and being surrounded by Chase's family was more perfect than I could have hoped for. We'd invited Brandon's mom, but she and Jeremy had flown back to Arizona for two weeks to spend with her family, and today would be my first time seeing her since right after Christmas.

Brandon continued to come every day and despite what we were both so obviously wanting, always kept it on a friendly level. Not saying that wasn't hard, but it's what we had to do. We hadn't brought up the day at the beach or my bathroom again, and he seemed happy just to be around. Every time I saw him he'd give me a hug, bend down so his face was almost pressed to my swollen belly and greet the baby. Sometimes just a "Hello" and "How are you treating your momma today?," and others he'd give a full recap of his and Konrad's morning surfing. It made my heart warm and stomach flip, but I wouldn't tell him that.

Like I'd suspected, Brandon was fighting again, and though I hated it, I kept my mouth shut. It wasn't my place, and it gave him a thrill and paid his bills, so who was I to voice my opinion? He still hadn't lost a fight, and thank God hadn't been back to the hospital. That didn't mean there wasn't a new bruise or cut brow every now and then though. Jeremy, Konrad, Bree and I went to every fight, I would sit there shaking and cringing until it was over, and after he'd showered and changed, would inspect his new injuries if there were any. Brandon laughed every time but let me do my inspections without complaint.

Breanna, Mom and I were coming back from another wonderful appointment of seeing my bear and getting a pedicure when my heart rate doubled. Brandon's Jeep was already in the driveway, and I couldn't wait to see him and show him the new ultrasound pictures. What was coming later, seeing his mom again, I definitely wasn't thrilled for. I'd cheated on Brandon weeks after last seeing her, and I'm sure she didn't like the fact that Brandon and I were friends again. I forced myself to walk slowly to the house, but I don't think I was fooling Mom or Bree. As soon as I was through the door, Brandon was hugging me and reaching for the pictures.

"Look at him! He was asleep, but look at him sucking his thumb!" I exclaimed. Mom and Bree giggled when they passed us. Yeah, not fooling them.

He dropped down to a squat and put his hands tenderly on my stomach, "Hey little man!" Brandon's deep husky voice was warm and melodic whenever he spoke to him. "How could you sleep through the whole appointment, huh? Your momma was hoping to see you moving around today. Next time, right buddy?"

I watched the one sided conversation, biting my lip to keep from grinning like an idiot. Brandon would be such a good father. *Whoa. Where did that come from? Don't go down that road Harper.*

Brandon stood back up and absentmindedly began tracing shapes along my stomach. "What did Dr. Lowdry say?"

"She said everything's great!" That was another thing, he always asked how I felt and how the appointments went. Even Konrad and Dad didn't do that, "I go back in another two weeks, she said he's still big, so there's a possibility she's going to put me on bedrest after my next appointment to try to keep him in there as long as possible."

"Bedrest?" His hazel eyes looked worried, "But she said everything is okay?"

I smoothed out his furrowed brow, and stared at his eyes. I'd finally figured them out. They were brown if he was shirtless, or wearing a brown or white shirt. Gray if he was wearing a black or gray shirt. Green was pretty self-explanatory, he had to be wearing green, and any other color would make his eyes the perfect mix of the three. "It's fine, don't worry about it. *If* I have to, it's just to make sure he doesn't come *too* early." He still looked nervous, "So! How about we go see your mom?"

After a few moments, all the worry left his eyes and a slow unsure smile spread across his face, "I have something for you, Harper."

"Really? What is it?"

He took my hand and started walking me down the hall, "Promise me something, if you don't like it, you have to tell me."

"I'm sure I'll love it . . . you have it in the nursery?" I asked confused when we walked up to the door.

"Promise."

"I promise." I squeezed his hand tight and opened the door. I didn't have to search around for it, or them should I say. "Oh my God. Brandon. Did you buy these?" Yes, I know that was a stupid question, but I couldn't believe this.

"Is that okay?"

"No, I mean yes, it is. But Brandon, that's a lot of money!" There was a dark cherry wood crib, dresser, changing table and a large leather glider chair. I remembered how much Brandon made from winning those fights, but I knew exactly how much these all cost since I was planning on buying them myself, and they definitely weren't cheap.

He shrugged, "I just need to know if you like them."

"I do, I absolutely love them." He'd even put the bedding in the crib that I'd bought. "You shouldn't be spending your money on this." I walked over to touch everything and picked up one of the baby blankets Bree had bought and draped it back over the edge of the crib.

Brandon came up behind me and turned me so I was facing him, "I wanted to do this for you."

"But that is really expensive Brandon."

"Harper," he smiled softly at me, "please don't worry about it."

I smiled and took a quick glance around me again, "Did you put them all together by yourself?"

He nodded, "Bree texted me as soon as you guys left this morning. I had just finished when she said you guys were down the street."

"And you set up the bedding too?"

"No," he huffed a laugh, "I'm pretty sure I would have messed that up. They must have ran in to do it while we were talking."

That made more sense. "Thank you," I reached up and kissed his cheek, "so much."

"You're more than welcome Harper," he roughly whispered. After a few minutes of us silently holding each other, his phone rang. "What's up? Yeah, we'll be there in an hour. Alright. Bye."

"Jeremy?" I guessed.

"Yeah, he said Mom's afraid we aren't going to show. So are you ready?"

I nodded but inside I was shaking my head furiously.

We said bye to the family and headed over to his mom's house, stopping to get some Golden Spoon for the four of us on the way since I'd been having ridiculous cravings for anything sweet lately, and secretly thought I needed to come with some form of a peace offering. I was shaking by the time we pulled up in front of the gorgeous house overlooking the beach, I hadn't even been this nervous when I first met her. Brandon was carrying the Golden Spoon bag full of frozen yogurt and toppings and I seriously considered ripping it out of his hands so I could use it as some sort of shield, but the door was already opening.

"Hi sweetie!" His mom smiled and pulled me into a warm hug. Guess the shield hadn't been necessary.

"Hey Mrs. Taylor."

Brandon chuckled softly and attempted to turn it into a cough, I guess he could hear the quiver in my voice.

"Oh come on now, you know you can call me Carrie."

That offer still stood? Good to know. I smiled and tried to sound normal this time, "How've you been? I love your new place, I'm so glad you decided to move here!"

"Us too! We needed a change and I love this side of the family." She gasped and her fingers flew to her mouth and then fluttered to my stomach, "Oh, look how big your belly is! How far along are you now?"

My jaw dropped, "Uh, thirty weeks." Did she think it was Brandon's baby or something? She was acting just the same as at Christmas.

"You're so close! Are you ready for him to finally be here?"

She even knew it was a boy? I shot a questioning look to Brandon but he was getting everything out of the bags and putting it on the counter. "Yes and no. I want to hold him and see him, but I think I'll miss this," I said pointing to where he was currently sleeping.

"That's exactly how I felt with both of them, I think that's normal." She rubbed her hand over it once more and turned to Brandon, "You got frozen yogurt! Oh my God it's like you read my mind! I've been craving it all day."

Apparently I'd been stressing out over nothing. This had definitely not gone as I'd feared. Brandon handed me my bowl and said he was going to check on Jeremy. Carrie sat down next to me at the table and gave my hand a quick squeeze.

"I've missed you girl! How are things? How are you doing after what happened to Chase? I was so sorry to hear about that."

"I'm okay, so is his family. We're just trying to move on, but it was really hard at first."

Her mouth tilted up in a sympathetic smile, "I know how hard that can be. Brandon was so worried about you, but you're strong, I knew you would make it through this."

"Um, Carrie? About Brandon." I gulped down an imaginary lump in my throat, "Why are you being so nice to me? I thought you would hate me."

She seemed to think about her next words for a minute, her smile now warm and her eyes bright, "Honestly, I was really hurt for my son when he told us what happened, but even then, I couldn't hate you. You'd made a mistake, and you were trying to deal with the consequences." Carrie glanced over her shoulder to where Brandon had left a few minutes ago, "One way or another, you and Brandon will always be in each other's lives. The way he looks at you is the same way Liam looked at me for fifteen years. You still look at my son that same way, even after all that has happened. How could I ever hate someone who loves my son and holds his heart?"

"But we aren't together," I whispered, it almost sounded like a question.

"Maybe it'll stay that way," she shrugged, "and maybe it won't."

I should have told her that we had to remain just friends, so she wouldn't continue to think that someday he and I might be together again, but I couldn't bring myself to say it.

"And don't think I didn't notice that you didn't deny being in love with him." She winked and took a big bite.

Crap.

Brandon came back a few minutes later, Jeremy rushed up to pull me in for a long hug, and the four of us hung out until later that night when my eyes started to get heavy. We said our goodbyes and hugged, Carrie made me promise to come around more often, and I was more than happy to agree. She was too bubbly and fun to not want to be around. The next thing I knew, my heavy eyelids slowly opened when Brandon lowered me to my bed.

"I'm sorry," I whispered, my voice raspy from the short nap, "I didn't mean to fall asleep."

He smiled and tucked a loose chunk of hair behind my ear, "Don't worry about it, you were tired."

"Mhmm. I had a great time though, thanks for taking me."

"Anytime, get some sleep." He leaned over and kissed my forehead softly once. As soon as his lips touched me, my gummy bear woke up.

I laughed once, "I don't think that will be happening, he's been asleep until now, he'll start kicking soon and won't stop for the next few hours."

Brandon slid onto the bed and put his hands under my shirt, resting them on my stomach. I sucked in a quick gasp but didn't say anything. We'd already gone way past our friend-only-touching-zone when he'd held me and I kissed him on the cheek this morning. He may talk to my gummy bear every day, but when his hands were on me, they were always over my shirt. Not now though. Now, I was lying in bed, he had his hands on my bare stomach, gently caressing it, and was looking at me from under thick black eyelashes. All I could think about was kissing him. My baby was going crazy, moving his legs and arms back and forth, and Brandon looked so happy I closed my eyes and pictured a world where this could be okay. A world where Brandon and I had stayed together, eventually gotten married and were now expecting.

After what must have been at the very least ten minutes later, Brandon leaned forward, his deep voice husky and hypnotic, "Be good to your mom little man, she needs to sleep," and then he kissed my stomach. So soft, so tender, I couldn't be sure if I'd imagined it. Then he straightened and came closer to me, "Good night, I'll see you tomorrow sweetheart."

I wrapped my hands around his neck and brought his face closer to mine. When our lips were barely an inch away I paused, giving both of us that opportunity to stop. We stared into each other's eyes for a few moments and I finally pressed my mouth to his. Our lips were still for a brief second before they began moving against each other in perfect unison. His tongue glided against my bottom lip and I opened my mouth to him, allowing us to explore each other for the first time in almost half a year. A wave of heat rushed through my body and I pulled him closer. Brandon moved his mouth in a line along my jaw to my ear and down my throat. He nipped at the hollow at the base of my neck and a soft moan escaped my mouth. I brought his face back up to mine, but our kisses slowed until he was barely brushing his lips against mine.

"I'll see you tomorrow Harper, sweet dreams," he whispered into my mouth before kissing me hard one last time.

On their own accord, my hands reached out for him, "Can you stay with me?"

Heat flashed through his hazel eyes, "Not tonight. I want to be sure this is what you want." I started to protest, but he stopped me with another mind blowing kiss, when he pulled back, both of us were breathless, "Sleep on it, we'll talk tomorrow."

I woke early the next morning and stayed in bed for almost two hours thinking about what I want. I know what I want, but I don't know if I can have that. I think I lost the right to have it, and how would the family feel if I were to start dating Brandon again? Would they think I'd never actually cared for Chase, and that every day I wasn't constantly wishing for another stupid time machine so I could go back and stop him? I felt like it would be one big *screw you* to them. I mentally kicked myself for letting myself act on my feelings for Brandon last night as I took a shower and walked downstairs for some breakfast.

"Hey Mom." I kissed her cheek and thanked her for the protein smoothie she'd made me. "Good timing . . . ?"

"I heard you in the shower, figured you'd be down here soon. How did everything go yesterday?"

"It was really nice. Like, oddly nice."

Mom tilted her head to the side and gave me her, *I'm thoroughly confused but know you're about to tell me anyway so I'll keep my mouth shut,* face and waited. I told her about the weird conversation with Carrie after we'd first gotten there and about the rest of the time with Brandon's family. I finished by lamely admitting that I'd kissed Brandon last night before he left.

She smiled and grabbed my hand, "I know you think you can't, but you *can* move on in that area of your life too. In fact, you should. Chase wouldn't want you to raise the baby and live your life alone."

"I won't be alone," I countered, "I'll have you guys."

"You will have us, always, but don't shut love out of your life. Chase would want you to have a husband, he would want the baby to have a father." She wiped a tear from her cheek.

"But isn't this too soon? I'm so confused, it's like when I was fighting my feelings for Chase when I was dating Brandon, only now I feel like I'm acting as if Chase didn't matter to me by even considering anything with Brandon."

"For a lot of people, two months is too soon. But your situation is entirely different because of what happened between the three of you before. So that doesn't exactly apply to you and Brandon now. If you're worried about us Harper, don't. We all want for you to be happy, and we agree Brandon makes you happy. We wouldn't have called him to help you out of your mourning if we were afraid you would eventually go back to him.

"If you want to do this on your own, then you should. But, if you want to be with him, don't miss your chance with him again. He's good for you, and though he has every right to be bitter about your baby, he already loves him more than we could ever hope a man in your life would." She paused for a minute and leaned back in her chair, "I know what Chase thought of him, and I promise he would be happy with your choice. He knew Brandon could take care of, and love you, better than anyone. That's why he didn't interfere with your relationship for so long."

We sat in silence a few minutes while I let that sink in. It's like she knew exactly what I needed to hear, to know the family wouldn't judge me, and most importantly, for someone to tell me Chase would want me to be happy and move on too. Claire leaned over and hugged me tight before speaking again, "I think the real question is, how did you feel after you kissed him?"

"Like I could finally breathe again," I answered honestly. "I still love him Mom."

"I know you do, sweetie."

"Is that wrong?"

"Not at all, and it doesn't dismiss the love you had, and still have for Chase. I know how you've always felt about both of them. Tell me," she switched directions, her face suddenly mischievous, "how *was* the kiss? He sure was up there longer than I thought he would be, seeing how he had to carry your sleeping butt up there."

Heat flooded my cheeks and a wide smile quickly stretched across my face. "Amazing," I said a little breathless, remembering his lips on mine and moving down my neck. Mom chuckled at my expression.

"Hmm . . ." Bree walked sluggishly in the kitchen with Konrad, "Mom's giggling, and Harper's blushing. I have to know what's going on here." She hugged me and sat on Konrad's lap in the seat next to mine.

"Harper kissed Brandon last night." Mom was leaning over the table like she was sharing some seriously juicy gossip.

"Well it's about damn time!" Bree said faking a little exasperation.

I looked at her stunned, "How can you even say that? It's only been two months Bree."

Her face fell to a sympathetic smile, "I know, but you're only holding back because you're afraid of letting go of Chase's memory. Tell me friend, has anything changed in your heart? If Brandon asked you right now to marry him, what would you say?"

Yes. I didn't even have to think about that or answer it for that matter, "But Bree—"

"Allowing yourself to be with Brandon isn't a bad thing. It's also not discarding what you had with Chase, and it's what he would want for you. We all do."

That's exactly what Mom had been saying, I looked between the three of them, my eyes narrowing. "Have you guys been talking about this? Why am I just finding this all out?"

"Because you needed the time to heal enough to the point where you would know if you wanted to be with Brandon or not. We didn't want to push you either way by saying it was okay too early," Mom said simply. "Sweetie, honestly, if you want to be with him you should. Don't let anything stop you from loving him and letting him love you and your baby."

"But I don't know how to go about this. What would be okay in a relationship with him?"

"What do you mean?" Bree asked.

"I mean—I don't know. This whole thing is just so weird and confusing. I already," I looked at them quickly, my cheeks heating with shame, "um, I already think about him playing Dad for Gummy Bear. He's so sweet with him and I find myself thinking how good of a father he would be. I'm afraid if I were to be with him again, I would just assume he would want to play that part and that isn't fair to Brandon. Or what if he didn't want that role at all? I can't pressure him into even having to make that kind of a decision."

"Kid," Konrad snorted, "I'm sorry, but really? You really think all that?"

"No. But I feel like I'm taking advantage of him or something."

"Okay, it's painfully obvious to us that he would be there for you and GB in a heartbeat. But hearing you say that, it's just so frustrating knowing that you two are doing this to each other. You sound just like Brandon."

"What do you mean?"

"I love you Kid, but God you're so dense sometimes. He freaking loves you. And I know you know that. But he's terrified that he's going to push you away with his feelings for you and GB. It doesn't help that you keep telling him you guys can't be together." He momentarily took a hand off Bree's thigh to stop me when my mouth opened, "I know why you say that, and he gets it too. But all of us are just waiting for the day when you guys finally acknowledge the fact that you can't live without each other. So you're sitting here telling us you're afraid of pushing him into something you think he might not want to go into, or you think he shouldn't have to. And when we go work out or surf, all he can talk about is wanting to take care of you and GB for the rest of your lives, but he's worried that if he says anything you'll shut him out for good. You know he told me he'd rather be your friend for the rest of his life than risk not being able to make sure you guys are happy and okay?"

"Oh Brandon," I whispered. "God I've been so selfish, he needs to go live his life. I need to make him leave."

"No, you've been stupid. I'm sorry," his hands went back in surrender as he looked at Mom, "but someone needs to say it to her. Harper," he waited until I was looking in his eyes, "you love him, and you want to be with him. He loves you and GB and would give anything to be with you. So stop fighting it, this is like ten times worse than you not telling Chase you were pregnant. And yeah, I knew then too." Bree, Mom and I all stared at him in shock, "I was with you and Bree all the time, it was obvious right away what was going on."

There was a knock on the door and the three of them turned to me with smirks on their faces.

"Konrad's right friend. If you really want this, then tell Brandon. You're the only one who's been stopping it."

I blushed and went to the door, heart fluttering. Brandon's gray eyes and wide smile were all I could look at when I opened the door. He hugged me quickly and crouched down to tell my gummy bear about how he'd gotten his ass handed to him by one of the guys at the gym because he'd been so distracted all morning. An elbow jabbed me and Brandon kissed where he'd felt it, then stood up and searched my eyes. If Konrad was right, and honestly I had no doubt that he was, then I *was* being stupid for trying to stop this. I loved him and the thought of not being with him for even another moment felt like the purest form of torture. I needed to change this. Fix it. Now.

"Morning." His warm voice was soft and unsure.

"I'm glad you're here, I was worried after last night you wouldn't come by again."

"Of course I'm here. Are you okay? After what happened, I mean. If I pushed you too much, you can tell me and I'll back off."

I smiled and grabbed his arm, "I seem to remember being the one who started it." Pulling him closer in, I leaned up on my toes and kissed him soundly.

"Harper," he rested his forehead against mine after we pulled away, "I need you to tell me what you're wanting from this. It would probably be a bad idea for me to just assume what's happening between us."

I took a deep breath and ran my fingers across the back of his neck, "I can't imagine my life without you in it, and I'll take that any way I can because I don't deserve you, but—" I huffed out a frustrated laugh, my earlier fears threatening to stop me, "It's not fair to even ask anything from you."

"Let me be the judge of that." He kissed my nose then rested his forehead against mine again.

He wants this too. He wants this too. And you're stopping it. I took another deep breath in and out before talking, "Even though I messed up before, I never stopped loving you, and I want to be with you in every way possible. The way you talk to him, and take care of us even though there's no reason for you to, well, I get flashes of you helping me raise him, as a family. And I want that. I want it bad. But I feel horrible for even telling you this. He's not yours, and what led to me getting pregnant is what broke your heart. So I can't ask you to do that. No matter how much I want it, I can't ask for a future with you because of what I did, it would be selfish."

"I tried to live without you Harper, I tried to let you go and I couldn't. To me, there is no one else, it's only been you since the day I met you. I love you, which means I love him too. Those flashes you get? I have them all the time." He cupped my face gently and leaned back to look in my eyes, "It doesn't matter to me that he isn't mine. If you let me, I'll raise him like he is, I'll take care of both of you for the rest of my life, and I promise I'll be right there with you to tell him about Chase, and how great his dad was."

Tears filled my eyes and eventually pooled over, I don't know what I ever did to deserve men like Chase and Brandon, and their families, but I was thanking God for putting all of them in my life. "If we do this," I warned, "you won't be able to get rid of me again." I laughed and kissed him softly. "I'm in this forever if you are," I whispered against his mouth.

"Forever." He agreed and scooped me into his arms, carrying me to the living room, our lips never parting.

When he sat on the couch, I pulled back slightly to smile at
him, and caught a glimpse of my family still sitting at the table.
I looked closer to see the three of them smiling at us, Bree and
Mom had tear-streaked faces. I remembered how much the entryway echoed and knew they'd heard everything. Having them
support me and being happy for us meant the world to me, as
I'm sure it did for Brandon.

Brandon had been looking at them as well, and turned to
smile at me, "I love you Harper."

If my heart could sing, it would be now. We'd told each other
in discussions that we still loved each other, but hearing him say
it right now, like this, was like the world was finally right again.
"I love you too." I trailed my fingertips down his hard jaw, and
reached up to kiss him again. "You're sure you want to do this?
Be a dad, early morning feedings, school and sports, teenage
years . . . be with me for the next sixty years?"

"I think we could try for seventy," he whispered, hovering
over my lips. Now that we'd had a taste of each other again, it
seemed like having our mouths apart from each other would
physically cause us pain. "And yes, to all of the above."

"Is everything okay Brandon?" I asked him a few hours later
as we sat near the pool after lunch. He'd gotten oddly quiet all of
a sudden.

He thought for a second before responding, "I'm afraid I'm
going to move too fast for you. You were with Chase and planning a future and family with him up until the accident. All I've
been able to think about is you, I knew there wouldn't ever be
anyone else. Over the last couple months, I tried to only be your
friend, and I would have stayed that way if you asked me to.
That didn't stop me from thinking of everything I would do if
I ever got you back though. But now that I have you again, the

only thing the time away from you did, was make me want you more. So now I'm right back to where I was before we broke up, wanting nothing more than to buy a house with you and marry you. But I don't know when it would be okay to do any of that because of what happened. And I know what you said about raising him with you, but I don't know if that's all you actually want me to do when it comes to him, just be the guy that helps you raise him. I want to be the *dad* that raises him, *his* dad. I just don't know if that's okay with you or if you think I'll be trying to take Chase's place."

"Brandon," I frowned a little, with what we'd been talking about earlier, I thought we were on the same page. Apparently not. "Okay let's clear this all up, so there's no more confusion. Considering everything we had before, I think we are way beyond worrying about moving too fast. I want to marry you, more than anything. But I don't care when that happens, it can happen tomorrow or it can happen two years from now. I had tried to explain it to Chase, but I don't think he actually understood that I didn't need to be married just because I was having a baby. With Chase though, I hadn't been planning a future with him until after he found out about the baby, I had already known way before that, that I wanted to marry you.

"I'll admit I was worried just being with you would be moving too fast after the accident for other people, but with the way I feel, and after talking to Mom, Bree and Konrad, I don't think we are. Mom was right, our situation is completely different, and it doesn't matter what other people think. This is our life together, not theirs." I laid down on my back, and put a hand over my eyes to shield the sun, "Answer me something before I continue. Being his dad, you really want that?"

He turned onto his side, his face hovering over mine, "I do."

"Good." I smiled and wrapped a hand around his neck, "I

don't want you to just be the guy that raises him. What you said this morning, was more than perfect. I want you to be his dad, I want him to be your son. I want you to be my husband and if we have more kids later on in life, I don't want *them* to be our kids, and *him*," I pointed to my stomach, "be my kid. I agree he needs to know about Chase, but you're going to be Dad to him, and he's going to be *ours*. Just like any other child we have.

"I want you to be at the rest of the appointments if you want to, and don't worry, Dr. Lowdry already knows about you. She pulled me aside during my second appointment and asked about the father, I ended up breaking down and telling her the whole story. I swear those Doctors are trained to be therapists too. She knows that Chase died, and she knows you've been there for me. Honestly, she's like Bree and Mom, I doubt she'll be surprised to see you there. So if you want to be there, then I would love for you to come with me. I want you to help me name him, and if it's okay, I want you in the room with me when I deliver. I'm telling you, I'm not going to pick and choose what you can and can't do, I want you there for everything. I've wanted you there for everything, but I've been denying myself of what I want and pushing my emotions away. Now that we're done pretending, I'm ready for it all, but you need to tell me if you're uncomfortable with any of this."

"If you were any other girl, I would be. But you're my world Harper, no matter how strange our situation may be, being with you and starting a family with you feels right."

"I completely agree," I whispered against his neck and pressed my lips there twice. "Are we all clear now? Anything else we need to cover?"

"Will you move in with me, let me take care of you and marry me?"

"Are you proposing Brandon Taylor?" I teased, looking up into his brown eyes.

He smiled and caught my lips with his, "Not until I have a ring for you sweetheart."

"Good because that would have been a horrible proposal. And in the words of the man I love, yes to all of the above."

15

BRANDON AND I had found a townhouse that weekend and were moving in tomorrow. It was a three bedroom, two and a half bath, two car garage with a backyard and it was perfect. It was less than ten minutes away from Mom and Dad's, and even though they were sad I wouldn't be living with them, they were really happy that Brandon and I were moving on with our lives. Mom said she was going to set up another nursery in the room anyway so she could babysit and to insure we would still come over often. Yesterday we had finished picking out and buying everything we needed to furnish our new place, and the things that weren't already stored in Mom and Dad's garage were being delivered tomorrow morning. We were currently starting the ultrasound at my first appointment with Brandon since he and I had gotten back together. As suspected, Dr. Lowdry wasn't surprised to see Brandon, and was genuinely happy he was there with me.

Brandon's breath caught and he squeezed my hand as soon

as Gummy Bear's heartbeat filled the room and he was on the screen. "Oh my God, Harper."

I smiled at him and looked back to the screen. Going through this right now was completely different than it had been with Chase. It had been almost magical with Chase, emotional since he died, and felt like a perfect new beginning with Brandon.

"Okay Harper, as you can see, the baby has already turned head down and dropped. That usually doesn't happen for a couple more weeks, so unfortunately I *am* going to have to put you on bedrest. He'll probably still come early, but honestly with how things are going it could happen at any time now. We need to make sure he stays in there at least a few more weeks so everything can be fully developed. If it comes down to it there are medicines we can use to help with that, but I'd prefer to not do that. So the less active you are now, the better." Dr. Lowdry turned to Brandon, "Now I'm counting on you to make sure she takes it easy, okay?"

He grinned at me, "I promise she'll be taken care of."

I rolled my eyes, he knew I could only handle being babied for so long before I started going crazy. I usually didn't make it past two days.

The next day was ridiculous, I wanted to be putting everything away in our new home, but once the furniture had been moved in, everyone made me lie on the couch and tell them where I wanted boxes to go. I continued to whine and complain until Brandon came back with another load of boxes and frozen yogurt from Golden Spoon for me. That shut me up and I decided to play nice the rest of the day. I ordered pizza for everyone that helped four hours later when they'd finished, and we had the house to ourselves by eight. Brandon and I walked from room to room so I could see how the furniture looked in the rooms, and I couldn't have been happier with how it turned out.

We had just left the new nursery when Brandon stopped me in the hall.

"Close your eyes sweetheart."

"Why?" I dragged out the word a bit.

Brandon stepped close and placed his lips to my ear, his fingers gently rubbing my swollen stomach. "I have a surprise for you, will you please close them?"

I obeyed and he took my hands to lead me to another room, my jaw dropped when I finally opened them. "When did you do this?" I glanced around at our bedroom that was dim, the only light coming from candles, and the huge bouquets of orange lilies. At least another two dozen lilies had the stems cut off and were lying on the bed.

He kissed me gently and walked me to the bed, "I made sure you were kept busy for a while. You really thought Bree wouldn't know where to put the nursery and kitchen items?" He sat me down and bent over, kissing me again.

"Thank you Brandon, for everything."

"Harper, I will love you forever, and I promise to take care of you and our kids for the rest of my life." He leaned over and pulled something out of a nightstand drawer, then dropped to one knee, my mouth popped open and my eyes widened. "Will you please marry me?"

Of course tears started streaming down my face as I nodded my head and managed to squeak out, "Yes!" I pulled Brandon's face to mine and kissed him until I couldn't think straight anymore.

I gasped when he opened the black box and there lay a thick white gold band with three large round diamonds on top. He pulled it out and gently placed it on the ring finger of my left hand. I laughed when the ring instantly fell to one side from the weight of it and pressed my lips to Brandon's, pulling him onto the bed with me. His large frame curled around my body as he kissed me passionately and slowly made his way to my stomach, which he kissed tenderly and told Gummy Bear that Mommy and Daddy were getting married. There was fire in his eyes when he brought his face back to mine and began unbuttoning my top. To be honest, with how big my stomach is, I thought he wouldn't even want me like that right now, but the way his lips moved over my throat and chest, and his fingers caressed my body, it didn't seem he thought the same. I was craving to be with him, but after a while he groaned and fell to his side on the bed, both of us breathing hard.

"Why did you stop?"

He'd been running a hand over his face and it stopped halfway down, "Wait, you're ready?" I nodded and blushed, he let out a frustrated laugh and pulled me close to his chest, "So once again you decide you're ready, and something stops us."

"No *you're* stopping us."

"Sweetheart, trust me when I say I don't want to stop, especially after you telling me this. But Dr. Lowdry told me we couldn't."

"What? When?!" I pulled myself up on my elbow and looked into his hazel eyes.

"When you went to the bathroom yesterday she told me two things. One, make sure you stay on the couch or bed. Two, do not have sex with you. She said normally, she encourages couples to have sex, but with how worried she is that you're going to go into labor too early, she said we had to refrain." Brandon smiled and kissed my cheek, "So naturally, you're ready."

"I'm sorry Brandon."

He cupped my face and looked at me with bright eyes, "Don't be. When we finally do, it's going to be amazing." He kissed my lips, then grabbed my hand to kiss the ring he'd just placed there. "It's been a long day, let's get some sleep baby."

* * *

I WOKE UP confused at first, but smiled and curled up even more into Brandon's arms when I realized we were in our place, in our room, in our bed. He had one arm under my head, the other wrapped lovingly around my stomach. I glanced at my ring and turned it every which way so the light streaming in through the blinds would catch perfectly on the diamonds. Brandon's hand started on slow circles when Gummy Bear's elbow skimmed across my side as he shifted.

"It has been way too long since I've woken up with you in my arms," he kissed the top of my head, "and I'm glad you like your ring."

"I love my ring, and I love you."

"I love you too, my beautiful fiancée."

I smiled and scooted away so I could roll over to face him, big stomachs tend to get in the way sometimes, "And I *love* that." I kissed under his jaw and his arms tightened around me, "How does Christmas time sound?"

Brandon started and looked down at me, "For what?"

"To get married. I don't want to be pregnant when we get married, I don't want it to look like a shotgun wedding. And I really want to wear a pretty dress, not a maternity dress."

"Four and a half months?" I nodded and he smiled wide, that dimple that I love so much flashed at me, "Sounds perfect." He kissed me chastely and got out of the bed, "I'm going to make us breakfast, you're going to turn our phones off and meet me in the kitchen when you're ready. Breanna's gonna hate me, but we're ignoring the outside world and not leaving our place for the rest of the weekend. They can find out about our engagement on Monday."

Brandon and I had done exactly what he said; I turned off the phones, grabbed a quick shower and dressed in comfortable pajama shorts and stretchy tank top. He made ham and cheese omelets, coffee for him, decaffeinated tea for me and cut up a melon. We sat at the kitchen table, my legs propped up on Brandon's lap, eating breakfast and staying long after it was gone just to talk and enjoy having our own place. The rest of the weekend was either spent on the couch watching movies, sitting out back in the evenings or curled up in bed. After complaining all throughout lunch the first day, he finally conceded to letting me stay standing long enough to help cook our meals, even though I did notice he seemed to make meals that didn't take much time to cook after he did allow my help. My family and his were coming for dinner Monday night to have everyone in our place now that it was completely done being decorated—Brandon had only let me work for five minutes an hour, and had done the rest himself, but I had to admit it looked amazing and I loved seeing him make our new place our home—and also to share our news.

There's something I had been thinking of since Brandon and I had decided to get back together, and after he asked me to marry him, all I have been able to do was think of a way to talk to him about it. I was sitting on the bed waiting for him to get out of the shower Monday evening, and as soon as he stepped into the bedroom in only a pair of jeans, I decided right now was as good a time as any.

"Hey, can I ask you something?"

"Of course," he crawled onto the bed and kissed me hard before sitting down and pulling me into his arms, "what's up?"

I bit my lip and took in his ridiculously handsome face. His eyes were full of love and joy when he looked at me, and coming from this intimidating looking guy, it made him just that much more attractive, "I've kind of been thinking about a name for him."

"Yeah?" His smile was playful and patient, we continued to go over the ten names Chase and I had decided on, and still couldn't narrow them down, Brandon thought it was hilarious, "And what have you been thinking?"

I took a deep breath and sat up, "You have to promise you'll tell me if this bothers you, okay?" I thought back to that day in his mom's kitchen in Arizona after Christmas, and how he'd looked in Chase's kitchen the day I told him I was having a boy.

His smile fell, "I promise babe."

"Well." My body was shaking, I couldn't believe how nervous I was about telling him this! He'd already told me he wanted a son named after his dad, and I knew he thought of Gummy Bear as his, but I didn't know if the baby not *actually* being his would make a difference to Brandon. "I was thinking we could name him Liam Chase Taylor."

Brandon's next intake of breath was audible, his mouth opening slightly. His brown eyes searched mine for what seemed like an eternity before he smiled and brought his mouth to mine, "Thank you Harper," he whispered against my lips and continued to kiss me fiercely. "I love you, thank you so much."

"I take it you like the name?" I asked a little breathlessly when he moved to my neck.

"I love it, it's perfect for him . . . for us." He cupped one side of my face and kissed my nose, "I understand why you would think it would bother me, but I promise I've never been happier than this weekend. I'm so lucky to have you Harper."

"I'm the lucky one," I whispered.

The doorbell rang, and he jumped off the bed to put a shirt on. "Can we tell them the name tonight too?" he asked pulling me toward the entryway.

"I think tonight would be perfect." I kissed his cheek and answered the door. I was engulfed in hugs and kisses from my family, Mom of course started asking why I was standing, "Mom, I'm fine. I literally just got off the bed when you guys got here." I hugged her tightly and Bree gasped.

"Oh my God! You're engaged?!" She screeched and hugged me again, bouncing over to Brandon to hug him too. She must have seen my hand on Mom's back.

"Congrats Kid." Konrad kissed the top of my head and shook Brandon's hand.

"Let me see, let me see!" Mom and Bree were holding my hand while Dad hugged both of us, "Konrad, are you seeing this? Take notes." Bree showed him my ring, then went back to inspecting it, "Did he just ask you?"

I raised an eyebrow at Brandon and smiled, "He asked me Friday night after everyone left."

Breanna dropped my hand, "Whoa wait, what? And I'm just hearing about this? You're supposed to tell me these things right away, not wait . . ." she counted on her fingers, "three days!"

"That would be my fault, I told Harper it was going to just be us during the weekend, I asked her to wait to tell you."

She turned her glare to Brandon, "For the next five minutes, we are not friends."

We all laughed and I drug her over to the living room. Before we could sit down the doorbell rang again and Brandon let in his mom and Jeremy.

"Oh Harper, look at your cute belly! You look like you've gotten bigger just over the weekend! You look great honey!" Carrie hugged me and when we pulled back I flashed my ring. She squealed and grabbed my hand, "Oh my goodness, con-gratulations you two!" She smacked Brandon on his arm, "How could you not tell your own mother that you were going to ask her! I would have given you pointers."

Jeremy hugged us and was smiling wide, "I'm really excited for you guys."

"Thanks Jeremy, and Carrie trust me, he did a great job!" I laughed and told everyone how he proposed while we walked them through the house to show off everything.

Everyone gushed over our home, and by the time the tour was finished, all the women were ushering me to the couch. I rolled my eyes but didn't say anything, I was just glad to have them there. The guys went out back to put the burgers on the grill, while I talked wedding with the women. They all loved the idea of a Christmas wedding and agreed that waiting until after the baby was born would be best. Carrie and Claire started discussing watching their grandson so Brandon and I could have some sort of a honeymoon, even if it was just a night or two alone in our house.

"Hey, Bree?"

"Yeah friend?"

"Are you mad at me for not telling you sooner?"

She snorted, "Not at all, I was joking. I'm so excited for you!"

"Well since you're *not* mad," I smiled and winked, "will you be my Maid of Honor?"

"Um, YES! Of course I will! Who else are you going to ask?"

"Just you. I know sometime while they're out there, Brandon is going to ask Konrad and Jeremy. It will be uneven, but I'm not really friends with anyone else other than everyone here. Brian and Marissa haven't talked to me since the funeral, so I can't ask her."

"I think it will be just fine to only have Bree. Either both guys can escort her up the aisle, or they can be with Brandon already and she can walk herself down," Carrie added.

"Do you think we'll be able to put something together by then? It really doesn't have to be anything extravagant. I just want to wear a dress, I want all of you there, and I want to marry him. Other than that, we can get married here for all I care."

"Oh no," Bree shook her head, "Mom has connections. It will be awesome."

"I do indeed!" Mom agreed, "We can definitely come up with an amazing wedding by then."

I smiled, "Okay! I think Brandon and I decided on December fifteenth, if we can't get that day, we can do the weekend before or after. Oh my word I can't believe all this is happening."

"Are you happy Harper?" Mom asked.

"I'm so *so* happy."

The three of them smiled wide at me and we went back to talking about the baby and wedding plans. When dinner was ready, we ate outside, adding the guys into our earlier conversation. Brandon had already asked Konrad and Jeremy to be in the wedding, we got the colors figured out, and figured out a few venues to look at this week. Most of Brandon's friends had graduated this year, and though we planned on sending them invitations, we weren't sure if they would all fly back out here. The majority of the guests would be his, and the Graysons, extended family. Mom said we could try to reach Sir again, but I wasn't going to get my hopes up. I hadn't received even an e-mail back from him since I told him I was pregnant, and didn't expect that to change now. After it got dark we went back to the living room and were all lost in different conversations when Brandon spoke up.

"So we have something to tell everyone."

"You're getting married?" Bree guessed.

I gasped, "How'd you know!" Everyone laughed and Brandon tried again.

"Okay we have something *else* to tell you." He looked at me and his face was so elated my breath caught, everyone snickered. "Sweetheart, you want to tell them?"

"We decided on a name for the baby." I was smiling so wide my cheeks were hurting, I tore my gaze away from Brandon to look at our family, "We're going to name him Liam Chase Taylor."

It sounded like they all gasped at once, and instantly started on how perfect it was, and how they loved it. Soon everyone was crying and hugging each other. When we all sat back down, Brandon held me tight.

"I don't think there could be a more perfect name for him," Robert said, and the rest of the group agreed.

"That's what we think too." Brandon responded, "Thank you all, for being there for us through everything. We've all gone through a lot of hard times to get to where we are now. But Harper and I are very thankful for your support, it means a lot to us."

I kissed his jaw and rested my head on his shoulder. I couldn't have said that better myself.

"Breanna," Mom leaned over and gave her a look, Bree quickly got out of her seat and walked toward the kitchen and came back with her large purse, "We made something for you two. Do you still plan on telling him about Chase?"

My throat locked up so Brandon answered for me, "We do. We think it's important for him to know."

Mom nodded while Bree handed us a large scrapbook. "If for whatever reason you didn't, that would be fine, no one would blame you for that. But in case you do, we made this so you could show Liam who Chase was, instead of just telling him stories."

Brandon sat the book on his lap and opened it, so the top was on mine. I gasped as we flipped through page after page of Chase. Pictures from right after he was born, to funny toddler, first day of school to sports and first time surfing. Watching him grow up right before my eyes was incredible, and as we neared the end, tears started falling down my face. This was the Chase I had known. The tall handsome tatted up artist. There were pictures of all the guys at the house he had rented for his friends to live in over the last two years, pictures of him and Bree, ones of him at the shop, and pictures of us together at the end. The first was on my birthday after Chase and I had come back downstairs. He was standing behind me, holding the picture of my second ultrasound on top of where my small bump had been and I had my neck craned up so we could kiss. A second was of us sitting on the tailgate of his truck with Bree and Konrad at the beach one day. The last two were hard for me, but I was so thankful they were in there. One was after Chase's last class of college, we had our arms wrapped around each other and foreheads pressed together. The next was of the last full night of his life, we were standing outside Mom and Dad's talking. I remember that conversation perfectly, he was giving me reasons for him not to go to the party, and I was standing my ground telling him he had to go. I hadn't even known someone took a picture of us, but it was beautiful. The sun was setting behind us, Chase was kneeling on the driveway and I was laughing while running my hands through his shaggy blond hair. He was holding my stomach with his face close enough that his nose was touching my belly button. Chase kept saying that if Gummy Bear kicked for him, he wasn't going to the party, so Chase had continued to talk to my belly, hoping the baby would wake up. But he hadn't and eventually Chase had left. That had been our last happy time together.

When we shut the book, Brandon turned to me and ran his thumbs over my cheeks, wiping the tears away and pressed a soft kiss to each cheek. He stood up and walked to the other side of the room, pulling Mom out of her chair, he wrapped his big arms around her and thanked her while she cried. This was one of the many reasons why I loved him. Beyond the tough guy exterior, was the most gentle and caring heart. What Chase and I had done had ultimately crushed Brandon. He had quietly stepped aside when he found out instead of taking it out on either of us. He had been there for me when I thought Chase broke my heart, and had helped me out of my catatonic mourning period when he died. He loved me and my baby, despite the mistakes I had made, and was now holding and thanking Chase's mother for a book to help us tell Liam stories of "how great his dad was," as Brandon had put it that day. After Mom finished crying, I hugged her tightly while Brandon hugged Bree, Dad and Konrad.

"Brandon," Mom croaked and cleared her throat, "I hope you know how much we love you too. We're so happy that you and Harper are together, we couldn't imagine her with anyone else. We know you'll take care of her and Liam."

"I will. Forever," he vowed.

16

I WAS UNCOMFORTABLE. I was tired of no one letting me do anything for myself. I was tired of constantly laying down, and I was just flat out tired. I was so big I felt like I looked like a whale, even though Brandon continuously told me how beautiful I was. He let me complain at all hours of the day, and always smiled at me. I knew he was working hard to hold back his laughter, and I was grateful for it. I knew how ridiculous I was being, I just couldn't seem to stop and if he had laughed, I'd probably snap at him.

We'd had another appointment two weeks ago, and Dr. Lowdry was even more concerned that I wouldn't make it much longer. Per her instructions, we already had the hospital bag packed, the rear facing car seat was already put in my Expedition and I was no longer allowed to help cook. I had the most absurd urge to get on my hands and knees, clean the entire house and go through all the drawers in the nursery to make sure everything was where I wanted it. Again. Of course I wasn't allowed, so I laid on the couch, and grumbled to myself or talked to my little Liam.

Brandon had started school again almost three weeks ago, but thankfully he'd talked to his academic adviser before the semester started and found out he only needed to take two more classes and he'd be able to graduate in December, a week before our wedding. He was absolutely amazing, he was always getting me anything I needed, and things I hadn't even thought to ask for. When he was at school, he made sure Carrie or Mom were here to keep me company because he knew how stir crazy I was getting. The only problem was the numerous fights he was doing. He'd told Crow once the baby was born he was going to take a couple months off from fighting, and even though we had more than enough money to get us by for a few years, he was doing fights every other night anywhere from L.A. to San Diego to save up as much as possible. I couldn't complain too much, he'd made over ten grand last week alone, but I didn't like the fights anyway, and he only let me come with everyone if it was going to be a lame match. He was afraid of the crowds with the bigger fights, so more often than not, I sat on the bed freaking out until he called to tell me he'd won.

He had dropped me off at Mom's this morning, so I could go to lunch and have a pedicure with her and Bree, and picked me back up for my thirty-six week appointment. Like I said, they wouldn't let me do anything for myself anymore. No driving and no painting my own toes, not like I usually did them or could reach them anyway, but still. I wasn't allowed.

"Well Harper, things look great, as does he. Continue to hold off on almost all activities and let's cross our fingers that you last at least another week. You'll technically be considered full term by then, but really he would be fine if he came out now. I want to start seeing you once a week now, though I don't know how many more appointments we'll get out of him." Dr. Lowdry's smile was warm as she spoke. "Are you both ready? Do you have any questions or concerns? Are you familiar with the hospital?"

"We took the tour and all of that earlier this week, and I don't think I have any questions. I'm just ready for him to be here. I don't sleep at all."

Dr. Lowdry laughed and patted my leg, "That's common to be uncomfortable, just think of it as your baby preparing you for waking up all hours of the night." She laughed again. "Brandon, what about you?"

"I think I'm good, I'm just worried she's going to go into labor and I'm not going to be at the house." He gripped my thigh, "I don't want her to be alone when that happens."

"I understand, but even if you aren't, most women won't have the baby for hours after their water breaks, so you'll have plenty of time to get to her and bring her to the hospital."

He nodded, but I knew that didn't help much. Every time he left for a fight he would tell Liam if he had to come into the world that night, at least wait until he was back from the fight. Brandon wouldn't even say hi to me when he called afterward, first thing out of his mouth was always, "I love you. Did anything happen? How are you feeling?" If I wasn't so afraid he'd come home with a broken something or other, I would laugh at him for simultaneously kicking the crap out of people and being terrified his fiancée was about to go into labor.

"Well!" Dr. Lowdry stood and gave me a hug, "If anything happens or you need anything at all, just call me. If not, I'll see you both in a week."

We thanked her and headed home for another fun filled night on the couch. Okay, I really needed to stop whining. Things could be so much worse. Brandon could not care, or he could be irritated with my moods, or worse, he could not be here at all. And I loved our nights at home, after dinner he would prop my feet up on his lap and rub them until the swelling went down. After, he would crawl next to me and press me close to his chest just so he could hold me while we watched TV. Like I said, he's amazing. I've just been super irritable lately.

"Brandon? Do you think we could do something tonight? Like maybe just go for a drive, or go to the beach? I'm not ready to be cooped up in the house again."

He bit the inside of his cheek and looked at me for a few seconds before reversing out of our driveway we'd just arrived in. "As long as you promise to tell me if you get tired."

I was already wide awake and practically bouncing in my seat knowing we were going somewhere, anywhere. "Promise! Where are we going?"

"Well it's your night, where do you want to go?"

"Beach and Pinkberry." Seriously, I had frozen yogurt or ice cream every day now. It was bad.

Brandon's husky laugh gave me goose bumps and I couldn't help but smile just listening to it, "Beach and Pinkberry it is."

He pulled the blanket out of the back of his Jeep and walked me toward the shore before laying it down and sitting me between his legs, my back pressed against him. After rolling my shirt up over my stomach, he started tracing delicate patterns on me. Liam instantly started wiggling as soon as Brandon's hands were on my bare skin.

"I'm so excited to meet him." His deep voice filled my body, "but I'm going to miss this. You're the most beautiful pregnant woman I've ever seen Harper."

I sighed and molded my body to his even more, "Have I told you how amazing you are and how much I love you recently?"

"I love you too." He brushed my hair away and pressed his lips to my neck. "What are you most excited for?"

"Watching you teach him things. Like how to throw a ball and surf . . ." I said quickly, I thought about that all day long. "You?"

"Everything."

"That's not fair babe! You have to say something."

He thought for a minute, "I want to see you hold him."

"You want to see me hold him?" I deadpanned.

"Yeah. The way you hold yourself whenever he moves or you're thinking about him, makes me fall in love with you that much more. It's tender, and full of love even though he isn't here yet. So I can't wait to see you actually hold him."

"Oh." And that right there made me fall in love with *him* more. I turned so I could face him and pressed a quick kiss to his neck, "You're going to be an amazing father Brandon. Your dad would be so proud of who you are."

"I hope so."

"I know he would."

He shrugged but was smiling at me, "I don't think he wanted me to fight for a living. He was a business man, I always thought I'd do that too."

"Do you want to? Someday, I mean."

"I'm really not sure. I should probably figure that out soon. I can't fight forever."

Thank God for that. "We have time, we have enough money to last us for a long time. I want you to just be with me for the first few months, I don't want you to worry about a career yet, okay?"

"Not likely, but thank you. I will stay home with you as much as possible for a while, but I've already been worrying about a career for some time now, I just don't know what I want to get into."

"We'll figure it out."

"Yes we will." He kissed me thoroughly before turning me so my back was pressed against his chest again.

We stayed out there until after the sun went down and were

now both lying on the blanket. My shirt was still rolled over my stomach and we each had a hand on it while our cramped baby tried to find a comfortable position to fall asleep in.

"It's getting late sweetheart, let's get some Pinkberry and get you home."

"Thank you for taking me here, even if I was still laying down for most of it, it was nice to be outside near the water." I let him pull me up and helped him fold the blanket back up.

We went to Pinkberry and my mouth was watering, Brandon thought my sugar cravings over the last few months were adorable, but I swear I turned into a crazed animal whenever I knew I was about to have some. Only problem was, if there were choices, I could never decide, which is why he usually went alone and picked for me. I stood there looking at everything and Brandon remained patient, he knew we'd be here a while. He wrapped his arms around my belly and planted his chin on top of my head, every now and then bringing his face down to kiss behind my ear and whisper how much he loved me and Liam. Then he'd start a trail of kisses down my neck and I'd have to start the decision making process all over.

"You're not helping babe." I reached my hand up to run my fingers over the back of his buzzed head, I knew that would keep him from distracting me for a while. I glanced to the right and saw two female workers sigh with a dopey-eyed look. Looking over my shoulder to see that the wall was the only thing next to us, I glanced again and saw they were indeed watching us. "Jeez, no matter what you do, women drool over you."

"What do you mean?"

"You fight in only a pair of shorts, and women practically climb over each other to get to you. You walk around at school or a store, and they trip over themselves to keep watching you. You talk or laugh, and their jaws drop and they get goose bumps.

Then you do something as sweet as wrap your arms around your very pregnant fiancée and whisper sweet nothings in her ear, and they start swooning."

His body tensed and I could practically feel his eyes looking everywhere, without moving his head, "That's kind of creepy. Wait, how do you notice this stuff?"

A quick glance to make sure they were still sighing and watching us together and I whispered, "I notice because I know what it's like to look at you, and I do the same thing. They're at our three o'clock, by the way."

"Does that bother you?" He teased, and when he shot a quick glance to our right he chuckled softly.

"Not at all, you're mine. It makes me laugh, knowing how much everyone else wants *my* man."

"I'm giving you fair warning, I'm about to show them how much I am yours."

I giggled, "Oh really now?"

"Hey if they want to watch, might as well give them a show." He turned me around and captured my mouth with his, moving his lips against mine.

I put a hand on either side of his neck so my thumbs could trace his jaw, knowing they could see my humongous ring and almost burst out laughing at how stupid I was being. Not that they had any doubt before, but they for sure knew we were to-gether now. I pulled away and smiled at him, "That was ridic-ulous." I grabbed his hand and pulled him toward the wall of yogurts.

"That was hilarious," he corrected.

"Yeah, except now they're going to fantasize about you kiss-ing them. Good job honey, I'm pretty sure they're goners now."

His deep laugh made me shudder and bite my lip, "I'm not going to lie, that was fun. I make sure guys know that you're mine all the time, it was fun to let girls know I'm taken."

"You do not." I smacked his chest playfully.

"I do. I thought guys stared at you too much when we first started dating, you should see it now. It's frustrating the hungry looks in their eyes when they look at you."

"Liar."

"Harper," he turned my chin so I was looking at his green eyes and talked soft and low, "maybe me telling you you're beautiful isn't helping, so let me try another way. I know you think you look bad, but you're sexy as hell. Pregnancy looks damn good on you. Trust me. It takes everything in me not to rip your clothes off and finally make you mine despite what the Doctor says. And when other guys look at you, I see that look on their faces, they're fantasizing about the exact same thing."

I rolled my eyes but planted a quick kiss to his lips anyway. After filling up my cup with frozen yogurt, I leaned into him and whispered, "It *was* a little fun. I flashed my ring their way when you kissed me."

Brandon's next laugh bounced off the walls, "That's my girl."

A male employee helped put the toppings on and took our cups to the register, there were now three girls huddled around it staring at Brandon. Brandon huffed a light laugh and shook his head as he wrapped an arm around me to pull me outside. We ate our Pinkberry in his Jeep in the parking lot and he had just turned the car back on when his phone rang. It was Scarecrow, Brandon put it on speaker.

"Man you gotta be there, this could make us more than we've ever got before. I already have a few bets and they're high."

"I'll be there, where is it?"

Scarecrow gave him an address and Brandon cursed, "I can't I have Harper with me, we're already ten minutes away, I wouldn't be able to get back in time if I took her home."

"Come on man, don't do this to me. The bets are only going to be this high if you're the opponent. I need you."

Brandon looked at me and took a deep breath in and out of his nose, "Fine. But you keep an eye on her, if anything happens to her, my next fight will be against you. Got it?"

"HELL YEAH! I knew my boy wouldn't let me down. See you in a bit." He hung up before Brandon could say anything else.

"I'm sorry sweetheart, but I have to take you. If you don't want me to go tonight, just tell me and I'll call him back."

"Well I don't, I never want you to go. But I know this means a lot to you."

He brushed his knuckles along my jaw, "Thank you. I love you."

"I love you too. Call your guys, I'll call Konrad and Jeremy."

By the time I was up on the platform with Crow, Breanna, Konrad, Jeremy and one of his friends were arriving and making their way toward us. They were surprised to see me at such a big fight, but after explaining our date and how he wouldn't have made it back they understood and the boys made a loose circle around Bree and I. I had accidentally been elbowed in the stomach pretty hard not too long ago, and that had been the last big fight Brandon took me to, ever since then I get boxed in whenever I'm allowed to come.

Scarecrow was jumping up and down and couldn't stop laughing and smiling. He finally leaned in and told me if Brandon won, he would be bringing home at least forty-five hundred. I blanched, that could only mean the guy he was fighting was really good. The most Brandon had ever made was three thousand. He introduced them, and the fight began along with my uncontrollable shaking. Bree held my hand, she knew how much I hated this. The fight seemed to go on forever, both fighters equally getting in good punches and kicks. Brandon finally got him on the ground and almost choked him out before the other guy, who went by the name "Demon," tapped out.

I breathed a huge sigh of relief, and Bree and I laughed shakily and hugged. Scarecrow hugged us hard and started out to the ring. I looked back at my fiancé who was riling up the crowd on the opposite side of the basement we were in. I saw Demon push someone away that had been yelling at him and charge toward Brandon, just as Brandon turned back around, Demon punched him so hard Brandon's body went stiff and fell to the ground. Demon sat on top of him and began punching him again and again until Scarecrow and some other guys pulled him off. Scarecrow rushed back over to Brandon but he wasn't getting up and he wasn't moving. I was screaming and trying to run to him, but there were multiple pairs of hands holding me where I stood. I kept getting flashes of Chase's limp body on the stretcher, his lifeless hand in mine. Bree's hand was gripping my arm so hard, I had no doubt she was seeing the same thing. A few guys helped Scarecrow pick up his body to carry him out of the room, and I broke away from whoever was holding me to get to Brandon. He was breathing, but he wasn't opening his eyes or responding to anything.

It probably wasn't the brightest idea, but there was a hospital less than a mile away so the guys carried him up the stairs and put him in the back of his Jeep. Jeremy jumped in with me so he could drive after tossing his keys to his friend. Konrad said he'd follow us there. Jeremy jumped out and ran into the E.R., when he came out he was followed closely by nurses with a stretcher. They took Brandon back to an exam room but made us stay in the waiting room. I collapsed into Jeremy's side and bawled my eyes out. I'd seen Brandon knock guys unconscious, but after a minute of smelling salts, they always woke up. Brandon didn't. There was no way this was happening.

Bree, Konrad and Jeremy's friend rushed in together, Bree was crying just as hard as me. Konrad's face was ashen and blank. This was too much for what we'd seen just over three months ago.

Jeremy's friend, Kevin, stood next to Jeremy and half whispered, "I get he was knocked out and all, but these people need to calm the eff down."

Konrad lunged at him but Jeremy jumped in between them. "I got this." He said calmly to Konrad and turned on his friend to push him toward the door, "Not cool man." I heard him say before they got outside.

Konrad sat on the couch and pulled Breanna onto his lap, she curled into him and soaked his shirt with her tears, his other arm went around me. None of us could say anything, the only sound was our sobs. My eyes seemed to not be able to leave his left arm that was holding Bree to his body. The thick pink scars from trying to get to Chase seemed to stand out even more now. Taunting me with alternating flashes of Chase dead on the ground and Brandon laying unresponsive. A few minutes later, Jeremy pulled me from Konrad and wrapped his arms around me, he was still in high school, but he was just as tall as his brother, though slightly lankier, and was able to hold me just as easily as Brandon.

"It's okay sis, it'll be okay." He softly crooned, "He's going to be fine."

An administrative nurse came up to us with a clipboard and paperwork to fill out for Brandon, and with the help of Jeremy, we got it completely filled out. When I sat back down on the couch, Kevin walked up, he'd been sitting in some chairs against another wall, and looked at us sheepishly.

"I'm really sorry. I didn't know about . . ." He looked around for a second, biting his lip.

"It's fine," I said hoarsely.

Scarecrow came running in and came right over to us, "Is he okay? Did he wake up?"

Bree and I started crying again at those questions. *He's not waking up!* I remembered Konrad's hysterical screaming from that night and my pleas for Chase to wake up when the EMT pulled me away from him.

Jeremy talked to him for a minute, and went back to trying to calm me down. Konrad wasn't having much more luck with Bree, but then again he looked like he was in shock. Scarecrow held a wad of cash in front of me and I looked up with disgust. I sucked in a deep breath to let him know what I thought about him and his money but Jeremy hugged me close, grabbed the money and shoved it in my purse while telling Scarecrow he needed to leave. He was a good brother for stopping me from saying something stupid.

"Sis, look at me," he ordered and I reluctantly looked up, "He's going to be fine. I know what this means for all of you, but he will be fine."

"Mr. Taylor?"

Jeremy and I jumped off the couch and rushed over to the Doctor.

"Are you family of Mr. Taylor?"

"I'm his brother, this is his fiancée," Jeremy answered, keeping a tight grip on my upper arm in case I fainted, which I definitely felt like I was about to do.

"He's awake, and you can see him. Only one person at a time, but I have some questions before you go back there. Can you tell me how this happened?"

Jeremy replayed what happened after the fight had ended for the Doctor who nodded and looked at his watch.

"We should have the X-ray back in a few minutes, if there's anything suspicious I'll be running more tests, but you may go in and see him now if you'd like."

After making sure I was going to stay vertical, Jeremy let go and walked back to the group.

"Miss? Do you need a wheelchair?" the Doctor asked looking at my swollen stomach and pale face.

"I'm fine, just please take me to see him."

We walked down two halls and into a room. Brandon sighed in relief and reached an arm toward me. "Come here sweetheart."

I grabbed his hand with both of mine, no longer caring about the tears still falling down my cheeks. "Are you okay?"

"I'm fine, just feel like I got my ass beat." He huffed a laugh.

"This isn't funny. You weren't waking up Brandon!"

"I know." He pulled my arm closer to his body, "Come here." He kissed me twice and held my face in his hands. "I'm sorry, he was dirty, I wasn't expecting that. I'll make sure it doesn't happen again though. That's the first time I've had someone do that."

I pulled away abruptly, "Again? No! Brandon, you can't fight again. Do you know what it was like seeing you like that? Unresponsive on the ground? I can't lose you too." I sobbed and fell into the chair next to the bed.

Brandon tried to get off the bed, but the IV was keeping him there. "You won't lose me sweetheart, I promise. I'll be more careful."

My entire body was shaking hard, I was trying to take calming breaths but it wasn't an easy thing to do. I thought watching Chase die on the ground was the worst thing I would ever experience in my life. I was wrong. Seeing Brandon like that, and thinking I was going to lose him too, that was the worst moment of my life by far.

There was a knock on the door, "Mr. Taylor?"

I looked up to see the Doctor walking in. I wish he had more emotion, his face looked like he could easily be delivering good news or bad news.

"It looks like you're going to be okay, you have a major concussion and we're going to have to keep you for a while to make sure nothing happens. But there isn't too much swelling, so that's a good thing. I do need to stress something though. You fight often, is that correct?"

Brandon nodded.

"I can't tell you what to do, but it would be wise for you to consider retiring from your fighting. Hits like the one you received tonight, can easily cause much more severe damage. Permanent damage. You were extremely lucky tonight, but since you suffered from a hit like the one tonight, even a minor one can cause damage if received the wrong way." He looked over a couple papers, and stayed looking at them as he spoke again, "We'll monitor you for the next four hours, and if you seem to be recovering fine, you can go home. Any questions?"

Brandon looked at me, and spoke softly. "No. Thank you Doctor." After he shut the door Brandon continued to watch me silently cry and hold my stomach for a few minutes, "Harper—"

I shook my head and moved farther from his reaching hand.

"Hey guys," Jeremy said as he walked in, "sis, you mind if I talk to him for a bit?"

I didn't say anything, I just stood up and walked out. Brandon called my name twice but I kept walking. When I got back to Konrad, Breanna and Kevin, I relayed what the Doctor said, and how Brandon planned to keep fighting. Konrad went to the bathroom and Bree held me while we waited for Jeremy to come back. Thankfully guys don't talk long, and he was walking back into the room in no time.

"He wants to talk to you."

I nodded and walked back down the halls, the door was cracked and I heard Brandon's rich voice filling the room.

"I'm sure it looked bad, but I really am fine."

"You don't get it man. You weren't there that night with Chase." I realized it was Konrad and stepped closer.

"I know that, but this is the first time something like this has happened, and it wasn't even during the fight. I make really good money, more than enough to support her and our family. I can't just stop because of one hit."

"You won't be supporting them if you take another hit like that and it paralyzes you."

"I won't." Brandon groaned.

"Look you can do whatever you want. Despite what Harper says tonight, she loves you enough that she would never actually stop you from doing something you wanted to do. But your girl wasn't the only one who thought you were gone. It was like a complete flashback of that night for all of us. People normally wake up from smelling salts, you didn't. You didn't even move."

"I didn't know they used them."

"Well they did, three different times. She has every right to be terrified that she's going to lose you like she lost Chase. Only this time, I don't know if she would be able to move on. I understand that you didn't see her side of things after you broke up, but we did. Everyone knew she was still madly in love with you, even Chase knew it but he never brought it up. We all knew he would never hold her heart the way you did. But you *did* see her the morning before he died, and you saw what that, and his death did to her."

"It was like she wasn't even there anymore," Brandon whispered.

"Exactly. *I* had to watch two police officers hold her down and she still escaped them to get to Chase. I watched her scream for him to wake up even though she knew he wouldn't. But tonight? Random guys standing near us even helped in trying to keep her away from the ring. She got away from four grown men tonight. Four! *And* she's about to have a baby. The fear in her eyes and voice, was like nothing I've ever seen before. It was as if her reason for existing was lying motionless on the floor. Losing you would kill her, I have no doubt about that. So do what you want, but consider her and your baby before you go out there again."

"I do consider them, I'm doing this to support them!"

"You can find another way to support them. Do you want her to always be worried that you won't come home one night from this?"

"No." Brandon took a few deep breaths in and out, "Seeing her like that tonight, I felt like someone stabbed me and kept turning the knife. I hate that I put her through that."

"Yet you still told her you weren't going to stop fighting?" Konrad challenged, "If you love her like you say you do, you'll take care of yourself so you can take care of them."

"I love her more than my own life," Brandon growled.

Konrad sighed, "I know you do man, I shouldn't have said that. You both mean a lot to me, I love you like family. I don't want to see either of you hurt." He took a couple steps toward the door and stopped. "Listen, she messed up with you once, and she's paying for it. She'll pay for it every day for the rest of her life. But she would never do anything again to hurt you. Think about that." Konrad stepped through the door and shut it behind him, he jerked back when he saw me. "Hey Kid."

I hugged him tight and cried on his shoulder.

"Did you uh, did you hear that?"

"Most of it."

"Aw hell. I'm sorry Kid, I didn't mean for you to hear that."

I wiped my cheeks and stood up straight, "It's fine. Thanks for talking to him, I really appreciate it." I traced some of the scars and his body started shaking when he looked down at them as well, "I appreciate everything you've ever done. And I love you too Konrad." I smiled and after another quick hug from him, waited until he rounded the corner before knocking and walking in.

"Hey sweetheart." Brandon's voice was thick with emotion, he could barely tilt his lips up in a smile.

"You feel okay?"

He shook his head slightly, "Not really, no."

"No?" I asked alarmed and rushed to his side. "What's wrong?"

"No, no. Nothing like that, I'm sorry I didn't mean to scare you," he sighed heavily, "again."

I pulled the chair back up toward his bed so I could still touch him. "I heard you and Konrad."

"You did?"

"Yeah," I breathed.

"Harper, I hope you know how much I love you."

"I do, trust me I do."

"I'm so sorry for putting you through this tonight. I didn't know how bad it had been. I didn't know how it all had gone down for everyone that was still awake."

I smiled and ran my hand over his buzzed hair, "You scared me. I thought I was going to lose my best friend and the love of my life."

"I know Harper, and I'm so sorry. I can't say that enough, you can't imagine how sorry I am. I shouldn't have gone tonight, and I won't go anymore. No amount of money is worth putting you through that."

"You and I, we've had too much loss in our lives already. Do you think we could attempt to not add to that?"

He nodded and pulled me to him, "I'm not going anywhere. I promised you forever, didn't I?"

"Forever," I agreed.

"Come here," he scooted to the far right side of the bed and rolled onto his left side, "you're still on bedrest, and I haven't been taking care of you tonight."

I lay down on my back and sighed at having Brandon's warm

body pressed against mine and finally relaxing. Dr. Lowdry may have a point to this whole bedrest thing, my entire body had been aching to lay down.

Brandon kissed me softly and placed a hand on my belly. "Are you two doing okay? Physically?"

"Yeah, he went to sleep right before I came in here the first time."

"Good, I want you to sleep too. I'll wake you up when we're going to go home."

I couldn't even protest, it had been a long day anyway, and what happened tonight had exhausted me to the point where I thought I could fall asleep standing. I felt Brandon's lips on my forehead and heard his whispers of his love for me, but I was out before I could respond.

17

"HOW ARE YOU feeling sweetheart?" Brandon asked popping his head into the bathroom where I was finishing my make-up.

"I feel great! I'm so excited to get out of the house again, you have no idea." Not that it had been long since we were out, we were just out Thursday night, the night of the fight, and it was only Monday. But I'd had so much energy the last two days, Brandon promised if I took a shower, got ready and was still feeling fine, he would take me out to dinner, then to see Mom and Dad.

He wrapped his arms around me and brushed his lips lightly against my neck, I almost groaned from the heated pleasure that instantly zinged through my body. "You look incredible."

"Not so bad yourself," I said a little breathless, remembering our first date and he laughed against my throat.

"Are you about ready to go? Because if we don't leave soon, I'm not sure we ever will." He pressed his body closer to mine and tightened his arms.

"I kind of hate Dr. Lowdry right now."

Brandon laughed and released me, "We've made it this long, we can wait a few more weeks. Go get changed, I'll be in the living room."

I pouted but left the bathroom and walked to the closet. I chose one of the shirts Bree had gotten me for my birthday. Those things had definitely lasted the entire pregnancy. I plucked the dark blue one and a flowy knee-length white cotton skirt from their hangers and walked back out of the closet. Hooking my thumbs into the waist band of my sweats, I started to pull them down when I felt something pop and my legs instantly got warm and wet. *Oh my God I just peed myself!* You have got to be kidding me, I've made it this far in the pregnancy without having an accident, and I get all cute for a date and I freaking pee on myself? I didn't even have to go. Frustrated, I threw my sweats into the hamper, walked back to the bathroom and hopped into the shower, being careful to keep my hair and face away from the water. I reached out to turn the water back off and froze. Oh. My. Word.

"BRANDON!" I stepped out of the shower and wrapped a towel around me, "Brandon!"

He came bursting through the door less than a second later, "What's wrong?!" His eyes were wide and panicked. "Are you okay?"

I laughed and nodded, "My water just broke!"

"Are you serious?" His face fell for a few beats then broke out into a wide grin. Closing the distance between us he kissed me until my knees were weak. When he pulled back, he cupped my cheeks tenderly and smiled. "So he's coming?"

"Guess so, you ready for this?"

Brandon suddenly gasped, "Wait, we have to go! That means we have to go!" He turned around and took off into the bedroom. By the time I dried myself off, I could hear him on the phone with either my family or his.

I felt strangely calm as I pulled on the dark blue shirt, and searched around for a clean pair of sweats. Brandon rushed out of the room with the hospital bag, I heard the front door open, close, open and close again before he came running back to me. I was sitting on the bed smiling at his behavior.

"Harper, we have to go. Come on sweetheart, is there anything else you can think of?"

"Phone chargers." I watched as he yanked both of ours from the wall. "Headphones, can you grab me one of your sweatshirts?" I didn't care if it was September, the nights were cool, and when we'd been in that hospital last week, it was freezing.

"What else?"

"I need you to kiss me, then calm down and drive us to the hospital." I smiled against his eager lips as he gently pulled me to my feet and led me out of our house.

As soon as we were driving, he was back on the phone calling the rest of our family. He was so excited, his smile stretched across his face farther than I'd ever seen it, and all I could do was sit there and stare at my favorite dimple. I reached out and ran my fingers over his buzzed hair and he looked over quickly before looking back to the road.

"Are you okay?" he asked as he set his phone down in one of the cup holders, "You're really quiet."

I shrugged, "I'm great. I was expecting it to hurt or something, or to freak out. But I'm just really happy. I feel peaceful. Is that weird or what?"

Yeah. That didn't last long. Right before I was taken to my room the contractions started getting really painful, another two hours later and they were even worse and coming much too often for my liking. I gripped Brandon's hand tight as another one started and he brushed a few loose strands of hair behind my ear before resting his forehead against mine.

"Good job Harper, it's almost done. I love you so much." His deep voice was slow and rhythmic, I'm pretty sure it was the only thing keeping me from screaming right now.

I blew out a deep breath when it was over and relaxed my hold on him. He kissed my lips softly and sat back in the chair, keeping his hand wrapped around mine. If there was ever a next time, I was definitely getting the epidural, I didn't care what they had to stick in my back. I looked around at my family and smiled at them. They were all caught in conversations, reading books, or talking on their phones to extended family and friends. Jeremy walked back in with bags and boxes from In N Out.

"I hate you," I grumbled as I caught a big whiff of the delicious food.

"Sorry sis," he grinned and started passing out the food, "I got you a cup of ice."

I narrowed my eyes and everyone but Brandon laughed. He shook his head when Jeremy passed him his food and I pulled my hand from his. "I know what you're doing, if you don't go eat, you're not staying in here when it's time." We obviously hadn't gone to dinner, so I was starving, and he hated that all he could do for me was get me more ice.

He looked at me for a moment, brow furrowed, then with a sigh walked to the side of the room where the food was. I put my headphones back in my ears and closed my eyes. When another contraction hit I gripped the side of the bed and tried not to inhale too deeply, I knew Brandon would come right back to my side if he knew what was going on. But since I couldn't hear them, I'd forgotten about the monitors and within seconds his hand pried my fingers from the thin mattress and held it tight until it was over. When I relaxed, he kissed my hand and went back to his dinner.

Another hour went by and everyone was now curled up on the couches and chairs watching something on the muted TV. Brandon helped me onto my side, and when I was comfortable he brought his chair around the bed so he could be facing me and rested his head next to my chest. One hand acting as his pillow, the other holding mine loosely for when I would need it again. I was glad he was going to get some sleep. I knew when I rolled to the side, he would think I was going to sleep as well, and would do the same. But that hadn't been my reasoning. I was now in so much pain, I couldn't hide it anymore and I didn't want the family to see. My face twisted when another one hit, but I kept my fingers from curling around Brandon's large hands. A few tears escaped my eyes and I let out a sigh when it was over again. Brandon's thumb started making slow circles against my palm and I opened my eyes to see him watching my face, his head still resting on his other hand. He looked like he was in as much pain as I was by just having to watch me.

He rose out of the chair, bending over to brush the tears off my cheeks, and then rest his forehead against mine. "Is there anything I can do for you sweetheart?"

"You're doing it," I replied. I wouldn't have been able to do even this part of it without him. He was my rock. "What time is it?"

Brandon glanced at his phone before shoving it back in his pocket, "Almost eleven. Try to sleep, he'll be here before you know it." He kissed me softly once, then pressed his lips harder to mine.

"As long as you get some sleep too."

He sat back in the chair and put his head back on his hand, this time it was next to mine, so our noses were touching. His other hand cupped my cheek and his jaw fell slack within minutes. I smiled at him and braced another fierce contraction before dozing off as well.

Loud persistent beeping jolted me out of my nap, Brandon jumped out of the chair and turned to look at the monitors. His eyes went wide and he ran to the door but a nurse was already coming through and began checking everything. She had me turn onto my back again and made everyone except Brandon and Mom leave. Another nurse came in and they spoke quickly back and forth while having me do certain things. Mom was holding one hand while Brandon gripped the other, keeping his gray eyes trained to mine. I felt like neither of us was breathing while we waited for the monitor to go back to normal, or for one of the nurses to tell us what was happening. Dr. Lowdry walked in and began speaking with the nurses and taking one of their spots, but I couldn't look at her. Brandon was now cupping my cheeks with both hands, and whispering to me, trying to calm me, but his own eyes looked terrified.

"Okay Harper, are you ready?" Dr. Lowdry asked from the end of the bed, Brandon released my face and I finally looked to her, "We're going to have to do this now, the umbilical cord is wrapped around his neck, but you're both going to be fine. Just do exactly as I say, and we'll have him out in a few minutes."

I nodded and took a deep breath, squeezing Brandon's hand like it was the only thing keeping me tied to this earth. Mom squeezed my other hand telling me everything would be fine, Brandon kissed me quick and hard and continued to say reassuring and loving words throughout the next six minutes. We all cried in relief when we heard little Liam's piercing wail. While they cleaned him and did a quick check to make sure he was okay, Brandon leaned over and alternated between kissing me sweetly through our smiles and pressing his cheek against mine to tell me how proud he was. As a nurse brought Liam over to us, she repeated information they'd been saying sporadically throughout their mini exam. Fourteen point three inches, six pounds six ounces, born at twelve oh three in the morning.

She handed me Liam and I knew I would never be the same. He was no longer crying, his wide eyes were staring right into mine while his mouth was shaped in a perfect little quivering

O, like he didn't know if he should cry again or stay silent. He was beautiful. Mom was standing near my head, silently crying, Brandon was bent close to us, lightly brushing his fingers up and down Liam's side. His eyes were bright and his smile breathtaking as he looked at our son.

"Hi Liam." My voice cracked as I smiled down at him.

He wiggled his hands out of his blanket and was clasping his long fingers around each other. While still brushing his fingers down his side, Brandon let his thumb brush against Liam's fists, and Liam instantly grabbed hold. Brandon's breath came out in a huff and we looked at each other, smiling wide before looking back down. Mom rubbed her fingers over where Liam was holding onto Brandon, before kissing each of us on the cheek and leaving the room to let the rest of the family know.

The nurse took him out of my arms and placed him in Brandon's while the Doctor did some last minute things with me. I understood immediately why Brandon wanted to see me hold him. Looking at Brandon, all six feet four inches, two hundred and forty pounds of pure muscle holding our six pound son was what finally had the tears rolling down my cheeks.

"Hey little man," He whispered as he stood a couple feet from the bed.

"Babe," his head snapped up to look at me, his smile the only thing I could focus on, "did you hear the nurse? About when he was born?"

Brandon nodded and looked back down to Liam, "You have pretty good timing son. You couldn't have come on a more perfect day."

I smiled at them and the nurse piped up, "Did you want him to be born on September eleventh?" she asked, her face gentle and sweet.

Looking over at Brandon, I saw the tears falling down his face and knew he wouldn't be able to respond, "It's not that we wanted it, we really weren't expecting him yet. But it's fitting for us and our family. He's named after Brandon's dad, Liam. He was on one of the planes that crashed into the twin towers," I said softly.

Dr. Lowdry and both of the nurses gasped and fell silent. After Dr. Lowdry was done fixing me up, she looked at the baby, still in Brandon's arms, and said, "This day will always be significant for you three. Loss and a gain, it's bittersweet, but I agree, it is perfect."

Brandon walked back over to me and gently placed Liam back in my arms. He kept one hand on him, the other on me. "You were amazing. I love you so much Harper."

"I love you too. So much." Liam let out a soft cry, and we both looked quickly back to him. "Look at him Brandon. He's perfect."

"He is." Brandon agreed, "He's finally here."

"I know, this is so surreal."

Liam started crying harder, sounding so precious, and so sad. But with his little arms waving and finally hearing him, I still couldn't stop smiling. Brandon put one of his fingers near his shaking hand, and as soon as Liam touched it, he grasped it again and fell silent.

"Daddy make everything better little Liam?"

Brandon looked at me, his expression full of pride, love and so much joy I started tearing up again. "I'm a dad." His voice was thick as he tried to speak around the lump in his throat. He pressed his lips to mine and pulled away slightly, "Thank you sweetheart, you have no idea how happy this makes me. How happy you make me."

With the hand that wasn't holding Liam, I ran my fingers down his jaw before cupping his cheek. "I think I have an idea. You are my world Brandon, I couldn't do any of this without you, nor would I want to."

Mom came back in then followed by Carrie. They both took turns holding him, and while they did, Brandon and I shared sweet kisses and meaningful glances. When he told his mom what time Liam was born, she smiled at us before seeming to understand what that meant. Her face fell soft, her eyes misting.

"Well hello Liam," she said like she was just seeing her husband for the first time in years. "You sure know how to make an entrance."

My heart tugged as I recalled stories she had shared with me. The night she first met Liam, it was pouring rain outside and she'd just been about to leave a coffee shop with her girlfriends. Liam opened the door and stepped in, his foot sliding on the wet tile floor and knocking into Carrie causing her to fall on him. They had laughed so hard it took them almost two minutes to finally get standing again and when they did he apologized and held out a hand to her, introducing himself.

She took his hand and shook it lightly saying, "Well you sure know how to make an entrance Liam Taylor."

When she turned to leave, Liam looked at her and said, "You're really going to leave after something brought us together like that?"

Instead of leaving with her girlfriends that night, she decided to take a chance on a stranger and had another coffee with him. They talked until the shop closed and were married six months later. That first sentence she spoke to him became a joke in their relationship as well as their family once the boys were born. And now, our little Liam was carrying it on for her.

"SWEETHEART," BRANDON GROANED, his voice was thick with sleep, "is it your turn or mine? What time is it?"

I turned my head toward where the clock sat on my nightstand, but couldn't open my eyes just yet. "I don't know. It's probably my turn though." Finally forcing my eyes open I blinked at the bright green numbers. It was a little after four in the morning, I smiled that at least he'd slept a little longer this time. Grabbing the comforter, I flung it off myself and onto Brandon. Before I could fall out of the bed though, he grabbed my forearm and held me down.

"If you think it's your turn, then it's most likely mine."

"I have to feed him anyway Brandon, he's been asleep for three hours. I'll go." I threw my legs off the bed and sat up. Brandon grabbed my shoulders and pulled me back down, crawling over until his head was hovering over mine.

"Then let me get him and bring him here for you." He kissed me softly, then pressed his lips to my throat. "Get comfortable, I'll be right back."

I sighed happily and propped the pillows up against the headboard and sat against them. Liam was a little over six weeks old, and while some nights we had to wake him up to feed him, tonight wasn't one of them. Brandon had been more than helpful with him, I couldn't believe how lucky I was to have him love and help me. I thought since I was the woman, I would be the one waking up every time to be with Liam, or be the one to change him. I was breastfeeding so of course I was the one doing all the feeding, but like now, Brandon would sometimes get him and bring him to me so I could stay in our bed. And we were always taking turns with everything else. Brandon was an amazing father. He loved Liam and was always so excited to see him, and the same went for our son. Whenever Brandon would talk to him, Liam went silent and just stared at him. If Brandon rained little kisses on him, or offered up his fingers to be gripped by his son, Liam smiled wide at his dad and my heart would melt watching them. They both made my days better, spending time with the two of them was what made me jump out of bed in the mornings, and although I wanted Brandon there as much as possible, I cherished my time alone with Liam whenever he went to his classes.

Brandon walked in holding him against his chest, and of course Liam was completely silent. "Someone's hungry, he kept trying to go for my chest."

"Did you tell him the restaurant is closed?" I snickered as he handed our son to me. I smiled widely back at the toothless smile facing me and kissed his forehead before setting him up to eat. Didn't matter that we were exhausted, I loved seeing my little man.

"I told him that restaurant had never even opened." Brandon laughed heartily and kissed both of us before climbing into bed next to me. He flipped on the TV and turned on the news, the only interesting thing on in the early mornings.

"How was your nap little Liam?" I played with his hand as he greedily ate, like he wouldn't ever get another meal.

Brandon placed a hand on my thigh and leaned over to be closer to us, "How was *your* nap Harper? You've been getting less sleep than I have."

"I know," I sighed and lay my head on his, "I can't help it though. Ever since he went to the nursery I feel like if I go to sleep, something will happen to him."

"He's fine, and he'll continue to be fine. But you need to sleep. Maybe—"

"No Brandon, I don't want to bother them."

"Harper." He moved his head out from under mine and tilted my chin so I was looking into his brown eyes. "You know you wouldn't be bothering them. They're here almost every day and they ask every time if they can babysit, so don't act like we can't call my mom or yours. Tell me what's really stopping you from asking them."

I looked down to my precious son before glancing back up to my amazing fiancé. Tears began rapidly filling my eyes.

"Sweetheart, you're crying? Why?"

"I can't Brandon . . . I can't." I choked on a sob and put my fist to my mouth to muffle it, Liam had started dozing off again.

"Harper what is wrong? Please tell me."

I was trying, I just couldn't speak yet so I held up a finger, silently asking him to give me a second to calm down a little, "I can't leave him. I'm terrified of what might happen if I do. Chase and your dad were gone just like that. I don't want to lose him and I don't want him to lose one or both of us. We know what it's like to be without a parent, I can't do that to him."

"Aw hell, sweetheart that won't happen. I know why you're scared, but we can't live like that. We can't let what's happened in our pasts, rule our lives now and in the future. That's not fair to us, and it's not fair to Liam. Nothing is going to happen, you need to allow yourself to enjoy our lives, as well as his. I don't want to be away from him either, but I will admit, I want alone time with you. We need to have time where it's just us. Even if it's just a couple hours, once a week."

"I'm sorry." I pulled Liam up to my chest and tried to burp him before taking him back to the nursery.

"For what?"

"For neglecting you. You're right, we do need time for us."

Brandon chuckled and removed the pillows from behind my back, so he could slide in behind me. "Harper, you haven't been neglecting me. Not at all. We've been extremely busy, and spending time as a family is more important to me than anything." His deep voice got even lower and he leaned forward to nibble at my ear, "But I'm selfish, and I want my girl for myself sometimes. Do you think we can figure out some us time?"

My heart started hammering from his lips brushing against my skin and I realized we hadn't had anything other than hugs and chaste kisses since Liam had been born. "I think we need to," I said a little breathless.

"Date night, every Thursday?"

"How convenient that it's Thursday." I smiled and nestled deeper into his chest.

Brandon lightly brushed his hand over Liam's head before he dropped both of them to my waist and then over where my stomach used to be.

"Do you miss it?" His hands had stilled for a second before sliding over my flat stomach again. I know, I know, I already have a lot of women that hate me. When we walk into the appointments for Liam, everyone asks if we adopted because within a week, my stomach went completely back to normal. It was mind blowing even to Brandon and me, and we definitely knew that my stomach had been close to the size of a beach ball not long before. I had one stretch mark, and it was mostly unnoticeable because it ran along a tip of one of my lilies. But if it weren't for that and my chest, I would think I'd made the entire pregnancy up and just stolen a baby from the hospital.

"You're the most beautiful woman I've ever seen either way." He shrugged and kissed the top of my head, "I do miss it, but I'm glad that he's here now. It will just take some time to get used to not having your stomach there. Like right now, I keep going to run my hands over it, and then they just continue to slide straight across and it throws me off for a second."

"Throws you off? Think about how I felt when I went to set that bowl on my stomach and it fell into my lap."

Brandon's husky laugh sent a shiver through me. "I'm sorry, but that was funny as hell. Your face was priceless."

Liam stirred and we both held our breaths until we were sure he was still asleep. "I'm going to put him back in his crib," I whispered. "I'll be right back."

I slid off the bed after letting Brandon kiss his forehead, and headed to the nursery. Rocking Liam for a minute, I pressed my lips to his head and put him down.

"I love you Liam Chase." After one last longing glance, I left the door cracked a bit, and went back to my other man.

"Did he wake up?"

I shook my head, crawling onto the bed and over to him. Grabbing the remote, I clicked off the TV and pressed my lips to the hollow at the base of his neck, letting my tongue glide over his collarbone. "Are you tired?"

Brandon groaned and wrapped his arms around me, "Not at all." He flipped me onto my back and hovered over me.

"I was thinking we could have a pre-date, date." I shivered as I wrapped my legs around him and pulled him closer.

"Harper," he spoke against my neck, "you have to tell me if anything has changed. We haven't done anything in a long time, and unless you set boundaries now, I don't know if I'll be able to stop once we've started."

"The only thing that has changed, is that I want you more now than I ever have before. I don't want to wait anymore, I want to be with you."

He crushed his mouth to mine and tugged lightly on my bottom lip, keeping his hold on it as he sat me up. In a move so fast, he pulled my shirt off and pressed me back down to the bed. Just having my bare chest against his was incredible and heat churned in my stomach. I arched my back into him as he started trailing down my neck to my chest. When he got to my stomach, he hooked his right hand into my shorts and started tugging down. My breathing was ragged as I waited in heated anticipation for what was finally going to happen between us. After my shorts and underwear joined my shirt on the floor, Brandon slowly explored my body with his lips and hands, but every time I tried to do my own search of him, he'd grasp my hands and pull them over my head. I was whimpering by the time he released his hold on my hands and put them on either side of my body, only leaving his mouth on me. Slowly I ran my hands down his muscled back, narrow waist and hips before gripping the top of his jersey shorts. His breath caught as I ran my fingers back and forth along the top and I laughed huskily when he quickly brought his lips back to mine. Before I could pull his shorts down, Liam woke back up and let out a long wail. Brandon cursed and fell to the side, pulling me on top of him. He held me tightly as we listened to him for a minute, both silently praying that he would fall right back to sleep. When he didn't, I pressed my forehead against his and sighed deeply.

Brandon was still trying to return his breathing to normal, his lips mashed into a tight line, his eyes shut. "Tonight," he said tightly, "*nothing* is stopping us. I'm going to take my time with you, and I'm going to make love to you all night."

"Tonight," I promised. Kissing his cheek, I rolled off him and the bed, got dressed and went to go get Liam.

When I walked into the room and brought him out of the crib, he cried even harder and it took a few minutes to calm him down. I walked around the dark room with him in my arms, trying to soothe him. Only after his long fingers grasped onto a chunk of my hair, did he finally stop crying. His eyes went wide and his mouth molded into that little O shape I love so much.

"Well hello grumpy." I cooed at him lovingly, "Thirty minutes is pretty short, even for you mister." I turned when I heard a noise from the hall, and watched Brandon as he leaned against the doorjamb. I took in his tan muscled body and bit my lip, thinking of our few moments we just shared, and the hours we would spend together tonight. My breaths were getting heavier and coming quicker as I thought about his body pressed to mine. It really had been too long since we'd kissed like that, let alone done anything more. The last time we'd gotten as far as we had now, had been before our horrible break up.

"Still my favorite thing," he said, breaking me out of my fantasy.

"What is babe?"

"Just watching you hold him." I smiled as he sauntered over to us. "How's he doing?"

"Good now. He was mad that it took me so long to come see him."

"Oh *he* was mad?" Brandon took him from my arms and kissed his head tenderly, immediately offering up his finger for Liam, "I hate to break it to you little man, but you interrupted my very important time with your mom."

I laughed and sat down in my glider chair, suddenly exhausted with the three and a half hours of sleep I'd gotten in the last forty eight hours. Watching them walk in circles for a few minutes, I fought to keep my eyes open. Brandon walked up to me and carefully bent over so I could kiss our now sleeping son before putting him back in his crib. When he was all settled, Brandon slid an arm under my knees, another behind my back, and carried me back to our bed. I tried to pull my shirt back off but Brandon stopped my hands and kissed me softly.

"Just sleep sweetheart. We can pick up where we left off tonight." Wrapping his arms around me, he pulled me tight into his chest and let out a content sigh. "I love you so much Harper."

I pressed my lips to his throat and whispered back my love for him. I was out in seconds.

LEAVING LIAM WITH Mom and Dad was incredibly difficult. Of course he didn't notice because he was sleeping, but it took me over five minutes to actually leave the house. I almost started crying when I got back in the car but forced myself to keep it in. I knew he would be fine with them, I wasn't worried about that at all. It's just that other than taking a shower and the few hours I did sleep, I hadn't been separated from him since we came home from the hospital. Taking a deep breath, I focused on Brandon and what we had planned for when he got back from his class. Glancing down at the clock, I cranked the car and drove home.

I enjoyed taking my time in the shower since I hadn't been able to do that in almost two months. All my showers were about five minutes these days, and I'd been in serious need of this. After I was done, I took my time doing my make-up and hair as well. I know Brandon loves me without make-up, but I was starting to feel like a slob since I never got ready anymore, and I wanted him to know that I wanted to look good for him. I stood in the closet for a few minutes trying to decide what to wear, but eventually ended up in matching hot pink and black lacy underwear and bra. I wasn't confident enough to just be naked when he got home, but I was pretty sure actually getting dressed was unnecessary. Running back into the bathroom, I studied my reflection to make sure I looked perfect. Tracing the lines of my tattoo, I was still beyond words that I'd just given birth a little over six weeks ago, and the only real physical evidence was my chest. Bree and I had gone shopping when my boobs grew two cup sizes during the pregnancy, and I was glad she'd forced me to get a few sexy bras, because everything else I had either wouldn't fit now, or would be anything but a turn on. I put a little bit of body spray on and turned to leave the bathroom when I heard the front door open. My heart picked up pace instantly as I forced myself not to run to my future husband.

"Harper? I'm ho—" He stopped short when he saw me, eyes bulging, "Dear Lord."

I smiled and slowly walked toward him, "Good or bad?"

"Good," he gripped my hips and pulled me to him, bringing his lips to mine, "definitely good." Picking me up, he carried me back to the bedroom and sat me on the edge of the bed.

Grabbing the bottom of his shirt, he helped me bring it over his head as he bent to kiss me again. I let my fingers trail over his chest, down his abs and to the button of his jeans. Like this morning, he sucked in a quick breath when I ran my fingers along the top of his pants and I laughed against his lips. After unbuttoning and pulling down the zipper, he stepped out of his jeans and brought his hands to my back to unclasp my bra. When it fell to the floor, he pushed my body back to the bed and let his lips trail over me. My chest was rising and falling quickly by the time he brought his mouth back to mine. I caught his boxers with my fingers and tugged slowly, groaning when he stopped me.

"Let me love you first," he whispered against my neck.

He pulled back, and put all his weight on his knees so he could slide me farther up the bed. Kissing me once more, he ran the tips of his fingers down my stomach, to my underwear. His eyes never left mine as he slid them down my legs, letting them fall to the floor too.

"You're so beautiful, Harper." Brandon said my name like a prayer as he ran his hands back up my legs.

My eyelids fluttered shut as his lips and hands loved me. When I didn't think I could handle any more, I brought his face back to mine and grabbed the top of his boxers thankful he didn't try to stop me as I added them to the pile of his clothes. He stayed hovering over me as I memorized every inch of him with my eyes, and spread out on the bed as my hands followed the path my eyes had just taken. I pressed my lips low on his stomach then made a trail up to his lips. Brandon flipped me onto my back just as my mouth found his and he nudged my legs apart with his knee. I thought I was going to go crazy as he stayed inches away from me and kept me from moving.

"You're sure you're ready?"

I ran my hands over his buzzed head and brought his face to mine, "I'm sure. I don't think I can describe the way I feel for you. 'I love you' just doesn't seem like enough, let me show you what you mean to me."

He pressed his lips to my forehead, then kept his eyes locked on mine as we showed each other feelings we couldn't put into words. He groaned and my breath caught when he finally pushed inside me and we stayed unmoving for a moment, just enjoying the feel of each other. We moved together like we'd been made for each other, each giving the other exactly what was needed. I didn't ever want it to end, I could spend an eternity loving Brandon in every way possible, and it still wouldn't be long enough for me. Our bodies remained intertwined when we were finished, and our lips and hands went back to their earlier exploration. We stared at one another, whispered our love for each other, laughed, wrestled, and kissed with such raw passion, that I felt like the first time blended right into the second and then the third. Each time different and more amazing than the previous.

We broke apart after the last time, exhausted in the most exhilarating way, breathing heavily and laughing huskily. Our alarms to go get Liam had gone off and we'd hit the snooze twice before both deciding it was time to get our son. When the third alarm went off, we shut it off and hopped in the shower quickly, the only thing keeping us from getting lost in each other in the shower was our aching bodies and the need to see Liam again. After we were dressed, Brandon pulled me in to kiss me roughly before leading me out to the Expedition. I called Mom to let her know we were on our way, and placed a hand over his resting on my thigh.

I was still smiling wide, and after a quick glance to my left, saw that Brandon was too. "That was—"

"Perfect," he finished for me. "That was absolutely perfect."

"It really was. I'm sorry it took us so long to get there."

"Don't be. If we hadn't waited and hadn't had this last year happen, it wouldn't have been the same. I'm not saying it wouldn't have still been more than amazing, but it just wouldn't have been like that."

I thought about it for a moment before agreeing, "I think you're right." I leaned over the console and kissed his cheek softly.

"I love you." He turned his head to press his lips to mine before I could sit back in my seat.

"I was made to love you Brandon."

His smile got even broader and he ran his thumb over my hand and across my engagement ring.

"And I can't wait to marry you."

"Other than you giving birth to Liam," the deep timbre of his voice got even lower, "marrying you will be the best moment of my life."

When we pulled up to Mom and Dad's, Brandon ran around to the passenger door and pulled me out of the SUV, pressing my back against the door after it was shut. These last six hours had gone by way too fast. "I'm not ready for our night to be over, but I can't wait to see him."

"Next Thursday can't come fast enough sweetheart." He skimmed his nose across my jaw before capturing my already swollen mouth with his. I moaned against his lips and wrapped my arms around his neck, letting him lift me up so I could secure my legs around his waist. We stayed like that, making out like we were teenagers dating in high school, not ready to separate for the evening. Our breaths were coming quicker, our grips harder and kisses rougher.

"I don't think I'm able to go for another round tonight baby. Besides, I don't think Mom and Dad's neighbors would appreciate the show."

He laughed and rested his forehead against mine, trying to calm down again, "Honestly, I don't know how I'm not collapsing right now. You wore me out Harper." He chuckled softly and placed me back on the ground. "Ready to get our son and go home?"

I smiled and pulled him up the driveway and into their house. Mom took one look at my swollen lips, messy hair and red neck from where Brandon's scruffy jaw had rubbed across too many times, and laughed softly.

She pulled me away from Robert and whispered in my ear, "So I'm guessing you two had a good date night?"

Blushing fiercely, I glanced back at Brandon and Dad talking, then back to her. "Oh my God, you have no idea." I had been seriously mortified the first time I heard Bree talking to her mom about anything sexual, but soon got over it and was glad to have another person to talk to. I looked around, "Where's Bree and Konrad?"

"They went to get ice cream, she'll have to wait to hear the juicy details until another time. What was this . . . the first time?"

I nodded and bit my lip to hide my smile.

"Oh, no way! I was kidding, I had no idea. You just looked too happy to not joke about it."

"Mom!" I hissed and shot a quick smile to the guys, "I told you we hadn't been like that before."

"Yeah, *before,* but you've been living together for months now."

"Like we've had time before tonight? I was super huge pregnant and Dr. Lowdry told us not to, then we've been taking care of Liam. We couldn't rush through these first few times, we'd waited too long to do that."

"Few!"

I grinned like the freaking Cheshire Cat as we made our way to the nursery.

"Well now that you've had those times, I assure you you'll find time *all* the time."

"Ha! Oh I can't even think about that right now. I'm too exhausted."

"Well just know, we're always available to babysit."

"We'll keep that in mind." I laughed softly and pulled my

sleeping baby out of the crib. My heart warmed when he was finally back in my arms. "I missed you little Gummy Bear," I whispered against his head and cradled him in my arms.

"He drank all three bottles you left us, but didn't sleep much, so hopefully you'll get a restful night tonight."

I nodded, hoping that was true. I needed time to recover from the night with Brandon. When we walked out into the living room, my future husband's smile made my heart skip a beat. I loved this man so much, and I couldn't believe he was mine. He walked over to us and lightly ran his hand over Liam's head before kissing him.

Liam yawned and blinked his eyes open to look at Brandon, "Hey little man. We missed you." After another yawn Liam's eyes slowly shut again, his mouth popping open slightly. "You ready to take him home Harper?"

I nodded and accepted kisses from Mom and Dad. "Are you guys still coming over Sunday?" In order to carry on family day, once a week everyone gathered at either Mom's, Carrie's or our house to have family time, and though they'd been skipping our place so I wouldn't have to worry about cleaning or playing hostess while trying to be a mom, I'd made them promise to let us have our week again.

"We'll be there, you two have *fun* until then," Mom said with a smile and a wink. Dad laughed out loud and Brandon actually blushed. I'd never seen him blush before, and I couldn't help but laugh too.

We got Liam fed, changed and asleep in his crib in record time. Crawling into bed, we kissed soft and slow, clinging to each other.

Brandon brought his lips to my ear, his deep voice making my body burn, "Harper . . ."

"Round four?" I asked with a grin.

His smile matched mine as he pulled me on top of him.

18

"BRANDON?" I ASKED roughly. His side of the bed was empty, and cold. Glancing around I noted I'd slept for six and a half hours and should probably go check on my little one.

I grabbed Brandon's shirt off the floor and slid it over my head before padding down the cool hallway. When I got closer I heard Brandon's warm animated voice and slowed, trying to hear whatever he was telling our son. I was already smiling to myself when I peeked around the slightly ajar door, he was talking to him about one of his surfing days. No . . . he was talking to him about one of *Chase's* surfing days. And he had the scrapbook of Chase's life on the dresser below them, pointing to one of the pictures. A soft gasp escaped my chest and I tried to slow my breathing so I could continue to listen without Brandon knowing I was here.

". . . he was always doing crazy stuff like that, it's why everyone loved him, but it got him in trouble more times than not. No one else would have continued to surf after that, and we were all trying to get him to come in. Brad and I rode out to force him to, since he had this huge cut on his eyebrow from where that guy punched him, but by the time we got out there he was already catching another wave and riding it in. I swear he knew how to piss us off too, because those guys weren't happy we started coming back out. Your dad could out-surf those guys, and I could fight them, but just a warning son, don't ever try to fight someone while on your surfboard out in the ocean. It doesn't really work out for anyone, and you look stupid trying to throw punches while treading water. We ended up laughing too hard and inviting them to the party that night, calling a truce."

Brandon flipped to the next page and chuckled lightly, pointing at one of the pictures again, "Like I said, he was crazy and always doing stupid crap," flipping the page again he pointed to one and said softly, "but your mom changed that."

I froze and tilted my head in even further.

"The day I met your mom, I knew she would be in my life forever. There was something about her and I knew I was already falling in love with her that first day. She made you want to be better, to attempt to be worthy of her love. Unfortunately your dad felt the same way; no one understood why he drastically changed, except for me. Even though she was with me, he stopped drinking, stopped sleeping with other girls, it's like she made him instantly mature into the guy he eventually wanted to be so he could have an opportunity with her. I was always afraid I'd lose her to him someday, it's like I knew it was a matter of when, not if. But your mom was different, I'd dated plenty of girls, but I hadn't really cared if they were there or not. It was just someone to try to fill the ache of losing my dad. So when I met her and realized my feelings, I fought to keep her as long as I could. Don't tell your momma, but Chase and I were constantly fighting over her when she wasn't around. Hell, we even fought over her when she *was* around. We knew either of us could have any girl we wanted, but we both only wanted Harper.

So of course, being us, words were used and fists flew whenever we were alone. I didn't tell her this, but I already knew what had happened with your dad before she told me. When I got home from break, and Chase never bothered me again, I knew something had happened. I just didn't know what yet. But you know what little man? I can't even be mad about it anymore, because if it hadn't happened, you wouldn't be here right now."

He gently kissed our three month old son who was completely enthralled in his stories and pointed to the last picture in the book. "And he loved you and your mom, so much. I'll always remind you of that, but I wish you could have met him."

I placed a hand over my mouth to stifle the sob rising in my throat and slowly backed away to our bedroom. Once I was under the covers, I let the tears spill down my face as I mourned the dad Liam would never meet, and my heart grew even more for the dad that was holding him now. I don't know how long I stayed there after I finished crying, but Brandon eventually got back in bed and stilled when he realized I was awake.

"Babe, what's wrong?"

"Do you know how much I love you?" He nodded and I continued, "Sometimes it's hard for me to even believe you're real, and that you're here with us."

He brushed back the hair covering my eyes and cupped my face, "I *am* here. I wouldn't want to be anywhere else."

"Exactly."

"Harper, please tell me what's wrong. Are you—are you getting cold feet?"

"No! I can't wait to marry you Brandon. You're so amazing, I wish I could tell you how wonderful you are and how much you mean to me. I just don't understand how you can be mine. I don't know what I did to deserve you."

He huffed a laugh and that dimple flashed at me, "Then why were you crying? I don't understand?"

"I— Thank you for telling him about Chase."

"I told you we would babe." He wrapped his arms around me and kissed the top of my head. "I'll always tell him about Chase."

"I know, just walking in and listening to you tell him stories was . . . I don't know how to explain it. It was wonderful, it made my heart happy," I said with a laugh.

His voice dropped lower, "You make my heart happy Harper." He pressed his full lips to mine, moving them slow. His left hand dropped under his shirt on my body, his fingers teasing my waist, stomach and hips. "Have I told you recently how much I love you in nothing but my shirt?"

"Have I told you recently how much I love you in nothing at all?" I countered huskily, letting my fingers drop to the band on his shorts.

Brandon moved my hand away from his body, placing our intertwined fingers above my head on the pillow. "Not now babe."

"What? Yes, now." I hitched a leg around his hip, pressing myself to him.

He moaned and moved his hips against me before stilling and pushing me away, "You're supposed to have sex after the wedding, not before it. Technically, I'm not supposed to see you today until you're walking down the aisle."

"And yet here you are." I grinned and brought our bodies back together suggestively.

"Here I am," he agreed.

He pushed me onto my back and let the hand that was still on my waist trail down. I whimpered and wrapped my hands around his neck, covering his lips with mine. When his mouth made a trail down my throat I reached for his shorts and the doorbell rang.

"That didn't happen." I kept my hands possessively on his body so he wouldn't move. The doorbell rang two more short times. I angrily slid out from under my fiancé and rushed to the door. "Are you serious?" I hissed when I flung the door open, "Liam's sleeping!"

Carrie, Mom, Bree and Konrad all stood at the door.

"Nice outfit," Bree snickered and her eyes widened when Brandon came to the door with a scowl on his insanely handsome face, "Oh hell no! No screwing until later!"

"Breanna!" My face got red, I could talk to her and Mom about our intimate life. But Konrad was definitely never around and neither was Carrie.

"It's kinda obvious friend." She stepped in and grabbed my hand, taking me to the bedroom. "Take a shower and put on something comfortable, we're going to be at the salon most of the day."

"I hope you realize you stopped us *before* it got to the best part. I'm going to be mad at you the rest of the day."

"No you're not. Wedding first, sex later."

I rolled my eyes and stepped into the shower, "You sound like Brandon. Why is Konrad here anyway? Is he going to the salon with us?" I laughed and rinsed the lather out of my hair.

"No he's here to hang out with Brandon until later. They'll take care of Liam."

My heart sank, "Oh, Liam."

"No, no! We are not starting this again. You will be just fine. You guys need a honeymoon, end of story. You'll regret it in a year or two if you don't."

"I know, but we're parents. I feel horrible!"

"Seriously, you guys won't even be gone that long. Most people take a week. You'll be gone three nights, including tonight. Just think of it like a long date night."

"Bree," I sighed, "I really do appreciate that you are all doing this for us, but we've only ever been away from him for the longest seven hours. This is way different. Do you know that I've packed his suitcase four different times?"

"That's just sad."

I stopped shaving for a moment and pointed the razor toward her, even though she couldn't see me, "When you have a baby, you'll see. And I'll be there to laugh at you for how ridiculous you are."

"Are you done yet? You were supposed to have done this before we even got here."

"Rude. Aren't you supposed to be nice to me today since I'm the Bride?"

"Aren't you supposed to be nice to me because I'm your best friend in the entire world, your Maid of Honor *and* I planned an awesome day for you?"

"True." I shut off the water and took the towel Bree was holding when I stepped out and grabbed her in a big hug, "You really are the best. I love you friend."

"I love you too."

Brandon walked in and when he saw us he held up his hands like he was surrendering and slowly backed back out. It wasn't weird to see Bree and I hug, but I usually wasn't naked.

"You're not supposed to see her!" Bree said over my shoulder, "You've already seen her too much this morning. Go hide until we can leave."

"Bree," I whined and looked at the empty doorway, "I love you Brandon!"

You could hear the smile in Brandon's voice, "I love you too sweetheart, I can't wait to marry you. Bree keep your hands off my wife, you already had your chance to make her gay . . . too late now."

Bree and I laughed so hard, tears were streaming down our faces. When I was finally able to take a normal breath, I wrapped the first towel around my body and grabbed another to get most of the water out of my hair.

After I was in my green Victoria's Secret PINK sweats, and

a plain button-up shirt so I wouldn't mess up my hair later, we were off to the salon. I'd heard of Bridezillas, and brides that were so nervous they threw up or continued to cry; but I was so blissed out, all I could do all day was smile and laugh with the women in my life. We had the most amazing time at the spa, we got massages, manicures and pedicures, had our hair and make-up done, and had an endless flow of water, champagne and fruit and cheese platters. I guess they didn't care that Bree and I were only nineteen.

We all looked amazing, and we weren't even in our dresses yet. Everyone's make-up was flawless, Carrie and Mom had up-dos, Breanna's shoulder length blond hair had loose spirals, with a braid going around the front right side of her hair, and mine was just as I'd pictured in my head. My long auburn hair was parted on the side, each side going into a soft braid down the side, coming together into a twist leading to a soft off-center bun low on my neck. After everyone that had helped us get ready for the day gave us hugs and said their congratulations, we were off in Bree's Lexus to the ceremony and reception site.

Even though they weren't thrilled, I'd eventually gotten my way and helped everyone set up for the wedding, so first thing we did when we got there was check both rooms to make sure everything still looked perfect. The room where we would have the ceremony had soft lighting, and twinkle lights inside tulle going down each side of the aisle. We didn't want too much in here, so other than large bouquets of white lilies, and some more lights, that was all there was in there. The room where we were having the reception was a different story. More white tulle filled with twinkle lights made soft arcs up to the middle of the room, making it look like we were in a large tent rather than a room. The tables had white table cloths, with green, silver and black tulle running along the top. Hurricanes filled with candles were spaced evenly in the tulle. Each seat had a little thing of bubbles for the end, and a favor of a short jar filled with things to make peppermint hot chocolate. The DJ was setting up his equipment, and there were tables in the back for where the food would be. The wedding cake was really just a top piece, white with swirls of black and green, and the next two layers were a hundred cup-cakes, all with the same type of designs. We were in one of the rooms in the back getting our dresses on when the guys showed up in their suits.

"Oh my gosh they're here!" I ran toward the window to watch them walk toward the building with a huge smile on my face. I don't know why, but I'd been holding my breath until I saw Brandon here. And he looked amazing, as did the rest of them. Dad was in a dark gray suit, with a black shirt, Konrad and Jeremy had on black suits with dark green button-ups, black vests and loose black ties. The love of my life was in all black with a loose green tie, in his arms was our bundled up son. I'm sure he'd dressed up for the funeral, but since I wasn't exactly aware of much going on at that point, this was the first time I'd ever seen Brandon in a tie, let alone a suit. His rugged looks in a suit made him look powerful and mysterious and oh so sexy. I was already biting my lip just thinking about taking it off him tonight. We watched them until they were in the building and it took an incredible amount of will power not to rush out to my almost husband.

When there was only twenty minutes left, the girls helped me into my dress, garter, and white Converse. There's no way I was wearing heels all night. My dress was simple and beautiful, strapless and form fitting until my hips where it lightly bunched and flared out to the floor, the back lacing up with thick ribbon. I looked at Mom and Carrie in their black and silver shimmery dresses, and my best friend in her dark green halter tea length dress. We all hugged and kissed each other on the cheek before they handed me my bouquet of white lilies and red roses, dark green ribbon holding them together, and heading out to meet the guys.

"Wow sis," Jeremy gently hugged me, afraid to mess anything up, and kissed my cheek, "you look awesome."

"Thanks Jer, you guys all look so handsome!" I squealed and accepted a hug from Konrad.

"You look beautiful Kid." He kissed my cheek as well before taking Bree in his arms.

"Thanks old man." I teased and gasped when I saw Dad and Liam, "Hi little one!" I kissed his soft head and played with his hands for a minute before Mom took him so she and Carrie could go sit down.

Jeremy and Konrad escorted them to their seats, then came back for Bree. She winked at me, and when the music started, the three of them left the room to take their places up front. Dad wrapped his arms around me and held me for a moment.

"You look so beautiful sweet girl. Thank you for asking me to give you away, it means so much that you've allowed us to be your family. We love you and are so proud of who you are and your choices."

I blinked back tears when he released me, "Thanks Dad. You guys mean everything to me, I wouldn't have been able to do any of this without you."

He held out his arm, and I placed my hand in the crook of it, "We're up, you ready for this?"

"So ready!" I did a little happy dance so Dad and I were both chuckling when we rounded the corner and started our walk down the aisle.

My eyes instantly found Brandon, and his expression made my body sing. A huge smile spread across his face, accentuating his dimple, his eyes were bright as he watched me walk toward him. If Dad didn't have a hold on me, I would have taken off running toward him, but we kept the slow pace, getting to Brandon seconds, that felt like an eternity later. When Dad gave me away, and put my hands in Brandon's, I smiled widely at him and we continued to stare at each other, letting everything else melt away.

Hi, he mouthed to me.

I smiled and mouthed back *I love you.*

I love you too. He squeezed my hands tight and looked at me with an expression I can only describe as pure joy.

We said our vows, repeated words after the pastor, exchanged rings and when asked, said "I do." The pastor announced us husband and wife, and Brandon tilted my face up toward him, capturing my mouth with his. In that moment, in that kiss, we promised each other forever and I felt like my life was finally complete. We reluctantly broke apart to face our family and friends before heading up the aisle and out of that room. As soon as we rounded the corner, Brandon took my face in his hands and pressed his lips to mine again.

"You look amazing Harper," he said around soft kisses, "so beautiful."

I ran my hands over his short hair when he pressed his forehead to mine, "We're married," I breathed a small laugh, "you're my husband."

"And you're my wife." He smiled as he pressed his mouth to my cheek, then my neck.

Our families found us then and we were bombarded with hugs from everyone. I was excited to see Brad and Derek had made it with their girlfriends, as well as some of Brandon's other friends from school. We took a few pictures; the photographer couldn't stop laughing because Brandon and I couldn't stop kissing, and finally said she'd just continue to take candid shots throughout the rest of the reception. We ate a bit, danced a lot, and by the end of the night I'd danced with all the men in my life, including little Liam Chase, a few times. I blushed fiercely when Brandon removed the garter with his teeth, and both Konrad and Bree caught the garter and bouquet. I winked at Konrad since I knew he was planning on proposing on Christmas Eve. When Brandon wrapped his arms around my waist and whispered softly in my ear, I hurried to say good-bye to our son and handed him over to Carrie, who was taking the first half of the watch. People blew bubbles at us as we made our way to the car, and we were off to our make-shift honeymoon.

Brandon rented a condo right on the beach not too far from where we lived, and we were there in no time, with Brandon carrying me through the door. He laid me on the bed before running back to my car and grabbing our bags, leaving them in the entryway and rushing back to me. His face was full of love and passion, his gray eyes burning. He stopped at the edge of the bed, and let his eyes take me in while I did the same. He'd taken off his jacket earlier in the night and rolled the sleeves of his black shirt up to his elbows, his green tie was still on but even looser than it had been when the wedding started. The shirt and pants fit him perfectly, stretching over his broad shoulders and chest, accentuating his narrow hips and falling perfectly down his long muscled legs. He looked like a god. An incredibly sexy god.

I sat up and scooted to the edge of the bed, grabbing his belt buckle I tugged him closer, a satisfied smirk stretching across his face, his dimple deeper than ever. When I had his pants and boxer briefs off, I stood up and took off his tie before slowly unbuttoning his vest and shirt, running my hands up his chest to his shoulders so I could slide it off as well. He pushed me back down onto the bed and brought one of my legs up, chuckling when he got to my Converse.

"This is just another reason why I love you," he said as he took it, and the other one off.

His hands left a trail of heat up and back down my legs as he removed my underwear and brought himself back between my legs.

"You're not going to take my dress off?"

Brandon kissed my neck and his deep voice gave me heated chills, "Maybe later." His brown eyes caught mine, and in them I could see everything he felt for me and I wondered how I could have ever been stupid enough to try to live without him. "I love you so much Harper," he said before he slid into me.

I gasped at the sensations that coursed through my body. Every time with him seemed to be better than the time before, and I didn't think I would ever get tired of these alone times with him. "Brandon," I cried when he rocked against me, "God I love you too."

"WAKE UP HARPER."

I grumbled and rolled onto my back, quickly slipping back into the place between sleep and waking. I felt something against my neck and tried to swat at it, when I didn't catch anything I figured it must have been my hair and sank deeper into the warm bed. Before I could drift back into my dreams, there was that brush against my neck again, but when it continued down my chest and stopped for a few seconds at the swell of my breast I tried to fully wake up to look at what I now knew was my husband. Brandon continued down my stomach, lightly biting my left hip, and crossing over to do the same to the right. My eyes flew open and I exhaled a breathy "oh" when his lips trailed to the inside of my thighs.

Brandon's low chuckle alone would have caused shivers, but his lips and tongue moving slowly against me were all my mind could comprehend right now. I ran my hands over his buzzed head and tried to keep my eyes open to watch him, but they fluttered shut again, a moan escaping my barely open lips. He slid two fingers in me as his tongue continued to work against my most sensitive area. A ball of limb-numbing pleasure was already spreading through my body and I had a feeling I wasn't going to be able to hang on much longer. My hips involuntarily rolled and his left hand gripped harder on the back of my hip, but didn't try to hinder my movements. He quickened his pace and after a few minutes I was extremely thankful there were no neighbors near us as the following cry tore out of my chest, my body surging with heat. Brandon hovered over my body and pushed into me when the next wave rushed through me and met my satisfied whimpers with a carnal growl as he moved against me, his lips and teeth nipping at the hollow at the base of my neck. Each bite a little rougher than the previous, matching his thrusts. My hands passed over the muscles in his shoulders and back as they bunched together with each hard drive into me. Our breaths were ragged and there was a thin sheen of sweat covering both of us when he collapsed on top of me some time later. He struggled to keep most of his body weight off me by resting on his forearms, and ended up rolling onto his back, pulling me with him so I could curl up against his side.

Intertwining our fingers, he brought my hand up to his mouth and placed a gentle kiss against it before kissing the inside of my wrist and rubbing a thumb across my newest tattoo. Brandon and I got "his and hers" tattoos, on my left wrist read "i love him," and on his right read "i love her." Cheesy? Definitely. But we love them. We'd gone to Chase's old workplace, and although I had been nervous to see them, we were welcomed with a lot of hugs from everyone, Trish no longer worked there. Jeff hadn't been able to stop hugging me, and Brian's eyes had actually started misting when he pulled back from a hug that rivaled Jeff's. We showed them pictures of Liam, and they loved his name just as much as our family had. We promised to have them over one night so they could meet him, and Brian had joked that he and Marissa would steal him. They already knew Brandon from parties and when he'd gone there to get some of his work done, and I was surprised when the guys had seemed genuinely happy we had gotten married. I learned guys gossip just as bad as girls do when they told me they'd known all about the drama involving Chase, Brandon and myself; even from way back when Brandon and I first started dating.

"These have been an amazing three days." I sighed happily. "Thank you for everything."

"Thank you for marrying me."

I nuzzled into his chest and smiled when his arm tightened around me, "I feel like everything is perfect now. Is that corny?"

He chuckled and kissed the top of my head, "Nope, because I feel the same way. Is it . . . is it bad that I'm really anxious to get back to Liam?"

"Oh my word me too. A big part of me can't imagine leaving this bed, but I'm aching to see our baby."

"Well then, let's go get him."

I crawled off the bed and goose bumps covered my body when I saw his eyes heat watching me walk around without any clothes on. I knew what he was thinking, because it couldn't be any different from what I thought when he did the same. Leaning back over him, I pressed my bare chest firmly to his and whispered suggestively in his ear, "I think I could use a shower first, care to join?" I raised an eyebrow at him before turning toward the bathroom, with my husband right behind me.

19

"YOU WANNA GO see Daddy?" I crooned at Liam as he smiled widely at me and whispered *Dada*. "Come on big boy." I groaned as I lifted him off the bed and onto my hip. "Oh my word, he is such a chunk!"

Bree laughed and rained kisses over his head, "Don't listen to your mom, you're the cutest baby ever, rolls and all."

"Of course he is," I scrunched my nose at him and play-gnawed on his fingers when he continued to press them to my lips, rewarding me with a belly laugh from Liam, "just because you have built in bracelets and anklets doesn't mean you aren't ridiculously adorable!"

"I got the bags, do you need anything else before we go?" Bree asked as she walked toward the front door.

"Nope! Let's go see them." We loaded Liam into his car seat and headed over to Brandon's gym.

Two months after our wedding, the gym that Brandon had continued his training at when he moved to San Diego, which led to his underground fighting, started going under since the owners went bankrupt. Brandon had been getting restless trying to figure out what he wanted to do with his life since he had stopped fighting. Not that we had to worry about money, but he felt like he wasn't doing his job as a husband and father by not bringing in more money. When he'd heard about McGowan's Gym going under, he'd rushed home and asked what I thought about it. He wouldn't put himself in danger of getting another hit like the one from Demon, but he missed fighting so much he thought owning the gym would be perfect. I couldn't have agreed more and the gym was his within the next month. Brandon was still on good terms with Scarecrow, since he was providing more fighters that he and Konrad helped train, and in the five months since he'd bought out the gym, they've more than doubled the amount of members and McGowan's had never been doing this well.

Bree and Konrad were engaged, were getting ready to move into a townhouse in the same complex where we lived and had recently started their Junior year at SDSU. They were getting married at the beginning of November and I couldn't be more excited for them. It always made me laugh thinking about how they'd both been when we'd started college. Konrad had been much the same as Bree and Chase, and wasn't looking for any type of relationship outside of a bed. But from the moment they first hung out, it was over for both of them. I could see that even if Bree kept him waiting on actually being his girlfriend. And now? Two years later and they were anxiously counting down the days until their wedding. Konrad worked for Brandon at McGowan's, and Brandon paid him *extremely* well. We both knew Breanna would never work, unless she could shop for a living, she didn't want to do anything that would take too much of her time, so Brandon made sure they were always taken care of. Just another one of the million reasons I loved him.

"Hey babe!" he called from the wall of punching bags. After

a quick word and instruction to the guy punching and kicking it, he jogged over to us and grabbed Liam out of my arms, swinging him up above his head and pulling him back down for a loud kiss. Liam squealed and chuckled. "How's my little man doing today?" Liam was still giggling as Brandon wrapped an arm around my waist and pulled me in for a long, slow kiss.

My body instantly warmed and it took Bree's high-pitched laugh to bring me back to the gym.

"And how's my wife?" His husky voice made my insides tighten and wish for our bed.

"I'm great." I smiled softly, my cheeks flushed. "How's it going today?"

Brandon's hazel eyes hardened for a quick moment, and lost all expression as he forced a smile, "Pretty good, we got a group of guys that came in and signed up for memberships together."

I frowned at his expression, "How many?"

"Eleven."

"Eleven? That's great Brandon! Why do you not seem happy about that?" There were days at a time that no new members came at all, eleven in one morning was unheard of.

"I am happy, so what brings you here?" He kissed my forehead and blew a raspberry on Liam's belly, Liam slapped down on Brandon's head and dissolved into a fit of giggles. We definitely had a happy baby.

"Well Bree and I have to go do some wedding stuff, but we were wondering if there's any way we could talk you guys into lunch?"

His rugged face softened and his hand dropped to my hip, giving it a small squeeze, "I can't leave Harper, Aaron called in this morning, so it's just me and Konrad until a little later. He can go with you though."

"I can go pick up some sandwiches from down the street and bring them back?" Bree volunteered.

Brandon's gaze flickered to something behind us, then to Konrad, and his face tightened again, "I'll go grab my card, Harper can you come wi—"

"Blaze."

The familiar voice had my body tensing and Brandon exhaled a curse. Turning slowly, I kept my eyes on Brandon's piercing hazel ones until I knew I needed to look ahead. Carter. My heart clenched and tears pricked my eyes. Why was I crying? Oh wait, that's right.

"Oh Blaze, no. Don't cry." He stepped forward and brought his hands up, probably to wipe the tears, but I slapped his hands away.

"Don't touch me."

A flash of hurt crossed his face before it slipped into his signature stone face. "Can we talk?"

"Why are you here Jason?"

"He's one of the eleven from this morning." Brandon's deep voice made its way through my body and helped calm me.

I leaned my back against Brandon's stomach, and he wrapped the arm that wasn't holding Liam around me again. "Why? Why would you drive *all* the way over here to come to this gym? I know for a fact you have all this on the base."

"I've been out for a month Blaze, my time there ended and I decided not to re-up."

"Then why are you still here?" I knew I was being rude, but seeing him again brought back the ache from losing his friendship, and the reason why it was lost.

"A good chunk of us were all getting out within a few months of each other. We're renting out a few houses in San Diego."

"What about your wife?"

He snorted and shook his head, "She drained my bank account when I was in Afghanistan, when I got back she was gone and there were papers for me to sign for the divorce on the table."

"I could have told you something like that would've happened. You really thought you could marry a base whore and she'd stay with you?"

"Harper," Brandon warned.

I looked up at his face and felt like a scolded child, "I'm sorry Cart— Jason, that was rude. And I'm sorry that's what you had to come back to, she didn't deserve you anyway."

Brandon flexed his grip on my hip to let me know that was better. He couldn't stand Jason Carter for obvious reasons, but of course he was still as polite as could be to him, just as he'd been with Chase.

"Carter," I sighed when a grin crossed his face from me using his last name, "why are you *here* though?" I made a loose circle with my finger, indicating the gym. There were tons of fighting gyms around San Diego, it was too much of a coincidence for him to choose this one.

"I uh—one of the guys that got out before us was already a member here before I moved, he told me the owner's name and I figured I could come here and talk to Brandon, see if he knew how you were. I didn't know if you guys were still together, or if you even spoke anymore. But you're my best friend Blaze, I needed to see you and this was my best shot. I was waiting for him to be done training that guy," he nodded his head toward the wall of punching bags, "and then you were here."

"That right there, what you just said, is a perfect example of how little of friends we actually are. We haven't spoken in over a year and a half, and even though you kind of lost the right to know anything about my life, if we were friends at all, you would have known that if you found Brandon, I wouldn't be far behind. You don't know anything about me anymore, and I don't know anything about you. So much has happened in the last year and a half with me, and you're clueless to all of it. That's saying something."

Carter glanced down to Brandon's hand on my hip and sighed, "Well it's obvious you are still together. And you're right, I don't know anything about your life now. But that doesn't change anything, you'll always be my best friend," he said softly.

Liam started getting fussy, so I turned and took him from Brandon. When I turned back around, Carter's eyes were wide and his jaw was dropped. He hadn't even realized Liam was there until then.

"You have a baby?"

The corners of my mouth curved up slightly, "Yes, and Brandon and I are married."

He looked at me quickly, then to Brandon and Liam and back to me. "Holy shit."

I rolled my eyes at him and hitched Liam higher up on my hip, "It was nice to see you Carter, but I have to go feed him." Bree handed me the diaper bag and I turned to go to Brandon's office.

"Blaze wait, can we talk sometime? I—I've missed you. We need to catch up. I know you're mad at me for what I did, but I hate not having you in my life somehow."

"Is your number still the same?"

"Yes." There was so much hope in that one word it was almost sad, but at the same time, I understood. If he had never crossed the line at that party, I would have craved our friendship too.

"I'll think about it Carter, and I'll let you know." Without another glance in his direction, I grabbed Brandon's hand and walked to his office.

"Are you okay Harper?" Brandon asked as soon as his door was shut.

"Yes, I just don't understand why he'd do this, and after not talking for so long. He could have just tried to call."

Brandon took Liam and sat down in his chair, sitting Liam on his lap so he was facing me while I got the food out of the bag.

"But he knows you would have ignored the call. You've got to hand it to him, the guy has balls for coming to my gym to ask about you."

I laughed and kissed his cheek before pulling up another chair in front of them. "So I'm guessing that's why you looked pissed off when I came in?"

"Yeah, I knew he was still in there, but I didn't know where and I didn't want him to see you. I'm sorry, I know that's immature, but he's not my favorite person in the world."

"Babe, I'm surprised you let him even become a member. I would have escorted him out as soon as I'd seen him." I smiled at Liam as he took another bite of baby food.

"The thought crossed my mind." He laughed softly, "Are you going to talk to him?"

I leaned back into the chair as I got another scoop of pureed carrots, "I don't know. If that night at the party wouldn't have happened, I would in a heartbeat. But he changed things, I don't think we can go back to being friends you know?" I shook my head, "God I still feel so stupid for not seeing it sooner."

He smirked at me, "You *were* the only person who didn't get it. Even with Bree constantly saying something to you, you were so sure she was wrong."

"He was my best friend! He treated me like every other guy in Sir's unit."

"Oh okay," he scoffed, " '*my* Blaze, *my* girl, I couldn't just let you go to California without me.' "

"Brandon Taylor . . . were you jealous of Carter?"

"Me? Jealous? Of my girl running away from me to throw herself in some random guy's arms? Not even close."

"Hmm," I fed Liam another scoop of nastiness, "I seem to remember yelling at him and telling him to leave before running into *your* arms and kissing you."

He smiled wide, "I don't remember that at all, you may need to remind me how that went."

His eyes had a wicked gleam in them as I leaned over Liam and stopped less than an inch away from his lips. "Brandon," I whispered low and sultry.

"Yeah?" He moved closer and I backed up a fraction of an inch.

I smiled when he growled and lightly brushed my mouth over his lips before sitting down, "Well if you don't remember it, I guess it never happened," I said cheerfully and went back to feeding our son.

"Tease."

"Oh yes, that's me . . . the tease." I winked and sat up for a chaste kiss.

"And to answer your question," he began after a few silent minutes, "I was never jealous of Carter. I knew if you were that clueless about his feelings that you didn't share them."

My stomach dropped knowing what he must be thinking about. I'd never shared Carter's feelings, but he'd known all along that there was something between me and Chase. I remembered listening to him telling Liam the morning of our wedding that Brandon knew it was a matter of when, not if. I took a deep breath in, held it for three seconds and then exhaled slowly.

"If you want your friend back Harper, I would never stop you. But if he tries anything again, I won't stop myself from hitting him this time."

"Thanks babe, but I'm really not sure if I even want him back in my life. You saw how he was after those few weeks of hanging out, and all those drunken voicemails he left me of the women he was with and stuff like that. That wasn't my friend, he completely changed when he got to California, and I don't know if that was a temporary thing or if that's who he really is now."

"Well I guess you won't know if you don't talk to him," Brandon offered.

"Do you *want* me to talk to him?"

He gently grabbed my chin and tilted it up, "I want you to do whatever you want to, I just didn't want you to think that I would be mad if you were friends again, and I know you miss the way you guys were before you moved."

I nodded, "Well I can see if he's still here? We can all talk?"

"If you want me there when you talk, that's fine."

"Brandon," I sighed and took off Liam's bib, "you're my husband, of course I want you there. If he has a problem with that, then that tells me all I need to know."

A flash of relief crossed his face and he smiled warmly at me, "Well then, we'll be right back." He stood up and kept Liam facing forward as he strode out the door with him.

I put everything away in the diaper bag, texted Bree back what sandwiches we wanted and sat in my chair just as the guys came back in.

Carter looked at me, then back to Brandon, "Uh, what's going on?"

"You said you wanted to talk," I gestured toward another chair, "so let's talk."

"I kind of hoped we could talk alone?"

"Anything you say to me, I will tell him, so you might as well just say it in front of both of us."

He looked uncomfortable, but sat down and wiped the sweat off his face with the bottom of his shirt, "I don't, um, really know where to start."

Well *I* do, "What happened to you? The Carter I knew didn't go to strip clubs and screw a bunch of girls, he didn't go and get wasted all the time, and he certainly didn't marry a base tramp that he had just met." I turned to look at Brandon, "I'm sorry, but there's really no other way to describe them." Looking back at Carter, I continued, "You were the first guy to make fun of those kinds of girls, and then you married one? Even without that though, you turned into such a douche Carter."

"I know, trust me I know. It wasn't the best few months of my life."

"And yet you continued to keep doing all of that, and for whatever reason you felt the need to always tell me what you were doing. I just don't understand."

He opened his mouth, eyed Brandon warily and quickly shut it again.

"Just say it."

"It's just," he exhaled loudly and sunk further into his chair, "I had to pull a lot of strings to move here with you, you have no idea how hard it was to do that. I get here, and you're with someone and my hopes of being with you were completely thrown out the window. I mean, I obviously was wrong, but I'd always thought you knew how I felt about you and thought you felt the same. So you can imagine how pissed off I was when I found out how wrong I was."

"We were just friends though, I don't know how many times you and I both said that."

"No, to *you* we were just friends. Yes, you were my best friend, but that wasn't it for me. You don't realize how much time I spent with your dad talking about you. He knew exactly how I felt, he knew why I wanted to follow you to California, he was the one who helped get my transfer pushed through."

"Sir did?" I deadpanned, "The same guy who wouldn't let me wear women's clothes?"

"Yep."

"I thought you said he wouldn't let you date Harper when you were in his unit, so why would he help you follow her here?" Brandon asked calmly.

"Uh yeah he did, but he was also the one to suggest the transfer."

"What?" Who was this guy Carter was talking about, and what did he do with my dad?

"I know, shocked me too. I'd already been thinking of a way to move out here when he called me into his office that Monday after you got your acceptance letter. He said something like, 'You know, Harper's leaving for California soon, she'll be near Pendleton. If you were there, you wouldn't be in my unit anymore.' And then he gave me that look, you know the one where he expects you to know what he's thinking? Then he said he'd start the paperwork if I was serious about being with you, and that was that."

"That just seems . . ." I trailed off not knowing what word to use.

"So unlike Sir?"

"Yeah."

"Shocked me too when it happened. So maybe you can understand why I was so miserable, and I guess I wanted you to know how miserable I was. I know how stupid that was, but I just couldn't stop. And Ashley, well, that was a mistake."

I shook my head slightly, "I still can't believe you did that, what were you thinking? Did you not learn how bad of an idea that was from any of the other guys in the unit? Like Ramos? You were there when he found out about his girl! You could have your pick of girls that would love you and would be faithful to you while you're deployed, instead you went for one of those skanks? They sit around waiting in the parking lots on base for a guy to come hit on them, when their guys go off on a deployment, you know they're waiting on base the very next weekend for another guy."

"I know Blaze," he snapped, "you think I don't fucking know that?!"

"I would strongly suggest you don't talk to my wife that way," Brandon said through clenched teeth.

Carter took a deep breath in to try to calm himself, "Sorry," he said to both of us, "Harper I know it was stupid, I knew what would most likely happen when I left, but she looked like you and I couldn't help myself."

Oh that's creepy.

Brandon's face hardened even more and he quickly turned his attention to our son. Thank God he was holding him. From the way the muscles in his arms were flexing, I knew Brandon was itching to hit something and Liam was the perfect thing to calm him down. I flashed a small smile at them before looking back at Carter.

"And now? After all that, what have you been doing this last year since you got back from Afghanistan? You still drinking all the time?"

"No, other than a beer or two with the guys every now and then, I don't do much of anything. I knew if I wanted any chance of getting you, I had to stop what I was doing. And then of course, I find you again, and you're married and have a baby." He leaned forward, resting his elbows on his knees and dropping his head in his hands. "I can't believe you have a freakin' baby," he whispered.

"I am sorry that you spent all this time, and moved to California, thinking that we would be together. I don't want to hurt you, but Carter I never saw you as anything more than my friend, and I'm sorry I didn't make that clear enough back in North Carolina. But I'm not going to be sorry for being with Brandon and having Liam, I can honestly tell you I've never been happier than I am now."

"Yeah, I'm starting to understand that. Congratulations, by the way." He said grimly, "How old is he anyway?"

"He'll be a year in two weeks." Brandon smiled down at him and bounced him up and down on his knee.

"Wow." Carter looked at him for a long time before looking back at me, "Really cute kid."

"We think so." I beamed. It got silent for a few awkward moments so I looked back at my old friend and sighed, "Well Carter, I don't know what you think about anything now that we've talked, but if you think we could go back to being friends, or I guess . . . what I thought was friends anyway, then I want that. But if that's not enough for you, then this is the last time I'm going to see you."

He furrowed his brow and leaned away slightly, "Blaze, I can't—I hate not having you there. I get that we're never going to happen. I know it took me probably too long for your liking to understand that, but I know now. I still want you around, or for me to be around I guess. Brandon, I wouldn't blame you if you didn't want that though. I know I acted pretty shitty before, but I would never try anything now that you're married. I'm not that much of a douche."

Bree and Konrad walked in with wide eyes when they saw Carter with us. "Uh, we have the food?" Bree said it like a question and mouthed *What the hell?* from behind Carter's back.

I shook my head at her and looked back at Brandon as he spoke again, "If you want, we're having some friends over for a barbecue next Saturday, you and your friends are more than welcome. Harper can text you our address."

My eyes widened.

Um, what?

Carter took that as his cue to leave and stood from the chair, "That'd be great, thanks man." He shook Brandon's hand and brushed his knuckles against Liam's arm. "Thanks for this Blaze." He hugged me tightly for a second and backed away, probably trying not to push his luck further. "Guess I'll see you next weekend?"

"Yeah, see you then."

With another awkward glance at everyone in the room, and a nod in the direction of Konrad, he walked out the door, shutting it behind him.

"Um, what just happened?" Bree asked as she handed out the sandwiches.

"We talked it out." I put my sandwich on the desk and grabbed Liam so Brandon could eat, "Brandon, why'd you invite them over? You really didn't have to do that."

He shrugged and took a big bite, speaking around his food, "People mess up and make mistakes all the time. Everyone deserves a second chance, right?"

It felt like someone punched me in the stomach. How was I any better than Carter? I'd slept with my boyfriend's friend and gotten pregnant. I'm practically the queen of getting second chances, especially from Brandon.

"Hey," he leaned over to whisper in my ear, "I didn't mean anything by that. I love you."

I nodded, "Love you too." I smiled when he pressed his full lips to my neck.

"So you guys are just back to being okay again?" Bree started searching for an explanation.

"Not at all, we're going to try though. He said he'd stop pursuing me or whatever now that he knows Brandon and I are married. So maybe eventually we will. I guess we'll see how everything goes next weekend."

"That's weird, do you not re—"

"So what wedding stuff are you girls doing today?" Konrad cut her off with a wink in my direction.

Bree's face lit up and she went into a detailed checklist of all we were going to get done. Or rather, what we'd already gotten done.

"Harper, if you don't want him to come over, he doesn't have to. I was just trying to help," Brandon said softly so we wouldn't interrupt Bree.

"No, I think it'll be good. Like I said, we'll see how it goes. If it doesn't seem like he's changed at all, then we don't have to see him again."

"Right. And if he pisses me off again, I now have his address from the membership card." He smiled wickedly, "What time will you be home today?"

I caught Bree smiling at me from the corner of my eye, "I'm not sure, late this afternoon, you'll probably make it home before I do, do you need me to pick something up or do something for you?"

"My mom offered to watch Liam for the night, she said she has enough things at her place that you wouldn't need to get a bag for him. You can drop him off on your way home."

"Hmm . . . date night? We haven't had one of those in a few weeks."

He leaned in close enough that his lips brushed against my ear, causing goose bumps to cover my body, "And it's long overdue."

Oh I definitely agree. "Well then, I'll get home as soon as I can."

"That's my girl." He picked Liam up and handed me my sandwich.

Bree and I winked at each other, oh if Brandon only knew. Carrie, Bree and I had already planned out this day, including the date night. Only Bree knew what was really going on, but Carrie had been the one to suggest acting like it was her idea. The only reason Carrie had enough things at her house was because we had Liam's bag already packed and ready for the night. We finished our food, and hung out with the guys for another few minutes before finally taking off. I'm not sure who was more anxious to leave, me or Breanna. But thankfully the guys picked up on our bouncing legs and shifting eyes toward the clock and practically pushed us out of the gym after hugs, kisses and a couple quick introductions to some of the regulars.

"HARPER, ARE YOU already home?"

My stomach erupted into a million butterflies when I heard his husky voice down the hall. I couldn't believe I was so nervous right now. Well not nervous, just really giddy. Okay, maybe a little nervous. I checked my outfit, or lack thereof, to make sure I looked okay. I was wearing black lace underwear and a blue silk spaghetti strap that I knew he loved. Fluffing my long hair that I'd loosely curled the bottoms of, I stood up straight at the end of the bed and waited. My palms started sweating and I was biting the crap out of my bottom lip when he walked in the bedroom door.

"God you're gorgeous." He took two large steps toward me and picked me up in his arms, since me standing on my tiptoes wasn't enough for him. "I didn't think you'd be here yet." He nuzzled against my neck.

"I could always leave and come back later . . . ?"

"Hell. No. I've been thinking about tonight all day, I'm not putting it off any longer than it takes for me to shower."

I smiled, this was exactly what I'd been planning on. "Well then hurry up," I pressed my body closer to his, "like you said earlier, this is long overdue."

He trailed his fingers lightly over my chest and down my waist before setting me down, "Three minutes." Capturing my bottom lip with his teeth, he tugged softly, then ran his tongue over it as he pushed me down onto the bed and headed for the bathroom.

I scooted up the bed until I was sitting against the headboard, legs crossed Indian style, and tried not to bounce up and down while I waited. Every second that passed felt like an hour and I held my breath, trying to listen to what he was doing. The water turned on and my heart sunk. Had he not noticed? I put it right next to the basket of towels, and he always grabbed a towel to bring it closer to the shower before he got in. I wrung my hands together and forced my bottom lip out from my teeth, which in turn made me start biting on the inside of my cheek. A few minutes passed, and then he was there, a towel wrapped around his hips, water still falling down his toned body, with wide eyes, a dropped jaw and clutching something in his hand.

"Harper, what is this?"

I shakily forced a smile onto my face. I didn't know how he would react, and unfortunately, I couldn't tell exactly what he was thinking right now.

"Is this—is this?" He ran a hand over his buzzed head and huffed a short laugh, "Is this what I think it is? Are you— sweetheart are we having a baby?"

I nodded and he practically flew at me with the biggest smile on his face. Capturing my face in his hands, he kissed me over and over, laughing in between each one.

"When did you find out?" he asked breathlessly and kissed me again.

I scrunched my nose and looked at him warily, "Two weeks ago?"

Thankfully he couldn't stop smiling, I had been worried he would be upset about that part, "And you're just now telling me?" He growled playfully and buried his face in my neck.

My breathing was getting ragged and I had to force myself to answer him, "Well I had my first appointment today, and I wanted to wait until I had that to tell you."

"Wait, today?" He sat back to look at me, "I thought you and Bree were doing wedding stuff."

"Yeah, we did all that yesterday. The appointment was all we had today. I was pretty positive I knew what the doctor was going to say, and I wanted to be alone with you when you found out, so I called your mom, asked her if she would watch Liam after we were done."

"So that was you? Not her?" He smiled and shook his head at me. "Wait, wait, wait. So Bree already knows?"

I laughed, "She was actually the one to make me take the test. I swear she has a built-in radar for pregnant women. I had no idea and she just showed up with a test one day and forced me into the bathroom."

"She would. Who else knows?"

"No one, and if Bree hadn't been literally waiting outside the door that day, you would have been the first to know, I promise."

"I can't blame you for Bree knowing, she's kind of a force all her own. She gets her way with everything."

"Pretty much." I smiled and pulled his face back to mine.

Pulling away, he lifted up the bottom of my silk shirt and placed soft kisses on my barely-there-bump, skimming his nose across it he kissed it one last time and made his way up my body. "When are you due?" he asked against my chest.

"May twenty-sixth, I'm ten weeks," I said breathlessly.

"I love you so much Harper, and I can't tell you how excited I am."

"Yeah?"

Brandon looked directly into my eyes, his brown eyes full of so much love, "Yeah."

Smiling, I kissed him once and let my head fall back onto the pillows while reaching for his towel, "I love you too."

20

"WELL I HEAR a congratulations is in order, huh Kid?" Konrad kissed the top of my head as he pulled me in for a hug.

"Why thank you! Your turn next, yeah?" I mock glared at Bree when he released me, but smiled when her jaw dropped.

"I swear I wasn't the one that told him!" she said with her hands raised, palms facing me.

"I told him," Brandon said as he walked up behind me, wrapping his arms around my waist, "It's only fair if Bree knew, he got to know too."

"You guys didn't tell Mom though, right?"

Konrad and Bree shook their heads and Bree said, "No, we know you're telling everyone at Liam's birthday party. I still can't believe you're going to have two kids before I even have one!"

"Hmm . . . guess you better get working on that then." I winked at her.

"No way, we're going to have our hands full playing with yours. Just keep popping them out, and we'll act like they're ours."

"Um, no! I think two is more than enough for now, I won't even be twenty-one and Brandon will be twenty-three when baby number two is born, if we have more I'm sure it can wait."

The doorbell rang and Brandon kissed my cheek before releasing me, "That's probably Jeremy, he's coming with a few cousins, so is it okay if we tone down the baby talk until they leave?"

"I thought you told Jeremy?"

"I did, because I know he won't say anything. My cousins on the other hand, don't know how to shut up. They'd probably call my mom before we could finish telling them." He chuckled and jogged off toward the door.

Bree leaned over the island in the middle of the kitchen and raised her brow, "So Jer knows too?"

"Yeah," I grunted and tried to reach for the stack of bowls on the top shelf, "I don't know why we're making such a big deal about not telling the parents yet, we've told practically everyone else. I guess we just want them all here at once, so they can find out at the same time."

I had just climbed on top of the counter when Konrad reached over me and grabbed the bowls, smirking when I glared at him. He didn't even have to go on the balls of his feet.

"Damn tall people," I muttered under my breath.

"Hey sis! Hey Bree," Jeremy hugged her quick, and turned to do a "guy hug" with Konrad, "Konrad, what's up man?" He stepped over to where I was still sitting on the counter and I frowned when I realized he was still taller than me even when I was up here, "Trying to reach the bowls again Harper?" He wrapped his arms around me and kissed me on the cheek before whispering, "Congrats sis. I'm really happy for you guys."

I hugged him tightly back, "Thanks Jer, and thanks for coming."

"I brought my girlfriend, is that okay?"

"Jeremy, you have a girlfriend?!" His face lit up and he had a huge grin, "Are you even old enough for one of those yet?" I laughed when he playfully punched my arm.

"I'm seventeen, not twelve."

I got all serious, "Oh yes, of course. How could I ever forget?" I looked around him, "Well where is she? I want to meet this girl who stole my brother-in-law's heart."

"She's with Laura and Kate, but she's really shy, so Bree," he turned to look at her, "go easy on her, okay?"

Bree put a hand to her chest, "Who me? Shy people are my specialty. Just ask Harper."

We all laughed and Jeremy eyed me curiously, "Sis, what the fuck are you doing?"

"Language!" I chastised him but started giggling uncontrollably when I still couldn't get down, "I can't get back down. I usually can't even jump up here. How the hell did I get up here Konrad?"

"Language!" Jeremy tried to mimic my pitch as he scooped me off the counter. "God you're so short."

"No, the rest of you are just freakishly tall." I pushed him away from me and went to stand by Bree, since she was much closer to my height.

"Aww, are they making fun of you again sweetheart?" Brandon was grinning when he rounded the corner, "I can't believe *anyone* would ever make fun of your height. Because you're average height, right?"

I glared at him until he wrapped his arms around me with my favorite smile and his dimple flashing at me, "Exactly." I reached up on my tiptoes and kissed him soundly.

"Uh, one, get a room. Two, Harper I want you to meet Aubrey."

I peeked around Brandon's side and saw a pretty girl with pale skin, raven black hair and wide brown eyes tucked under Jeremy's arm. Oh my word they were cute together. "Hi Aubrey!" I walked over to them and hugged her quickly, dropping my arms and stepping back when I remembered how much I hated being hugged before Bree socialized me.

"Aubrey, this is my sister-in-law, Harper."

She gave a small wave and blushed when she smiled, oh yeah, we were going to get along just fine. "Nice to meet you Harper, you have a beautiful home."

"Thank you! Aubrey, this is my best friend Breanna and her fiancé Konrad." I waited until they said their *hellos* and stepped back into Brandon's arms, "And I'm guessing you just met Brandon?"

She nodded and bit her lower lip, trying to curl further into Jeremy's arm.

"Um, no! Where is the little munchkin?" one of the twins called from the dining room.

I laughed and when Kate and Laura walked into the kitchen, I went to hug them both. "He's at Mom and Dad's for the night, figured this would be a little much for him. You girls remember Konrad and Bree?"

Laura jumped over to Bree's side for a hug and Kate crossed her arms and failed at glaring at me, "I wanted to see my little Liam though." She pouted and drug her feet to hug Bree.

"Next time," I promised them, "besides, we have four or five single guys fresh out of the Marine Corps coming today, you really want to be playing with a baby that whole time?"

"Oh my God, really?!" they both said at the same time.

I laughed and nodded. The twins were Brandon and Jeremy's cousins, only a year younger than myself and insanely beautiful. They had a good half foot on me, had blue eyes and unnatural blond hair, but they rocked it pretty well. Other than their eyes, I still hadn't found a way to tell them apart, thank God Kate had one eye that was half blue and half brown, or I'd always wonder who I was talking to.

"Well then!" Kate said and grabbed her sister's hand, "We're going to go change into our bikinis!"

"You do realize we don't have a pool, right?" I called to their retreating forms.

"Don't care!"

"I'm going to end up punching someone, aren't I?" Brandon grumbled from behind me.

"Probably." I sighed and looked up at him, glad to see he was smiling. "When are you going to start the grill?"

"Already did after I let them in. I'll put the burgers on a bit after everyone else gets here."

"Thank you." I kissed his soft lips and relaxed further into his chest, "And thank you for this, I think it'll be a good day."

"I think you're right." He lifted me up and sat me on the counter, gave me another kiss that almost reduced me to a puddle and walked over to Jeremy, "Come help me with the ice chests."

"Brandon! I just barely got down from the counter, and Jeremy had to help me!"

"I know." He smiled wickedly and walked out to the garage.

I turned to Konrad, "Care to help?"

"Ya know, I forgot to get the ice from the store . . . wanna go with me baby?" He grabbed Bree's hand and led her quickly out of the kitchen.

Jerks.

Looking to the only person left in the room I added dryly, "Want to join?"

Aubrey walked up next to me and had to jump three times before she got enough leverage to lift herself all the way up.

"They're really high up, right? It's not just me?"

"No, it's definitely not just you," she said softly and tucked her hair behind her ears. "Thank you so much for having us, this is really sweet of you."

"Of course! It's fun to do. I apologize in advance if it gets rowdy. I don't know much about the guys coming."

She laughed and swung her legs back and forth, "That's fine."

Man, did I talk this soft too? "So tell me, how did you meet Jeremy?"

"Um, school."

"Oh yeah? How long have you been dating?"

Aubrey blushed fiercely and looked over to the door leading to the garage, "Only a week. He asked me out a few times last year, we were Chemistry partners, but I don't know . . . he scared me."

"What? Why?"

"Well I mean, besides his size, he's really popular and outgoing. He was already popular after his first week at the school, and I knew a lot of girls liked him. I don't know. Guys like him don't date girls like me, I thought it was a joke."

The first half of that didn't surprise me one bit. He'd really filled out in the last year, was built just like Brandon, and looked exactly like him. Their size was intimidating, and they were incredibly handsome. But what the hell? "I'm sorry, I must be missing something, girls like you?"

"He plays football and is the captain of the soccer team, I'm not into sports or anything school related really."

"If he's dating you, then I'm pretty sure that doesn't matter at all to him. You're gorgeous Aubrey, and you seem really sweet, it's not hard to see why he likes you. Jeremy doesn't just date girls . . . actually, he hasn't had a girlfriend in the two years that I've been with Brandon. So for him to ask you out is a big thing for him. And those boys don't have a cruel bone in their body, he would never date you as a joke. He's just like his brother, they're extremely protective and devoted to the girls in their life. Nothing less."

She blushed again, "You and Brandon are so perfect together.

Jeremy's told me so much about you both, and seeing you together is cute. It's obvious how much you love each other."

I smiled and leaned back on my hands, "We are definitely in
love."

Brandon and Jeremy walked through carrying two ice chests
and smiled widely upon seeing us on the counter. Jeremy
couldn't tear his eyes from Aubrey. Oh he was such a goner.

"So then, you're not into sports, what *are* you into?"

Aubrey was looking at Jeremy's back and biting the corner of
her bottom lip, "Um, what?" She blinked her doe-like eyes at me.

"Interests," I laughed and nudged her side, "what are your interests? Besides Jeremy."

"Oh," there goes that blush again, I think I've met my match
in the blushing department, "well I like photography, and I read
a lot."

"What do you read?" I never got into reading, the only books
in my house growing up were by Stephen E. Ambrose, R. Lee
Ermey or Tom Clancy and those didn't exactly pique my interest.

"Anything with a love story. I *love* love triangles."

How is that exciting? I was in the middle of a love triangle
not long ago. It wasn't exactly fun. I just nodded my head, "And
photography?"

She touched the large bag at her side, I'm guessing she had her
camera in there, "Anything really. Scenery, people, flowers . . ."
She trailed off.

"I'd like to see them sometime, if that's okay with you."

"See what?" Jeremy asked as he jogged back into the kitchen,
planting himself between Aubrey's legs, his hands resting lightly
on her waist.

"She said she likes photography."

Jeremy glanced up at me briefly, "Oh man sis, you should see
her stuff, she's really good. She has her camera with her, why
don't you show her what you have on there Aubrey?"

Kate and Laura chose that moment to come back in and Aubrey's blush instantly left her face as she took her hand back out of her bag.

"Later," I whispered and she nodded her head in relief.

Brandon walked into the kitchen talking on my phone, even though I saw it in his hands, I still patted my shorts to make sure I didn't have it on me, "Yeah, you'll see a white truck and black Jeep out front, just walk on in. We're in the kitchen. See ya." He tapped the screen and handed it to me.

"Carter?"

"Yep, they just pulled onto the street. Where'd Konrad go?"

I rolled my eyes, "Jerk said he forgot to get ice and left me on the counter. Thankfully *someone* is nice enough and agreed to join me up here after everyone ditched me."

Brandon looked at Jeremy and started laughing, "Sweetheart, he didn't forget the ice, we just dumped it all in the ice chests with the drinks."

Konrad and Bree walked back in the kitchen, Bree looked completely ravished. I narrowed my eyes at him and pointed at his chest, "Ice, huh? Asshole."

He gave a sheepish grin and shrugged, "I'm sorry, but it's too funny that you can't get down."

"You're on my list Konrad Anderson. You are on. My. List." Everyone was laughing loudly when we heard a voice from somewhere in the front.

"Hello?"

"In here." Brandon called and the twins started smiling.

Carter rounded the corner, closely followed by a few guys, "What's up man?" He shook Konrad and Brandon's hands and looked at me awkwardly as he came in for a hug, "What's wrong with you?"

"Nothing," I grumbled.

"She's mad because Brandon put her up there, and no one

would help her off." Konrad smirked and leaned up against another counter, with Bree in his arms.

"Well duh Blaze. That way they don't have to worry about you getting into trouble."

I glared at him and scooted toward the edge, but quickly went back. Aubrey did the same and Jeremy eventually helped her down. She was at least three inches taller than me, and even she wouldn't jump down.

Carter walked back into the dining room when he heard more of his friends come into the house and Brandon sauntered over to me, "It's just because you're so damn cute up there." He kissed me and pulled me down, making it so my chest was pressed hard against his as I slowly slid down his body. His gray eyes heated and my body instantly responded. Stupid barbecue.

Carter came back in, making a total of six Marines, two of them had girlfriends with them, and we started the long process of introducing everyone. Brandon introduced us before Carter introduced himself and his friends. Kate caught my eye as she shamelessly stared at Carter, mouth partially open. I don't know if it was her expression, but Carter definitely did a double take when he saw her too. He passed over Aubrey and Jeremy and when he caught sight of Laura, his brow furrowed and he quickly glanced over to Kate, back to Laura and finally rested on Kate again. When he looked over to me, I raised an eyebrow at him with a wide smile and I swear he blushed as he stumbled over his introductions.

"Did you see that?" Brandon whispered low in my ear. So I wasn't crazy.

"Mhmm."

"Huh." He kissed my head and stood up straighter. "Interesting."

It was quiet when Carter finished with their names and thankfully Brandon said he was going to start the food, so all the guys shuffled out with him and the hamburger patties. It was adorable to see Jeremy hesitate and look between the guys and Aubrey a few times before she pushed him out the door. I started getting cheese ready for Brandon and slicing up tomatoes and onions for when the food would be done. Bree and Aubrey helped me as the other four girls sat on barstools and talked chattily.

"Hey Blaze, your hubby said he needed cheese." Carter walked toward me but looked at Kate over his shoulder quickly before thanking Bree for the plate of separated cheese she was holding out to him.

"You're drooling Kate." I smiled at her after Carter went back outside.

She smiled mischievously and glanced back quickly before leaning forward like we were sharing secrets, her elbows resting on the counter. "He's cute, huh?"

Bree and I grinned and rolled our eyes at each other while Laura agreed. Aubrey just nodded her head silently next to us.

"So, you're *the* Blaze?" one of the girlfriends asked.

Stifling a groan, I plastered a smile on my face, "That I am."

"I heard a lot about you, Craig lives with Jason."

The name Craig wasn't ringing a bell, I was trying to remember which guy had been next to her, "All bad things, I'm sure?" I smirked and turned to grab the sliced produce, "Aubrey, can you help me with the plates and bowls?"

"From what he said, you two are close?" Craig's girlfriend continued.

"Uh, kind of. We were best friends back home, but that was a while ago."

"Cute pet name he has for you," she goaded.

I set the plates back down a little harder than I should have, and tried to stay smiling as I tilted my head to the side, "Not really. I wouldn't call making fun of how much I blush 'cute.'"

"He doesn't have a nickname for anyone else."

"Oh my God, he has a nickname for his best friend. Big effing deal." Bree slapped her palms down to her sides in exasperation. "Can we eat now? I'm starving."

Dear Lord I loved Bree.

"You were the reason Ashley left him, you know."

I bit down on my tongue and counted to five before saying anything else, "I'm sorry, what was your name again?"

"Lauren."

"Lauren, right. Can you come here for a sec?" I led her into the living room, thankful Bree made everyone else stay in the kitchen, "I'm guessing you're a friend of Ashley's?"

She raised a dark brow in confirmation.

"I'm sure you have a reason for trying to stand up for your friend that was *sweet* enough to empty Carter's bank account and let him come back from war to find divorce papers, but I can assure you I had nothing to do with said divorce. Whether she believes that or not, is her problem. But if you still feel the need to be in the middle of it, feel free to ask Carter when the last time was that we spoke before last week. He'll tell you it was *months* before he even met Ashley. I knew they got married, but I found out through a text."

"I'm sure, I know you were still around and I've heard enough about you to know what kind of girl you are."

"I doubt that."

"You weren't always surrounded by Marines? Sleeping with half the guys in Jason's unit? From the way he talks about you, you're still screwing him. Does your husband know you've fucked most of the infantrymen in Lejeune?"

"Excuse me? Who the hell do you think you are coming in *my* house, accusing me of—"

"Being a home-wrecker? It's about time someone informed you of what you are! Do you know how heartbroken Ash was that her husband told her she'd never be you?"

"What happened between me and Ashley is between us." Carter came up beside me and I felt Brandon's large frame step behind me. "And whatever has happened since then is none of your business either."

"It is my business when I had to listen to my friend cry for hours on end about some slut!"

"Shit." A mumbled voice came through the back door, "Lo, what the fuck is wrong with you?" A lean guy I'm guessing was Craig pushed through us and grabbed her arm, whispered to her for a second and watched her storm out the door. "Y'all, I'm so sorry. I'm gonna take her home. Harper, Brandon, please forgive that. She's— she's . . . well what she said wasn't right. Y-you're not a, uh, slut Harper. I'm real sorry."

My blood was boiling and my body was shaking, but I forced my voice to stay even, "Feel free to come back, but don't bring her."

Craig nodded at me and looked up to Brandon, "Brandon, I'm—"

"It's fine," Brandon raised a hand to stop him, "but Harper's right, don't bring her back to our house again. We'll save you some food if you decide to come back."

He waved awkwardly and bolted for the front door.

The three of us stood there for a moment looking at the shut door and I brought my hands up with a soft clap, "Well, she was lovely. Burgers, anyone?"

Carter smirked and punched my arm, "Hell yeah, bet I can still eat you under the table."

Like that was hard to do. I patted my stomach and winked at Brandon before looking back at Carter, "I don't know about that, I've been awfully hungry lately."

"This isn't ice cream Blaze, you know you can't beat me unless it's that."

"True." I sighed and wrapped my arms around Brandon's

waist, looking up at his amused expression, "Aren't you supposed to be manning the grill?"

"Everything's practically done, but Jer's got it covered. Bree
said we needed to save you."

I rolled my eyes, "I was handling it just fine . . . okay maybe
not."

"You handled that better than I would have expected anyone
to. You're kind of amazing, you know?" Brandon's gray eyes ran
over my face, resting on my lips.

"And you're kind of ridiculously handsome, you know?"

He leaned down and gave me a soft kiss, smiling against my
mouth when another happy sigh escaped my lips.

"Gah, you guys are disgustingly cute." Carter gave us a
crooked smile and shook his head.

"You know Carter, Kate's single . . ." I pursed my lips and
raised my eyebrows.

"The one with the awesome eyes?"

Brandon and I laughed, "Yep."

"Oh really now? Well then, please excuse me." After rounding the corner, he poked his head back in and looked at me with
mock disappointment, "I know for a fact you perfected your
right hook, I expect to see it next time someone calls you a
slut. Prokowski wasn't your punching bag for nothing, make us
proud Blaze!"

Carter didn't leave Kate's side for the rest of the afternoon, and
although it helped me breathe easier, I know Brandon wasn't completely comfortable with him yet. It took me a bit to realize why
he kept pulling me closer to him than I already was until I noticed
the longing glances Carter seemed to still be sending my way.

"You need help in here?"

Turning, I saw Carter standing behind the breakfast bar with
a sheepish grin on his face, "There's not much left, I'll be back
out there soon."

The chair scraped against the floor before he sat down, his body slumping into the chair as he brought his beer to his lips, "So today has been fun."

"Mhmm. Glad you guys could come. It was nice to be surrounded by jarheads, it's been too long."

"I knew you'd miss us. It was so different when you left for school. I mean, we had a lot that we were always doing, but it still felt like we had nothing to do or look forward to without you there."

"It was weird for me too, especially with Bree. I've never been around girls, but she's great, she was the perfect roommate and friend for me. And all the guys that we hung out with reminded me of you all, so it made it easier. Going my whole life being surrounded by Sir's unit, I felt like everyone in there before you got there, and during, was my real family. You guys were my home."

"Even Jacobs?" He gave me his crooked grin and I rolled my eyes remembering the perverted creep.

"Okay maybe not *all* of you. I think I told you when you first got here, I felt like I went from one family of brothers to another, and that really is the best way to explain it. It wasn't you, or Prokowski and Sanders, but they were still protective and funny like the rest of you, so it felt like I was back home being around them. The house and Bree made moving an easy transition." I turned to put the rest of the crème pie in the fridge, and my heart ached when I saw his lonely expression, "It really has been good to see you Carter. I've missed you."

"I've missed you too Blaze. These last couple years have gone," he took another swig and sighed deeply, "a lot different than I thought they were going to."

"For me too." I leaned onto the island and shook my head, laughing softly, "I didn't think I would be married or have a baby, that's for sure."

"I did, but I definitely thought it would be with me. I had it all planned out, I was gonna sweep you off your feet, you were going to drop out of college and marry me immediately." He puffed a small laugh and ran a hand through his short hair.

"Well, obviously that didn't happen." I smirked at him.

"*Obviously*. What did you see yourself doing?"

"Continuing school, trying to enjoy the 'college experience,' I guess. I don't really know Carter, I just wanted to get away, be me, or find out who I was."

"And then you met Brandon, and your whole world changed?" He looked sad, even through his smile, "I've gotta admit, I thought getting you to marry me anytime soon was a long shot, but I couldn't believe the girl I knew was already head over heels for some guy she'd just met. You were so different when I got here, confident, feminine and outgoing. I had to keep reminding myself that you *were* my Blaze. I'd already lost you to everyone here though. It was painfully obvious after those first few minutes on the beach. And seeing you with him, I just—I don't know. It shocked the hell out of me and killed me."

"To be honest, I wasn't even thinking about dating when I left home. I mean, I figured I would, but never thought I'd meet someone I wanted to spend the rest of my life with after just two weeks of being here, ya know?" I laughed softly and the corners of my mouth tilted up, "Definitely thought marriage and babies would happen sometime *after* graduation. Like you said though, life doesn't always go as planned, does it? It caused me to grow up, too soon probably, but I'm fine with that because it was the result of my actions. I just hate that those actions forced the people closest to me to grow up too." Silence filled the kitchen for a few moments before I continued, "And while I can't regret anything that brought Brandon and I to where we are now, I wish I could have spared Brandon and Chase a lot of the pain that we went through to get here."

"Chase? That tatted up guy . . . Bree's brother right?"

I nodded and watched him try to figure it out.

"I knew it! I knew there was something going on there, he was way too possessive of you for you to just be friends. He was worse than Brandon and me combined. Where is he anyway?"

"He died."

"Oh damn. When?"

"Over a year ago, he ran a red light and was hit by an eighteen wheeler. I was five and a half months pregnant with Liam. Chase was the father."

"The fuck?" He leaned over the countertop and whispered, "Does Brandon know about this?!"

"Yes Carter, Brandon knows everything, I promise. I uh, I cheated on Brandon with Chase not long after you left for Afghanistan, but trust me when I say it is way too long and FUBAR'd to even try to explain tonight."

"Blaze, you can't just say something like that and not tell me what happened."

My vision got blurry and I blinked back the tears, "Not tonight, kay Carter?"

"Yeah, alright." He shook his head in disbelief, "But he just acts like Liam's his son?"

"Chase was the father, but Brandon *is* Liam's dad. He loves him like he's his own." I walked over and sat in the seat next to him, "I don't expect you to understand what that means, it's hard to explain it to anyone who wasn't there for everything that happened."

Carter continued to stare at me with wide unblinking eyes, "Jeez Blaze."

"I know."

"One day, we're sitting down and you're telling me the whole damn thing."

"Okay Carter. Will you tell me all about you too?"

He sat forward, resting his elbows on his knees, "Hell, I'll tell you it all right now. I pretty much lost it after that night at the party, slept with a new girl every weekend, went to strip clubs every Friday night and was wasted all weekend, every weekend. One Friday, I'm walking out to my car with some of my boys and I see this girl sitting on the tailgate of a big truck. Swear to God I thought it was you. Walked over and saw it wasn't, but by that point she had seen she caught my attention and started laying it on pretty thick. Honestly it was pathetic, but at that point I didn't care. Made the guys find their own way and spent the afternoon with her, drove to Vegas late that night and married her the next day. Stupidest damn thing I've ever done, and God she drove me crazy. Anytime we were out, she'd try to get me to have my dog tags outside my shirt, and would always wear a 'Marine's wife' shirt. Wouldn't even call me by my name, always called me Sergeant and let everyone she talked to know she was married to a guy in the military. I mean like literally, it was the first thing she said. Even the other people would look at her weird for just bringing it up like that. She didn't care about me just the same as I didn't care about her. We were both using each other for something, and I think that's the only reason we tolerated each other for the month before I left."

"And what Lauren said about you and her?"

He scoffed and rolled his eyes, "I accidentally called her Blaze one night, and she got all excited that I gave her a nickname, I was drunk and straight up told her, 'That name's not for you, you'll never be her.' "

"Jason Carter!" My mouth popped open wide, "I can't believe you actually said that to your wife." I know it was awful, but I burst out laughing and couldn't stop.

Carter was shaking with silent laughter, "And yet, here you are laughing about it."

"I'm sorry," I wiped tears from my cheeks and laughed louder, "but I was picturing what her face would have looked like when you said that."

"Oh God she was mad. Slapped me across the face in front of everyone, hurt like sin too!"

"You were in front of other people?!"

"We were at a bonfire with some friends. That night didn't end well, that's for sure."

"Good God, Carter. That's terrible." My chuckling made it obvious I thought anything but that.

He shrugged, "Needless to say, that marriage didn't work out."

"Oh, I wonder why?" I winked and a smile stretched across my face briefly before faltering when I saw the pissed off expressions on most of the people that had just walked through the back door. Brandon was first, shrugging off Konrad's halting arm with one hand, the other had his phone pressed to his ear. Bree, Jeremy and Aubrey followed behind him, the first two brooding, Aubrey was nervously looking between Brandon and me. "Babe?"

"Let me call you right back," he said quietly and slid his phone into his pocket, "Harper, I gotta talk to you."

"No, you don't!" Konrad said harshly and my eyes widened in surprise.

"I can't believe you're even considering this, you arrogant asshole!" Bree shoved him roughly from behind, Brandon didn't even spare a glance at her.

"Sweetheart, that was—"

"You're smiling?! Are you kidding me?" Jeremy's face was bright red as his voice continued to rise, "How can you be happy right now? You're going to destroy her!" He grabbed Brandon's collar as he started walking toward the back door again.

"Back off Jer." Brandon growled and roughly removed his brother's hand before turning back to me.

"What are we missing?" Carter leaned over and half-whispered to me.

"I have no idea." My eyes went even wider as Jeremy tried to put Brandon in a headlock.

"I said back the fuck off!" Brandon maneuvered out of the hold and shoved Jeremy into the wall, Jeremy charged Brandon again but Konrad caught him and held him back.

"Brandon Taylor!" I hissed, mortified. "What is wrong with you?"

Even with Konrad holding Jeremy back, Brandon stepped right up to Jeremy, their noses touching as they stared each other down.

"Stop!" I hopped off the tall chair and forced my way between them, both hands on Brandon's chest, "Everyone calm down!" Once Konrad released Jeremy and Brandon was finally looking at me, I narrowed my eyes at my husband and spoke softly, "Apologize to Jeremy."

Brandon scoffed, but after registering my expression muttered an apology.

"Now tell me what's going on."

"That was Scarecrow on the phone." Brandon's face stretched into a smile again.

"Okay, and . . . ?" Everyone's anger and Brandon's hopeful expression suddenly clicked and I recoiled from him, "Oh my God, you're not serious, are you?"

"Harper, just hear me out." He reached his arms to me and I stepped back until I ran into either Konrad or Jeremy.

"You're serious?!"

"What is going on?" Carter asked exasperated.

"Sweetheart, please just listen. They want a re-match, his people *alone* are offering *double* for a re-match. That plus whatever else from the bets, do you know how much I could bring in?"

"His people? Who is he?" But I had a sinking feeling I already knew who. There aren't many people who would want to go up against Brandon again.

"Demon."

"NO!"

"I would make eight grand off his trainers and manager! Eight grand Harper!"

I shook my head and stared at him incredulously, "We don't need that money Brandon."

"It wouldn't hurt either, five minutes and I could walk out with an easy ten thousand dollars. Maybe more."

"Why are you doing this?" My voice broke at the end and he stepped toward me again, this time succeeding in wrapping his arms around me.

"What's going on?" someone asked from the back door.

"Great question." Carter sounded annoyed.

"He got a call to go fight," Konrad said softly.

"Well what's wrong with that?" Carter eyed me warily before facing Konrad again, "He hadn't lost a match when I used to hang out with you, right?"

"He's never lost, period. But the last one, the guy he fought wasn't happy that he lost, so he went after Brandon again, hit him so hard it almost caused severe damage. Doctors said he wouldn't be so lucky next time he got another hit to the head. This fight's against the same guy."

Hearing Konrad gloss over that awful night gave me chills, Brandon brought me back to his chest, kissing the top of my head.

"Let's just talk about this," Brandon whispered against my hair.

I pushed back and looked up at him, searching his gray eyes, my heart broke at the determination there. "You've already made up your mind."

Brandon grimaced, "Nothing bad will happen, I promise."

Shaking my head, I stepped out of his embrace, "Then go Brandon. If you're so sure about this, just go."

"Sweetheart, don't be like that."

"I said go." Without another glance in his direction, I pushed past the group of people in the dining room and walked toward the bedrooms. Stopping in the nursery, I barely made it over to the chair before my legs gave out and the sobs shook my body. I could hear yelling from the dining and living room for a few minutes before Brandon came into the room, picking me up off the chair and wrapping his arms around me tight.

"Please don't be mad at me."

Was he serious? Did he expect me to just be okay with this? "Why would you do this? To Liam and me? To our baby? Why!"

"I'm sorry, but that's a lot of money. I would be stupid to just pass on that. Please come with me, I need you there."

"There is no way I would go back to an Underground fight! Not after what I saw last time. Don't do this," I begged, "what if something happens to you? Do you not care about us at all?"

He stepped back, looking like I'd slapped him, "How could you even ask me something like that?"

"Brandon! Do you not remember what happened after your last fight at all? You promised me you wouldn't fight again. You *swore* you would never do something that could risk us losing you. And one phone call from Crow and you're just going to jump back into it? This isn't some ridiculous excuse for a fight, this is Demon. *Demon!* I'd never been more terrified watching you fight someone than I was that night, he was good then and I have no doubt he's been training."

Brandon's eyes narrowed slightly, "I beat him once, I ca—"

"I wasn't saying you weren't good, or that you can't still win a fight. But damn it babe! Does none of this just scream *bad idea* to you? Liam will be one in less than a week, your last fight was a year ago tomorrow. Doesn't that seem like a bad omen?"

He breathed heavily through his nose, "It's one fight. It'll be over before you know it."

"Brandon—"

"I need to do this Harper." If the finality of his tone hadn't broken through, the expression on his face would have let me know this discussion was over.

Biting back a sob, I somehow managed to nod my head and keep the next wave of tears back until he kissed me chastely and said he'd call me as soon as it was over. He hadn't heard one word I'd said. Did he really miss fighting that bad? Was it just because it was Demon? Because I knew it wasn't for the money.

Konrad and Jeremy opened our bedroom door before shutting it and barging into the nursery, closely followed by Bree.

"He's going?" she asked softly as she sat on the glider's ottoman.

Nodding, I eyed the boys, "Will you please go to the fight? Make sure nothing happens to him?"

"We're staying with you." Bree answered for the three of them.

"I need to be alone right now, and I need you there in case it gets bad. Please keep me updated."

Konrad's phone chimed and he cleared his throat, "Fight's confirmed, it's already going around who's fighting and where."

"Go," I pleaded.

The boys hugged me before walking out, but Bree lingered.

"I want to know who won as soon as it's over. Okay?" When she didn't say anything I hugged her tightly and walked her out to the hallway, "Can you apologize to Carter for me? Tell him I'll talk to him later."

Bree sighed, but kissed my cheek and made her way to the living room while I went to the bedroom and started packing a few things. Grabbing money, my toiletries, pajamas, a change of clothes and everything Liam would need for two days, I was out of the house ten minutes after everyone left. Mom was surprised to see me, but after saying everyone was having a good time at our place, and I didn't want to pick up Liam too late, she gave me a quick kiss and sent me on my way with my son. Bree texted me that the fight had started only ten minutes after I had us settled into a hotel room and I held Liam tight as I paced back and forth for twelve excruciatingly long minutes. As soon as she let me know that Brandon won, and all of them were safely in their cars and headed back to our house, I powered down my phone and curled onto the bed, letting loose the flood of tears that had been threatening to spill over since I walked out my door.

21

Looking at Liam in my rearview mirror, I bit my bottom lip nervously as I tried to calm my body's shaking. It was Monday afternoon, and in the day and a half since I'd been gone, I still had yet to turn on my phone or speak to anyone and was now five minutes from the house. Brandon was supposed to be working today, but I had a feeling he'd be home when we got there, and I was trying to mentally prepare myself for whatever was waiting for me there.

I knew it was stupid to leave the way I did, and not leave a way for anyone to get ahold of me. But I had known I wouldn't be gone more than two days, and I needed time for Brandon and myself to think separately. The fact that he was so willing to go back to fighting after everything we went through last year, and all his promises, killed me. And I still had no idea what I thought about it, or why I thought he had done it. My mind kept screaming at me that if he would do this, then our family really didn't mean that much to him, but I knew that wasn't true. Brandon loved us fiercely. Which kept leading me to the question that had been bothering me, why would he risk getting hurt, or worse, if he cared about us as much as I knew he did?

My stomach dropped when I saw Brandon's Jeep in the driveway. Not bothering with the garage, in case I felt the need to make a hasty retreat again, I put my Expedition in park and just stared at the door. He was going to be so pissed. The few times I'd ever seen him truly angry were terrifying, and his anger hadn't even been directed at me. Glancing down to my knotted hands in my lap, I was surprised when a tear fell onto my arm. Brushing the wetness from my cheeks I took a deep shuddering breath and got Liam and myself out of the car. I'd barely shut the front door when I heard Brandon running down the hallway. He skidded to a stop when he saw us and I inhaled a gasp. He wasn't pissed, but he looked terrible. His eyes were puffy and bloodshot with dark half circles underneath. One hand was steadying himself against the wall while the other was clutching at his bare chest, rising and falling quickly with labored breaths.

"You—you're—" He cursed softly and pressed his lips tightly together.

Liam started wiggling against me and asking for his dad, so I set him on the floor, watching as he quickly crawled toward Brandon. Brandon dropped hard to his knees and scooped him up in a tight hug, a sob breaking out of his chest. My chest tightened, I'd seen Brandon cry before, but he was always silent and as controlled as could be during those times. To watch his shoulders shake mercilessly and hear him continue to choke on his tears broke my heart worse than I thought possible. He rolled over until he was propped up against the wall and curled his body around Liam, murmuring things too low for me to hear.

On shaky legs, I walked into the hall and sat down against the wall opposite them, my knees barely brushing Brandon's feet. At the contact, he abruptly stood up with our son and walked into the nursery. A wave of nausea rolled through me, but with the lack of morning sickness this pregnancy, I figured it had a lot more to do with the fact that I'd screwed up this situation even more, than with the pregnancy itself. The nursery door shut some time later, and Brandon's hand stopped in front of me in offering. Placing my hand in his, I let him help me up, where he proceeded to lift me into his arms and carry me to our bedroom. Each step was careful as his brown eyes bore into my gray ones, when we reached the bed he laid me down so gently, as if he thought I would break from anything more. Without breaking contact from my eyes, he crawled in next to me, and rolled me onto my side so we were facing each other. I reached up to brush the remaining tears from his face, and traced the shadows under his eyes. Catching my hand, he kissed my palm, then the tattoo on my wrist before releasing my hand so he could cradle my face.

"Brandon, I—"

He brushed his thumb over my lips and slowly shook his head, "I was stupid." His voice was soft but rougher than usual, "So stupid. I missed fighting, and hated that people thought I stopped because I was scared. When he called—" his eyes briefly left mine as he tried to search for words, "it was like what happened last year was nothing, just another minor injury. I felt like I needed to prove something to myself, to Scarecrow, to Demon . . . everyone. I knew leaving was about the worst thing I could do, and I knew you would hate me when I got home, but I couldn't stop. I had to go, I had to fight.

"I felt sick as soon as the fight was over, I knew I'd fucked up. I should have felt that the minute you stepped away from me when you realized what was happening, but I'd been too wrapped up in it all to even absorb what you were saying to me until it was done. I got here as fast as possible, ready to get on my knees and beg you to forgive me for doing that to you . . . it never occurred to me you'd be gone." The pain in his eyes was tearing at me and he had to take a few deep breaths before continuing, "We tried calling you dozens of times, Jeremy went to Mom's house to look for you, the rest of us went to Robert and Claire's. Claire lost it when she realized she'd let both of you just leave. No one had any idea where you would have gone. God Harper, I thought I'd never see you or Liam again. You, Liam and the baby are my world. I don't know how to live without you. I know I messed up, I know I hurt you, but please don't do that to me again. I love you more than my own life Harper. I'm so sorry for hurting you."

I studied his face as I spoke, "I felt like you didn't care about us enough, if you would go and do something like that, without a thought as to how it could hurt our family."

Brandon's eyes shut tight and he dropped his head into the crook of my neck, breathing in deep. "That couldn't be fur—"

"Brandon? Harper?!"

We sat up at Bree's shrill voice and were off the bed before she got to the room. Taking four long steps toward us, her palm connected with my face before I even registered her hand swinging back.

"Breanna!" Konrad yelled and reached for her.

Brandon cupped my cheeks gently, his eyes wide with shock, fear and anger. Before he could say or do anything, Bree was pulling me into her arms for a too-tight embrace.

"You can't do that." She cried and clutched me even tighter, "You can't leave. We thought—we thought you were gone for good. You made me go so you could leave! Why wouldn't you tell me? You're my sister, you can't just leave. I've been going crazy looking for you, Mom and Dad are so upset—" She continued to ramble until her body was shaking.

"Shh." I ran my hand through her short hair, "It's okay Bree. I'm not going anywhere." After sitting both of us on the bed, I rubbed small circles on her back and let her cry. Looking at

Konrad and Brandon, I realized how much every one of us in our ever-growing, mismatched family needed each other. There was so much loss for everyone that we all clung to each other for one reason or another. Anything we did immediately affected the rest of us, something I should have taken into consideration before trying to avoid my husband for a little over a day.

Bree's sobs turned to hiccups not long after and she pulled back to look at me, "I'm sorry for slapping you, I can't believe I did that."

The corners of my mouth tilted up, "I think I deserved that one friend."

"Okay, yeah. You really did." She made a weak attempt at laughing, "When did you come back?"

"About half an hour before you showed up. Sorry for worrying all of you."

"Oh! We have to call Mom and Dad!" She started scrambling around for her purse.

"I let them know," Konrad said from the doorjamb where he was talking to Brandon.

"Mom and Jer know too." Brandon added, "I'm guessing we have another twenty or so minutes before they all start getting here to talk to you. Would you two give us a minute?"

Bree took Konrad's outstretched hand before turning back to look at me, "Where's Liam?"

"He's napping," Brandon answered and said something low to Konrad, who nodded and led Bree from the room.

Walking to me slowly, he brushed his fingers across the cheek that still stung and pressed his lips there softly. "Are you okay?"

"I'm fine. Are you?"

"You're back, so yes I am." His fingers gently tilted my head back so I was looking into his eyes, "I love you Harper Taylor, and I love our family. Please don't ever doubt that again."

I wrapped my hands around his neck and brought his face

closer to mine, "I won't." My body buzzed when I pressed my lips to his for the first time since Saturday.

Brandon lowered us onto the bed, careful to keep most of his weight off me while still pressing his firm body to mine. He grabbed my left hand with his right, placing our intertwined fingers above my head, his lips moving down to my neck. When I reached for his shirt with my free hand, he rolled so I couldn't move it and whispered against my skin, "Just let me convince myself that you're here."

My arm wrapped around his broad shoulders when his mouth covered mine again, and we continued to lay there kissing soft and slow until our families started arriving. With one last lingering kiss, we left the comfort of our bedroom and went to face our extremely upset families.

And I'd thought Bree had been mad.

After thirty minutes of Carrie, Jeremy, Dad and Mom yelling at me for leaving the way I did, then crying that I was back, everyone finally calmed down enough to actually talk things out rationally. Apparently Brandon had been ripped into by every member of our family Saturday night and yesterday for being stupid enough for even considering the fight, let alone going. No one cared that he won or that he'd made a lot of money, the risk of him getting hit in the face again was just too great for him to have taken so carelessly. And I was glad I wasn't the only one who seemed to be pissed off at him for taking it. But my disappearance had taken over most of everyone's anger as they all searched for me and Liam.

They'd looked early into the morning Sunday, and Brandon continued to every motel and hotel in the immediate area until the family gathered again early Sunday afternoon. After dividing up the lists of numbers, each person called the same places he'd checked, as well as the rest of the hotels, motels, inns and bed and breakfasts within one hundred miles. By the time the family left again Sunday night, Brandon went back out looking for my car because he guessed correctly that by using cash I'd gotten a room under an alias. When that still brought no results, he'd called Carter *and* driven by his house to see if he'd been lying when he informed Brandon he hadn't heard from me. Coming up empty again, he'd come back home at ten this morning and had been lying on the floor of Liam's bedroom calling my phone every five minutes, waiting for it to be turned back on. He hadn't slept since Friday night, and it showed in everything he was currently doing.

Seeing his exhaustion, our family started trickling out of the house, each one feeling the need to reprimand Brandon and me one last time for both being careless. After going back and forth with Carrie, she finally got her way and took a sleeping Liam home with her for the night. Brandon panicked at the thought of his son being gone from him again, but Carrie looked up at Brandon with an I'm-still-your-mother-don't-mess-with-me face and told him after we'd gotten some much needed sleep, she'd be back in the morning with him. Konrad told Brandon he'd take care of the gym tomorrow, and with a final hug from him and Bree, we were alone.

I grabbed my husband's hand and led him to our bedroom. He hadn't put a shirt on when everyone got here, so after undressing myself and helping him out of his jeans, I helped him fall onto the bed and climbed in beside him. He threw an arm over my waist and buried his head into my neck, pressing a soft kiss there. The muscles in his back and shoulders relaxed when I began running the tips of my fingers over his buzzed head and down his neck. With a muffled "I love you," he was sound asleep within a minute. His deep rhythmic breathing had my eyes heavy and closing not long after.

* * *

MY BODY JERKED awake and I sat up confused when I didn't hear Liam crying, either of our phones going off, and Brandon's breaths were still heavy and relaxed. Being careful not to move Brandon, I crept down the hall to Liam's room and almost had a heart attack when his crib was empty. Before I could scream for Brandon, I remembered Carrie took him home this afternoon and started back for my bed. I froze when I heard the door knocker, and my already increased heart rate took off in a dead sprint. Tiptoeing to the bedroom and throwing on one of Brandon's shirts, I crept back down the hall and warily took a peak at the side windows.

"Jesus Carter," I sighed and swung the door open, "you scared the crap out o—" my words and breath rushed out when he squeezed me tightly.

"Thank God you're okay."

I tapped his shoulder until he let me go with an awkward grin, "I'm fine. What are you doing here? What time is it?" It wasn't fully dark outside, but that didn't help much.

"Almost eight?" He looked at me like I should know this.

"Brandon and I were sleeping, your knocking woke me up."

"Is he still asleep?"

"Mhmm." Which reminds me . . . I'm standing in a darkened house with Carter in nothing but a shirt. No bra, no underwear. Just a shirt that grazes the top of my thighs. Folding my arms somewhat under, but still over my chest, I looked down to make sure the rest of me was still covered and asked again, "What are you doing here Carter?"

"I wanted to talk to you, alone if that's okay."

Mashing my lips together, I stepped out of the way and waved him in. I led him to the living room, turning on a few lamps on the way and sat on the chair opposite the sofa he was seated on. "So let's talk."

"Are you okay?"

"Carter, I told you I'm fine."

"Okay, I know. But you were really upset Saturday night, and then you just disappear? Obviously this fight was something Brandon shouldn't have done if you'd leave, so I was surprised when Konrad said you were back."

"Leaving was a really immature thing to do."

"But you did it Blaze. And that's why I need to talk to you."

Oh no.

"Look," he began again and rested his elbows on his knees, "I know I said I wouldn't do anything since you're married, but if you feel like you need to get out Blaze, I'll help you with that. If you're afraid of Brandon, all you have to do is tell me and I'll do everything I can to get you away from here."

"Oh my God. Carter. You have taken this way out of proportion. I do not want to get out of my marriage and I definitely don't want to leave Brandon."

"You *left*. People don't just leave their husbands unless something is wrong Blaze."

I wanted to tell him he should know, but I kept that back, "I didn't leave Brandon, I just needed a minute to think."

"About how bad he is for you? He hurt you, that was extremely apparent Saturday night. And did you see him throw his brother into the wall? I know we've talked about this before, but he's dangerous Harper. He's a fucking bomb just waiting to explode."

"You're wrong." I whispered and shook my head, "You're so wrong Carter. The few times you've hung out with him haven't been the best times, but even you should see how wrong you are. That night at the party, he didn't hit you when he had every right to. He let you become a member at his gym and invited you to our home for a barbecue. I have the sweetest, most caring and selfless husband in the world. Yes, he likes to fight, and yes he's extremely protective of his family. But I love that he is."

"Blaze, the way he is with you—"

I held up my hand to stop him, "Don't finish that. Do you not remember me telling you I cheated on him and got pregnant with his friend and housemate? He didn't even yell at me when he found out Carter. He was devastated, but he didn't raise his voice or call me a million things that I was already calling myself. Then he took care of me when I wouldn't take care of myself, and despite everything I did to him, he's still here with me."

"So that's it. You're with him out of guilt? You feel like you owe him something?"

"Of course not!" I hissed and narrowed my eyes at him, "I love him more than anything. He is everything to me. When we broke up, I felt so lost. I tried moving on with my life the way I knew I should, and I would have happily, had Chase not died. But no matter what, being happy with Chase or not, a few months without Brandon by my side was painful and incomplete. I couldn't even imagine a life without him."

"Alright, I'm sorry I shouldn't have said that. But that doesn't change the way he is with you. He doesn't let a guy even come near you without threatening to beat him to a pulp."

I rolled my eyes at his dramatics, "Not true, only you and Chase. You know how I am Carter, I need to be surrounded by guys. And not in a slutty way. Growing up with hundreds of brothers, it was only natural for me to find all that here. Other than Bree and the girls in her and Brandon's families, I don't have female friends. They are all male, and Brandon doesn't have a problem with that because he knows that's home for me. There have even been a few that have flirted, and Brandon didn't do anything other than laugh about it. But you? Well you openly admitted to everyone that you followed me across the country and that you were in love with me. Even if you lied about it, and I bought it, he knew from the beginning what was going on.

And to make it worse, he and Chase were already constantly fighting over me. Which I also had no idea about. I found that out not long ago by accident." Taking a deep breath, I sank into the cushions and covered myself with a blanket, "So he tried to keep the two guys that also loved me away from me, what boyfriend wouldn't?"

"He's possessive. That can be dangerous."

I made a pfft sound and smirked at him, "Possessive? Hardly. He knew I didn't like you in that way, so he made sure to keep you the hell off me, which I really appreciated. If you want to take that as possessive, be my guest. But he had every right to at least punch you that night, and he didn't do anything other than keep you away. And you know what? He knew I was in love with Chase too, and without even confronting Chase, he quietly stepped back so we could be together. I'm pretty sure that's the exact opposite of a possessive man."

"Seriously?"

I nodded and smiled at his taken aback expression.

He thought for a few minutes and finally blurted out, "Did you have to marry a damn saint Blaze?"

"Saint, huh? I thought he was a possessive ticking time bomb?"

"Well, it was supposed to help my argument." He winked and laughed softly.

"Oh, Carter. What am I going to do with you?"

"Love me?"

"Uh . . . no." I laughed at his playfully hurt expression, "Nice try though." When our laughter quieted, I said in a soft voice, "He really is amazing Carter."

"I know." The corner of his mouth tilted up in a sad smile, "I wish it were me Blaze. I'll always wish it was me instead of him. But I know he's good for you and your baby."

"Babies."

"What? You're pregnant again?" His face was pained through his smile for me, "Well damn. I guess I really don't have a shot with you now."

I knew he was joking, but I stayed serious, "You need to find someone who is good for you too. I know she's out there somewhere."

"But all I see is you. For the last three years, all I've seen was you Blaze."

"You have to stop. You need to know that it's never going to happen between us, and start living your life for you. And not a life where you wait for something to separate Brandon and me, because that will never happen. Get out there, date some girls, and find the one that was meant for you. I *do* love you Carter, but it's never been the way you want it. So find someone that you love, and loves you the way Brandon and I love each other."

"Maybe one day I will," he said doubtfully.

"I hope you do." I yawned and got off the couch, wrapping the blanket tighter around me, "Now get out of my house so I can go back to sleep with my husband or *I'll* kick your ass."

"Puh-lease. Preggos aren't supposed to kick ass. Isn't it bad for the baby or something?"

"Well fine, then I'll let Brandon do it."

"Alright, alright. I'm leaving!" He hugged me close, and kept me in his arms a little too long for comfort, "I really am glad you're happy Blaze. Believe it or not, that's all I really want for you."

"I want that for you too."

"Maybe someday." Kissing the top of my head, he released me and grabbed the doorknob. "Will I get to see you again soon?"

"We're having Liam's birthday party Saturday at two."

He smiled and chuckled, "Birthday party, alright sounds good."

"Kate will be there."

"Yeah?" His eyes flashed and his smile changed into something I'd seen thousands of times from Chase and Brandon, "I uh—I got her number. Would that bother you if I called her?"

"Why else do you think I'd invite you to a family party?"

His eyes unfocused for a minute, when they came back to me, he grimaced, "Blaze . . ."

"Don't Carter. If you have no interest in Kate, that's fine and don't feel forced to come on Saturday. But you need to start moving on."

"I do. Like her, I mean. She was great to hang out with, she's really funny and gorgeous. But—never mind. You're right. I'll be here Saturday." With one last longing glance, he half waved and opened the door, "Night Blaze."

"Bye." I shut the door behind him with a tired sigh and went about shutting off the lights. When I turned toward the hall, Brandon was leaning against the wall in nothing but a pair of dark boxer briefs. Dear Lord my husband is sexy.

"Once again, I have to give him credit, the guy has got serious balls for bashing me in my own house." His smile was wide as he pulled me into his arms.

"He's ridiculous. Sorry if we were too loud, I didn't know who was at the door and when I saw it was him I figured I'd let you keep sleeping."

"You didn't wake me up, my stomach did. I haven't eaten since you left."

"Brandon!"

"I couldn't. I couldn't do anything Harper. All I could do or think about was finding you and hating myself for pushing you away."

"I was being rash," I whispered into his chest, "I shouldn't have left, it was immature and hateful. I just thought if you would put yourself in a position where we could lose you, I wanted you to know what it felt like to have us gone."

His breath caught in his throat and his arms tightened around me.

"I'm so sorry baby, but I also needed you to have time to figure out if you would rather have a life without us. Because that's what it felt like you wanted when you made your mind up. And so, of course, I made it worse by trying to hurt you back, instead of talking it out with you."

"Don't apologize. Don't leave me again, but don't apologize."

"I'm—"

"Nope." He pressed his lips against my own, and spoke around our kiss, "No more *sorrys*."

I grumbled but leaned up onto the balls of my feet to deepen the kiss until his stomach growled, "Okay. Food. What do you want?"

"Uh—" He raised his hands above his head to stretch and my eyes hungrily raked over his long toned body, "You if you keep looking at me like that."

Grinning, I placed a soft kiss right below his chest, but pulled away before I got lost in his body, "You need actual food first, how does Chinese sound?"

His stomach growled again in response and he led me into the kitchen to find the take out menu. I scowled at Brandon when he sat me back on the counter, but ordered our food and handed him the phone when I was done.

"They'll be here within thirty minutes."

"Half an hour?" He mused and his eyes heated as he scooted me forward so my bottom was barely on the edge of the counter. My breaths came quicker when he pressed himself against me and moved the collar of his shirt I was wearing to nibble his way from my neck to shoulder. Catching the band of his boxer briefs with my toe, I pushed down and a sound that warmed my body escaped his chest, "That should be enough time."

22

"DID YOU GET that?" I asked Aubrey as Liam smashed his cake onto his face.

"Oh yeah." She brought her expensive camera back to her face and leaned her body back as she continued to take shots of him.

Aubrey really was amazing with that camera. Brandon, Liam and I had visited his mom yesterday and Aubrey had been over for dinner. She showed me a lot of her pictures and when I sent a couple dozen to Bree she called and begged Aubrey to shoot her wedding. It was the first time she was going to get paid for what she loved to do, and with all her shyness she just blushed fiercely with a huge smile on her face. When I'd gotten a minute alone with her, I asked if she would take pregnancy photos when I got big again and she looked like I'd just offered her the moon. She is so sweet, and I hope she and Jeremy stay together. They're absolutely perfect for each other.

Brandon wrapped his arm around me and discreetly brushed his hand over my stomach. I was only twelve weeks and I was already showing enough to know my bump was a baby . . . not a big meal. Hell, it wasn't even a bump, my whole stomach was already rounding. We'd seen Dr. Lowdry yesterday, and she said it was normal to show quickly after your first pregnancy. Apparently something about your body already knowing what was going to happen, so it responded quicker. All that did was make me frown. I'd been massive by the time Liam was born, if I already had a ridiculously defined baby bump that decided to pop up out of nowhere this last Thursday, I could only imagine what I would look like by the time I delivered this one. So I'd worn a loose shirt last night and today since the parents were still in the dark. We could have told them Monday, but everyone's emotions were so all over the place with Brandon's fight and my disappearing act, that we decided it was best to continue with our plan to wait until today.

"Girl," he whispered softly in my ear as he caressed my belly again.

I turned to plant a kiss on his cheek and whispered back, "Boy."

Liam screeched and spoke gibberish before shoving more cake in his mouth and hair. Everyone laughed with him and Brandon kissed my neck before going to pick Liam up out of his high chair and bring him over to the sink. That boy was covered in cake and frosting. I took his onesie off and rinsed it off in the sink so all the food would go down the drain instead of the washer, then helped Brandon attempt to wipe him down. We gave up not even two minutes later and Brandon rushed to give him a bath and put him in new clothes. I smiled at my guys when they walked back out, Brandon with a huge smile taking small steps behind Liam who was speed crawling back toward me.

"How's my birthday boy?" I scrunched my nose at him when he did the same with his somewhat toothy grin.

"Not taking a nap anytime soon, that's for sure," Brandon grumbled, but with his dimpled smile and bright eyes I knew he was anything but frustrated. He'd let Liam get away with no naps if he could.

Liam turned and dipped all the way to the side as he reached for someone else, making me almost lose my hold on him and I rolled my eyes as I gave him over to Carter. Of course Liam would be in love with Carter. Since he'd shown up this afternoon, it was the only person he wanted to be with. If I had any doubt that Carter wouldn't give Kate a chance, that was quickly demolished when they each saw the other hold Liam. Kate had swooned and an hour later Carter's eyes had taken on a dazed heat when Kate had scooped him up and kissed Liam resulting in a fit of laughter from my son. It wasn't ten minutes later that Carter asked if he could take Kate on a date this evening.

Opening presents was the cutest, and longest process of the day. Each present took about three minutes to open and then we'd go through the process of getting him to stop eating the wrapping and tissue paper so he could start on the next present. By the end I was exhausted but blissfully happy, and getting more excited by the second now that the extended family was starting to head out. We'd been picking up and cleaning as the party went, so thankfully we were ready to relax with our family by the time Carter and Kate left together.

"What'd he say?" I asked Brandon as I watched Liam play with a big dump truck.

"He asked if I would be okay with him dating my cousin."

My eyes widened, "He asked *you* that?"

"Right? I told him it wasn't my place to say whether or not he could and that she could make her own decisions. So he says, 'I know, but I know you're not my biggest fan. And I don't want to piss you off more than I already have.'"

"Oh. That's thoughtful, I guess. What'd you say?"

Brandon shrugged and laughed when Liam didn't understand

how the truck had gotten away from him, "I said as long as he treats her well, I didn't have a problem with it."

Huh. Brandon really is too nice and forgiving of people.

"I may have also said that if it kept him from going after you . . ." he trailed off.

I hugged his waist and smiled into his chest. "That sounds more like you, but that's why I love you. I'm all grimy and covered in cake, I'm going to change really quick."

"Put on a tight shirt."

"Is that how you want to tell them? Just show them?"

He smiled and looked back to make sure no one was near us, "Just act like nothing's different, see how long it takes them. I think it'd be fun Mrs. Taylor, don't you?"

"I have to agree with you Mr. Taylor. I'll be right back."

Changing into a bright blue racer-back stretchy tank, and a clean pair of jeans, I made my way back to the living room and tried to wipe the smile off my face.

"You look amazing Harper." Brandon pulled me into his arms again and kissed my neck softly. "I'm sorry, I know you get self-conscious, but you pregnant is a breathtaking sight."

I grabbed each side of his face, and pulled him down to me as I stood on my toes, "Thank you." I kissed him quickly twice, barely pulling away to look in his eyes, "I love you."

"And I love you." Our next kiss was anything but quick.

"Okay you two, get a room," Dad called from one of the couches.

Blushing, I leaned around Brandon's side and grinned through my embarrassment at our audience. Liam had crawled over to us and pulled himself up on my leg, gripping my pants with one hand and reaching relentlessly with the other. I pulled him up and settled him on my hip before making my way to a chair. Mom, Dad and Carrie were making fun of me and Brandon so they didn't even notice when I walked by them. I frowned but sat down, knowing it wouldn't be much longer before someone noticed.

I was wrong.

It took another hour and a half.

Brandon had even taken Liam from me so he wouldn't be blocking my stomach, I had gotten up numerous times to get and refill drinks, as well as to go to the bathroom. It took Bree commenting on the color of my shirt for Carrie to gasp and Mom to jump up and literally squeal.

"Oh my God! Oh my God, are you pregnant?! Please tell us you're pregnant!" Mom rushed over and placed her hands on my rounding stomach.

"Well it'd sure be awkward right now if I weren't." I laughed and accepted her numerous hugs and kisses on the cheeks, only to be replaced by the same from Carrie and Dad. At least Dad was more controlled with only one gentle hug and kiss for me, and a big man hug for Brandon.

"You're already so big!" Carrie was crying happily as she kissed her son and turned back to my stomach, "How far along are you?"

"I'm twelve weeks, and trust me, I had the smallest of bumps until Thursday morning, and then all of a sudden this was here."

"Twelve weeks! Oh my goodness, congratulations! Jeremy Allen Taylor, get your butt over here and congratulate them."

"Mom," Jeremy huffed a laugh and pulled Aubrey closer to his side, "already beat you to it. You guys are a little behind on the news."

That, of course, got me a couple glares and Brandon a smack on the back of his head, but soon we were all sitting down arguing over whether I was having a girl or boy. Brandon shifted Liam back onto my lap and excused himself when he got a phone call. When he came back five minutes later with a nervous expression, I was worried about who that had been, but tried to keep shut until he was ready to tell me. It didn't help that he continued to check his phone every few minutes, and my patience soon ran out.

Hugging Liam close to me, I leaned into Brandon and waited until he looked directly at me before speaking low, "Was that Scarecrow?"

"What?"

"On the phone. Was that him?"

His eyes softened and he kissed my temple, "No. I told Crow on Sunday to delete my number and that I was done with the Underground."

"You did?" I couldn't stop the smile that crossed my face.

"Of course. I know I messed up, I'm not about to do it again. Him calling would just be a temptation that I don't need."

I took a deep, relieving breath and thanked God again for giving me a man like Brandon. "Well then who called, you look nervous."

He opened his mouth, shut it, and quirked the corner of his mouth up, "Is it okay if we talk about it later?"

Maybe my thanks had come too soon. "Uh, should I be worried?"

Brandon checked his phone again and searched my face, "No, I don't think so."

My heart dropped, "Babe that doesn't exactly help!" I hissed between clenched teeth.

"I'm sorry. Don't be worried, it'll be fine." He leaned forward to kiss me, but when the doorbell rang he paused and blew out a deep breath. Mumbling something, he put a hand on my shoulder and said he would get the door.

"Are you expecting someone baby girl?"

"No Dad . . . we aren't." I turned to look at the door, but Brandon had stepped outside, the door barely cracked and all I could see was his back blocking whoever was out there. Standing up,

I repositioned Liam on my hip and turned just as Brandon stepped back into the house, followed by a fit older man with salt and pepper hair and a stern, weathered face. All the air left my body with a loud whoosh and my hand covered my mouth.

Brandon watched me with worried eyes before stepping around the chair to stand by my side and grasp my hand. "Harper?"

What was he doing here? How did he even know where I was? The stiff-postured man holding a faded olive-drab colored seabag in his right hand stared at me silently, and I seemed to only be able to do the same. I vaguely registered Brandon taking Liam and passing him off to a family member behind us so he could pull me close to his body.

"Sweetheart, please say something." When my voice continued to fail me, he leaned closer and spoke in my ear, "If you don't want him here, just tell me."

Brandon knew about this, I realized. This is who called him, why he was so nervous. Why wouldn't he tell me? I mentally thought about the way I looked, trying to figure out if anything was unacceptable. My make-up was light, but probably still a drastic change, and thank God I'd taken my Monroe piercing out when Liam continued to grab at, or head butt it. Was my tank top too revealing? What is he thinking and why isn't he saying anything?

"Brandon," Dad cleared his throat and stepped up to my other side, "who is that?"

"Th-that—" I paused for a moment to collect myself, determined to not start crying. With my hormones all over the place already, it's safe to say I was having a difficult time, "That's Sir. That's my father."

The room fell quiet for about three whole seconds. "And may I ask what makes you think you're welcome here?"

My jaw dropped and Dad audibly inhaled. You just didn't talk to Sir that way.

"Please forgive my wife." Dad started and shifted a fraction closer to me, "I'm Robert Grayson, that is my wife Claire," he gestured over to Bree, "my daughter Breanna and her fiancé Konrad."

Sir nodded and cleared his throat, "The ones that called and e-mailed," he stated. "I appreciate what you've done for Harper."

Brandon left my side to take Sir's bag and set it down in the hallway, "You can sit, can I get you anything to eat or drink?"

"No thank you, I'm fine." With an outstretched hand he closed the distance between us, "Harper. You look well."

I took a step away from him and looked at my husband, "You knew about this?"

His face was tense but his eyes were full of worry. Before he could answer, Sir did it for him.

"He's been writing me at least once a month for over a year now. The last one he sent with an airline ticket."

I couldn't hold back anymore, I was about to finish what Mom had just started, "So that's the only reason you would come see me or talk to me? Because my husband bought you a ticket here? What makes you think I wanted to see you? You dis-owned me!" My voice was shaky but raising, "You cut me out of your life, you wanted nothing to do with me or Liam." He took a step toward me and again I took one back, "You've *never* wanted anything to do with me!"

"That's not true." Sir's voice wavered and it stopped me where I stood.

Had the world just stopped turning? Had hell frozen over? The Sir I knew was emotionless. The man in front of me looked pained and his chin was quivering slightly.

"Do you know that in the last two years I've felt more love from this family," I pointed toward where everyone was sitting behind me, "than I ever felt from you?"

"Mom," Brandon said softly and gave her a look.

"Oh. Right, we'll be outside," she said and everyone started standing.

Turning, I saw Bree holding Liam and reached my arms out. "Please Bree." I needed to hold my son, I needed that comfort of having him in my arms. Bree gladly handed him over and was the last one to walk into the backyard.

"Babe, do you want me to go out too?"

I grabbed Brandon's hand and gripped tight, "Don't you dare leave me right now." Looking directly into his eyes, I shook my head, "I can't believe you would do this without telling me."

"Harper I—even with everything that's happened, I know you wish you had a different relationship with him. You were devastated when there was no response from him again last summer, I couldn't just stop trying to reach him yet. There was never any word from him and I sent him an open ended ticket over a month ago, with the last letter I was going to send him, and I told him that. He called me a week and a half ago, we talked for a bit and he decided he would come." He cupped one cheek and brought his other arm around both Liam and me, "I know this is hard for you, and Robert is a great Dad Harper, but you need Sir in your life too. Please understand why I continued to try to reach him."

Oh Brandon. Of course I understood. I just wish he would have given me some warning. I pressed my lips to his for a few seconds and gave him a small smile, "Thank you. You're right, thank you so much." Brandon's relief was palpable and it helped ease the tension in the room. Turning to Sir, I gestured behind him, "You're more than welcome to sit, Sir. We can talk."

He offered a smile much like the one I had just given Brandon and sat down in the chair closest to him. Brandon and I sat on the couch facing him, and I kept a tight grip on Liam as I tried to figure out what would make Sir want to be in my life suddenly.

"He sure looks a lot like you." Sir said after a few awkward minutes of silence. His gaze was fixed on Liam and . . . was that a smile?

Clearing my throat, I instinctively hugged Liam closer. I'd never seen baby photos of myself, but my son definitely didn't look anything like his father. Other than his eyes, there wasn't a trace of Chase in him. And even those were different, Chase's had been a darker electric blue, Liam's were such a pale blue that people did a double take and then were completely mesmerized by them. They looked like a Siberian husky's eyes.

"I know I'm late, but congratulations on the wedding and him . . . it's Liam, right?"

I nodded, "Liam Chase Taylor."

"Brandon told me the significance of his name, that's a great way of honoring their lives."

"And what else did Brandon tell you?" I asked through clenched teeth. This man wanted nothing to do with my life, and he thinks he can comment on why we named him Liam Chase?

"Sweetheart," Brandon said softly.

"No, I want to know what all you've told him." Looking back over to Sir, I continued, "And I want to know why you're here. This is the longest conversation we've had in years, I haven't heard back from you in over a year and a half, then all of a sudden you're in our home!"

"I've told him everything," Brandon pulled me closer to his side, "Chase, my fighting, Liam's birth, our wedding, the gym . . . other than what's happened in the last month, he knows everything."

"Well then, let me fill you in." I seethed, I couldn't seem to control my anger right now, "Brandon and I are having another baby, Brandon fought again, and I disappeared for a day."

Sir's eyes dropped to my stomach and Brandon looked like he was regretting not telling me about this. As he should.

"Oh!" I started again, "And Jason Carter came back into our lives and told me how you helped him come here so he could be with me. Thanks for that by the way, it's nice to know you two tried to plan out my life without asking me first."

Sir shook his head, his eyes narrowing slightly, "That was never my intention, from my conversations with Sergeant Carter, it was implied that you shared his feelings, I was simply helping."

"Helping? Nice." I had barely found out that Carter had been ranked Sergeant when his service ended. How did Sir know that? Were they still in touch?

"Harper," Brandon whispered close to my ear, "baby try to calm down. He wants to talk to you."

"Then talk," I directed at Sir.

Brandon sighed and ran a hand over his face, keeping it there for a moment. Sir shifted forward in his chair just watching me until my anger slowly started to subside.

"I know I wasn't the best father, and I know there are a lot of things I should have handled differently since you moved here." He stopped to clear his throat, "But I always wanted you Harper, you were the only thing that kept me going when Janet di—when she died."

His eyes watering finished off my almost non-existent anger. My chest ached watching the strongest—emotionally—man I knew slowly start to break down.

"If it weren't for you, I don't know how I would have continued my life, but I didn't know what to do with a baby, especially a girl. Her family hadn't approved of our relationship, and I'd run away from mine when I joined the military. Your life wasn't ideal for you, I'm sure, but that's all I thought I could do for you. You being there was what made me get up every day, and I know I wasn't around much, but you look and act so much like your mother it killed me to be around you. Not that that constitutes as an excuse, nothing excuses my behavior. It wasn't your fault you reminded me of her, and I should have embraced it rather than pull away from you.

"When you left for school, I had a hard time adjusting, and hearing your voice over the phone made it harder. I started working more, staying on base longer, and only communicated with you via e-mail. I thought distancing myself further would help me cope with you leaving."

My head was swimming, I couldn't believe everything he was telling me. I hadn't known anything different until I moved here, so I hadn't hated my life growing up until I started hanging around with the Graysons. I started hating Sir for how distant he'd been, and though I'd always figured it was because of my mother, I had no idea how much her death still affected him to this day. Hearing his words made it difficult to continue hating this man at all. My arms were twitching, wanting to wrap around Sir for the first time in my life, but he didn't usually say this much to me during one month of living together, and I was afraid if I moved or said anything, it would all stop.

"I will never forgive myself for the way I responded to the e-mail you sent when you found out you were pregnant." Sir whispered, his tear-filled eyes never leaving mine, "It was the exact same thing Janet's parents told her when we found out she was pregnant with you. They hated that she was with someone in the military, hated me even though I'd never spoken to, or seen them. We hadn't been together long, but I knew I wanted to marry her, and the only thing that stopped us was her parents. When they disowned her for not aborting you, we married that next weekend and I'd never been happier. We were so young, she was barely eighteen and I was nineteen, but we were on top of the world and I couldn't wait for you to come along.

"I was terrified for you when I read that e-mail, and I stupidly thought I could keep you safe if I could stop you from going down the same path your mother and I had been on. As soon as I sent the e-mail, I wanted to die. I couldn't believe I'd done that, I knew you would never do something so heartless, and that you would probably never forgive me either. Claire Grayson called me that day, and to put it mildly, she didn't hold anything back. I was glad you had a family that loved you the way I'd never shown you, and figured you not forgiving me would be for the best. So that's why I stayed silent, even after you all tried to reach me before Liam was born and for your wedding. I thought staying away would be the best thing for you and your new family. Brandon's letters helped me with that; I was able to know more than I probably would have if we'd continued talking the way we always have. But when he said he wasn't going to continue writing me, I panicked. I thought I was helping you, but I know all I've done was hurt you. I do love you Harper, I've always loved you."

My jaw dropped. That was the first time he'd ever said that to me.

"I'm proud of the woman you've become. You have handled everything life has thrown at you in a way not many could, and I'm thankful you didn't let certain things ruin your life the way I let them do mine. You have a great family, I couldn't be happier with your choice in Brandon. It's obvious how much he loves you and Liam, and if it weren't for him, I wouldn't be here now." He looked over at Brandon, "Thank you son, for everything."

Brandon simply nodded and continued making lazy circles on my upper arm. Shifting Liam over to Brandon's lap, I shakily stood up and walked toward Sir. He stood and stiffened momentarily when I wrapped my arms around his waist, before awkwardly placing his own around me.

"I love you too." I said through the lump in my throat.

"Oh Harper," his own voice was gruff with emotion, "will you ever forgive me?"

A laugh that sounded more like a sob escaped my throat and I stepped back, "This family is all about second chances, you don't even have to ask."

He hesitated a bit, but wrapped his arms around me again and hugged me tight, "I have missed you so much. Nothing was the same after you left."

I had no idea what to say. This conversation has been so unlike anything I've ever had with Sir, and it changes everything that's happened over the last twenty years, especially the last two. I couldn't miss my life with the old Sir, but if the man that just explained his actions throughout my life were to leave, I would miss him greatly. We stepped away from each other after minutes of holding each other, "Would you, uh, would you like to meet your grandson?"

Sir's eyes filled with tears again as Brandon brought Liam over to us.

"This is your grandpa, little man," Brandon said as he held Liam's squirming body to his chest. "Can you say 'hi' to Grandpa?"

"Go bye bye!" Liam said with a toothy, scrunched-up nose grin. Didn't matter if we were saying hello or good-bye, it was always *go bye bye* with him.

Sir didn't respond, his jaw was slack and the corners of his mouth were twitching up.

Liam looked at me and patted Sir's chest. I nodded and said "Grandpa" again.

Looking back at Sir, Liam patted his chest again and said, "Go bye bye Grapa!"

"He's waiting for you to say 'hi' back to him," I explained.

"Oh!" Sir huffed, "Hi Liam. It's good to finally meet you."

"He wants you to hold him," Brandon said awkwardly, "is that okay with you?"

"Of course, uh—" he held his arms like he was going to cradle him and I laughed.

"Sir, you can hold him differently, he's not an infant anymore, just hold him like this." I demonstrated without actually taking Liam.

Sir carefully took him from Brandon and a large smile crossed his face when Liam started talking nonsense a mile a minute and looking at Sir like he was speaking English and carrying on a well thought out conversation. My heart warmed and squeezed watching Sir hold him. I never thought I would see this, never thought I would introduce Liam to my cold, distant father, and definitely never thought I'd see Sir act like this. I didn't know he even had the capability of smiling, hugging or crying. And now all of the above had happened within twenty minutes. I couldn't be more dumbfounded, or happier.

Figuring Mom was more annoyed than I had been that Brandon went behind our backs, I left the three men in the house and went out back to explain everything that had just been said inside. Like I knew they would, because my family was just amazing like that, everyone agreed happily to make Sir feel like he was welcome. As the people I loved started heading back inside, I grabbed Dad's arm and made him stay back for a second. When we were alone I hugged him tight and didn't let go.

"You will always be my dad. You may not have raised me, but then again neither did Sir. You and Mom have shown me love like I never knew, and took me in as another daughter without question. Because of that, *you* are my dad."

"Oh baby girl." He laughed once and kissed the top of my head, "You really are precious to us. I love you."

"Love you too." I squeezed him once more and let go to walk back inside.

"Was my jealousy that obvious?" he mock whispered. "That why you're giving your old man some peace of mind?"

I winked at him, "Not at all." Yes it was. "Just wanted you to know how I felt before you could start to have any doubts."

"WHAT A DAY," I said with a sigh as I curled into Brandon's side that night.

"I second that."

Just throwing a birthday party for my little monster was hard work, but having Sir show up had taken me on an emotional ride that left me feeling drained yet strangely alive. The whole family stayed well past midnight and after hours of just talking with everyone, I think Sir was finally feeling a little more comfortable with them. His tense shoulders had shown his worry about their judgments of him, but holding and playing with Liam all night, and my family's ability to love everyone, had him relaxing and laughing as the night wore on. He was sleeping in our guest room now, and we were going to talk in the morning about the possibility of him moving here. Apparently he had retired from the Marine Corps a few months ago after twenty-two years of service, and with how the day had gone, wanted to be closer to us. I still couldn't believe that this wasn't a dream.

"Are you still mad at me?" Brandon pulled away slightly so he could face me on his side.

"No, I'm not. I'm glad you did what you did, I just couldn't believe you'd kept something like that from me."

"I know I should have told you about the letters and his coming, but I was afraid I would get your hopes up and he wouldn't ever respond or show up. I thought it was better to deal with you angry for having not told you, than watch you be crushed if he let you down again."

"You really are too good to me Brandon Taylor."

Shaking his head, he brushed some hair behind my ear and cupped my cheek, "All I want is to make you happy. I'll do anything for you Harper."

"I know. Thank you." I kissed his lips softly and held his gaze, "I love you so much."

"And I love you."

23

Two and a half years later.

"COME ON GUYS, it's time to go to Grandma and Grandpa's."

Liam and his sister set down their flowers and rushed back to Brandon and me.

"Bye Unca Chase!"

"See ya Uncle Chase!"

It was the fourth anniversary of Chase's death, and like every month, we were here to say our *hellos* and leave orange lilies on his grave. Brandon and I still told stories of him all the time, and though Liam and our daughter Kristi didn't fully understand what we meant when we told them he was gone, or that he was Liam's father, they loved hearing his stories. Trying to explain that he was Liam's father was even worse than explaining they wouldn't meet him, so for now they affectionately knew him as Uncle Chase and looked forward to our visits every month.

I hitched Kristi up on my hip, grabbed Liam's hand and watched Brandon as he said a few quiet words to Chase. He did this every time, and I loved him for it. I'd asked him a while ago what he always said, and he simply explained he was thanking Chase for his part in our family and letting him know he would always take care of us.

Brandon took Kristi and wrapped his other arm around me as we walked back to the SUV. "How are you holding up Sweetheart?"

"I just can't believe it's been four years." I smiled softly at my husband and rested my head against his shoulder. "It feels like it's been longer, but at the same time like it just happened." My body shivered as a flash of that night played through my mind.

He rubbed his hand up and down my arm and kissed my forehead, "I know baby." He responded to both my statement and remembrance of that night, "I miss him too."

We drove to Mom and Dad's for our annual night of celebrating Chase's life and I took a deep breath before we walked in. Our crazy family was all already there, as well as the new additions. Kristi and Liam tried to tackle Sir, who actually preferred to be called Papa now, and he gladly went down and let them jump on him. He was a completely different man from the Sir I'd grown up with, but he was great with the kids, and Brandon and I spent a lot of nights with him. He'd moved to California just as soon as he'd left from his first visit and after a lot of pushing on Carrie and Mom's part, was now dating a great lady named Veronica.

Konrad hugged Brandon and gave me a kiss on the cheek before rushing a plate of food to an extremely pregnant and moody Bree. Their little girl Cadence was helping our kids tickle Sir, and girl number two was due any day. Aubrey and Jeremy were curled up on each other on one of the chairs and deliriously in love. They were definitely still in the honeymoon stage . . . seeing as they'd just gotten back from their honeymoon three days ago. Carrie's new husband Bruce was helping Dad bring in the food off the grill and Kate almost knocked into him as she came storming around the corner.

"Harper! Oh my God, how do you deal with him?" She pressed the tips of her fingers to her forehead and shook her head, "He's impossible!"

Brandon and I smiled at each other and rolled our eyes, "What'd he do now?"

"He wants to name him AIDIEAS."

"It's better than freaking Wrinkles!" Carter mocked as he rounded the corner with their new English Bulldog puppy. "Baby, you can't name a male bulldog Wrinkles."

Can't argue with that. "What kind of name is Ideas?"

Carter hugged me and clapped Brandon on the shoulder, "No, it's said AY-DIAS. All I Do Is Eat And Shit."

Brandon and I burst into laughter. Oh dear.

Carter set down the squirmy ball of wrinkles and he took off running toward the screeching and laughing kids, crashing into a chair on his way. "We can always call him crash?"

"Oh! I like Crash," Kate said with a little clap.

"Yeah? Well, I like you." Carter's voice went deep and husky causing Brandon and me to back away.

Kate launched herself at Carter and we groaned as we tried to step around them. Those two couldn't have been more perfect for each other. Apparently Carter didn't learn much since not even a month after their first date they eloped in Vegas, but at least this marriage was still going strong. They fought on a daily basis, but their fights never lasted more than ten minutes and always ended in everyone else within seeing distance yelling at them to get a room while they attacked each other with lips and searching hands.

Once we were away from the love fest, we made our way

around the house hugging and kissing everyone as we passed them. Mom's eyes were bright with unshed tears and she kept me in a hug for a long time before sending me to the table with another platter of food. When I was done, I stood off to the side and watched our large mismatched family and smiled.

"What are you thinking?" Brandon's deep voice still made my heart pick up its pace and warmed my body. His lips on my neck and hands pulling me closer to his body weren't helping much either.

A soft moan escaped my lips and he laughed against my skin. "Um—well before my husband started distracting me, I was thinking about how much I love this." I gestured out to everyone around us, "I love our family . . . I love our life."

Brandon grunted in agreement and rested his chin on top of my head. "It took a lot for all of us to get here, but I think that's what makes all of us put together, perfect."

As always, I couldn't have said it better myself. Turning in his arms, I reached up on the balls of my feet and he leaned down to press our lips together. I sighed contentedly and rested my forehead against his, "I couldn't agree more."

Acknowledgments

OF COURSE, I have to give a big thank you to my husband for helping me believe I could do this and always encouraging me in my stories. He's put up with the laundry not being done, groceries not bought, and the house not being cleaned on more than one occasion so I could immerse myself in my books. I appreciate his bemused looks when I would start fighting with something one of my characters was currently doing in the book and his endless patience as I would talk for hours about them like they were friends. Whether or not I thought he was paying attention, he could always tell me what was going on between whom, would read any chapter I put in front of him and always gave his honest opinion. He's my best friend, and I couldn't have done any of this without him. I love you babe!

Don't judge, but I have to thank my furry daughter who would lay in bed with me when I couldn't even waste time getting out of my pajamas because I was too wrapped up in my writing. Other than the few times she'd drop the tennis ball next to me, or ask for a belly rub, she would lay there with her head on my arm and stare at the screen like she was completely enthralled with whatever was going on.

To Katie, Angie and Michelle, thank you for getting as excited about my books as I am while listening to me ramble on about the drama and relationships, and go through ridiculous ideas that were quickly nixed, or noted on paper or my phone. You guys made me feel like I wasn't crazy and gave me motivation when needed.

BOOKS BY MOLLY McADAMS

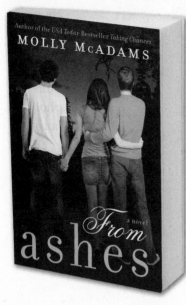

FROM ASHES
A Novel
Available in Paperback and eBook

Cassidy has only ever trusted two men: her father, and her best friend Tyler—until she meets Gage... And there's something about Cassidy that makes Gage want to protect her—and make her his own.

For a year and a half, Gage and Cassidy dance around their feelings for each other as Tyler tries to keep them apart; until one day Tyler unknowingly pushes Cassidy right into Gage's arms...

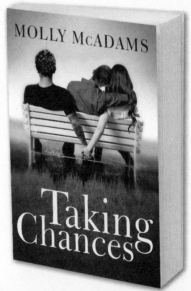

TAKING CHANCES
A Novel
Available in Paperback and eBook

Eighteen-year-old Harper is ready to live life her own way, escaping from under her career-Marine father's thumb and heading to college in San Diego. But soon, she finds herself torn between two men...and after one weekend of giving into her desires, everything changes...